The Secrets We Keep

A J WILLS

Cherry Tree Publishing

The Secrets We Keep
AJ Wills

Copyright © A J Wills 2022

All rights reserved. No part of this publication may be reproduced, stored in a retrieval system, or transmitted, in any form or by any other means, without the prior written permission of the author, nor be otherwise circulated in any form of binding or cover other than that in which it is published and without a similar condition being imposed on the purchaser.

This book is a work of fiction. Any resemblance to actual persons, living or dead is purely coincidental.

CALL HANDLER: Police, what's your emergency?

CALLER: It's my daughter. She's missing.

CALL HANDLER: How old is she?

CALLER: Ten. She'll be eleven next month. We've looked everywhere, but I can't find her. I don't know what to do. Please, you have to help us.

CALL HANDLER: Try to stay calm. When did you last see her?

CALLER: She left for school this morning, but she never came home. She should have been back hours ago.

CALL HANDLER: Have there been any arguments at home? Anything that might explain why she's not come home tonight?

CALLER: No, nothing like that. I'm worried someone might have taken her.

CALL HANDLER: Have you tried contacting all her friends? Are there any family members she might be with?

CALLER: No, we've checked with everybody.

CALL HANDLER: Does your daughter have a phone?

CALLER: Yes, but she left it at home. She must have forgotten to take it this morning.

CALL HANDLER: So, there's no way to call her?

CALLER: No. I'm going out of my mind with worry. What if... ?

CALL HANDLER: Please, you have to stay calm. It's not going to help your daughter if you start panicking. You've done the right thing by calling. We're going to help you find her, okay?

CALLER: But what if something's happened? What if someone *has* taken her?

CALL HANDLER: Has she ever gone missing before?

CALLER: No, never. It's not like her. That's why I know something terrible has happened.

CALL HANDLER: And there's nothing to intimate where she might have gone?

CALLER: How many times? No. We've looked everywhere we can think of and spoken to everyone who knows her. Nobody's seen her since she left school this afternoon. You have to do something. Please, I'm begging you.

CALL HANDLER: And what's her name?

CALLER: It's Annie. Her name's Annie Warren.

MONDAY

Chapter 1

CATHY

A creeping rot of unease twists in the pit of my stomach. Something dreadful has happened. I just know it has.

We've spent the last few hours scouring the estate behind the house, looking in the places where Annie could be hiding, and contacting all her friends and their parents. But it's been an exercise in futility. There's no sign of her.

She's vanished.

Gone.

Missing.

Now I'm left with a gut-wrenching, insidious, hollow feeling of utter despair and helplessness that no parent should ever have to experience.

Nobody teaches you what to do if your child goes missing. They didn't cover it at our antenatal classes. There are no helpful posters on the walls at the GP surgery or useful cut-out-and-keep articles in those glossy magazines for parents. And when the topic does crop up on Mumsnet, it's never with any actionable advice, just a load of frantic parents winding each other up into a frenzy about something that will probably never happen to them.

I never thought it would happen to us either, and I have absolutely no idea what I'm supposed to do.

'We should be out there, looking for her. Not sitting around waiting.' Kit jumps off the edge of the sofa where he's been perched for the last five minutes, his foot tapping furiously, chewing his fingernails down to the skin.

The house aches with emptiness. We're so used to Annie filling it with her noise. Singing and chatting incessantly. The TV on too loud. Her feet thumping up and down the stairs.

'The police said we should wait for them to arrive,' I say, my stomach tight.

Time ticks perilously slowly. It seems like hours ago that I made the call to report my daughter missing. I couldn't believe how calmly and dispassionately the woman took all my details, asking whether we'd had any arguments at home and if we'd tried to contact Annie's friends to check whether they'd seen her.

Do they think we're stupid or something?

'Did you tell them she's only ten?' Kit asks.

'Of course I did,' I snap back.

'So why aren't they here yet?'

'I don't know.'

'Didn't you explain how serious it is?'

He's pacing up and down now, his shoulders hunched up to his ears, hands shoved into his pockets. A bundle of nervous energy.

'For god's sake, Kit, sit down, will you? You'll wear a hole in the carpet. She said they're sending someone. I'm sure they're on the way.'

'And what are we supposed to do in the meantime? Sit here and make polite conversation? Kick back and watch a film?'

I hate it when he gets like this, all antsy and sarcastic, taking it out on me when he knows full well this is not my fault.

'They'll be here,' I tell him. 'There's no point getting worked up about it. It's not going to help.'

I always thought Kit would be good in a crisis. He's usually so calm and collected, the person who keeps his head while everyone else runs around flapping and clucking. But he's wound up so tightly tonight, it's infectious. I just about held it together when I dialled 999, but his agitation is getting under my skin, ratcheting up my own anxiety.

I've always looked up to Kit and defer to him on most things, maybe because he's older than me. A lot older. Not quite old enough to be my father, but not far off it.

Before him, I'd been through a string of unsuitable boyfriends, all too immature and self-obsessed to amount to anything more than a bit of fun. There was something different about Kit. At forty-two, he was fifteen years my senior, but the age difference barely registered. I was attracted to him because of his relaxed self-confidence. Not arrogant or cocky, but a man happy in his own skin. He had nothing to prove to himself or anyone else, and that was utterly alluring.

It was entirely by chance that we met. One of those weird quirks of fate. I'd travelled into Canterbury to meet up with a friend for lunch and happened to be walking past the register office at the precise moment Kit was passing in the opposite direction. I might never have looked at him twice, other than for a young couple getting married who needed two witnesses. Kit and I were in the right place at the right time and, much to our mutual amusement, we were dragged off the street to assist with the formalities, like something out of a Hugh Grant movie.

Afterwards, Kit asked me to join him for a drink. He told me he'd only popped out of his office to grab some lunch. It became his little joke, telling anyone who wanted to know how we met it was the most expensive sandwich of his life. One drink became several and when he finally realised the time and had to rush back, I happily gave him my number.

We were married within the year, and I fell pregnant with Annie, our little miracle, four years after that. She came as a surprise to us both. Kit already had grown-up children of his own from a previous marriage and I'd been told by doctors it was highly unlikely I'd ever conceive again. So when I did, unexpectedly, I had no way of knowing how he was going to react.

I was terrified of telling him, but I had nothing to fear. Kit was delighted, although I think more for my sake than at the thought of being a father again. I cooked him his favourite meal and when he asked me how my day had been, I placed the plastic pregnancy stick in the middle of the table.

'What's that?' he said, glancing at it briefly, like he didn't know.

I waited.

'Are you... ?'

I nodded. 'Pregnant.'

'Are you serious?'

'Look for yourself.'

'But... how?'

'I thought after two kids you might have worked that out,' I laughed.

'Yes, but I mean – I thought you couldn't, you know, after...'

'I thought so too.'

I was only nineteen when I'd first fallen pregnant. Too young to be a mother. I still don't know what went wrong, only that there'd been "complications."

'Darling, that's wonderful news.' He pushed back his chair and hurried around the table to hug me.

'Are you sure?'

'Am I sure what?'

'Are you sure you're happy? We've not talked properly about having a baby.'

'Of course I'm pleased. I know how much this means to you,' he said.

Nine months later, and after a textbook pregnancy, I nearly gave birth in the café. My waters broke while I was chatting by the counter to Fiona, my friend and co-owner. She had to shoo the customers out to close up early and drive me to the hospital.

I couldn't reach Kit on his mobile, but I left a message between my contractions as we drove, praying he'd make it on time.

They wheeled me straight into a delivery room where I gulped down great lungfuls of gas and air. Fiona stayed with me, gripping my hand, until finally Kit made it. He'd cut it fine, but he crashed into the room seconds before Annie was born.

'It's a girl,' he announced, his face beaming with joy. 'And she's perfect.'

I lifted my head to see, sweat pouring off my brow. Gingerly, the midwife placed her on my chest. And in that exquisite moment, I thought my body was going to explode with happiness and love.

Her face was red and wrinkled and she was grumbling like she was working up to scream. Kit was right, she *was* perfect. The miracle I never thought would happen.

'She has my eyes,' Kit said, leaning over us both. He planted a delicate kiss on the top of her head.

'Have you thought of a name yet?' the midwife asked.

'Annie,' I said without hesitation.

Kit and I had discussed names a few times but hadn't been able to agree.

'Really?' he said. 'Annie?'

'It was my grandmother's name,' I explained to the midwife. 'My father's mother.'

I didn't tell Kit that Annie didn't have *his* eyes. It's what fathers always think. Annie had *my* father's eyes. They're an identical shape, like almond teardrops.

I wish he could have been there to share that moment with us. He would have been so proud. And he'd have loved having a granddaughter.

But now she's gone and it's like my whole world is disintegrating. Again.

'Call them back and find out why they're taking so long,' Kit grumbles, running stiff fingers through his hair.

'I can't call them again. I told you, they'll be here any minute now.'

'This is killing me. I can't stand it,' he says.

I know what he means. I feel it too. We're in limbo, a hellish purgatory between our old, happy life and this new reality. I wish I could click my fingers and magically make Annie return. To make everything go back to normal. The three of us together without a care in the world. That all seems like a distant hope right now.

Maybe I *should* try calling again. Perhaps I didn't make it clear how serious this is. But how much more serious can it get than a ten-year-old girl going missing in broad daylight on her way home from school? The town should be flooded with search parties and dogs and bright lights by now. What the hell is keeping them?

'I'm going out again,' Kit growls, turning on his heel, heading for the hall to grab his coat and boots.

'Don't go,' I plead. 'They'll be here any second and they'll want to talk to you too. I don't want to be here on my own with them.'

He shakes his head. 'I can't sit around here doing nothing.'

'Fine,' I say, throwing up a hand in exasperation. 'Go, then.'

And then there's a sharp tap at the door and we both freeze, staring at each other, blinking.

Chapter 2

The two police officers standing on the doorstep don't possess a grey hair between them. She's slightly taller than him and attractive without make-up. Her hair is pulled back tightly in a ponytail, and she has rich, chocolate-coloured eyes and a dainty freckled nose. He's all muscle, brawn and hair gel, obviously trying to make up for his lack of stature with hours spent in the gym.

'Mrs Warren? We're here about your daughter,' she says, shooting me a tight, professional smile. 'May we come in?'

I open the door and stand back to let them through. Kit's waiting in the lounge. He looks them both up and down. They're not what I had in mind either. I'd imagined they'd send some senior detectives. Hard-bitten cops who'd seen it all and wouldn't muck about when it came to finding a missing ten-year-old girl.

Kit glances at me with a 'what the hell?' kind of a look. At least they're here.

'Please, take a seat,' I say.

They sit next to each other on the sofa. She pulls out a notebook and pen while he rests his hands on his knees and stares at us with a grim but polite smile. I guess it's supposed to let us know he appreciates the seriousness of the situation. In which case, why did they only send two young PCs?

She asks me Annie's full name, age and circumstances of her disappearance.

'We've given you all these details on the phone already,' Kit huffs crossly. 'Why aren't you out there looking for her?'

The female officer stops writing and studies my husband. 'I understand your frustration, Mr Warren, but it's important we gather all the relevant information about your daughter. Rest assured, we're doing everything in our power to find her. Now, when was she last seen?'

I explain again that the last we'd seen of her was when she'd left the house that morning to walk to school.

'And how was she when she left home?'

'Happy,' I say.

'You'd not had any arguments or cross words?'

I shake my head and fold my arms over my chest, hugging myself tightly. 'I spoke to the school when she didn't arrive home and they confirmed she'd been there all day. I mean, otherwise they would have called me, wouldn't they?'

The female officer smiles and nods. 'Does Annie have any health issues, either physical or mental?'

I glance at Kit. 'No, nothing like that.'

'Does she have a mobile phone or any other electronic devices, like an iPad or a laptop?'

'Yes, she has a phone in case she needs to contact us, but she forgot it this morning,' I say. 'I found it in her room.'

'May we take a look?'

'Umm - yes, I guess.'

Kit jumps up. 'I'll get it,' he mumbles.

'And her passport?'

'What?'

'Does Annie have her own passport? If so, is it missing?'

They think she's run away. After everything I've told them and the danger she could be in right now, they actually think a ten-year-old girl who's never gone missing before has decided to run off to another country. Dover and the cross-Channel ferries to France aren't far from here, but I don't think Annie would have a clue how to get there on her own, let alone how to make it to an airport alone. And besides, what would she do in another country? She doesn't have any money.

'No,' I sigh. 'We've never taken her abroad.'

She makes another note in her little black book.

'Can you give us a description of Annie?'

'She's about so tall,' I say, holding my hand at shoulder height above the floor, a lump balling in my throat as I think about my precious little girl.

'So roughly four foot seven?'

'I guess.'

'Hair? Eyes?'

'Brown eyes and dark brown, shoulder-length hair.'

'Any distinguishing features?'

She doesn't have any birthmarks or unusually shaped moles, if that what she means, but I could tell her a million things about Annie that make her unique, like the way she always sits on her hands, rocking back and forth when she's watching TV. How she sticks out her tongue between the gap in her two front teeth when she's concentrating on her homework. How a rash of freckles on the bridge of her nose only becomes visible in the summer sun, and how she gives this peculiar lop-sided, goofy smile whenever she's in the vicinity of a cute animal. But it's not what she wants to hear. 'No,' I say.

'And she was wearing school uniform when she was last seen?'

'Yes, a grey pinafore dress, white blouse and a green cardigan.'

'Any other clothes missing from her room?'

'No.'

'Great, that's helpful, Mrs Warren. Thank you.'

Kit clumps down the stairs and reappears with Annie's phone. It's only a cheap model. Ironically, we bought it for her so she'd be safe when she was out on her own. She can text and call, but we've set it up with tight parental controls to stop her accessing inappropriate websites.

The male officer takes it and asks for the passcode.

'0905,' Kit says. 'Annie's birthday.'

'Does she have access to any social media accounts?' he asks, spooling through the phone. I crane my neck to see what he's looking at, but he's holding it at an angle and I can't see.

'She's not supposed to,' I say.

The male officer glances up and raises an eyebrow. 'We'll get the experts to take a proper look at this. Mind if we hold on to it for now?'

'Sure, if you think it'll help.'

'I'd also like to take a quick look around the house,' he says. 'If you have no objections?'

'What do you need to look around the house for?' Kit wrings his hands. 'She's not here. She's out there somewhere.' He waves in the air. 'You should be out there looking for her.'

'It's nothing to worry about.' The male officer stands and tugs his stab vest down towards his hips.

'Fine.' Kit bows his head in surrender. There's no point fighting it. We don't have anything in the house to hide and the sooner they get on with it, the sooner they can get out on the streets looking for Annie.

'Do you have a loft?' the male officer asks.

Kit nods.

'I'll need access to that. And any outbuildings? Sheds? Cabins? Anything like that?'

'I'll show you.' Kit leads him out of the room, leaving me alone with the female officer.

For the next ten minutes, she grills me about Annie's mood and behaviour and our family circumstances. Has she experienced any bullying at school? Have we noticed any unusual bruising or marks on her body recently? Has her behaviour changed in recent weeks?

There hasn't been anything like that. Red flags, I guess you'd call them. This morning, everything had been perfectly normal. Annie was happy and excited about school. We'd all sat around the kitchen table for breakfast, Annie humming and singing the same pop tune over and over with her book propped open against the jam pots and a sticky finger holding the pages open. She was so engrossed in the story, she was almost late. I had to remind her of the time. She raced upstairs to clean her teeth and flew back down, dragging her bag behind her. She snatched her sandwiches from me and I snagged her for a kiss before she pulled away, laughing.

'And that was the last I saw of her,' I tell the officer, as I go through the events of the morning for what seems like the twentieth time.

Finally, she snaps her notebook shut as Kit and the male officer return to the room. The two officers exchange a glance, and he gives her an almost imperceptible shake of his head. Their smiles have dropped, and they both seem tense.

'I'm going to call this in,' he says to her, slipping out of the room, reaching for the radio attached to his protective vest.

'What happens now?' I ask.

She folds her hands in her lap and leans towards me. Her expression has softened. She's concerned. Whatever preconceived notion they had when they turned up here, it's gone. Now she's worried, which means they're taking it seriously.

'My colleague's passing on the details to a senior officer,' she says. 'We might need to bring in some additional resources.'

I breathe out heavily through my nose with relief. Finally.

'What kind of resources?' Kit asks.

'That'll be up to the senior team to decide, but certainly more officers to search for Annie.'

'What about a media appeal?' Kit sits back down on the sofa at my side. I grab his hand for comfort. It's hot and clammy.

The officer cocks her head, her eyes widening. 'I was about to come onto that.'

'It's important to get the word out quickly, isn't it?' Kit says. 'Especially in the first twenty-four hours.'

'Yes,' she agrees. 'We'll pass on all the information about Annie to our press liaison team and hopefully the local media can put out the appeal.'

'When?'

'I don't know. Hopefully, it'll make it onto some of the late-night bulletins, but we will need a photo of Annie,' she says. 'Ideally something recent that is a good likeness of her.' She grimaces as if it's an imposition to have to ask, but we're a step ahead of her.

Kit disappears into the kitchen and comes back with the photo of Annie we selected earlier, already out of its wooden frame. He lays it on the coffee table as the male officer returns to the room.

It was only taken last year, the most recent school photo we have of Annie. She's grinning into the camera, happy and carefree, her bottle green school cardigan slinking off her shoulders, a dark spot on her blouse above her collar bone that could be jam or paint or blood.

She looks off balance, like she's falling from the stool and is about to make a run for it. So typical of her, never still for one moment, even when she's having her picture taken. I love this photo. It really captures her cheeky side. Her irrepressible spirit. It looks natural. Not posed, even though it is.

'That's a lovely picture,' the female officer says, picking up the image and studying it.

I know we have to do this for Annie's sake, but by handing the photo over, we're making her public property. If she's not found soon, that image is going to be everywhere. All over the news. In the papers. On websites. Social media. We'll have lost our little girl all over again, and we'll never get her back as our own.

I still remember that photo of Sarah Payne, the little girl who was abducted and murdered years ago. And Holly and Jessica. Milly. And so many others, immortalised in the photos their parents shared with the police and the press when there was still hope they'd be found alive.

'Do you have any others?' the officer asks.

There's a load on my phone. I quickly scroll through them, suggest a couple of my favourites, and AirDrop them to her.

'Will those do?'

'They're perfect. I'll get them over to the press office now,' she says, as she uses her phone to take a snap of the printed school photograph.

'And then what?'

And then hell is unleashed.

The longer time marches on and Annie isn't found, the bigger the story is likely to become. I know exactly how this is going to go. It's always the same when a pretty, young, white girl from a decent, hardworking family, with no history of absconding, goes missing. It's irresistible fodder for the press. They'll be onto the story like wasps around a honeypot.

My heart pumps hard in my chest, my breath shallow and laboured like I've just sprinted up the stairs. There's no going back now. We have to do this. It's the price we have to pay.

'I should warn you,' the officer says, 'there might be some interest from the press when we release the information, especially if Annie isn't found soon.'

I bury my head in my hands as the room begins to spin. Kit rubs my back as my stomach cramps.

The thought of having anything to do with the press makes my body turn inside out with disgust and nausea.

I've been here before.

I know the damage they do.

I blame the media for killing my father and I'll never forgive them for that.

Chapter 3

YANNICK

'What are we leading on tonight?' I adjust my earpiece as I hop onto the stool in front of a bank of blinking TV screens in the newsroom, the microphone wire I've fed under my shirt cold against my skin. 'Tell me we've found something more interesting to replace the housing crisis story.'

'There *is* nothing else,' Tasha mumbles in my ear from the gallery.

'Come on, there *has* to be something better.' It's the same story we led on in the main programme at six. That was four-and-a-half hours ago, and even then it was dull.

But that's so typical of Tasha. She'll always go for the easy option, rehashing the same news we put out at six rather than looking for something new and exciting, because that would mean actually putting in some effort.

It's crazy that we're both on the same pay grade. We're both production journalists, responsible for overseeing the bulletins during the day, but while she's fresh out of university, I've been around long enough to get a crack at some of the presenting shifts. Not often on the main programme, but at lunch and on the late bulletins, mainly.

Tasha's a few years younger than me and should be bubbling with ideas and enthusiasm, but she's hopelessly out of her depth and lacking any ambition or spark. What are they teaching them at college these days?

It would help if she didn't spend most of her time glued to her phone messaging her friends, and used it for what it was designed for - speaking to people. The kids coming through these days seem to have an in-built aversion to talking to anyone, if they can text or email instead. Bernstein and Woodward didn't break Watergate by emailing. You need to talk to people to win their trust. To get them to open up. To persuade them to tell you the stories they'd otherwise keep close to their chest.

Tasha is typical of the new generation with no aptitude for life in a busy regional newsroom. Two weeks ago, she mixed up the names of the defendant and the victim in a high-profile murder trial. And a month before that, she downloaded a photo from Facebook that was supposed to be of a young mother killed in a motorway pile-up, only for one of the keen-eyed directors to spot it was the wrong woman as we were going on air.

I've no idea why Tasha even decided on a career in journalism. She probably thought she'd waltz in here and within a few weeks would be in front of the camera. But don't they all? It seems like everyone who joins these days thinks they're going to be the next big thing. I blame all those *Love Island* wannabes who end up with daytime TV slots even though most of them can't even read an autocue.

But news is a cut-throat business and most of the jobs are the unsung ones behind the scenes. I should know. I've been battling to work my way up for the last six years, and here I am still picking up the crumbs of the occasional presenting shift on the late evening bulletin.

'There's nothing else, Yannick,' Tasha repeats, stifling a yawn in my ear. Delightful.

'Have you even looked at the wires? Checked the police press line?'

I can imagine her rolling her eyes at the others in the gallery.

'Shall we have a quick rehearsal?' the director, Una, says as I glance through the sheaf of scripts on my lap. They're my security blanket. A back-up in case the autocue fails, which it's liable to do at any time. We're hardly operating with cutting-edge technology. Budgets in the regions have been squeezed by the network for years. We run everything on a shoestring these days. Even the late bulletin is run by a skeleton crew.

Tonight, there are only four of us. Me, Tasha, who's producing the bulletin, Una, our long-in-the-tooth director who was supposed to retire years ago but who keeps coming back to plug the gaps, and a vision mixer. He's a technical geek who spends most of his day locked away in one of the back rooms with a soldering iron and a pile of broken kit to fix.

'Just look into the camera for me, Yannick,' Una instructs.

I straighten my back, put on my serious newsreader's face and stare into an unblinking, unmanned camera lens partially hidden by the scrolling amber text of the autocue.

The late-night bulletin used to be presented from the studio where the main evening programme is hosted, but the head of news wanted to mix things up and thinks it looks more authentic to have the late presenter sitting in the newsroom, like we're in the thick of the action. What she's forgotten is that we have so few staff that by ten thirty at night, the newsroom is deserted. It's like presenting on the deck of the *Marie Celeste*.

'Let's go in ten,' Una says, starting a countdown to the rehearsal.

She rolls the titles and cues me in. I look up from my scripts and gallop through the world's dullest five minutes of news.

'Good evening. The region is facing an unprecedented housing crisis with an estimated twenty thousand homes needing to be built within the next five years to meet demand, according to campaigners,' I read, trying to inject some enthusiasm into my voice, but it really is the most tedious story.

Where's the human interest? The blood and the tears?

I'm not sure how much more of these shifts I can take. There must be better opportunities out there somewhere if they're not going to give me a shot at presenting the main show.

I rattle through the rest of the bulletin, my mind drifting to a brighter future on the network. I'm not wedded to staying in current affairs, although I could see myself anchoring the national evening news. I wouldn't do anything too lightweight, though. Maybe my own investigative series. Or documentaries.

I race through the rest of the run order and feel a little bit of me die inside when I reach the 'and finally' item, a story about an overgrown pig rescued from a house in Maidstone and rehomed at a wildlife park on the Kent Downs.

'And I guess you could say that for Pippa, she's finally had her bacon. Now, let's see if it's going to be the weather for pigs. Here's Raheem with your forecast,' I say, throwing one of my winning smiles at the camera.

'You'll need to slow down a bit, Yannick,' Tasha says as the end titles roll. 'We came out with thirty seconds in hand.'

I silently grind my teeth. Of course I'll slow it down when we're on air. I do know what I'm doing. And I'm bloody good at it. I only wish they'd let me prove it. They keep promising I'll get my opportunity, but there's only so long I can flog myself to death on these late shifts. I'm not getting any younger. I'll be twenty-eight next year. Another year closer to the big three-oh. But it's dead men's shoes around here. Our main presenters have been in post for years and don't look like they're going anywhere soon. And the management won't shake things up for the sake of it. They're too worried about the ratings.

'Five minutes to air,' Una tells everyone.

I reach for a scratched mirror on an adjacent desk. Someone's written 'ugly' across the glass with an indelible black marker. I check my hair. I have great hair for TV, although is that the first hint of grey tingeing my temples? And those creases at the corners of my eyes are definitely getting deeper, no matter how slavishly I apply that expensive cream before bed every night. Maybe it's not such a bad thing. I've always had youthful looks, but maybe a more distinguished, veteran look might get me noticed and taken more seriously.

I glance down at the monitor showing the off-air feed from the national news team. The presenter, a blonde woman with a suspiciously smooth, high forehead, is running through the front pages of tomorrow's newspapers.

'Four minutes to air,' Una announces.

Everyone's quiet now. We're all ready and primed. It's only five minutes of television. It's hardly putting a rocket into space or performing open heart surgery. No one's going to die if we make a mistake, but we're all professionals. We all want a clean bulletin.

'Three minutes. Yannick, can you adjust your earpiece? I can see it poking out behind your collar.'

I reach over my shoulder and tuck the curly wire out of sight before checking my laptop on the desk by my legs one last time.

I open the Press Association wires and I'm immediately drawn to a line flashing in red, indicating a breaking story of high importance.

'1 GIRL MISSING'

Mostly these alerts are of no interest to us in the regions. Usually, they're in someone else's patch.

But tonight, when I see that red flashing story, my heart skitters.

'Two minutes to air.'

I click it open and scan the brief details. There's not much. A name, an age and a location. A little girl who's gone missing on the way home from school. More information to follow.

My mouth goes dry and the world around me shrinks away. I double-check the name. Keep breathing. This isn't the time to lose it.

'Tash, have you seen this?' I glance at the camera, as if I can see her through the lens. 'There's a girl missing in Faversham.'

The story dropped twenty minutes ago. Twenty minutes it's been sitting there, flashing red, and she's not spotted it. What is she playing at?

'Yeah, but it's a bit late to get it on now,' she says in a bored drawl.

I could throttle her. It's a big breaking news story. The sort of story every self-respecting journalist prays for. Something to sink their teeth into and a chance to be first with the news.

'It's not too late,' I say. 'Come on, we need to get it into the bulletin. Police have released a picture. Can you get that mounted?'

'There isn't time,' Tasha says, sounding exasperated. 'We're about to go live.'

'One minute to air. Good luck, everyone,' Una says.

If she won't make the call, I'll have to take control. It would be unforgivable if we missed the story, and it won't only be Tasha's head on the block. It'll be mine. 'Change at the top of the programme,' I say. Maybe Tasha will even thank me later when she realises I've saved her from a tongue-lashing from our news editor, Tim. 'We're leading on the missing girl.'

'I don't have time to write it up *and* mount the picture,' Tasha complains, a nervous tension in her voice.

'Don't worry about writing it up. I'll take it straight from the wires. You concentrate on sorting out that photo. Make sure it's ready.'

'We'll have to drop something to make room.'

'Drop that stupid pig story.' I'm virtually yelling at her now, my adrenaline pumping.

'Thirty seconds. Standby, everyone,' Una says.

'Okay, okay.' Tasha's breathing heavily. She's starting to panic under the pressure, but I need her calm and in control to guide me through. I can't have her going to pieces in my ear.

'What's happening, everyone?' Una asks. 'Talk to me, people. Are we changing the run order or what?'

'Ummm - I don't know,' Tasha replies.

'Yes,' I scream. 'We're leading on the missing girl. Don't worry about autocue, I'll ad lib.'

'Okay, story one now missing girl. Housing crisis becomes story two,' Una says. 'Let's get on air and we'll sort out the timings in a moment. On air in ten, nine...'

I place the laptop on my legs, pull my shoulders back and clear my throat. My heart's racing far too fast. I take three deep breaths to calm my nerves. No one wants to see a flustered newsreader. I need to stay professional and push my personal feelings aside.

'...eight, seven, six, five...'

I glance down at the two brief lines of copy on the wires. This is really happening.

'...four, three, two, one... and cue titles.'

Upbeat music plays and the title sequence unfolds on the monitor at my feet, a montage of images showing off the best of the region.

'And cue Yannick,' Una says.

Chapter 4

There's nothing like the buzz of live TV and a breaking news story. I glance up from my laptop, looking serious. Not quite frowning, but resisting the urge to smile. It's important to set the right tone. A newsreader shouldn't appear happy with a run order of misery, tragedy and injustice.

'Good evening. We start with some breaking news tonight. A major search is underway for a missing ten-year-old girl who vanished on her way home from school in Faversham earlier this afternoon. Police say they are extremely concerned for the safety of Annie Warren, who was last seen leaving school at around three thirty but who failed to arrive home. Anyone with information about Annie's disappearance is being urged to contact Kent Police. And of course, we'll keep you up to date with any developments on that story as they happen.'

I pause for a beat, but as I attempt to subtly slide my laptop back onto the desk, I knock the autocue controls. The text in front of the camera jumps ahead to the end of the next link.

There's no point panicking. These things happen. It's how you navigate out of them that matters. It's what separates the ordinary newsreaders from the great ones. Fortunately, I still have my pile of scripts on my lap. I glance down and read from the top, with adrenaline still racing through my veins. It's only two short sentences. A boring link into the housing crisis item, but my mind's stuck on the previous story. The missing girl. Annie Warren.

I skip through the link and throw into a pre-recorded film that's been cut down from a longer version that was shown on the main programme.

'And on package,' Una says in my ear. 'Great job, Yannick.'

'How are you getting on with that picture, Tash?' I ask.

'Nearly there,' she says.

'Is it going to make?'

'Should do.'

'Good job.' There's no point ranting while we're on air, telling her she should have been across the story. I need that picture ready for a recap at the end of the bulletin. 'And how are we doing for time?'

'Thirty seconds over,' she says.

'And we've dropped the pig story?' I say, flicking through my scripts.

'Yes.'

'Let's lose story five as well, the knife crime figures.'

'The knife crime story? Don't you think - ?'

'Just do it!' I don't mean to shout, but honestly, we don't have the time to argue.

'Back to you in ten, Yannick,' Una informs me in my ear.

I rattle through the remaining stories, keeping up the pace to buy myself some time for the recap on missing Annie. I'm still not confident Tasha is going to have that photo ready. If necessary, we'll go without it.

'Picture's in,' she gasps, much to my surprise.

'Now back to tonight's breaking story,' I say with due solemnity, 'and police have released a photo of the missing ten-year-old, Annie Warren, who has sparked a major police search this evening after vanishing on her way home from school in Faversham.'

'On picture,' Una says.

The screen at my feet fills with an image of a happy, smiling girl with a smattering of freckles across her nose and sandy hair tied into two bunches. It's one of those ubiquitous school photographs taken against a blurry tortoiseshell background. Her shoulders are back and she's lifting her chin like she's fizzing with pride while leaning towards the camera, almost as if she's been caught in the act of running away. Her bright red school tie is slightly askew and there's a fuzzy white mark on her jumper that might be toothpaste or yogurt. It's hard to tell.

'Police say Annie left school at around three thirty and was expected home by four, but her parents raised the alarm after she failed to turn up. If anyone has any information about Annie's whereabouts, they're asked to contact Kent Police as a matter of urgency.'

'Back on you,' Una says, as the image of Annie vanishes from the screen.

'Of course, we'll keep you updated on developments with that story through the night on our website.' It's a lie. We don't have the resources to update the web pages out of hours, but who's going to be checking? 'And we'll bring you all the latest on the search in our breakfast bulletins with Maggie from six forty-five. But that's all from us this evening. Goodnight.'

Una counts us off air and I pretend to shuffle my scripts as the newsroom lights go down.

The wait for the final clear seems to take an age, the camera fixed on me.

'And we're off air,' Una announces at last.

I let out a sigh of relief and my shoulders slump.

'Great job, team. Well done, everyone,' she adds.

I jump off the stool and pull out my earpiece. Una swaggers out of the gallery and across the newsroom with an exaggerated sway of her hips. 'Great bulletin. And good to get that missing girl story in,' she says.

'No thanks to that useless waste of space producing tonight.' I nod towards the darkened gallery at the edge of the newsroom where Tasha's still hiding out.

Una's eyes narrow. She points at the microphone still attached to the lapel of my jacket. Tasha's probably heard every word. Oh well, it's nothing I wouldn't say to her face, although maybe not so bluntly.

I peel off the mic and lay it on the stool before returning to my desk. A few minutes later, Tasha skulks sheepishly out of the gallery, staring at the floor. I guess my microphone wasn't muted.

She flops in her chair at her desk and prods lethargically at her keyboard and mouse until her computer monitor wakes up. She's supposed to leave a handover for the breakfast producer as well as a selection of ready-written news items, so I suspect she'll be here for a while longer yet.

As I'm cleaning the make-up off my face with a baby wipe, the phone on her desk rings. No prizes for guessing who that'll be. I chance a surreptitious glance in her direction.

The colour drains from her face as she picks up the handset and listens.

'Right,' she says, chewing her lip. 'Okay. But - '

It'll be Tim, our ever-vigilant news editor. He'll have been watching the bulletin and seen us breaking the story about the missing girl.

'Yes, sure,' she says, 'but I still need to finish the overnights.'

I wander around to her side of the desk as Una hurries out of the building, waving over her shoulder. She can't get out quick enough. 'Night, everyone.'

'Is it Tim? What's he want?' I mouth to Tasha as I catch her eye. 'Let me speak to him.' I hold my hand out for the phone. I don't want her taking all the credit for getting the story on air tonight.

She shrugs. 'Yannick's here. He wants a word.'

'Tim?'

'Yannick, well done on breaking the story,' he says with a nasal drawl. If you didn't know him, you'd think he was disinterested, but it's just Tim. He rarely sounds excited about anything.

'No problem. It broke just as we were going to air, so it was a team effort,' I say humbly. I don't want to look like I'm crowing.

'It could be a big one. We need someone out there tonight news gathering. I've scrambled a camera and I've told Tasha to get her arse across there pronto.'

'Tasha? Why?' I say, momentarily forgetting she's sitting right in front of me. I turn my back on her as her lips curl and she raises an eyebrow. I'm not having her stealing my story from under my nose.

'Because she's on the late shift and there's no one else.'

'Do you think she's up to taking on a big story like this?' I say, lowering my voice to a whisper.

'I don't have any alternative, Yannick, unless you want to go? I've spoken to the police and there's already a big search going on. I want us there talking to people. Plus, national want some pictures too, although they might send their own reporter if the story develops,' Tim says.

'I'll go.'

I glance over my shoulder. Tasha is staring at me with her arms folded across her chest. I'm doing her a favour. She should be pleased. And anyway, she doesn't understand the significance of the story. It's going to be huge. It's not every day a ten-year-old girl gets abducted in broad daylight. It's going to be all over the papers tomorrow, so we need to be on the scene before the hordes from the London nationals descend on the town.

'Great. Get there as soon as you can,' Tim says. 'Start digging around. See what you can find out. And make sure you get some pictures sent back for the breakfast bulletins.'

'Of course. I won't let you down.'

When I hang up, Tasha is staring at me with ill-concealed disdain, her lips pursed and her eyes narrowed.

'Tim asked *me* to go,' she says.

'I'm doing you a favour.' I hurry back to my desk and start packing my bag. 'Haven't you still got the overnights to write?'

'That's not fair.'

'Life's not fair.' I'm not going to stand here arguing with her. This is my story and I'm not about to share the glory with anyone else.

Chapter 5

CATHY

The two police officers left about forty minutes ago, and now the house feels hollow again. We rattle around inside it like two spare parts, not sure what to do with ourselves. It feels wrong to be doing nothing, but the police were adamant. Imagine if by some miracle Annie turned up and we weren't home, or she somehow managed to get to a phone and there was no one here to answer.

Kit's pacing up and down the lounge chewing his fingernails, the floorboards creaking under his feet, while I sit on the edge of the sofa staring into space, my mind numb. We're both too preoccupied with our own thoughts to speak. Annie's never been out this late on her own. Wherever she is, she must be terrified.

Not knowing is the worst thing. My mind's already started filling in the blanks, conjuring up terrible images of Annie's little body, bloodied and pale at the bottom of a water-filled ditch or cowering in the footwell of some stranger's car. I know that doesn't help and I need to stay positive, but I can't control it. The dark thoughts control me.

'Can you get onto the internet?' Kit says, scratching his head as he pores over his phone. 'I was trying to see if they've released Annie's picture.'

'I don't know.' I pick up my phone and open a browser, but a stark message informs me it can't connect to the internet. 'No, it's not working.'

'Bloody hell. That's all we need right now, on top of everything else.'

Neither of us is much good with technology. I usually find if you wait long enough, invariably these things tend to fix themselves, but why did it have to happen tonight of all nights?

Kit dives behind the TV to check the router, but he's interrupted by a knock at the door. We both freeze and stare at each other. Kit's the first to react, marching purposefully into the hall.

I hold my breath.

But it's not Annie.

It's another police officer in civilian clothes who flashes a warrant card and introduces herself as a family liaison officer, a FLO, she says, who's been assigned to stay with us during this difficult time.

'My name's PC Zara Slotkowski.' She has a practised friendly smile, which I guess is designed to put families like us at ease. 'But please, call me Zara. I'm here to support you while we try to find your daughter. I can answer any questions you might have and I'll do my best to keep you up to date on any progress in the search for Annie.'

'Is there any news?' I gasp.

She lowers her gaze. 'No, not yet, Mrs Warren, but as soon as I hear anything, you'll be the first to know.'

She seems nice enough, but I could do without a stranger in the house right now, even if she is here to help. I don't have the mental capacity for it.

'Shall I put the kettle on?' she says. 'Make us all a nice cup of tea? Just point me in the direction of the kitchen.'

I nod and indicate to the door off the hall. She might as well make herself useful while she's here.

Another long, slow hour passes.

My mug of tea sits cold and untouched on the coffee table in the middle of the room. Zara's on the sofa opposite, occupied with her phone.

'Sorry, the internet seems to be down at the moment,' I tell her.

She shrugs and carries on tapping away. 'It's okay. I have unlimited data.' Lucky her. We get terrible coverage with our provider.

'Has the media appeal gone out yet?'

'Yeah, several of the local news websites are running it.' She holds her phone up to show me.

The sight of Annie's happy, carefree face staring back at me brings a lump to my throat.

It's a little past ten thirty when the phone rings. It's so loud in the silence that's settled between us that we all jump and my heart catapults into my mouth.

'Hello?'

'Cathy, darling, it's Fiona. I've just seen the news about Annie. How awful. How are you coping, you poor thing? You must be worried out of your mind.'

A long breath seeps out of my lungs. 'Hi, Fiona.'

I should have called Fiona earlier and let her know, but I've not been thinking straight all evening.

'What can I do to help?' She's taken on that officious tone of hers when she's on a deadline or thinks she has to organise people.

'Right now, get off the phone. We need to keep this line clear in case Annie calls,' I explain. 'Sorry.' I can be blunt with Fiona. She's one of my best friends and my business partner in the coffee shop we've run together in the town centre for the last ten years.

'Right, yes, of course. I wasn't thinking.'

She hangs up immediately, but ten minutes later she's at the door, hammering at it like there's a raging fire.

'Fiona, you didn't need to come over. It's late. You should be in bed,' I say, but secretly I'm pleased to see a friendly face.

She throws herself at me, wrapping her arms around me, hugging me tightly. 'We saw it on the late news as we were turning in,' she says. 'Honey, you must be going out of your mind with worry. You should have called.'

As she peels herself off me, I notice she's brought her dreadful boyfriend. He's hanging back outside the door, rocking awkwardly from one foot to the other in the street, hands shoved in his pockets, collar turned up. He's the latest in a long string of inappropriate partners she's been through since her divorce.

'Come on, Demetri.' She waves him inside. 'Don't hang about in the cold.'

'Hallo, Cathy,' he says, with a heavy Eastern European accent. I've met him a couple of times, when he's popped in to see Fiona in the coffee shop, but I still can't get over the tattoos that spill out from the cuffs of his jacket over the back of his hands and creep out from his collar and up his neck. I'm hardly one to criticise, but he seems so much younger than her. He can't be much more than mid-twenties. Fiona's pushing fifty.

'Right, tell me everything,' she says, grabbing both my hands and fixing my gaze. 'When did you last see her?'

I tell Fiona everything I've told the police, how Annie seems to have vanished into thin air after she walked out of school this afternoon and that the police are at least taking it seriously. I introduce her to Zara, who's still on her phone on the sofa. She smiles and gives a friendly wave.

'Any idea where she might have gone?' Fiona asks.

I shake my head and bite my lip, trying to hold back my tears. 'No,' I whimper, 'but what if someone's taken her?'

'Hey, don't even think like that,' Fiona says sternly. 'I'm sure she's fine. You've called around all her friends, I take it?'

'Yes, of course. Nobody's seen her. What the hell am I going to do?'

She slips off her coat, hangs it on the newel post at the bottom of the stairs and pushes up her sleeves, all business-like. 'Right, well, there's no point moping around being miserable about it, is there? We need to get on it, start mobilising people.'

Kit shakes his head. 'I should be out there, looking for her, but the police want us to stay in the house in case Annie tries to get in touch,' he says.

Fiona waves his concerns away. 'Leave that to them. They know what they're doing. There's plenty we can do from here.' She slips on a pair of thick, black glasses and holds her phone at arm's length. 'I take it you've already posted something online? Facebook? Instagram? Twitter?'

It's not even occurred to me. I rarely share anything on social media. Why would I want people prying into our lives? 'No, not yet,' I mumble.

She arches an eyebrow. 'Come on, Cathy. We need to start raising awareness. You know how important the first few hours are, don't you? If we can get everyone sharing your posts, we'll reach far more people than the police can.'

'I'm sure you're right, but you know how much I hate it.'

'I don't care. Not tonight. If you want to find Annie, we need to spread the word,' Fiona insists, making my insides crawl.

Fiona is a dear friend, but she can also be a monumental pain in the arse. She's the most loyal, funny, caring person I know, but she has a tendency to be bossy and controlling. I fear tonight is going to bring out the worst in her.

I warmed to her immediately when we met as newbies at a yoga class in the community centre in town. It was run by a skinny-arsed, oat milk-drinking vegan with a long grey plait that spilled down her spine, who told us all to breathe through our feet and shin bones. We thought it was the funniest thing we'd ever heard and ended up in a giggling mess at the back of the class like two naughty schoolgirls, neither of us with a clue how to do any of the stretches.

'The only stretch I've mastered is yawning,' Fiona told me over half a pint of lager in the pub afterwards.

We never went back to the yoga class, but we've stayed friends ever since. I can't remember how the subject of life goals came up, but several months later we discovered a common dream of owning our own coffee shop. Fiona had a young daughter and hadn't worked since she was born. She was getting itchy feet to do something meaningful with her life, while I was still working as a waitress, supported by Kit's rather more successful career.

When I mentioned it to him, he was wildly enthusiastic and offered to put up half of the money if Fiona covered the rest. And that's how the *Skinny Latte Coffee Shop* was born.

'A video post is probably the best idea. A tearful appeal from you,' Fiona says. 'I'll tag all my friends and family. We'll get it going viral in no time.'

'I'm not doing that, Fiona. Be serious.'

'I am serious. Come on.' She holds up her phone and points it at me. 'What the hell's wrong with your internet? I can't get any wifi.'

Every cloud. 'Ah, yeah, there's a problem with it. Sorry,' I say.

'That's no good.' Fiona lowers her phone and scowls at me. 'You're going to need decent broadband or we won't get anywhere.'

I shrug. I don't have a clue what's wrong with it. I just want my Annie home.

Fiona turns to Demetri, who's standing in the corner looking bored. He sticks out his bottom lip in a gesture which suggests he doesn't have a clue either.

'I know, I'll call Jake. He'll be able to fix it.'

'Fiona, no! He'll probably be in bed,' I cry, but it's too late. She's already found his number and has her phone to her ear. She holds an outstretched hand towards me, fingers splayed, holding me back.

Jake Maginnis is another ex-boyfriend. The first after her divorce, although he was still married at the time. They only lasted five months until he called it off and they both agreed it had been a mistake. They split amicably and have remained good friends, which is just as well as we've relied on him since we opened the coffee shop. He's a plumber by trade, but also an all-round Mr Fixit. There's not much he can't turn his hand to.

'Jake, it's Fiona. I'm with Cathy. Did you hear about Annie?' she says.

It's a mistake asking Jake to come around. The house is already full.

'There's a problem with her broadband and she desperately needs to be online tonight to sort out the social media appeals. Any chance you could pop around and take a look? Ah, brilliant. You're an angel.' She hangs up and smiles. 'He'll be here in ten minutes.'

Chapter 6

This is so typical of Fiona, waltzing in and taking over. She loves a crisis. Never more in her element than when a drama's unfolding.

She was the same when her sister's husband walked out a few years ago and she took it on herself to set up a profile on a dozen dating websites for the poor woman, determined to get her matched up with another "more suitable" man, as if she couldn't be trusted to do it herself.

Or like when I had my stalker. He wasn't really any trouble, just an older guy who developed a weird fixation with me. He kept coming into the coffee shop and telling me how beautiful I was. It was all harmless enough, although a bit creepy, until one evening I found him waiting for me outside with a bunch of flowers while I was locking up. I was handling it, but Fiona thought she knew better and had to interfere. It was lucky he could still walk after she arranged for her friend's son to put him in hospital for a week as a warning.

And that's what she's like. She can't keep her nose out of anyone else's business, unless there's a genuine problem and then she flounders around, waving her arms in the air and wailing like the world is ending. It was me who negotiated a better deal on the lease on the coffee shop when the landlord wanted to double the rent. It was me who called in pest control when Fiona spotted a rat in the rubbish in the back yard. And it was me who found Jake in the first place, the night before we were due to open and had the near disaster of the boiler packing up.

He was the only plumber who'd come out at short notice and happily work through the evening to ensure our grand opening could go ahead the next day. A few weeks later he was back to replace all the ageing pipework, which he said was another catastrophe waiting to happen. And that's how he became our go-to guy for anything that needed repairing or replacing. He could turn his hand to anything, including, it turned out, Fiona.

'You look a bit pasty,' she says, fussing over me, stroking strands of hair behind my ear. 'Maybe a touch of lipstick. Something for your cheeks. Nothing too over the top. Kit, what do you think?'

Kit's eyes widen. He glances at me and back to Fiona. 'Yeah, I don't know. Whatever you think.'

I swat her hand away. 'Fiona, stop it.'

She glares at me like she's my mother or something. 'Cathy, I'm only trying to help.'

'Cathy, can I use toilet?' Demetri asks, looking pained.

'Sure, it's upstairs. First door on the left.' I waft a hand in the direction of the stairs, and he slopes off.

'Have you thought about what you're going to say? Keep it natural. Speak from the heart.' Fiona thumps her chest with her fist. 'We're all about winning hearts and minds. And don't smile. Look sad.'

I let out a gasp of exasperation. Why can't she just leave me alone?

I'm almost grateful when Jake finally turns up. He whips off a baseball cap when I answer the door and usher him inside. He hasn't shaved and smells faintly of stale sweat. His eyes dart nervously around the room.

'Hey,' he says sheepishly.

'Thanks for coming. I told Fiona not to call.'

'It's fine.'

Fiona rushes out of the lounge like a whirlwind. 'Oh, Jakey, you're here. Well done. We're all so worried about little Annie.' She pouts. 'Poor Cathy is beside herself. We were going to post some social media appeals, but her internet's not working. Would you be a dear and see if you can fix it? You're so good with things like that.'

Is she flirting? I shake my head. There's a time and place and it isn't now.

'Where's the router?' Jake asks.

'Behind the TV in the lounge.'

He kicks off his boots and places them neatly under the rack of coats in the hall. Kit shows him through, while I'm left stuck with Fiona prattling in my ear.

'Perhaps you could hold up a picture of Annie,' she says. 'Do you have one we could use? And I don't know if this would help, but if you give me your logins and passwords, I could run your accounts for you. You know, to take some of the pressure off while you've got other things on your mind.'

'Yeah, whatever.'

'I mean, say if you'd rather not, but I thought it might be a good idea.'

'Yes, it's fine. I'll write them down for you.'

Where the hell is Demetri? He's been gone for ages. I hope he's not upstairs poking around. I know he's Fiona's boyfriend, but I hardly know him.

'And what about a hashtag? We need to agree on something we'll all use. What about "hashtag-Find-Annie"?'

'Sure. Whatever you think.' I know she's right. We need to do everything we can to find Annie, but I can't think about all this stuff right now, with all these people in the house and Fiona going on and on.

'Or maybe "hashtag-Bring-Annie-Home"? What do you think?'

'Yes,' I say.

'Yes, what?'

'Hmmmmm?'

'Okay, try that now. It should be working,' Jake shouts through from the lounge.

I check my phone. The local news webpage I was trying to look at earlier loads instantly. The search for Annie is their top story. I wander into the lounge with Fiona trailing behind me like a lamb. 'What did you do?'

'Rebooted the router, that's all,' Jake explains. 'Sometimes they get jammed up and stop working.'

'Brilliant. Thanks so much.'

He glances down at his shoeless feet and wriggles his toes. 'It's okay.'

'Bravo, Jake,' Fiona says, beaming. 'Right, let's crack on, shall we? Jake, you must have loads of followers. Can you make sure you share all this stuff?'

His smile looks more like a grimace. 'Sure.'

'Why don't you sit down on the sofa,' Fiona tells me, pushing the coffee table out of the way. She kneels on the floor with her phone held up in front of her face.

Above our heads, the floorboards creak. What *is* Demetri doing?

'Where? Here?' I ask, lining up in front of Fiona's phone. I don't want to do this, but if it gets her off my back and can help in any way to get Annie home, I have no choice but to go along with it.

'Okay, recording,' she says with a nod.

I feel everyone's eyes on me. Waiting to hear what I have to say.

'Errr, hello everyone. This is Cathy Warren.' I stare unblinking into the lens. 'Thanks for watching. I was just wondering if anyone has seen my daughter, Annie.'

Fiona lowers her phone, her face painted with disappointment. 'No, no, no,' she says, like she thinks she's Martin bloody Scorsese. 'With passion, Cathy. Try again.'

She holds her phone up once more and I clear my throat. In the corner of my eye, I see Kit watching with his arms crossed and Jake at his side, running his tongue around the inside of his mouth, looking like he'd rather be anywhere but here.

'If anyone's seen my daughter, Annie Warren, please let us know – '

'You didn't introduce yourself,' Fiona snaps. 'Try again.'

'Hello, I'm Cathy Warren. My daughter Annie went missing on her way home from school today and her dad and I are really worried.'

'That's it, keep the passion going. Don't be afraid to cry,' Fiona encourages me.

'If anyone knows where she is, or if you've seen her, please contact the police,' I continue. This is awful. I hate being the centre of attention and I've never liked having a camera pointed in my face. 'She's only ten.'

'Ask people to like and share.'

'So if you could like this message and share it, we'd be most grateful.'

Demetri finally reappears, his hulking presence looming large in the doorframe. He leans against it and folds his arms over his chest, smirking at me. I really can't understand what Fiona sees in him. He gives me the creeps.

'Do it one more time. Remember to look sad,' Fiona instructs me.

My head feels like it's in a vice. The room unexpectedly hot and sweaty. I can't think. I can't breathe.

'One more time. Cathy? What's wrong?'

The room starts to spin. My chest is tight, my ribs crushing my lungs.

'Cathy?' Fiona's voice is a distant whine.

I can't stand it anymore. I can't do this.

I jump up and Fiona rocks back on her haunches, eyes widening in surprise.

'Enough,' I say. 'It's too much. I can't bear it. I want everyone out. Now.'

When no one moves, I raise my voice and scream. 'I said everyone out! Get out of my house and leave me alone!'

Fiona stands, watching me warily. 'Cathy, we're only trying to help.'

'But you're not helping, Fiona. You're interfering, like you always do, trying to take over. Get out of my house!'

She blinks rapidly and swallows as everyone finally falls silent.

'Fine, I know when I'm not wanted. Demetri, come on, we're going.'

She strides out into the hall and snatches her coat off the stairs with her boyfriend lumbering like a sulky teenager behind her. Jake, head down, slides past me.

'I'm sorry,' he mumbles. 'I shouldn't have come.'

He pulls on his boots as Fiona flings open the door.

'I was only trying to help,' she hisses.

And then they're gone. Jake pulls the door closed behind them and I collapse onto the sofa with my head in my hands and let out a long, deep breath of relief, conscious that sitting opposite, Zara, our liaison officer, has been wordlessly watching everything.

Chapter 7

YANNICK

It's almost midnight when I arrive in Faversham, a smart market town on the north coast of Kent, half an hour's drive from the TV studio in Ashford. I head straight for Annie's school, St Jude's Primary, which, according to the map on my phone, is on the northeastern side of the town, near the marshes at Oare.

The town should be deserted at this time of night, but as I pull off the motorway and head north into the neighbourhood where Annie was last seen, there's a buzz of activity. Worried-looking people wrapped up against the chill trawl the streets with torches, peering into gardens and behind bushes, calling Annie's name. The lights are on in many of the houses and as I drive slowly on, taking it all in, I can sense the collective fear, like static in the air before an electrical storm. People are worried. A child is missing. They all want to help, but I know what they're thinking. Something bad has happened to her. At worst, she's been abducted. Someone, maybe even someone they know, has snatched her from the street. It's a terrifying thought.

At the school, the playground is brightly illuminated under fierce floodlights that have been erected to assist the search. There's a significant police presence. Swarms of officers in fluorescent yellow jackets are everywhere.

It's already turned into a full-scale operation and Annie's only been missing for a few hours.

I park close to the school, a brown brick single-storey Victorian building with an incongruous-looking bellcote above the apex of a tiled roof. I kill the engine and grab my phone. I've missed several calls from Harry Collier, the cameraman Tim scrambled. I call him back and we arrange to meet by my car.

Harry can be cantankerous and difficult when his heart's not in it. I guess he's been doing the job too long, but I'm hoping this story will get him excited, even though it's late. While most of the staff cameramen were let go a few years ago in another round of budget cuts, and the reporters issued with camera kits to self-shoot their own stories, Harry managed to cling on. We're only supposed to use him when it's a big story or the circumstances make it a difficult shoot, like tonight when we'll need to be agile and ready for any developments.

'Bloody hell, they must be desperate!' Harry shouts when he spots me clambering out of my car, ignoring the fact it's the middle of the night. He's staggering along with a camera in one hand and a tripod slung over his shoulder.

'I thought Tim was going to send me a decent camera,' I retort.

'It's not like you to get your hands dirty on an actual story.'

'You're right, they were desperate.' I clasp his meaty hand as he drops the tripod on the ground with an unconscious groan. 'Can you get some general shots of the activity and I'll see if I can grab some people to talk to.'

'I've already shot a bit,' he says with a grin. 'But what about the parents? Are they speaking yet?'

He knows the drill. On stories like this, it's like following a formula. We'll need shots of the school where Annie was last seen, some images of the search, vox pops with some volunteers, a soundbite from the police and possibly a piece-to-camera from me. But we both know the real prize is an interview with Annie's parents, with tears and genuine emotion. Even though we'll no doubt get complaints that we've intruded on their grief later, it's what everyone wants to see because we're all voyeurs at heart. Whether we admit it or not, we want to see the pain and the heartache laid bare, to truly understand what it must be like to lose a child. It's a parent's worst nightmare and every mother and father watching will be asking the same questions. What if it was me? What would I do?

'We'll get to them,' I say. There's no rush. I'm confident Annie's parents are not going to be speaking to anyone apart from us, so we can afford to take our time. And anyway, it would look suspicious if we turned up at the house too soon.

I nod towards the school where a white marquee has been thrown up in the playground. Inside, two women are serving hot drinks from a large metal urn to police officers and volunteers. 'Can you get some of that activity first?'

I've not seen any other journalists so far, but it won't be long before the town is overrun with reporters and news crews, especially if Annie's not found by the morning. A ten-year-old girl missing overnight is news gold. We need to move quickly.

As Harry sets up to grab a wide shot of the school, I spot a woman in an oversized high-viz jacket circling around the playground. She's clutching a notepad and pen and looks a little lost. A reflective strip on her back confirms my suspicions. She's a police media officer, dispatched to assist communications between the police and the press who they'll be relying on to broadcast appeals for information about Annie.

I plaster a smile on my face. 'Yannick Kellor,' I say as I approach. 'We're with the local TV news. Is there someone who can do a quick interview for us about the search?'

She looks startled, her eyes opening wide. She looks me up and down and fingers a stray strand of hair off her forehead.

'I'm afraid everyone's a bit tied up at the moment. What did you need exactly?'

'Just a few words about the latest on the search.'

'I'll see what I can do,' she says. 'Have you seen our latest press release?'

She hands me a piece of paper, but there's not much new in it other than a tantalising snippet that the force has drafted in two hundred officers to assist with the search. It's a great new line for the breakfast bulletins and proof of how big the story is panning out to be. They wouldn't divert that many officers to the search unless they were seriously concerned for Annie's safety. This story is getting better and better by the minute.

'Can you call me when you have someone available?' I hand her my card. 'We're going to get a few shots of the search. Do you know the way Annie walked home? I was hoping to retrace her footsteps.'

'Sadly not,' the media officer says. 'There are at least three different routes she could have taken, but nobody saw her and there's not much CCTV around this part of the town. At the moment, we're concentrating our efforts in and around the estate.' She points over my shoulder.

It makes sense. I had a quick look at the map of Faversham on my phone before I left the studio and there are countless routes Annie could have taken if she was heading home from school towards the creek, the narrow stretch of tidal water that divides the town.

The most obvious are through the housing estate, a warren of back streets and alleys, or along the main road from St Jude's, past a long row of terraced houses, a newsagent and a church. She could even have taken a longer, more scenic route out over the marshes, past several deep-water lakes. I bet the police are already thinking about bringing in a dive team. Now that would make great pictures.

Harry brushes past me to grab some close-up shots of the women in the marquee. He kneels at the end of the table and shoots low, creating an interesting angle, focusing on the women's hands. He might be a grumpy old sod at times, but he's a creative cameraman when he puts his mind to it.

'Harry, do you have the mic? Let's grab some voxes.'

He tosses me a scruffy black rucksack. I pull out a shotgun mic and approach a middle-aged couple in walking boots, woollen hats and hiking jackets, who are milling around cradling hot mugs of tea.

'Can we have a quick word?' I say, with Harry at my elbow, the camera on his shoulder, its top light blinding them.

I smile sweetly as I shove the mic under the woman's nose. Women, in my experience, are far more likely to speak to the likes of me and Harry in situations like this.

She glances at the man. Her husband, I presume. He looks tired and drawn.

'How concerned are you about Annie Warren's safety?' I ask.

'Well, of course, everyone's terribly worried,' the woman says.

'It's incredible to see so many people turning out to help the police with the search. What do you think's happened to her?'

'Hopefully, she's safe and someone's looking after her, but of course, with all the marshes and the bogs around here, anything could have happened.'

It's not the answer I'm looking for. I try again.

'Are you worried she might have been abducted?'

The woman's jaw tightens. 'Gosh, I hope not.'

'But it's possible?'

'It would be awful if it's true, but it does happen, doesn't it? You hear about these things on the news, but you just don't think it's going to happen on your own doorstep.'

I lower the microphone and touch her arm. 'That was great, thank you. But can I get you to say that last answer again, so we don't have to edit it later?'

She looks at me blankly.

'So if I ask you again what you think has happened to Annie, could you say you're really concerned she might have been abducted?'

Her husband steps away and I sense Harry moving behind me, framing the woman's face tightly. I ask the question again before she has time to say no.

'Of course we're really worried about little Annie,' she says as I nod enthusiastically, 'especially if she's been abducted. You don't expect that sort of thing to happen around here, do you? Is that alright?'

'Perfect. Thank you.'

There's nothing more to be gained from hanging around at the school, so I suggest to Harry that we head into the estate.

There are so many people out, either chatting on their doorsteps with their neighbours or working in pairs, combing through the undergrowth and poking their heads into darkened alleys, that it could be the middle of the day rather than the small hours of the night. Groups of teenagers are loitering with cigarettes, footballs and bikes, watching with amused detachment. A police patrol car crawls along, its headlights dipped. A bleary-eyed young woman with dishevelled bed hair appears at her door wrapped in a towelling dressing gown.

In between the masses of houses, mostly post-war semi-detached cheap stock, we find a rudimentary football pitch with a pair of rusty, paint-flaking goalposts, alongside a fenced off children's play area. It's the perfect location to record an as-live for the breakfast bulletins. It's not something I've been asked for, and it probably won't be used, but if we keep it short, it'll at least give the producer an option and I'm keen to show I've gone the extra mile.

Harry shoulders his camera. I hold the microphone below my waist, out of shot. I stare into the lens, count to three and begin.

'Police have drafted in around two hundred officers to help with the search for missing ten-year-old Annie Warren here in Faversham, their numbers bolstered by countless volunteers from the community. Although it's too early to speculate what has happened, many here tonight fear the worst, that an innocent little girl has been snatched off the streets by a monster living in their midst.'

I lower my eyes and speak directly into the mic with some directions for the breakfast producer. 'Drop in the vox here with the female volunteer talking about her concerns Annie might have been abducted.'

Nobody knows what's happened to Annie for sure. She might have wandered off and had an accident or been snatched off the street by a stranger in a van. Either way, it's a great story.

I clear my throat, straighten my tie and lower the mic out of shot again.

'As you can see behind me, people have turned out in their droves, torches in hand, to scour the area, unwilling to give up until Annie's been found. Unfortunately, the police have yet to piece together the exact route she took on her way home, which is hampering their efforts and forcing them to widen their search, in a location peppered with boggy marshland and open water. It's unclear at this stage whether police will be drafting in divers to help with their search, but many here tonight will be hoping it won't come to that.'

I hold my gaze into the camera for a count of three, looking suitably concerned, until Harry lowers the camera and switches off the top light. I don't want to appear callous and uncaring, but it's important to get the facts across impartially. I'm not here to weep and wail. I'll leave that to Annie's parents.

'Great, I'll get that sent back to base before we leave. So do you want to try the parents now?' Harry asks.

I glance at the time on my phone. It's pushing on towards one, but there's no chance they'll be sleeping. Not with their daughter missing and half of Kent Police searching the town for her. Now is as good a time as any.

'Sure,' I say. 'We'll go in your car.'

'Do you have an address for them?' Harry frowns.

'They're on the creek.'

If he's surprised I know where they live, he doesn't show it. The police haven't released their names or address yet, but any journalist with a modicum of talent could track them down with Annie's name in the public domain. You can find out almost anything if you dig deep enough.

I only hope they're not being cosseted by an overly protective team of police officers. If I can speak to them directly, I'm sure they'll agree to an interview. But that's only part of the deal I'm here to strike a deal. I want an exclusive. I don't want them talking to any other journalists. I know they'll be worried sick about their daughter, and it's not a conversation they'll want to have right now, but I'll be doing them a massive favour. If they agree, they won't have to deal with any other reporters. It's a way of minimising their stress while keeping the story alive. A win-win for us both.

It's less than a two-minute journey by car to the Warrens' house. We pull up in a pub car park overlooking the creek. The tide's out, leaving a channel of thick, gloopy mud into which several small pleasure craft and yachts have partially sunk.

We aim for an anonymous-looking whitewashed house with a door that opens directly onto a private road. Three people, two men and a woman, have just come out. They don't look like police, but you never know. One of the men, with tattoos curling up his neck, brushes my shoulder as he barges past, knocking me off my stride. But none of them stop. They keep walking away.

All the lights are on in the house, but thankfully no police are standing guard outside. There's no one to stop me from knocking.

I hammer with my fist and step back. A bubble of voices from inside falls silent and footsteps creak across the floor.

The door opens and a woman stands silhouetted by the lights inside. It only takes a second for the spark of recognition to flit across her face.

'Hello, Aunty Cath,' I say with a sympathetic smile. 'I heard about Annie. Can I come in?'

Chapter 8

YANNICK

'Yannick? What are you doing here?'

'I was worried. I thought you'd appreciate a friendly face,' I say. I wasn't expecting quite such a frosty reception. Apart from Kit, I'm about the only family Aunty Cath has left, although we've not been close for years. And of course, she hates that I'm a journalist. She still sees my choice of career as a personal affront, but I suppose you can't blame her after what she went through with her father.

'It's not a good time.' My aunt yanks a chunky-knit cardigan back onto her shoulders.

She's not hysterical, like I expected, or shedding a flood of tears, although I'm sure they'll come. She's holding it together well, probably still in shock and not yet contemplating the worst. But her face is pale, like she's seen a ghost float through the walls, and she's knotted with tension, clawing at the back of her hands as if her skin is crawling.

'I heard about Annie. How are you coping?'

'Fine.'

'Really?'

'Look, Yannick, what do you want?'

'I told you, I was worried about you. And Annie,' I say.

'It's one o'clock in the morning.'

'I was on the late shift when the news broke. I thought I could help.' I chew my lip, trying to hold my irritation in check while Aunt Cathy keeps me standing on the doorstep like a stranger.

'Cathy?' Uncle Kit's voice calls from inside the house. 'Who is it?'

His heavy footsteps on the wooden floor herald his appearance. When he sees it's me, his face freezes in an expression I struggle to read. I'm not sure whether he's pleased or not. He rests a protective hand on Aunt Cathy's shoulder. 'Yannick,' he says, forcing a smile. 'It's cold out there. Why don't you come in?'

Cathy glances at him, unsure, but steps aside. She's never stood up to him in all the years they've been together.

'This is my colleague, Harry,' I say, remembering my cameraman waiting discreetly behind me. He raises an apologetic hand in greeting as he follows me in.

Kit shows us into the cosy sitting room at the front of the house where a woman with wiry black hair tied in a bun is sitting on a sofa. She nods a tight-lipped greeting as Kit introduces me. She looks me up and down, clocking the tripod I'm carrying. And then, when she notices Harry's camera, her eyes widen with alarm.

'Mr and Mrs Warren, I'm not sure it's a good idea inviting the press in at this early stage,' she says.

'Yannick's family,' Uncle Kit says firmly.

'Even so – '

'This is still my house. I'll decide who I invite in and who I don't,' he says pointedly. 'PC Slotkowski is a police liaison officer. She's keeping us up to date with developments.'

I nod and smile. So much for catching Cathy and Kit on their own. It's going to make negotiating an interview with them that much harder, but there's not much I can do about it. These so-called liaison officers invariably overstep the mark. Too often they think they're there as a barrier to hold back the media, which is utter nonsense.

PC Slotkowski begrudgingly makes room for us on a long, low sofa. Harry and I sit side by side opposite my aunt and uncle. A TV is on low in the corner, tuned to one of the rolling 24-hour news stations. A tickertape scrolling along the bottom of the screen routinely flashes up news of Annie's disappearance. I keep half an eye on the screen to check whether the channel has considered it a big enough story to warrant sending a crew yet.

'When did you last see her?' I ask.

Cathy stares at the floor, twirling her wedding ring around her finger, and sighs. 'This morning.'

Kit takes her hand and squeezes it. He glances at Slotkowski. She's obviously heard the details already. 'She didn't come home,' he says. 'We think something happened to her on her way back from school.'

Poor Annie. I've hardly seen her since she was a baby, but this must be tough on my aunt and uncle. No one expects their child to go missing in broad daylight. It's at times like these I'm glad I don't have kids. Not that I could ever see myself as a father. It's something that's never held any appeal for me.

'I'm sure they'll find her,' Harry says, turning on the charm with a warm smile. 'We've just been through the estate and the place is teeming with police and volunteers. She's probably just hiding out somewhere, totally oblivious to all the fuss she's caused.'

They're the words of comfort I should be saying, but I don't do sympathy. I never seem to be able to find the right words. And besides, it makes me cringe when people wear their hearts on their sleeves. Like crying in public. Awful.

Cathy looks up at Harry through dark lashes, her eyes narrowing. She's about to say something when there's a sharp, officious knock at the door.

Kit hurries out to answer it. The sound of a deep, male voice carries through from the hall and a few moments later two men in dark suits appear, giving off the distinctive air of authority, their presence mildly intimidating. The small room suddenly feels hot and crowded.

'DS Monkton.' The first man flashes a warrant card as he surveys the room. He's tall and stiff-backed but with rounded, sloping shoulders as if he's trying and failing to carry the weight of the world. 'This is DC Shears. We need to ask you a few questions about Annie, if you don't mind.'

When he notices the camera on Harry's lap, he raises an inquisitive eyebrow. 'And you are?'

Harry struggles up from the sofa where he's sunk into the soft cushions. 'Harry Collier,' he says, holding out a hand, which Monkton ignores. 'We're with the local news.'

I spring up onto my feet. 'Annie's my cousin,' I add. He's less likely to throw us out if he knows I'm family.

Monkton looks to Kit for confirmation. He nods.

'I'd rather we did this in private,' the detective says.

'We have nothing to hide.' Kit crosses his arms defensively.

'Even so, this is a delicate matter, and I don't want it splashed across the media. That's not going to be helpful in getting Annie home.'

'Yannick stays,' Kit says.

I feel a smirk creep across my face. Kit and Cathy don't want me here waving cameras in their faces any more than the police do, but Kit isn't one to be told what to do. And Annie is my cousin, after all.

'Don't mind us,' I say. 'We just wanted to grab a few words from my aunt and uncle for the breakfast bulletins tomorrow. I think it will help raise the profile of the appeal to hear directly from them, don't you? And it would be great to get a few words from yourself too.'

An uneasy silence descends on the room. Monkton's clearly not a man who likes being backed into a corner. He's used to calling the shots and not being told no.

'Fine,' he growls at last. 'But everything said in here tonight remains confidential.' He stares at Harry. 'And the camera stays off. Got it?'

Harry nods enthusiastically, like a puppy trying to please its owner.

Monkton asks the questions, perched on a dining room chair Kit fetches for him, while Shears stays silent, taking notes.

'Mrs Warren, walk us through what happened this morning before Annie left for school.'

Cathy sighs and rolls her eyes to the ceiling. 'I've been through this a dozen times already,' she says, sounding exasperated. 'Why do you keep asking me the same questions over and over?'

'One more time, please,' Monkton says. 'It's important we understand your daughter's state of mind when you last saw her.'

'Like I've already explained, we had breakfast as usual, and Annie left the house at about eight thirty. That was the last we saw of her.'

'And she usually walks to and from school on her own?'

'Since the beginning of this school year, yes. It's not far and she's become so independent lately, I didn't think it would be an issue. Lots of her friends walk on their own,' Aunty Cath says.

'Ten is still quite young.'

Uncle Kit bristles. 'Are you here to lay blame or are you actually interested in finding our daughter?'

'Just trying to establish the facts,' Monkton says. 'And how did she seem when she left? Was she in a good mood?'

'As far as I could tell, yes,' Cathy says.

'Anything on her mind? Any problems at school?'

'No.'

'Any cross words between you?'

'No, nothing like that.'

'Has she ever gone missing before?' Monkton crosses his legs and rests his hands on his knees. He's staring at Aunt Cathy like he's studying a map, watching how she responds as closely as he's listening to what she says. Does he think she's holding something back?

'Never. It's totally out of character.'

'Do you know which way she normally walked home?'

'When I used to pick her up when she was younger, we always came home past the church. It was the way I taught her to come.'

'You mean down Brent Hill and past the factory?' Monkton asks.

'Yes.'

I picture the route in my mind, recalling the map I studied on my phone. Cutting through the estate is probably slightly quicker, but I doubt there's much in it.

'Is there a chance she might have gone through the fields behind the industrial estate?' Monkton asks, his finger tapping out a frantic rhythm on the back of his hand, like he's wired on too much coffee.

'I don't think so.' Cathy shakes her head. 'That would be a long way to walk home. And she has no reason to go that way.'

'But it's not impossible?'

'I guess not.'

'Look, how is this helping?' I can see Uncle Kit's getting agitated with all the questions. 'Shouldn't you be out there looking for Annie instead of giving us the third degree? In fact, we should all be out there looking for her.'

Monkton shakes his head. 'I want you both to remain at the house in case Annie turns up or tries to contact you. I understand she has a phone, but she left it at home this morning?'

'One of your colleagues took it earlier,' Aunty Cath says.

Interesting. And certainly a good line to keep up my sleeve. Something I can drop into a package or reveal during a live. To hell with confidentiality. People are fascinated by that sort of tidbit. Of course, there'll be the usual cohort of conspiracy theorists who'll read more into it than it just being a forgetful ten-year-old with other things on her mind.

'Could we take a look in Annie's room?' Shears asks. It's the first thing he's said since he arrived. He has the sort of weaselly voice that would grate on you if you had to spend any time alone with him.

'Why?' Kit asks. He sits up straight with the muscle in his jaw twitching.

'It's routine in these sorts of investigations. There might be something Annie's left behind that could be useful.'

'And we'll need to take Annie's toothbrush,' Monkton adds with an apologetic grimace.

'Toothbrush?' Kit frowns.

'We need a sample of her DNA.' Monkton lowers his gaze. At least he has the decency to look sheepish.

The room falls silent as the implication becomes clear. It's obviously in case they find a body and need to identify it quickly. A lump balloons in my throat as I imagine little Annie's body being dragged from a marshy pond, her face blue and bloated, her hair tangled with weeds. It's a horrible thought.

I glance at Aunty Cath. She looks as wizened as an old lady, folding in on herself, as if she wants nothing more than to curl up in a ball on the floor with her own misery and despair. Maybe I have misjudged the timing. It's too early. We should have waited until the morning when it wasn't so raw. But if it wasn't me knocking on the door, it would have been someone else. At least I can try to keep the wolves at bay if they agree to an exclusive with me. It'll give them a good excuse to turn the rest of the media pack away, especially if we agree to feed some selected clips to the other broadcasters in return for respecting my aunt and uncle's privacy.

Uncle Kit gets up with a weary sigh. The stairs in the old house creak as he and Shears head for Annie's room, the floorboards above us wheezing under their weight.

Monkton smiles at Cathy as they wait, but her eyes are vacant. 'We have two hundred officers out looking for your daughter right now,' he says, trying to make her feel better. 'And there are probably several hundred more volunteers from the community helping. We've already started door-to-door enquiries. If she's out there, we'll find her. I promise.' He doesn't sound convinced, but he's trying to divert her thoughts from the alternative. That Annie is already dead and that they're looking for a body.

Aunt Cathy sniffs and wipes her nose with a tissue she has clenched in her fist, but she's clearly not ready to accept that Annie might be dead.

'Someone's taken her, haven't they?' she says, echoing my immediate thoughts when I saw the news break as we were going on air.

Monkton blinks rapidly. His fingers stop tapping on the back of his hand as he holds her gaze. 'It's a bit early to speculate,' he says.

'But that's the most likely scenario, isn't it?'

'Not necessarily.'

The stairs groan, heralding the return of Uncle Kit and DC Shears. All the eyes in the room are drawn to the transparent plastic bag in his hand. Inside, a solitary, pink toothbrush adorned with rainbows, glittering stars and prancing unicorns, its bristles splayed.

If ever there was an image that captured the essence of the story, that's it right there. I'm sorely tempted to sneak a photo on my phone, but even I can see how insensitive that would be.

'I'm afraid we'll also need to take any computers or laptops in the house,' Monkton says, directing his demand at Uncle Kit.

'What for?' my uncle grumbles.

I'm not surprised he's pissed off. They're treating them like they're suspects rather than victims.

'It's a formality. And we'll need your passwords, of course.'

'I don't see what this has got to do with finding Annie.' Uncle Kit's voice rises, and his face reddens.

'There might be something useful on them that could lead us to finding your daughter,' Monkton says calmly, unmoved by Uncle Kit's growing indignation. 'Something you might have overlooked.'

'You think we have something to do with this?' Uncle Kit thumps the arm of the sofa, making us all jump. 'You think we're involved in Annie's disappearance, don't you? Why don't you have the balls to come out and say it?'

'It's purely routine.'

'I can't believe this.' Uncle Kit runs a hand through his hair. 'You seriously think we could be involved in the disappearance of our own child?'

I wince. It's the elephant in the room we've all been trying to ignore. The police always suspect the parents when a child goes missing. Everyone knows that, because statistically a child is far more likely to fall victim to someone they know than a complete stranger. But I wish, for Uncle Kit's sake, he hadn't voiced it out loud.

His words hang in the air like a foul odour. I have no doubt social media is going to be full of that kind of speculation the longer Annie is missing. I suppose it's a good thing that he at least recognises that's what's going on here. That they're both going to be under suspicion by the police and the public.

'Nobody's saying that,' Monkton says.

'You don't have to. Instead of getting out there and finding Annie, you're more interested in pinning this on us. You're a disgrace.'

'Please, Mr Warren – '

'You disgust me.' A spray of spittle flies from Uncle Kit's mouth. 'What kind of parents do you think we are that we could do that?'

'Nobody's accusing you of anything, but we will need to take a look at your computers.'

'You're serious, aren't you?'

'Absolutely.'

Chapter 9

CATHY

August, 1990

It's Mother who takes us to school and picks us up, cooks our dinners, keeps the house clean, does all the shopping and nags us to finish our homework before bed. We hardly ever see Daddy, but that's because he's usually helping his patients.

He's not just any kind of doctor. He's a special doctor, a surgeon, which means he has to cut people open to make them better and that's why he has to spend so much time at the hospital.

It sounds yucky to me. Who would want to cut someone open, even if it is to make them better? But Mother says it's an important job, and it's why we live in such a nice house, near the sea, and I have my own bedroom and I don't have to share with Monica, my older sister. I only wish he was around more often. But even when he is home, he's usually too tired to play or read stories and Mother shoos us away if we try to bother him.

But this summer, it's different. Daddy is at home all the time. Mother says it's because he's taking a holiday, but I'm not sure that's true.

I usually love the long summer holidays. No school. No getting up early. No homework. The whole day to do what I want. But something's wrong with Daddy. He seems so sad. He spends most of his time sitting in his favourite chair, just staring out of the window, his face dark and scratchy where he hasn't shaved.

This morning when I came down for breakfast, he was in the kitchen with a newspaper spread out across the table and his head in his hands. It's not the paper he normally buys which is so big he has to fold it in half to read it, and at weekends lands heavily through the letterbox, bulging with extra sections and magazines. This one is half its size with lots of pictures and big headlines.

'Can we go to the beach today?' I ask, helping myself to a bowl and filling it to the brim with cornflakes.

The beach and the pier, with all its bright lights, noisy arcade games and promise of fun, are only a short walk from the house, but we hardly ever go there, which is a shame.

Daddy glances up, his eyes all glassy and red, like he hasn't even noticed me.

'Not today, sweetheart,' he says. His hair is all messy and he's wearing a scruffy T-shirt and his gardening trousers. He usually looks so smart.

'Please,' I beg, grabbing his arm, trying to pull him off his chair. 'We never go to the beach.'

Mother and Monica are both out, so it would only be the two of us. We could even buy a bag of candy floss to share from the man in the wooden hut by the pier.

'I said, not today,' he repeats, his voice more of a growl. He yanks his arm out of my grip and, shocked, I stumble backwards.

Why's he being like this?

'But it's a lovely sunny day. It'll be fun.'

'Catherine, how many times do I have to tell you, we're not going to the beach today. Just go outside and play, will you, and leave me in peace.'

'You never want to play with me,' I cry. 'It's not fair.'

'Enough with your whining and whingeing,' he yells, jumping from his chair. It topples backwards, crashing noisily onto the tiled floor. 'We're not going to the beach!' His fists are clenched, and his face turns red with anger.

I flinch, a chill running through my bones. I'm used to Mother losing her temper with us all the time, but I've never seen my father angry like this. I don't like it at all.

'Daddy, don't shout,' I whimper, confused.

'Go on, get out! I don't want to see you for the rest of the day.'

Tears bubble up into my eyes and my throat feels thick, like I can't swallow.

'I hate you!' I scream at him, then turn and run for the back door, grabbing my trainers on the way out.

He's not normally this grumpy. All I wanted to do was go to the beach. What's so terrible about that?

Fine. If he doesn't want to see me, I don't want to see him either. Let's see how he likes it.

I run the length of the garden, not once stopping to look back until I reach the wooden gate that leads into the woods behind the house. It's my special place. It's where I've spent most of the holidays on my own, playing.

I pull back the bolt and scurry out, wiping my cheeks with my sleeve.

Why did he have to be so horrible?

I put my head down and run as fast as my legs will go, through the dense mass of trees and the thick knots of brambles and thistles, not stopping until I reach my den.

I started building it at the beginning of the summer using fallen branches propped up against the low-hanging bough of a tree, well away from the trodden paths where the only sound comes from the hidden wildlife and the rustle of wind through the leaves.

There's an old horse chestnut tree that opens up like a hand in the middle of the wood that would have been perfect for a treehouse. Its branches are like enormous fingers spiralling out from a human palm. And at first, I thought that's where I'd like to have my den, except I'm not very good with heights. I can't stomach the thought of climbing trees. Even thinking about it makes my tummy squirm and my head go all funny.

That's why I decided to build my den on the ground. In the last few days, I've covered it in ferns to make a roof and laid down handfuls of moss for a carpet. From outside, it's almost invisible, unless you know it's there and you're looking for it. It's the perfect place to hide, where no one can find me.

I climb inside and lay on my back, watching a spider busy repairing its web, and listening to the sounds of nature. Birds chirruping and caw-cawing. The rustle of mice in the undergrowth. A squirrel scratching up a tree trunk. They're the sounds I love. The sounds that make me happy.

I'll stay in my den all day, well away from my father and his terrible temper. I might not even go home until it's dark and my parents have started worrying about me. That will show them. I expect Daddy will pace up and down in the lounge with his forehead wrinkled, chewing his fingernails while my mother is on the phone calling all my friends' parents to see if anyone knows where I am. But they won't find me. And it will serve them right.

But after a few hours, and with my stomach rumbling, my resolve weakens, and boredom sets in. I should have thought to have grabbed some food. Some packets of crisps and a chocolate bar, at least.

I try to take my mind off it by adding another layer of sticks to the roof of my den, hunting for branches that are just the right length and collecting a bunch of pretty flowers to hang from the ceiling. Pink mallows, yellow buttercups and long-stemmed daisies.

An inquisitive rabbit sticks its head out of a hole beneath the trunk of an oak tree, its whiskers twitching, nose sniffing the air. I try to coax it closer, rubbing my fingers together and sucking the air through my teeth in what I think is an encouraging sound that says I'm friendly. But when she sees me, she freezes and then bops away, her tail zigzagging into the weeds.

I've no idea how long I've stayed out, but the sun is high in the sky when my hunger finally gets the better of me. I'm still cross about the way Daddy shouted at me, but I can probably sneak back into the house and grab some food without him seeing me. I'm not ready to speak to him yet, and I can't face him shouting again.

As I walk back towards the house, dragging my feet through the dirt, kicking up puffs of dust and dried mud, dappled sunlight streams through the branches above. The air is heavy with the scent of pine. It's so peaceful in the woods, I think I could live here forever. Maybe when I'm grown up, I'll build a cabin and hunt wild rabbits for my dinner.

I'm not sure what makes me stop and look up as I reach the edge of the woods, where the path curls and twists like a ribbon towards the back gate. A feeling that something is wrong? Whatever it is, a nasty feeling hollows my tummy.

Ahead, through the dappled light and shadows, something is hanging from a tree. It's swinging and twirling. I can't make out what it is, but it's something that doesn't belong there. It doesn't look right.

I force one foot in front of the other, curious but afraid. In my chest, my heart is thudding, banging against my ribs. As I get closer, I recognise Daddy's shoes. The ones he wears in the garden on Sundays, all scuffed and covered in mud, a hole above his big toe where the leather has worn thin.

They rotate slowly, attached to a pair of legs. A branch creaks and as I look up through a halo of sunlight and blink, I see my father's arms hanging limply by his side, his head resting on his chest, his eyes bulging behind his closed lids.

I open my mouth to scream, backing away in horror, but nothing comes out.

'Daddy?' I gasp, clamping a hand over my mouth.

I turn and run. As fast and as hard as my legs will move, trying to get far away, scrambling through the clawing fingers of brambles and tripping over tree roots.

I stumble and fall, grazing my knees and kicking dust into my mouth. I have to get up. I have to keep running.

And I don't stop until I'm back at my den. I throw myself inside and bury my head under my hands, squeezing my eyes shut, trying to make the horrible image of what I've just seen go away. But it stays in my head and it's all I can think about.

Has my father done that to himself? Was it because of what I said?

The last words I screamed at him come back to haunt me.

I hate you.

Why had I said that?

Stupid.

Stupid. Stupid.

Stupid. Stupid. Stupid.

I bang my fists against my skull. This is all my fault. And nobody is ever going to forgive me.

Chapter 10

CATHY

I can't breathe. It's as if all these people in the house are sucking the air out of the room. Eyes are staring at me. Watching me. The police asking the same questions over and over again. Yannick sitting there pretending he cares. A stranger with a TV camera on his lap smiling sympathetically. And all I want is my baby back. My beautiful little girl. I want to scream at everyone to leave us alone. But, of course, I can't. How would that look? They already think we have something to do with Annie going missing. I can hear it in their questions and the way they're looking at me.

So instead of saying anything, I sit quietly, twisting the cuff of my cardigan around my fingers, my gaze fixed on a stain on the rug. I can't take much more of this. It's killing me.

And it's not just me. I've never seen Kit so worked up. He's boiling with fury. I'm angry too, but what's the point of yelling? Annie's only been missing for a few hours, although it already feels like a lifetime. You'd think they'd be a bit more sympathetic.

And that stunt with Annie's toothbrush. What the hell was that all about? Some kind of sick psychological trick designed to test us? To see how we'd react to the idea that she's dead? I'm not playing that game. Annie's alive.

Mothers have an instinct for these things, like twins who know what each other is thinking. She's not dead, she's been taken. It's obvious. Snatched off the street by some sick deviant. Don't they realise the clock is ticking? They should be out there looking for her, not in our house trying to pin it on me and Kit.

'What exactly do you expect to find?' Kit shouts at the older detective, Monkton. He's a grisly, age-ravaged cop with a heavy five o'clock shadow and a way of looking at everyone like they're guilty of something.

'It's purely routine, Mr Warren,' he replies.

If he says "purely routine" one more time, I'm going to scream.

'Kit, just give them to him,' I say.

Kit falls silent. 'What?'

'Just give them the computers if they think it's going to help them find Annie.'

I don't care what they do with them, I just want these men gone. I want everyone gone. And besides, there's nothing on the laptops that we have to hide. Arguing about it is only going to make us look guilty.

'Fine,' Kit huffs, 'but I really don't see why this is necessary.' He storms off into the dining room and returns with our two laptops. One is Kit's work computer. The other is our own personal machine. He hands them both over and writes the passwords on a yellow sticky note.

'We'll get them back to you as soon as we can,' Monkton says, tucking them under his arm.

'I'd like to be alone now,' I say.

'Of course. We'll be on our way, but we'll let you know the moment we hear anything.' Monkton leads the way out with Shears on his heel.

Finally, they're leaving. I don't stand up or offer to shake their hands. I let Kit show them to the door and find a snag of skin around the base of my thumbnail to occupy my fingers. When I hear the door slam shut, I breathe a sigh of relief.

Now I just need to deal with Yannick, who's making out like he's here for my benefit, when I know full well what's really on his mind. It's all one big act with him. Pretending he's worried about Annie. About me. He's never cared about anyone in his life, other than himself. There's only one reason he's here with a cameraman in tow. Bloody journalists. They're all the same. Ghouls feeding off the torment of others. I should throw him out, but it's a bit late now, especially with that awful liaison woman watching our every move.

'Aunt Cathy, are you okay?' Yannick's voice makes me jump.

'Yes, I'm fine.' I need some air. I stand up, heading for the kitchen and an escape into the back garden for a few minutes.

But Yannick leaps up in front of me, blocking my way. 'I know this is bad timing but now the police have gone I wondered – '

'Yannick, please. Don't.'

He has the gall to look affronted. 'What?' he says, eyes wide with innocence.

'You're going to ask me to do an interview.'

'It would only take a minute. A mother's plea for her daughter's safe return could make all the difference. You know, if someone's watching and they know what's happened to Annie.'

'No,' I say firmly, wrapping my cardigan around my chest. 'Absolutely not.'

'Come on, Aunty Cath. One quick soundbite, that's all. And then we'll be gone.'

'No,' I repeat firmly. 'I'm not doing it.'

Kit returns to the room, brushes past me and turns up the volume on the TV as he notices a reporter broadcasting live from outside the pub up the road.

'Why not?'

'You know why,' I hiss, with a glance at Zara, the liaison officer. She's looking at her phone, pretending not to take any notice.

'Because of what happened to Granddad? But that was years ago.'

It's been over thirty years, but my anger and resentment still burn fiercely. For a long time, I blamed myself for my father's death. But it wasn't anything I'd done. It was the scurrilous lies and half-truths the papers printed about him. They took his name, and they destroyed his reputation when he hadn't even been found guilty of anything. I'm sure Monica would be turning in her grave if she knew Yannick was here in my house begging me to sell my soul after all these years of hurt.

'I don't talk to journalists,' I say. 'You of all people should know that.'

'But we're family. You can trust me.'

I shake my head. 'I'm sorry, Yannick.'

'Aunty Cath – '

'You can leave now,' I tell him.

'One soundbite. Please,' he begs. As if that's going to change my mind. He really doesn't know me at all.

The cameraman jumps up off the sofa and for a horrible moment I think they're going to gang up on me. But instead, he steps in front of Yannick, like he's breaking up a bar brawl.

'Come on, she said no. You're not going to change her mind,' he says. 'Let's get these shots played back to the studio.'

Yannick sighs. 'Maybe tomorrow, when things are a bit clearer then?' he says.

'Goodnight, Yannick,' I say. I'm tired and I'm not in the mood for an argument right now. I want them both out of the house and I want my daughter home and safe.

'Uncle Kit?' Yannick turns his back on me. 'I really need this interview. And if you speak to us, I can keep the rest of them from bothering you.'

Kit glances over his shoulder, still distracted by what's on the TV. 'Maybe tomorrow, Yannick, yeah? It's late and everyone's exhausted. It's been a long day.'

'Come on, Uncle Kit.'

'Yannick, I said not now.'

The cameraman puts a hand on Yannick's shoulder and attempts to guide him away, but he shrugs it off crossly. 'Come on, mate. Let's leave it for now.'

'Right. Fine,' Yannick fumes. He storms out in a huff, followed by the cameraman, who shoots me an apologetic smile.

And suddenly the house feels empty again. Too empty. Too quiet. I ache for my daughter. I sink into the sofa, feeling like crawling under a rock and staying there until this is all over, a wave of fatigue washing over me.

It's only been a few hours, but I miss Annie so much. Her absence has torn my heart apart. I miss her mess and the noise and chaos. With her gone, the house is eerily silent. Deathly.

'Shall I make us all a cup of tea?' Zara asks, putting her phone down on the arm of the sofa like she's at home.

What's she really doing here? Has she been sent to keep an eye on us? When she arrived earlier, she behaved like a long-lost friend, telling us to call her by her first name and that she was here to do anything she could to help during this difficult period.

Difficult period? Huh! She has no idea what we're going through. How could she?

And the way those two detectives were asking all sorts of questions, it wouldn't surprise me if she's been sent to spy on us. To listen to our conversations and observe our behaviour. I don't know. Maybe I'm being paranoid. I'm so tired, I can hardly think straight.

'Actually, I think my husband and I could do with some time by ourselves,' I say. 'It's been a stressful few hours.'

Her friendly smile slips. 'That's entirely your decision, but most people in this situation find it's useful to have someone around they can talk to and guide them. And if there are any developments, the team will let me know straightaway and I can keep you informed.'

'I need some space,' I say.

Kit turns down the volume on the TV, takes my hand and places it in his lap. 'It's going to be okay, Cath. I promise,' he says. 'The police are going to find whoever's taken Annie and they're going to bring her home.'

'Would it help if I made myself scarce for a bit?' Zara says. 'Why don't I take myself off into the kitchen and leave you two to it?'

'I'd rather you came back in the morning,' I say, as another knock at the door makes us all start. 'Who the hell is that now?'

If it's another journalist, I'm going to give it to them with both barrels. It's been like an open house since we reported Annie missing, with people coming and going as they please. Whatever happened to our privacy?

'Whoever it is, tell them to go away,' Kit says.

I drag myself wearily to the door and pause for a second before opening it, gathering my strength.

There's a woman I don't recognise standing on the doorstep. She doesn't look like a police officer or a reporter.

'Yes?' I snap.

She's about my age. Shorter though, and heavier, with streaks of grey running through her shoulder-length hair. I eye her with suspicion, ready to slam the door in her face.

'I'm Pam Buckley, chair of the residents' association. I live on the estate.' She waves a hand at the sprawling network of houses in the road behind our house. 'I saw the police leaving and the lights still on, so I thought I'd pop my head in and see if there's anything you need.' She smiles so sweetly, I feel bad about the tone I've taken with her. 'I'm so sorry about what's happened.'

She glances down the road, towards the rows of houses along the creek and the boats sitting lopsided in the mud. 'Almost everyone's turned out to look,' she says. 'It's a real community effort. I'm sure we'll find Annie soon enough. Anyway, I just wanted to let you know we're doing everything we can. People are going to keep looking through the night.'

'All night?' It seems extraordinary that people who don't even know us are prepared to go to such incredible lengths, giving up their time and sleep.

'People are distraught that something like this could have happened on their doorsteps. I've got groups all around the lakes and three more concentrating on the marsh. Plus, there are countless others going around the estate, checking gardens and sheds, that sort of thing, while the police are concentrating mostly on knocking on doors.'

'You've organised all that?'

Pam shrugs. 'We look after our own around here. We can't imagine what you must be going through. It's awful.'

I've never met Pam before. I didn't even know there was a residents' association, even though we've been in the house for over two years. But we're private people. We don't even have much to do with our neighbours, other than a friendly hello if we happen to see them out. I can't believe she's gone to so much trouble coordinating a public search for my daughter.

'I don't know what to say.'

'You don't have to say anything,' Pam says. 'It's what we'd do for anyone. It's what I hope someone would do for me.'

'You have children?'

'A daughter. Phillipa. She's a couple of years younger than Annie, but she knows her from school. She's staying with my brother tonight.'

She catches me glancing at her hand, looking for a ring.

'Her father didn't stick around for the birth,' she says, 'but I reckon we're better off without him, anyway.'

My shoulders slump and tears spring from nowhere. I've held them in all night, trying to be brave. Trying to stay strong as everyone was firing questions at me. Now, in the face of such compassion and kindness, I can't help myself.

'I'm sorry,' I say, wiping my cheeks with a tissue.

'You don't need to apologise. You let it out.'

'Thank you for everything you're doing,' I say. 'But I don't think you're going to find her.'

Pam scowls. 'Why not?'

'I think she's been taken by someone, and they'll be long gone by now.'

'You mustn't think like that. It's still early days, and anyway, I heard the police have set up roadblocks on all the roads out of town.'

'And if someone took her by boat? She could be halfway to France by now.'

'Cathy? Who is it?' Kit calls from the lounge.

Before I can answer, he's at my side, an arm draped over my shoulder.

'This is Pam. She's coordinating all the volunteers looking for Annie.'

Kit nods and Pam smiles.

'What can we do for you?' he asks rudely.

My cheeks burn with embarrassment. 'Pam was just telling me that everyone's turned out to look for Annie,' I say. 'And they're going to keep searching for her through the night.'

'Right.' Kit eyes her suspiciously. 'Thanks.'

Pam shoves her hands in her pockets and puffs out her cheeks. 'I suppose I'd better get back to it. These volunteers aren't going to organise themselves.'

'Would you like to come in?' I ask, as Kit steps back inside. I hear him telling Zara it's "just some do-gooder from the estate".

I'm fairly sure Pam hears him too. 'No, thank you,' she says.

She bites her lower lip and looks down at the ground as if there's something else on her mind.

'Thank you for popping by,' I say. 'I really appreciate it.'

'No problem. You must let me know if there's anything else I can do to help.'

I step back to close the door, but she remains rooted on the doorstep. 'Was there something else?'

'Actually, do you fancy getting some fresh air?' she says. She shoots a glance over her shoulder to where the news crew Kit was watching on the TV are packing up their equipment. I shrink back out of their view. I don't want them spotting me after I've only just managed to get rid of Yannick.

'I'm pretty tired,' I say.

'Just for a few minutes.'

'And the police have asked us not to leave the house in case there's any news from Annie.'

Pam draws in a deep breath and lets it out slowly. 'Look,' she says, poking her tongue into her cheek. 'There's something you really need to know.'

TUESDAY

Chapter 11

YANNICK

Bleary-eyed and irritable, I haul myself out of bed and make a strong black coffee in the machine in my kitchen and crash with it on the sofa in front of the TV to catch up on the breakfast news bulletins. I've only managed to snatch a few hours' sleep and I'm still fuming over the way Aunty Cath and Uncle Kit treated me last night. All I needed was a few words on camera about how worried they were about Annie. Would it have killed them? We are family, after all. Instead, I had to suffer the indignation of being thrown out of the house in front of Harry. I'm never going to live that down.

To be fair to him, he didn't say anything as he dropped me back at my car. We drove in silence, and he must have sensed the foul mood I was in. He didn't even ask why I'd not told him Annie was my cousin, which I guess was a shock when we knocked on the door. I don't suppose it will be long before word gets back to the newsroom.

There have been no new developments overnight, but all the main channels are leading on the story this morning. Most of them have dispatched reporters to Faversham to deliver live slots into the broadcasts. Some are on the estate where volunteers are still out on the streets, others down by the old quay with the creek and the boats in the background, the sun rising over the towering spire of St Mary's Church. It makes the as-live I recorded look a little out of date, but at least no one's identified Annie's home address yet. But it's only a matter of time. I have to get Cathy and Kit to agree to an interview before the vultures descend.

With the TV still on in the background, I grab my iPad and flick through the online news sites. No surprise that they're all awash with the missing Annie story. All of them have her happy, smiling face in that school photo, alongside images of police conducting house-to-house inquiries or searching around the town and the marshes. Everyone is going crazy for the story.

It's no surprise. Annie is a pretty, middle-class girl from a decent home. Her parents, respectably married, are well-educated and have good jobs. Uncle Kit is the chief executive of a charity supporting refugees and Aunt Cathy runs a coffee shop. They look like the perfect couple. It's a news editor's dream story.

Gina Priestly, our head of news, calls my mobile as I'm finishing my coffee and contemplating making another. She's the last person I expected to be ringing so early.

'Did I wake you?' she asks.

'No, I was watching the coverage from Faversham.'

'Great job last night. Well done. I have Tim and Holly on the line. Hang on a minute, let me see if I can patch them in.'

There's a silence as Gina dials in Tim, our news editor, and Holly, the programme producer.

'Right, can everyone hear me?' Gina asks.

I'm not usually privy to the editorial discussions that take place amongst the senior editorial team, so it's a privilege to be invited in, and maybe a sign they're taking me more seriously. Perhaps another step towards a shot at presenting the main programme. It's certainly an encouraging development.

'Great coverage last night, Yannick,' Tim says. 'Thanks for turning out.'

'Glad to be involved.' It's nice to feel appreciated for a change.

'Right,' Gina says, plaudits done and now sounding all businesslike. 'I wanted an early chat about what we're doing to move this story forward. I want us all over it today. It's going to be huge. I've asked Yannick to join us as he was in Faversham last night and can give us a better sense of what's going on. So, Holly, what are your plans?'

Holly clears her throat. 'Assuming Annie's still missing, I want to anchor a special from the town tonight. Even if she is found, it's still a big story. I'll put together a dedicated title sequence.'

'Okay, good,' Gina says. 'Tim, what resources can you put on it? Do you have enough people?'

'I'll stand everything else down and reroute all the reporters and cameras. I was thinking we need pieces on the family, the search, the volunteer response, and maybe something from the school, as well as a backgrounder on Annie. You know, what she's like, what she likes to do, with a montage of any pictures we can source from social media. I suggest we get someone senior from the police live on the show too.'

'Excellent,' Gina says. 'And can we get graphics working on a timeline and a map showing Annie's last known movements?'

'The problem is, nobody knows for sure which way she walked home,' I interject. 'There are three possible routes she could have reasonably taken.'

'Great, good intel, Yannick. Let's get graphics to map all three possible options. Anything else?'

'What about the parents?' Holly asks. 'Are they talking yet? If we can get a tearful interview in the bag, we can build everything else around that, and it would be great for titles and teases, of course. Any suggestion from the police that they're going to speak?'

'The police aren't saying much other than the standard lines at the moment,' Tim says. He sounds frustrated. 'No indication yet that they're putting the family up for interviews.'

'Not even on a pool basis?' Gina asks.

'Can we get to them directly, independent of the police?' Holly chimes in. 'I mean, we know Annie's name and the rough area she lives. Surely we can track the family down.'

'We'll do our best,' Tim says.

My heart sinks. I can't sit here and say nothing. They'd never forgive me. I'd wanted to deliver an interview with Kit and Cathy ready for the breakfast bulletins, and well ahead of the opposition. That would have made Gina sit up and take notice of me. Instead, I'm going to have to tell them the truth about last night. I cough to get their attention.

'Yannick? Do you have something to add?' Gina asks.

'Actually,' I say, my mouth dry, 'I spoke to Annie's parents last night, but they were too upset to speak on camera.'

There's a moment's silence on the line. 'You tracked them down last night?' Gina asks, sounding surprised.

I take a deep breath. 'Annie's my cousin.'

Stunned silence. I take it as a cue to keep talking.

'I went to the house hoping I could persuade them to talk on camera, but they didn't want to. Not yet.'

'Are you serious?' Tim asks. 'Why didn't you say something before?'

'Sorry.'

'I don't understand,' he continues. 'Why wouldn't they speak to you? I mean, you're family.'

'It was bad timing, I guess. When I got there, a couple of detectives turned up to give them a grilling.'

'Are they being treated as suspects, then?' I can almost hear the cogs turning in Tim's head.

'I don't think so, no. I mean, I don't know for sure, but I think they were just trying to eliminate them from suspicion.'

'Even so, that's another great line to explore,' Tim says. 'Great stuff, Yannick.'

It's a waste of time going down that road, and it's only going to further antagonise Cathy and Kit if we insinuate they're somehow involved. Then they'll never give me an interview, but I know better than to argue with Tim. He's been the station's news editor for more than ten years, and for good reason. He's ferocious. I've seen how he chews up and spits out reporters who try to stand up to him. It's not worth the grief, so I let it go, hoping he'll forget about it.

'Is there anything else you can tell us from last night?' Gina asks.

'Not really.'

She breathes out heavily through her nose. 'Right, well, this changes things significantly. I want the Warrens talking to us exclusively. I don't want anyone else to get a sniff with them, is that understood? We've got a fantastic opportunity here, thanks to Yannick. Let's not fuck this up. Yannick, that's your number one priority. Do whatever it takes to get your aunt and uncle speaking to us. Got it? And above all, make sure they don't talk to anyone else.'

'I - I - I'm not sure it's going to be that easy,' I stammer. Trust Gina to pile on the pressure. As if I needed the additional stress. Perhaps I shouldn't have said anything. But Harry knows now that Annie's my cousin, so it was only a matter of time before he shot his mouth off.

'Do they want their daughter back or not? See if she'll make a direct appeal,' Gina says.

'It's complicated,' I explain. 'My aunt, Cathy, had a bad experience with the press when she was a child.'

'What kind of bad experience?'

'My grandfather was a vascular surgeon who was suspended pending an investigation after a series of alleged botched operations. The tabloids got hold of the story and did a hatchet job on him.' I pause for a second. 'He hanged himself and Cathy found his body.'

'I'm sorry to hear that,' Gina says, not sounding remotely regretful. 'But it could be good news for us. She's less likely to talk to the papers. Persuade her that talking to the local TV is different, and that if Annie has been abducted, it's her opportunity to speak directly to whoever's taken her. I want Cathy crying a mother's tears for her missing daughter. Can you deliver that, Yannick?'

'I'll do my best,' I say.

'Put it this way, deliver that interview for me and we'll talk about those presenting shifts you keep pestering me about.'

Chapter 12

There's no point hanging around at home with the weight of Gina's expectations on my shoulders. So I hastily shower, dress and jump in my car to head back to Faversham. Time isn't on my side.

I arrive just before ten to find the town crawling with journalists. Far more than I imagined there would be. Satellite vans and radio cars are parked on every corner near Annie's school. Photographers with long lenses and haggard faces are stalking around like hungry packs of wolves and reporters with notebooks are stopping people in the street to grab interviews and information.

I park a short distance from Cathy and Kit's house, conscious of being recognised and potentially giving away where they live. That would be a disaster. I put my head down and shove my hands in my trouser pockets, trying to look inconspicuous as I shuffle past a young couple with a toddler in a pushchair. They don't look at me twice. I'm on the TV at least three nights a week these days, but I still rarely get recognised. I guess that's regional television for you. It's different with the local press. We all tend to know each other.

I jog across the road, ahead of an oncoming car whose driver is distracted by something going on down by the creek. As I round a corner into Cathy and Kit's street, I immediately see what's caught his attention. My aunt and uncle's house is under siege. I've no idea how the press pack has found it, but it totally scuppers my plans.

What do I do now? I can hardly walk up and knock on the door.

The only consolation is that they're all outside. Cathy and Kit clearly haven't opened the door to them, which means my hopes for an exclusive interview remain intact, for now. Still, it's a concerning development with Gina and Tim breathing down my neck.

I'll have to come back later when hopefully they've lost interest or have headed off chasing their tails at the first sign someone's found a new angle. But maybe it's not such a bad thing. It gives me the opportunity to do some digging of my own. The town's bound to be awash with gossip and innuendo. Someone will have heard something on the grapevine. It could give me a lead to chase and a juicy new line on the story for tonight, just in case I can't get the interview with Cathy and Kit. Everyone knows everyone's business in a town like this. I just need to find someone willing to talk.

But where to start?

The school seems a good place. So that's where I head first.

The marquee is still up and there are a handful of volunteers hanging around, cradling steaming polystyrene cups. I straighten my jacket and run my tongue over my teeth before approaching a couple of the women with my best newsreader's smile.

'Excuse me. Sorry to trouble you. I'm from the local TV news station...'

But the words are barely out of my mouth before they've moved swiftly away, holding up their hands as if to ward me off.

It's been less than twenty-four hours, but they've already grown weary of the press attention around here.

An older man with thinning grey hair, a rounded back and shuffling gait, turns off the street and into the playground. His boots are caked in mud. It's a fair bet he's been out on the marshes all night.

'Excuse me,' I say, stepping towards him, stooping to his height to make myself appear less threatening.

He looks up at me with frightened eyes and hurries on.

This is hopeless. I'm in the wrong place. I need to go where they've not been pestered a thousand times by reporters already. Maybe the estate is where I should be, and particularly the ring of houses on the outer fringes that haven't been bombarded by journalists and the police yet. A place where the tittle-tattle of a big story has been fermenting.

The first three doors I knock on go unanswered, but at the fourth house, my luck changes. The door is opened by a balding man in his mid-sixties, with spindly arms and wizened, sun-damaged skin.

'Sorry to bother you. I'm with the local news,' I explain. 'We're following the story of the missing girl, Annie Warren.'

'Oh, aye,' he says, raising his chin and studying me through narrow slits for eyes.

'I imagine you've heard all about it?'

'Little girl on her way home from school, was it?'

'That's right,' I say. 'Everyone's looking for her.'

'I didn't see nothing,' he says gruffly.

'Have you heard anything? Any whispers about what might have happened?'

He sucks in his cheeks while he thinks and then shakes his head. He doesn't know anything.

I get a similar response from his next-door neighbour, a nervous, spotty man with a baseball cap covering greasy hair. There's a strong smell of cannabis when he furtively opens the door, his eyes as black as coal. He's probably spent the night high, killing Nazis on *Call of Duty*.

He nods across the road to a house with a small front garden planted with garish, plastic-looking flowers. 'Try Julia,' he says, sniffing. 'She knows everything that's going on round here.'

Another knock-back, but I'm getting closer. I can feel it. You just need to keep asking the questions and wearing out the shoe leather. If you speak to enough people, more often than not, you turn up something useful.

Julia is a dumpy woman in faded leggings and rolls of stomach fat accentuated by a tight fuchsia pink T-shirt. She sucks on a cigarette and blows smoke out of the corner of her mouth as she stands on the doorstep listening while I explain that I'm looking for information about my missing cousin. Although I don't tell her we're related, of course.

'Oh yeah,' she says. 'Poor little mite. We was out for a few hours last night looking, but if you ask me, they ain't going to find her.'

'Why's that?'

'Little girl like that. You seen the picture? Sweet little thing, in't she? Some filthy paedo's taken her. You'll see. Problem is, this place is full of 'em.'

Her words are like a hammer blow to my chest. They snatch the breath from my lungs and steal the strength from my legs. It's bad enough thinking of Annie's body being pulled lifeless from the frigid waters on the marsh. But to imagine she might have been taken by a child molester is horrific. The worst thing. Worse even than death. I swallow down my emotions and take a lungful of air.

'If I was the police,' she continues, 'there are a few doors I'd be banging on pretty smartish.'

I frown. Has she heard something or is she speculating?

'Which doors?' I ask.

'It used to be a nice estate. Everybody knew everyone. We used to look out for each other.'

I brace myself for the inevitable tirade of hate and intolerance.

'I'll welcome anyone here who's decent and hard working.' That wasn't what I expected her to say at all. 'But...' She leans towards me conspiratorially and lowers her tobacco-tinged voice to a hissed whisper. Here we go. 'The council's been dumping all these sex offenders here for years. It's disgusting.' Her mouth curls and she wrinkles her nose.

'Is that true?'

It's a hell of a story if it stands up, but it sounds like the sort of rumour that goes around small communities like this. Sex offender or not, I suppose they've got to live somewhere, but it would be a national scandal if the council was housing them all in one residential estate. I make a mental note to do some digging.

'I *know* it's true. They're everywhere round here.'

Surely not. 'Okay, like who? Do you have any names?' I ask.

Julia stubs the end of her cigarette out on the wall and licks her lips. 'Guy who lives in the next road along.' She points over my shoulder and gives me an address. 'Blair Black. You want to be checking him out for a start.'

'He's a registered sex offender?'

'Interested in little girls, I heard. You only have to look at him to see what he's like. Creepy bloke.'

I raise an eyebrow. 'Creepy? How?'

'I dunno. He looks evil,' she says, shuddering.

'What do you know about him?'

'Not much. Keeps himself to himself, mostly. Always has his curtains closed, like he's got something to hide.'

Something to hide? A fizz of excitement spreads from my stomach and up my spine. This is good. This is something I can work with.

'Give me that address one more time,' I say, making a note on a scrap of paper.

'I hope they find her,' Julia says, slipping back inside the house, 'for her parents' sake. They must be going through hell, but honestly, I've got a really bad feeling about it. I only hope I'm wrong.'

Blair Black. He's got to be worth checking out as a suspect. Who knows, if I play it right, I might even talk him into giving me an interview.

I hurry back into the street and find a quiet spot under a telegraph pole to call Tim on the newsdesk.

'I've got a lead,' I say. 'Some bloke the neighbours are pointing a finger at. He's on the sex offenders' list. Into little girls, apparently. I want to doorstep him and see if I can get him on camera.'

Tim listens attentively, but I sense he doesn't share my enthusiasm. 'Right, and what about the Warrens? Have you spoken to them yet? I've got a crew on standby. We really need that interview for tonight's programme.'

'I've not had the chance to speak to them yet. The house is surrounded by journalists. I'm trying them again later. But, listen, this guy, he's called Blair Black. Perhaps you can get someone to do some digging into his background for me. Is there a camera I can use?'

Tim sighs wearily. 'Where's he live?'

'About five minutes' walk from Annie's school. Please, let me have a camera. I won't let you down.'

Tim falls silent for a moment, and I hear the hubbub of a noisy newsroom in the background. 'Fine. You can use Harry. Give him a call. He's already in Faversham. He should be free.'

'Thanks, Tim. You won't regret this.'

'I'd better not, or I wouldn't show your face in the newsroom for a while.'

He hangs up, leaving with me my phone pressed to my ear, listening to static. I know he has no faith in me, but I'm going to prove to him I know what I'm doing.

Chapter 13

Blair Black's house is a blot on an otherwise respectable street, with filthy wooden windows in frames that are cracked and peeling, bulging rubbish bags heaped up in the garden and frayed blackout blinds, pockmarked with mould. I can see what Julia meant. Sex offender or not, the house looks deeply suspicious. What's he hiding in there? I guess there's only one way to find out.

Harry's joined me. I've told him I want to knock at the door with the camera rolling to capture Black's reaction when he's confronted. It might be the only chance we get to film him, and if it later turns out he did have something to do with Annie's disappearance, the footage is going to be priceless.

My nerves flutter in my stomach as I clutch a fluffy microphone around the corner from the house where we can't be seen from the property.

'Ready?'

Harry gives me a thumbs up and we march to the door, brushing through long fingers of grass that have spilled across a cracked path from an overgrown and neglected lawn.

I bang with my fist. It echoes through the house. My throat's dry and perspiration beads on my forehead. I wipe it with my sleeve and knock again. This is what it's all about. All my senses alive and my heart going so fast it feels like it's going to gallop out of my chest.

Everyone else is focused on the search for Annie, but we're a step ahead of them all. I've found the first legitimate suspect who might have had something to do with her abduction. It's like my old journalism lecturer used to tell us at college. There's no story without a villain. Yes, there's Cathy and Kit's anguish. The mystery of what has happened to Annie. But no one's pointing the finger of blame. Until now. If I've got this right, forget presenting shifts on regional TV. I'm heading for the big time. A reporting job with the national network, at least. And who knows what might follow on from that?

Who knows, we might even find Annie. Now that would be a coup.

After what feels like an eternity, a lock clicks, and the door opens a crack.

I shove the microphone into the gap.

'Mr Black, I'm Yannick Kellor from the local news. I wanted to ask you about the missing girl, Annie Warren.'

I step to one side to give Harry an unobstructed view, hoping his camera can pick out Black's face in the shadows. All I can see is a shock of long, grey hair and an unkempt beard.

'Mr Black, do you have anything to say about Annie's disappearance? Do you know anything about what happened to her?'

I feared he would slam the door in our faces, but to my surprise he opens it wide, blinking as the sunlight hits his craggy face.

He's at least six foot tall, lean and sinewy, but stooped, like he's spent his life ducking under doorways and low arches to avoid banging his head. He has a crooked nose and furtive, dark eyes set deep under a thickset brow. His hoary beard hides his mouth and he's let his hair grow so long, it's tied back in a straggly ponytail. He's exactly what I imagine a man with an unhealthy interest in little girls might look like.

My stomach rolls with disgust.

'Sorry, who are you?' he asks, his voice a croaky whisper.

'The local news.' I glance at Harry to make sure he's getting a nice, tight shot. 'I assume you've heard about Annie Warren, the girl who's gone missing?' My heart's still racing, but his calm reaction has dulled my excitement. He's not acting like he's guilty of anything, but that doesn't mean much. 'She's only ten years old. She vanished on her way home from the school up the road. You must have heard about it?'

Black shakes his head as he strokes his beard. 'No, I haven't. Sorry,' he says. 'I don't have a TV. When did it happen?'

'At about half-three yesterday.'

'Right.' He nods slowly, his eyes glassy, as if he's thinking it through. 'Well, I didn't see her.'

'Are you sure?' I find the photo of Annie on my phone and hold it up. 'She's only ten.'

He's as cool as a mountain stream. Totally unfazed as he stares at the happy, smiling little girl with her green cardigan slipping off her shoulders in the school photo all the media outlets are using. 'I've never seen her before,' he says.

'Where were you yesterday afternoon?' I ask.

His gaze shoots from my phone to my face. He recognises the accusation and edges back into the house. There's a strong odour coming from inside, of stale urine and sweat, like the place could do with a few windows opened.

'I was in the house all day. I don't go out much. I'm not as mobile as I used to be.' He slaps his thigh and shifts to one side to reveal a mobility scooter in the hall. Beyond it are dusty piles of books and newspapers, yellowing with age.

'You're standing okay now,' I say.

He looks down at his legs and back up at me. 'Are you going to use this on the news?' He nods at Harry's camera.

'Probably,' I say, although he's not given me much to use. All I've got is a creepy old guy denying anything to do with Annie's disappearance. If Tim can't confirm he's on the sex offenders register, there's not much I can do with the footage. Unless I can get the police to confirm they're investigating him. It would have been better if he had slammed the door in my face. At least it would have made him look like he was hiding something.

'Do you have a message for Annie's family?' I blurt out as he begins to close the door.

'What kind of message?'

'I don't know. Anything you want to say?' I'm desperate now. I need to keep him talking, to see if I can trip him up and make him say something incriminating that I can use.

'Not really,' he mumbles. 'I'm sorry, I have to go.'

'One more question.'

He hesitates, and I shove the microphone under his chin.

'Why do you keep all your curtains closed?' It's the best I can come up with. It certainly looks suspicious when there's a little girl missing in the area.

He shrugs and frowns. 'I guess I don't like people sticking their noses into my business.'

'People on the estate say you're a child abuser. Are you a paedophile, Mr Black?' Nothing left to lose. Time to go for broke. 'Did you abduct Annie Warren?'

His face clouds over and he shoves the door shut in our faces.

I wet my dry lips with my tongue. 'I guess that's no comment. Did you get all that?' I ask, turning to Harry.

He rolls the camera off his shoulder. 'Yeah, but what are you going to do with it? You can't just go accusing him.'

He unplugs the microphone, and I wrap the lead around my hand as we pick our way down the overgrown footpath and back onto the street towards his car.

'I need to watch it back and hear what he said again.' I look back at the house. Did the curtain at a window on the first floor just twitch? Or did I imagine it? 'Did you hear anything strange while you were filming?'

Harry frowns and gives a slight shake of his head. 'Don't think so. Like what?'

'I thought I heard banging.' I don't know what makes me say it. Desperation? I need something from Blair Black, else I have nothing for tonight, especially if I can't change Aunt Cathy's mind about giving me an interview. If I can persuade Harry there's something untoward going on in that house, it'll be easier to justify why I've singled out Blair Black.

Harry stops walking and stares at me. 'From inside the house?'

'I think so.'

'Bloody hell. I didn't hear anything, but I can play the footage back and see if the mic picked up anything.'

The hairs on the back of my neck stand on end and I get a chill sense that we're being watched. I glance up and spot a figure across the road, standing near a tree on a patch of grass between the row of houses and the creek. It's a man wearing a baseball cap pulled down over his eyes. Scruffy jeans. A zip-up top. Lean. Athletic. Just looking at us. Staring at me. He looks familiar. I've seen him before, but I can't think where.

You'd think I'd be used to it by now. It's always a source of fascination when we turn up anywhere with the camera. It's a like a beacon advertising something extraordinary is happening in the neighbourhood.

But this feels different. It's more than just mawkish curiosity. He's standing back, trying not to be seen, almost like he's stalking us. Most people just come right up to us and ask what we're doing.

At first, he doesn't move or avert his gaze when he sees he's been spotted. Is there something he wants to tell me? Sometimes people are reluctant to come forward and speak on camera, even when, inside, they're dying to talk.

I raise a hand and wave.

'Hey,' I call, stepping into the road towards him. I've spent the morning hunting down information about Annie and maybe this guy has what I've been looking for all along.

An approaching car blasts its horn and I have to jump back onto the pavement to avoid being run down.

When I look back, the man has vanished, like he's clicked his fingers and disappeared into thin air.

'Did you see that guy?'

Harry nods. 'Just another rubbernecker,' he says, blipping open his car and sliding the camera into the boot.

'I don't think so,' I say, shaking my head. 'I think he wanted to talk to me.'

Harry laughs. 'You think everyone wants to talk to you. Do you want to listen back to this recording or what?' He plugs a pair of headphones into the camera. They look like a relic from the last century.

He scrolls back through the footage but is interrupted when his phone rings. He wedges it between his shoulder and his cheek as he answers it, keeping his hands free for the camera.

'Yup, right, I'm on my way,' he says, and hangs up.

His clipped tone tells me something urgent has occurred. 'What is it?'

'The newsdesk. The police are holding a press conference at the house in twenty minutes.'

'What house?'

'The Warrens'. It looks like they're going to make a direct appeal for Annie's safe return.'

My stomach plummets into my boots. 'No,' I gasp, 'that can't be right.' They can't be doing this. It's my exclusive. My family. Why would they do this to me? It feels like my whole world is imploding out of control. Gina and Tim are going to kill me. 'Are you certain?'

'I'm sorry, Yannick. I know you were hoping to bag them for yourself. Are you coming or what?'

But I can't speak. This is a total and utter disaster.

Chapter 14

'Bring the sticks!' Harry shouts as we bundle out of the car.

He grabs the camera as I throw the tripod over my shoulder and trudge wearily down to the creek towards Kit and Cathy's house, where there's a buzz of excitement in the air from the swelling press pack jostling for position.

Normally, I'd be excited too, but this shouldn't be happening. Cathy and Kit have no right taking part in a press conference when they refused to talk to me last night. I'm Cathy's nephew, for pity's sake. What a betrayal. Well, good luck to them. I hope they realise they're going to be bombarded with media requests now and I'm not going to be around to fend them off on their behalf. They should have taken the deal I offered them last night. Now they're on their own.

Harry waves as a familiar face steps towards us.

Luke bloody Braithwaite. I might have known. He's been with the station for longer than I can remember. He's one of those career journalists, a solid, safe pair of hands they usually put on all the biggest stories. So not only have I lost my exclusive, but Tim's punishing me by taking me off the story entirely. He could have at least had the decency to let me know.

Luke nods in my direction, but he's more interested in getting Harry into place than acknowledging that he's stolen my story.

My gut twists with resentment. A few hours ago, I was finally being promised that shot at presenting the main programme, being told what a brilliant job I'd done last night. And now I've been dumped. I'm half minded to call Tim and tell him exactly where he can shove his job. It's only regional bloody TV.

Luke grabs the tripod out of my hands and shoves Harry through the throng of photographers and camera crews until he's at the front with an unobstructed view of the door where Cathy and Kit are expected to speak.

Has anyone even briefed them on what to say? I hope they're not going to make it up on the spot and trot out some hackneyed clichés dressed up with a few tears and sniffles. This is why they need me, to guide them on what to say and how to say it. The whole nation's going to be watching. If they're not careful, they'll end up looking foolish.

I should leave. Go and drown my sorrows and forget about it. But I can't. I need to hear what they say.

And I suppose there's a chance all might not be lost. If they keep it brief and stick to a simple appeal for information about Annie, a longer, more in-depth interview with them might still be possible. But if they take questions, it's going to seriously undervalue any deal I can strike with them.

It's not long before two uniformed officers who've been stationed outside the house step to one side and the door opens. I stand on my tiptoes to get a better view over all the heads and flashing cameras. Another officer steps out of the house, clutching a notepad in one hand. I immediately recognise the assistant chief constable. The crowd of reporters close in on him like the jaws of a python around the twitching body of a doomed rabbit.

Elbows fly. Microphones appear from nowhere. People jostle and push. Everyone wants an unobstructed shot. Everyone wants to hear what he has to say.

It should be me in the thick of it, not standing here at the back. But like a deep-sea diver in the middle of the desert, my presence here is redundant. This is all Cathy's doing. And all because of what happened to Granddad. I hope Uncle Kit can talk some sense into her.

'Good morning, ladies and gentlemen.' A hush settles over the press pack. 'My name is Neville Mikelson, the assistant chief constable of Kent. I have a brief update for you on the inquiry into missing Annie Warren. Then Annie's parents would like to make a short appeal for information.

'As you will know, Annie was last seen leaving school at approximately three-thirty yesterday afternoon, but failed to make it home. We have mobilised more than two hundred officers and my teams have been carrying out extensive door-to-door inquiries throughout the night, with the search supported by members of the local community.

'We are now becoming increasingly concerned for Annie's welfare and considering all possibilities, including that Annie may have been abducted. I would urge anyone with information concerning Annie's whereabouts to urgently contact the police. If you know anything, no matter how trivial it may seem, please call. You don't have to give your name, but the information you provide may be crucial.'

Hands shoot up and several journalists shout out questions without waiting to be asked.

'Do you have any specific intelligence to suggest Annie *has* been abducted?'

'Do you have any suspects?'

Mikelson waves the questions away.

'I'm now going to invite Annie's parents, Cathy and Kit Warren, to say a few words,' he says. 'They'll be making a short statement but won't be taking questions.'

At least that's something. If they keep it brief and to the point, there's still hope I can pull this disaster back from the brink.

Uncle Kit emerges from the house hand in hand with Aunt Cathy, both of them wearing grim expressions like they're stepping up to face the gallows.

As the click of cameras becomes a continuous hum, they stare blankly into the sea of strange faces. They both look exhausted, with dark rings around their eyes and a haunted air of despair hanging over their heads. I could almost feel sorry for them. The last twenty-four hours have broken them. They're hollow shells of the people I know. What a shame they stabbed me in the back.

Cathy catches my eye and gazes at me vacantly. Her face is washed out and pale, her hair ruffled. And now I really look, I can see she's not wearing make-up, which isn't like her, especially having to face all these people.

She's always put on a touch of eyeliner, added a lick of mascara and worn a subtle shade of lipstick, even when she isn't leaving the house. Appearing without make-up lends her a vulnerability that's going to strike a chord with every parent. It's exactly what I would have advised, if she'd have let me. Most women faced with appearing before TV cameras would slap it on, probably too thickly. But without make-up, you can read the anguish in Aunt Cathy's face, in the sallow dip of her cheeks and in the bruised bags under her eyes.

Appearing in full make-up and with perfect hair would have been the worst thing she could have done if she wanted to win the public's sympathy. We want to see our victims suffering, as we imagine we would suffer in the same situation. She's the perfect image of a mother in torment. A mother who's lost her child.

The air crackles with anticipation as Aunty Cath opens her mouth to speak.

'We just want our Annie home,' she says in a voice so quiet and timid it's almost carried away on the breeze. 'We can't eat. We can't sleep. We can't do anything while she's missing. If you're out there somewhere, sweetheart, we just want you back here with us. We miss you so much.'

She wipes a tear from under her eye and Uncle Kit rubs a comforting hand along her forearm.

'If someone's taken her, I'm pleading with you, please don't hurt her. Just bring her back to us, where she belongs,' she says, then lowers her head and lets the hair fall over her eyes as her shoulders begin to rock.

I will her to lift her face, to let the cameras see her tears. The country needs to feel her pain, although there's something endearing about the way she looks so uncomfortable in front of such intense scrutiny.

In contrast, Uncle Kit looks more poised and in control. As Cathy sobs at his side, he looks into each and every camera lens, like he knows exactly what he's doing.

'If you're listening to this and you've taken our daughter, please, it's not too late to bring her home,' he says. 'It's not too late to do the right thing. Let her go.'

Reporters fire a volley of questions at them, despite the assistant chief constable's warning.

'Has she ever run away before?' someone shouts.

'Are you hopeful Annie's still alive?' another yells out insensitively.

'How are you both coping?'

I hold my breath, hoping they keep to their word and don't answer any of the questions. It'll leave more for me to explore when I finally persuade them to sit down and talk. Now they've faced the cameras once, it's going to be harder for Aunt Cathy to refuse to do a longer interview with me.

The couple turn and walk back into the house, shepherded protectively by the assistant chief constable. The door clicks shut, and the media throng begins to disperse. It was short and sweet, but it's enough to guarantee it will be leading the news bulletins for the rest of the day.

I feel my phone buzzing in my pocket and my guts lurch when I see it's Tim.

'Did you see they've held a press conference?' he yells down the line at me so loudly I have to hold the phone away from my ear. 'What happened to the exclusive you promised?'

A prickle of heat circles around my collar. 'I'm not sure I promised – '

'I had to send Luke across to cover it, as you clearly can't be trusted.'

That's harsh. I'm not sure what more I could have done to talk Cathy and Kit into giving me that interview. No one else was knocking on their door at one o'clock in the morning.

'I'm sorry,' I mumble. There's no point arguing with him when he's ranting like this.

'It's your aunt and uncle. How difficult can it be?'

'Tim, I want that interview as much as you, but I need more time.'

'You don't have time, Yannick,' he says and hangs up before I can utter another word.

He really can be an arsehole sometimes. I know he's under pressure from Gina to deliver, but I can't perform miracles.

I slip my phone back into my pocket and tap my foot impatiently on the ground as I watch Harry struggling with his camera and tripod back to his car. In fact, everyone's leaving, heading in opposite directions, scurrying off to feed footage back for the lunchtime bulletins or write up their copy for the print deadlines.

Outside Cathy and Kit's house, it's now the quietest I've seen it all day, like everyone's had their feed and with their stomachs full, all the reporters and news crews have grown indolent. The two uniformed officers have resumed their guard positions outside the door and a few journalists are setting up to do lives with the house in the background. But that's it. If ever there was a perfect opportunity to catch my aunt and uncle, it's now.

Except the assistant chief constable's still inside with them.

I wait patiently, biding my time, and twenty minutes later he reappears at the door. An unmarked car sweeps up to the house and he's bustled inside before it takes off at speed. A few of the reporters left in the vicinity attempt to chase after him, shouting questions. It's a perfect diversion. While they're all preoccupied, I take my chances and sneak around the back of the house.

No one pays any attention as I approach the rickety wooden fence that surrounds Cathy and Kit's narrow rear garden. I try the gate, rattling it in frustration, but it's locked from the inside. Typical. Nothing's ever easy.

I step back and look for an alternative way in. The fence towers a good foot above my head, but there's no other option than to climb it. Not that I'm dressed for climbing fences. This is an expensive suit, and if it gets ruined, I'm sending Tim an expenses claim for a new one.

I reach up, grasp the top of the nearest panel and try to pull myself over. But it's hopeless. I don't have the strength in my arms and I can't find any purchase with my stiff brown brogues. I need something to climb on. A bin or a box. Of course, there's nothing like that around.

All I can see are a couple of traffic cones on the other side of the road that have been left by a building firm refurbishing the house opposite. One of those will have to do.

I scurry across the road, grab one and place it at the foot of the fence. Thankfully, it takes my weight and gives me the leg up I need to haul myself inelegantly up and over, into the garden, where I land clumsily, turning over my ankle.

I wince with pain and limp towards the house. Fortunately, I think it's twisted rather than sprained. No lasting damage.

The back of the house is in darkness, until I knock loudly on the kitchen door and a light comes on. Aunty Cath appears and frowns when she sees it's me.

'Yannick? What are you doing out here?' she asks, clearly not pleased to see me. I can't blame her. We've never been close, especially as I've hardly had anything to do with her in ten years, not since she took me in when my mother died. I only stayed with them for a few months while I finished my exams and then I was off to university, and I never came back. I was too keen to make my own way in life.

'The front's crawling with reporters,' I explain. 'I just wanted to talk.'

'Please, Yannick, let's not do this.'

Up close, she looks worse than she did when she appeared for the cameras. Her skin is pale and blotchy, her eyes bloodshot. It's a shame her attitude's not mellowed. I thought now she'd faced the press she'd be more amenable to doing an interview with me.

Uncle Kit walks through from the hall carrying three empty mugs and does a double take when he sees me.

'Yannick?'

'Have the police gone?' I ask.

'Zara's in the lounge,' he says.

And then she appears, like a genie, summoned by the sound of her name. She looks at me suspiciously.

'I thought I heard voices. It's Yannick, right?'

Like an annoying fly on a warm summer's day, I try to ignore her. 'I thought you did a great job just now, Aunty Cath,' I say.

She shrugs, her eyes still rimmed red with tears.

'You didn't answer my question,' she says. 'I don't suppose you're here to see how we're doing.'

I put a hand to my heart as if she's fired an arrow into my chest. 'Aunty Cath, how could you say that?' She raises an eyebrow. 'You know I care.'

'Do you?'

'Of course. It must be awful what you're going through. And poor little Annie. I just want to help,' I say, softening my tone.

'You can help by leaving us in peace.' Aunty Cath folds her arms across her chest and lifts her chin defiantly.

'Please, don't be like that. I know you don't approve of my job, and I understand why, but I really think this is a big opportunity you're missing. We have to make sure as many people know what's happened to Annie as possible, to spread the word, because someone out there knows what's happened to her. And the best way of doing that is to do a proper interview, not just a few words outside the house.'

'I can't.'

'Yes, you can. It won't take long, and I'll be here to hold your hand. It'll be so much easier than what you've just done, facing all those cameras at once,' I explain.

'I didn't want to do that either, but your Uncle Kit insisted.'

That's interesting. I thought he was on my side, that he understood why I wanted them to do an exclusive interview with me rather than an insincere press conference for everyone.

'If you do this interview, it's going to make headlines across the country,' I say. 'And that means more people are going to hear about Annie. And the more people who hear what's happened, the greater the chance of someone coming forward with information.'

Uncle Kit places a hand on Aunty Cath's shoulder. 'I think we should do it,' he says quietly. 'He's right, we need the publicity. And if we're going to talk to anyone, it might as well be Yannick.'

Aunty Cath shakes her head, her bottom lip protruding. 'I can't,' she repeats.

I sigh. I never thought it would be this hard, but I can't walk away for a second time. How would I ever hold my head up in the newsroom again?

'You don't want people thinking you have something to hide, do you?' I say.

'What?'

'Well, if you stay hidden behind closed doors, people are going to naturally start asking questions.'

I watch Zara out of the corner of my eye. She's pretending not to listen, but I see her stiffen.

'But I have nothing to hide!' Cathy snaps. 'All I want is to get Annie back.' Tears bubble up in her eyes again.

'And you will, I promise. But you need to do this interview.'

'No,' she screams. 'I'm not doing an interview. Not with you. Not with anyone.'

Chapter 15

CATHY

I've not been able to stop thinking about what Pam Buckley, that woman from the residents' association who's been organising all the search volunteers, told me. I had no idea there were so many evil people out there, living on our doorstep.

'I don't want to worry you, but I think it's better you know,' she said, as we strolled along the narrow path by the creek, shoulder to shoulder like a pair of co-conspirators, our heads bowed, our coats buttoned up to our necks. 'And this might have nothing at all to do with Annie's disappearance.'

'Please, if you know anything at all, tell me,' I pleaded.

Whatever she had to say, she was hedging around it, which is how I knew it was bad.

'The thing is, I have a contact in the police, who tipped me off a while ago because she thought I ought to know, as the residents' association chair,' she said.

I stopped in my tracks, turned and looked her in the eye. 'Just say it.'

She sucked in a deep breath and glanced up at the starry night. 'She told me they've housed almost twenty registered sex offenders within a five-mile radius of the estate.'

'Twenty?' I couldn't believe what she was telling me. That's twenty suspects who could all have had something to do with Annie's abduction. 'That's ... unbelievable. Why are you telling me this?'

What did she expect me to do with that kind of information? Couldn't she see how cruel it was to share it with me? To make me think Annie might have been snatched off the street by any number of sick, depraved predators living in the town. It didn't help at all, it just made me even more anxious.

And yet, I still don't want to do an interview with Yannick. It's as simple as that. He might be family, but I don't trust him. Isn't that awful? My own nephew and I don't believe he won't twist and manipulate my words and paint me as someone or something I'm not. Maybe he is here with our best interests at heart, but he's a journalist. I don't think he cares at all about me. Or Annie.

I've made allowances in the past because of his upbringing. He never knew his father. Monica fell pregnant when she was only nineteen. She insisted she could raise him on her own, but she never had any more children, and Yannick became the centre of her universe. Until her death, snatched from us too young by breast cancer, she spoilt him rotten. He was only with us for a few months, and that was long enough. He was a self-centred, arrogant brat and neither of us were sad to see him leave. I certainly wasn't surprised when he didn't come back after he finished university.

'Don't you want Annie back?' Yannick says. It's a cheap shot.

'Of course I want her back. I hate her not being here. It's like a piece of my soul is missing.'

'Then do the interview. Show everyone the pain and heartache you're going through. It's your chance to tell them all about Annie and what she's like. At the moment, she's just a photograph. A two-dimensional image. But you can bring her to life. Do you have any recent videos we can use? That would really help.'

He spits the words out like they're bullets from a machine gun. Fast and furious. Unrelenting. As if he thinks the sheer weight of his enthusiasm is going to win me around. I hate the way he keeps glancing at Kit, as if they're in on this together, ganging up on me.

'Come on, love. What harm could it possibly do?' Kit says. 'I'm sure Yannick knows what he's talking about.'

He's changed his tune, but he doesn't know what he's saying. We don't *need* to do this. The story is already making headlines. It's everywhere.

I grab a pile of letters and business cards that have been shoved through the letterbox from journalists and producers, begging us to talk. I wave them in front of Yannick's face.

'We have every news outlet in the country hammering on the door, wanting to speak to us. If I wanted to do an interview, if I thought it would help, I'd have done it by now. I only agreed to do the press conference earlier because I was told it would get you all off my back.'

'One interview,' Kit says. He puts on that soppy voice he uses when he's trying to convince me of something against my better judgement. 'That's all Yannick's asking.'

'If you're so keen, why don't you do the bloody interview yourself?' I say.

Yannick shakes his head and lowers his gaze. 'You're Annie's mother. It's you people want to see.'

They're backing me into a corner, making me sound unreasonable. I'm not stupid. I understand why Yannick's pressing me so hard. Ours is the kind of story that sells papers and boosts viewing figures. I've seen these interviews before. The worried parents, clutching each other's hands, pale and frightened, talking in a darkened room, spotlit like they're actors on a stage. They do it because it's supposed to elicit empathy and raise the profile of the case, which the police have been at pains to explain is vital in the first few hours of a child going missing. I get it. But I still don't want to do it.

'I don't care,' I say.

'Please, Cathy. Do this for me. For Annie.' Kit squeezes my hand tightly.

I yank it away. I've deferred to him on all the important things in our lives for the entirety of our marriage. But not this time. I'm not giving in.

'You know why I can't do this,' I hiss. It's not that I don't want Annie back. Of course I do. It's what I want more than anything in the world, but I'm not selling my soul to further Yannick's career. They'll edit my words and distort the truth. That's how they work, isn't it? They all have an agenda. It won't matter what I say or think. They'll manipulate it into the story they want it to be, and I'll have no control over what gets said. That's the truth of it.

Kit throws his hands up in exasperation. 'Not this again. That was years ago, and anyway, this would be different. This would be Yannick, your own nephew.'

He makes it sound like I'm a stuck record, going on and on about my father, but the papers destroyed him with their lies. I'm sure he'd still be alive today if it wasn't for what they published about him. I shudder at the memory of the headline in the paper he left strewn across the kitchen table before taking himself into the woods with a length of rope.

The Butcher of Brighton.

Can you believe it? Like he was a sadistic dictator or a murderer. He was a surgeon. All he ever wanted was to help people. Of course patients sometimes died. It was a difficult and complex job. But someone claimed there was a pattern of failures and the hospital said it was left with no choice but to suspend him while he fought to clear his name.

None of the papers gave him that chance, of course. They all vilified him like he was already guilty, painting him out to be a villain. His reputation was left in tatters. And he saw only one way out.

Then they went after me.

I was ten years old, the same age Annie is now, struggling to comprehend the loss of my father. I had no reason to doubt the motives of the sympathetic stranger who approached me as I walked home from school a few weeks after my father's funeral. She wore bright red lipstick, had the most beautiful russet hair and floated around on high heels under a sweet cloud of Chanel No 5. She knew all about my father's death, told me how sorry she was and that she'd also lost her father when she was young. She wanted to know how I was coping, how my mother was, and whether I thought we'd stay in the house.

She bought me a hot chocolate in a quiet backstreet café and the words tripped off my tongue as I spilled out all our family secrets. I told her I was worried about Mother, who was drinking heavily by then, and my sister Monica, who was still only fifteen but seemed to have gone off the rails.

The following weekend, it was all in the papers. As if they hadn't already done enough damage. Mother accused me of all sorts of horrible things, that I did it for the attention. But I would never have done that.

'I don't think you should do the interview either.' I'd almost forgotten Zara was in the room, listening. 'At least not without speaking to the press office first. Do you want me to call them and have a chat?'

It sounds as though she's on my side, but I'm wary of her. I don't think she's who she's pretending to be.

'It's entirely up to my aunt to decide if she's going to give an interview,' Yannick snaps at her. 'It has nothing to do with you.'

'Yannick, don't take that tone, please.' There's no need to be rude to her. I don't like her, but while she's under our roof, she deserves to be treated with civility.

He rolls his eyes like a petulant child. He never did like being told what to do.

'Look, I want Annie to be found as much as you do, but there's something else,' he says, fixing me with puppy dog eyes, as if I'm that easily swayed. 'My news editor's given me an ultimatum. He's as good as told me there's no job for me if I can't get you to agree to an interview.'

Oh, please. Are there no depths to which he won't sink? 'Don't be so melodramatic.'

'It's true. I need this interview, Aunty Cath. But you need it too if you're going to get Annie back. This could help us both.'

At least he's being honest now. 'This isn't about your career, for god's sake. This is about Annie. She could be anywhere, with anyone, and you're worried about your job? Show some respect, Yannick.'

'Please, I really need this. We both do.'

'Just stop!'

'Okay, I'm sorry.' Yannick takes a physical step backwards, away from me. 'You're right, this isn't about me, but let me help you take control of the story. This is completely different to what happened with Granddad. This is about using the media for good. All you need to do is be open and honest, and the public will love you.'

'I don't need their love.' This is like water torture, the way he keeps going on and on and on. I wish he'd just stop, but he's not going to until he's got his way, is he?

'No, you don't,' he says. 'But you need them to help find Annie. You need them on your side if you're ever going to get her back safely.'

Chapter 16

YANNICK

Uncle Kit unlocks the back gate and I sneak away, unable to suppress the huge grin on my face, so wide it makes my cheeks ache. I was beginning to doubt whether I could ever change Aunt Cathy's mind about the interview. I know why she's reluctant, but it's the right thing to do, for her and Uncle Kit, for me and for Annie. She can't lock herself away and expect the police to perform some kind of miracle. They clearly don't have a clue. She needs maximum press exposure.

I rush back to my car, eager to call Tim with the good news.

'She'll do it,' I announce breathlessly. 'Cathy's agreed to the interview.'

'Brilliant. Well done, Yannick. I knew you wouldn't let me down.'

A scratching on the line as his voice becomes muffled suggests he's holding the receiver against his chest. I hear him talking to Holly, the programme producer, letting her know the interview's as good as in the bag.

I know Aunty Cath had a hard time with the press when her father died. Mum told me what the papers printed about him, how they'd portrayed him as some kind of murderous psychopath, and how Aunt Cathy blamed them for his death and never got over it. But like I told her, this isn't the same. This is using the media to her advantage. Raising awareness and getting Annie home, safe and unharmed. And who better to hold her hand through the whole process than me?

My stomach bubbles with excitement. Everyone's talking about Annie's disappearance. Finally, this interview, if I get it right, could be my fast track to a network job. No more reading the regional news on the graveyard shift. This could be my ticket to the big time.

'I've got a camera on standby. When can she do it?' Tim asks.

'She'll need a bit of time to get herself ready, but soon.'

'Early evening? It would be good to get this in the can tonight.'

'Should be fine,' I say, checking my appearance in the rear-view mirror. The lack of sleep hasn't done me any favours. My eyes look puffy and bloodshot. 'And it gives me time to get my questions together.' My mind spins with the opportunities this is going to open up. I've always fancied having my own documentary series. And although I've never been much of a dancer, if *Strictly* came knocking, what the hell, I'd happily do it.

'Great. Immy's on standby. We'll get her in a car over to you as soon as she's wrapped up this evening's programme.'

'What?'

'We'll get Immy over to Faversham as soon as she's finished here. I think she'll have a great rapport with your aunt, especially as she's a mum too.'

'No,' I say, stunned. 'Imogen's not doing the interview.'

Imogen Moon, one half of the evening programme presenting duo, is adored by our viewers, but she's a total airhead. All teeth and blonde hair. Such a cliché. She wouldn't know a news story if it came and bit her on her perfectly gym-toned ass. She's not taking over my story. No way.

'Of course she's doing the interview. Why wouldn't she?'

My cheeks flush with a fury that rages from my chest. They can't do this to me. I won't let them. It's my Aunty Cath. I've spent all this time and energy talking her into it. This is my interview. My exclusive.

'That's not fair.' I must sound like a whiny prima donna, but that's how I feel.

'It's what Gina's asked for. It was all agreed in the meeting earlier,' Tim says, as if that somehow justifies Imogen Moon stealing my scoop. 'But listen, we'll need you to produce the item and oversee the edit.'

'Oversee the edit?'

'Problem?' Tim says.

I can't let this happen. I won't. After all the hard work I put into persuading Aunty Cath to do the interview, there's no way I'm letting Imogen Moon waltz in on her six-inch Louboutins and steal the glory. I don't care that she's the programme's anchor with a legion of adoring fans. She's not taking my story.

'Cathy won't speak to anyone other than me,' I say, thinking on my feet. 'It was the one stipulation she had. I'm sorry.'

'Seriously?'

'Yup.' It's a good job Tim can't see my face. It must have "liar" written right across it.

'Let's get Immy over to have a chat with her anyway. I'm sure when Cathy meets her, she'll be more than happy to let her do the interview, especially if you're there to oversee things.'

I shake my head violently, even though he can't see me. 'Sorry, Tim. She was absolutely insistent. She won't speak to anyone other than me. It's a waste of Imogen's time sending her over here.'

'Perhaps I can have a word with her? Give me her number.'

'No, Tim. Look, do you want this interview or not? It took a lot of persuasion to get her to agree to do it and to be honest, she's wavering. If you start putting the pressure on her, or you send Imogen out here, she'll pull the plug on the whole thing. I'm not kidding.' It's a desperate, last-ditch attempt to salvage a brewing disaster. I couldn't stand to be in the same room as Imogen Moon, asking *my* questions to *my* aunt about *my* story.

Tim sighs. He'll be standing at his desk, because he always stands when he's stressed, running a hand through his thinning hair.

Holly will probably have already started building tomorrow's programme around the interview, with Imogen no doubt anchoring live from the town, linking in and out of her exclusive. It's not my problem that she's going to have to rip up her plans and start again.

'Can you talk to her and explain?'

'It won't do any good. It's me or no one.'

'Just try, will you?' Tim barks, his patience snapping. 'We're all relying on you.'

Chapter 17

CATHY

'Can we see Annie's room?' Yannick asks.

Family or not, I don't want him upstairs poking through our things. It's bad enough that the police have turned the house upside down, nosing through our belongings and taking liberties with our privacy. It's not as if Yannick and I are close. I haven't heard from him in years. He's only crawled out of the woodwork now there's something in it for him. 'I - I - I'm not sure,' I stammer.

The cameraman, I think he's called Harry, nods. 'Yeah, some shots in Anne's room would be ideal,' he says.

I knew I shouldn't have agreed to this, but Yannick kept going on and on and in the end, I didn't have the strength to keep arguing. But it's a mistake. I can't stand them being in the house, opening up our most intimate selves for the world to see. I just don't have the emotional energy for it right now, not while Annie's missing.

Before I can stop them, Yannick's off up the stairs with the cameraman trailing behind, his dirty boots leaving dried mud all over the carpet. I glance at Kit, who just shrugs and follows them up.

They all march into Annie's room without considering that I might not want them in there, but how can I stop them?

I cringe with embarrassment as the cameraman takes shots of the unmade bed, Annie's pink unicorn duvet cover a crumpled heap on top of a wrinkled white sheet. I've not touched her room since she disappeared. I couldn't bring myself to do it. I want it to be exactly how she left it for when she comes home, like nothing has happened and we can all return to the lives we were living before this nightmare began.

Then he focuses on a row of her soft toys and sweeps the camera around towards her collection of gymnastics medals hanging off a hook and the poster of that Korean boy band she loves. All the little reminders of what I've lost, my precious baby girl who's always singing and laughing or practising her gym tumbles on the lounge floor.

Meanwhile, Yannick sifts through Annie's desk, shuffling through her drawings and notebooks. He knocks a felt-tip pen onto the floor and doesn't even bother to pick it up. Then he heads for her chest of drawers.

'Don't go in there,' I snap, launching myself across the room and elbowing him out of the way. I'm not having him pawing through her clothes. It's bad enough they're in her room.

He makes an exaggerated protest of innocence, holding his hands up in surrender as if this is all a big game.

'Aunty Cath, why don't you sit on the bed and maybe pick up one of Annie's soft toys? Uncle Kit, sit with her and could the two of you look up out of the window as if you're thinking about her?'

This is what I was afraid of, how he's going to make it as if all we've been doing is sitting around, staring soulfully out of the window, pining for her return. It's ridiculous. I can't see how this is going to help get her back.

'I'm not sure – ' I mumble.

'We want people to empathise with what you're going through,' Yannick says. 'It's just a way of presenting the trauma you're dealing with in a visual way.'

With a sigh of resignation, I reluctantly sit on the edge of the mattress, feeling self-conscious and vaguely stupid. I'm certainly stupid for letting Yannick talk me into this.

Harry kneels down in front of me with his camera on his shoulder and one eye squeezed shut, staring through the viewfinder, painfully close. I wrinkle my nose at the sour haze of body odour radiating off him as he flicks on a dazzling top light.

Kit comes over and sits at my side, our thighs and shoulders pressed together, unnaturally close. He shoots me a tight half smile. Is that his way of apologising? After all, it's partly his fault Yannick's here at all. He was the one badgering me to do this.

On Yannick's instruction, I've not bothered with any make-up, and I've only roughly run a brush through my hair. He says it would give off the wrong impression if I was "dolled-up". Better that I look "haggard and exhausted". Ha! Not difficult the way I'm feeling right now.

'Which is Annie's favourite?' Yannick asks, pointing at the teddy bears, dolls and assorted soft toys behind us.

'This one, Rocky,' I say, plucking out a sad-looking bear with matted fur and mournful button eyes.

I sit him on my lap and straighten his blue felt jacket. I can't remember where he came from, whether he was a present or even if Kit and I bought him for Annie.

'That's great,' Harry says. 'Don't look at the camera, but keep playing with the bear and sort of looking wistful, like you're worried about Annie and what's happened to her. And maybe now glance up out of the window for me. Perfect.'

It all seems so staged. The light on top of the camera reflects off the windowpane and I glimpse a distorted image of the four of us crammed into the room. What the hell are we doing? We should be out there, looking for my daughter, not posing for the TV cameras. This feels so wrong.

But for the next twenty minutes, I'm entirely at Yannick's mercy as Harry films me and Kit with different items of Annie's belongings. Dolls, books, medals and even looking through her wardrobe. We've not even started the interview yet.

Eventually, Harry declares he has enough footage, and we all trudge back downstairs to the lounge. I'm exhausted and irritable. I just want my house back and Yannick and his cameraman gone.

Harry pulls the curtains closed, puts his camera on a tripod, sets up some lights and asks me and Kit to sit together on the sofa. Yannick grabs a chair from the kitchen and sits opposite, preening himself, as if this is all about him and nothing to do with saving Annie. At least Zara's not here breathing down our necks, monitoring every word and how we say it. I've asked her for some space this evening and she didn't protest. I'm sure she'll quiz us about it when she's back tomorrow.

It seems to take an age for Harry to set up everything just as he wants it, every second we wait ratcheting up my nerves, until I'm a tightly coiled spring. This is worse than anything I imagined. Adrenaline races through my veins like molten lava, my stomach churns and my head swims with a dizzying lightness. What would my father say if he could see me now, selling out so cheaply? I hope he'd understand I'm only doing this for the sake of Annie and my family.

Finally, we're ready to begin.

'Let's start with the morning you last saw Annie,' Yannick says. 'What do you remember about the day and how Annie seemed?'

'She seemed fine.' I glance at Kit. He's wringing his hands in his lap, no less jittery than I feel. 'Happy. Looking forward to school.'

'Nothing unusual or different about her behaviour or demeanour that morning, then?'

'No.'

'What time did she leave the house?'

'About eight thirty.'

'And that was the last time you saw her?'

'Yes.' I didn't want to cry on camera, but my tears seem to have a mind of their own, dampening my eyes. I dab them with a tissue and try to compose myself. I don't want to appear like a blubbering wreck, although I have the feeling that's exactly what Yannick wants.

'Tell me a bit about Annie. What's she like?' Yannick pinches his chin between his fingers, leaning forwards with an encouraging smile. I suppose he's only trying to put me at my ease.

'She's always happy. Smiling. Laughing. She loves music and is forever singing around the house. She's just a beautiful little girl. Every parent's dream,' I say. Of course, we have cross words. I don't like the way she talks to me sometimes and she's definitely becoming more stroppy the older she gets. We're clashing more than we used to, but I guess that's just a sign she's growing up.

'I was admiring the gymnastics medals you showed me in her room earlier.'

'That's right, she's quite an accomplished gymnast, but like most little girls her age, she's into all sorts of things. She loves her pop music. And dancing. She's always dancing.'

Yannick nods enthusiastically.

'I just want her home.' My bottom lip wobbles. 'Here with us, where she belongs.'

Yannick glances at a notebook he's holding in one hand. 'I understand the day she disappeared she'd walked to school by herself?'

'It's not far.'

'And she usually walks home on her own, does she?'

'Yes.'

'Remind me how old she is?'

I don't like the turn his questions have taken. Alarm bells are going off in my head. 'Ten. Eleven next month,' I say. 'But you'd know that if you'd bothered to remember her birthday.' The barb comes out before I can stop it.

Yannick's eyes widen for the briefest moment, but he quickly regains his composure. 'Don't you think that's a bit young to be letting her walk home on her own?'

I bite the corner of my lip. I can see what he's doing, trying to get a rise out of me. I knew I couldn't trust him. Why didn't I listen to my gut and tell him what he could do with his interview? 'Not really. Most of her friends walk home without their parents.' I hope the camera can't pick up that I'm grinding my back teeth.

'Some would say you're an irresponsible parent.'

I swallow a lump in my throat as sweat beads on my forehead under the harsh lights. 'Plenty of children walk alone to school at the age of ten, but this isn't a busy inner city. This is a quiet market town. We thought she'd be safe,' I say.

I take another glance at Kit, hoping he'll back me up. Why is he staying so quiet? I'm the one being painted as the bad parent here, even though it was a joint decision to let her walk by herself when she'd pestered us to let her have more independence. In fact, it was Kit who pushed for it when I wasn't sure it was a good idea.

'If you could turn back the clock, would you still let Annie walk to school alone?' Yannick asks.

'What kind of a question's that? Of course I wouldn't.'

'So you accept you were wrong?'

'That's not what I said. You're twisting it.'

I might have known Yannick had something like this up his sleeve. He never could stick to his word.

He looks down at his notes again.

'Was there any kind of argument before she left home?'

I don't know why everyone keeps asking us that. 'No,' I say firmly.

'No reason you can think of at all why she might have run away?'

'I don't think she's run away. I think someone's taken her.'

'You're convinced Annie's been abducted, then?' Yannick asks.

A solitary tear rolls down my cheek, the floodgates threatening to open. 'Yes,' I croak. 'Otherwise, I think she'd have been found by now.'

'Would you describe her as a happy child?'

'Yes, of course.'

Yannick takes a deep breath and looks to the ceiling, his eyes narrowing as he composes his next question. What the hell is he going to ask now? He's working up to something. I can see it. I'm sure the camera must be able to see my heart thudding against my ribs and the tremor in my hands I'm trying to steady by gripping them tightly in my lap. How much longer is this going to go on?

'But your own childhood wasn't a happy one, was it?'

I breathe heavily through my nose with the sensation of the floor opening up beneath me and that I'm plunging down a deep, dark pit. Surely, he's not seriously going to bring up my past?

'Your father died when you were the same age as Annie, and that severely affected your relationship with your own mother, didn't it?' Yannick says.

I can't breathe. Does he really think I'm going to answer that? That I'm going to discuss my family history in front of a TV camera?

Kit stiffens. He knows Yannick's overstepped the mark, so why doesn't he say something?

'Yannick, don't,' I whimper. 'Please.'

'It's a reasonable question, given the circumstances, isn't it? Your mother was devastated by your father's suicide, and she became withdrawn and distant. That's true, isn't it? All I'm wondering is what kind of impact that must have had on you, and subsequently bringing up a child of your own?'

'That's enough.'

'You didn't feel loved by your own mother after your father's death, did you? I wonder, do you think Annie felt loved by you?'

My fingers wrap around themselves so tightly my knuckles turn white.

'That's enough.' I glance at the cameraman, trusting he'll take pity on me and stop the shoot, but he keeps filming.

'Do you think Annie felt loved?' Yannick repeats.

'I'm serious, Yannick, this isn't what I agreed to. Stop filming.'

Kit's hand finds my knee. 'Come on, Yannick. Don't be an arse.'

Yannick's eyebrows shoot up. 'Seriously? I'm only doing my job.'

'I thought we were going to talk about Annie,' I say.

'And we have,' Yannick says. 'But I think it's also important to explore the relationship between you and your own parents, and how your past might have influenced your relationship with Annie.'

'None of that has anything to do with Annie going missing.'

'Doesn't it? Is it why you didn't have any more children?' Yannick presses.

I flush hot and cold.

'Was it because your relationship with Annie was so difficult? Did you see history repeating itself?'

'Stop it!' I shout. I jump up, my fingers reaching for the microphone clipped to the inside of my blouse. My instinct is to rip it off and walk away. 'I'm done,' I say. 'I don't need this, Yannick. The interview's over.'

'Keep rolling,' he says to Harry.

I freeze, staring at my nephew. It's a threat. If I don't cooperate, he'll use the footage of me storming off, making me look like one of those dodgy politicians caught by their own lies. Even Yannick wouldn't stoop that low, would he?

Yes, I can see it in his eyes. He would happily hang me out to dry. If only his mother could see him now.

I sit back down and try to regain some semblance of calm. I need to win back control.

'Perhaps we could try a different tack,' Kit says, finally. 'It's not fair bringing up Cathy's past.'

I thought he was going to sit there, say nothing, and let me fry. He's always been quick to defend my honour in the past. Maybe it's the camera. He looks cool and collected, but maybe his nerves have got to him more than I realised.

'It's all in the public records, Aunty Cath, and it's only going to be a matter of time before someone else digs it up. I thought we might as well deal with it here and now. Get it out in the open, you know?'

'I don't want it out in the open.'

'Fine, let's move on.' He has a stupid grin on his face. No matter how much I protest, he's going to use the footage anyway, unless I can talk him around. Give him something better.

'Let's talk some more about Annie,' he says.

Okay, this is more like it. We're back on track. Safer territory. I smile wistfully. 'Like I said, she's a happy girl. Always singing and laughing, but she's also kind and caring. She loves animals. She was always begging us for a kitten or a puppy. And she's popular at school. And clever.'

As I go on, Yannick looks increasingly bored, and eventually he cuts me off.

'And if, as you believe, someone *is* holding Annie against her will,' he says, leaning forwards, pointing at me with a bent finger, 'what message do you have for them?'

It's the one question I've prepared for. The one I was expecting. I take a moment to dry my eyes, sniff and look directly into the lens of the camera.

'Please,' I say, 'we just want our daughter back. Her dad and I are worried sick about her. We've hardly slept since she vanished and if anything happened to her, I'd never forgive myself. Please, let her go. She needs to be with her family. I'm begging you. Do the right thing. Bring her back to us.'

WEDNESDAY

Chapter 18

YANNICK

Holly, the programme editor, is hunched over a small monitor at her desk in the newsroom, wearing a pair of headphones as she watches the interview I spent most of the night editing. Tim, at the next desk along, is lounging in his chair with a phone clamped to his ear, completely oblivious. I'm not sure he even notices me. But then, the reception I've received generally since I walked into the building has been decidedly underwhelming. A few perfunctory "good mornings". The odd nod of acknowledgement from some of the reporters huddled around the kettle in the kitchen. One of the other production journalists even asked if I'd watched that new comedy on Netflix everyone's raving about and didn't mention my interview at all. I wasn't expecting a red carpet, but some recognition that I've just landed the station's biggest scoop in years would have been nice.

'Everything okay with the piece?' I ask, sidling up to Holly. At least she'll appreciate what I've achieved.

A broad smile lights up her face and she knocks the headphones off one ear as she notices me standing by her desk. 'This is brilliant. Well done, Yannick.'

I do my best to look humble. 'Thanks. Have you had a chance to watch the whole thing through?'

'Yeah, yeah, I was just going through it again to see where we can tighten it up,' she says.

My shoulders tense. 'Tighten it up?'

The edit *had* come in slightly longer than I'd planned, but it's worth every second. Everyone wants to hear Cathy and Kit's story and I've included plenty of the cutaways we shot in Annie's bedroom and some previously unseen video footage of her I persuaded Aunty Cath to download for me from her phone.

'It's running a bit long at the moment,' Holly says. 'I need to get it down to about six or seven minutes at most.'

Typical. I've handed her the scoop of the year and she wants to hack it down.

'It's all good material, Holly. Isn't there anything else you can lose from the show to make space?'

'I can't give over eleven minutes to a single package. It's about the pace of the programme, Yannick. We only have thirty minutes on air.'

'Not even for the parents of a missing child who are attracting international headlines and giving their only media interview to us?'

Tim slams down the phone and swivels in his chair to face me.

'Great job with the Warrens,' he says. He always manages to carry off that rugged, just-stepped-out-of-bed look. His clothes look like he's slept in them. His shirt is open at the neck, his tie a token effort hanging midway down his chest and his face is darkened with at least two days worth of stubble. 'That was the network,' he says, nodding at the phone.

I knew they'd be interested. 'I pushed over some clips for them to use last night, like you asked,' I say.

'Yeah, yeah, they've got those. They've taken the rushes as well so they can cut their own piece, but they're really interested in doing their own interview,' he says.

'No, they can't.' I'm not having them bulldozing in and taking all the glory. This is my story. My exclusive. I'm not sharing it with anyone.

'I can't tell them no. It's the network.'

'You know the deal. Cathy will only speak to me. If they want to run the package, they'll have to cut it from my footage.'

At the end of the interview, I'd made sure Harry had shot plenty of me nodding sagely as Cathy and Kit answered my questions. Plus, I had him shoot some wide shots of the three of us sitting in the lounge together. It means if the network wants to take my interview, it's going to be almost impossible to cut me out. And they'll hate that. They always want their own people on the big stories. There's no place for the "regional Reggies" like me.

But I have to get noticed somehow.

'Can you give her a call and at least see if she'll entertain the idea?' Tim asks. 'Or let their desk speak to her directly?'

'She won't do it. You know she doesn't trust the press. She didn't even want to speak to me, but I assured her she wouldn't be pestered by anyone else if she did.'

From the corner of my eye, I catch Gina, our head of news, striding out of her office towards the newsdesk.

'Fantastic interview, Yannick,' she says, making a beeline for me, a pair of glasses on a chain looped around her neck bouncing up and down on her chest. 'It's got award written all over it. Can you all come through? I want to chat about tonight's programme.'

In her office, Holly, Tim and I take seats on a hard, grey L-shaped sofa facing Gina's desk. Holly hands out the provisional run order printed on A4 sheets of white paper and outlines her vision of how the show is going to look.

'I commissioned a special opening title sequence,' she says, 'with all five headlines focused on missing Annie, obviously.'

'Do we know what they are yet?' Gina asks, chewing the arm of her glasses.

'Top headline, a mother's anguish, with a clip from Cathy Warren. I'll also take something else from her interview for title two. Not sure exactly what yet, but she said some interesting things worthy of titling. The rest will be updates on the search, depending on what the police say and if there are any more updates, and finally how the town's coping. Luke spent the night out with the volunteers and is putting together a nice piece.'

'Okay, great,' Gina says, nodding. 'Give them space, Holly. No need to rush them.'

'Sure.'

'And the lead is obviously Yannick's interview?' Gina asks.

I bite my bottom lip to stop myself from smiling. I don't want to look smug.

'Yeah, so the plan is to have Imogen anchor the programme live from Faversham. She'll set the scene and walk us briefly through the timeline of events then bring us up to date on the latest on the search, before throwing into Yannick's package,' Holly explains.

It's a shame they're planning on sending Imogen for the lives tonight, but at least it's my face all over the top story.

'What about Yannick?' Gina asks. 'How are you using him?'

Holly stares at her blankly.

'Let's have him here in the studio chatting about his relationship with Cathy, Kit and Annie. He's the only one who has any intimate knowledge of the family. It would be a shame not to take advantage of that. Are you okay with that?' she asks me.

I nod. Of course it's alright. It's the chance to star centre stage in the biggest story of the year.

Holly frowns and scribbles a note on her notepad. 'Fine,' she says. 'At the moment, the package is running at over eleven minutes, but I'm aiming to get it down to more like six or seven.'

'Why?' Gina asks, looking up from the run order. 'If it's good stuff and we have the exclusive on it, why would you chop it?'

'Well, because otherwise I can't get everything else in the show.'

The smug grin of self-satisfaction I was trying to hold in check finally breaks free and I have to put my hand across my mouth, stroking my chin thoughtfully, to hide it. If Gina says my interview needs to run in its entirety, Holly's going to have to back down.

'I don't care about anything else,' Gina says. 'I could listen to Cathy Warren talking about her lost kid for the whole show. Let it breathe. Don't be shy, Holly. Everyone's going to be watching. They all want to hear what she has to say for herself. Plus, Yannick's done a great job digging into some of her demons. In fact, Tim, have we got someone looking at the story of what happened to her father?'

I glance up at Gina with a slight pang of guilt. I couldn't ignore my grandfather's suicide and how it's affected Aunty Cath's relationship with Annie. I wouldn't have been doing my job if I'd sidestepped it, but now it's going to be laid bare to the nation and with Tim digging further into the background of the case, making a big deal of it, there's a danger it's going to be blown out of all proportion. And Aunty Cath has more than enough on her plate to deal with right now.

Tim pulls out a pencil from behind his ear and jots down a note on a scrap of paper. 'We can do.'

'Let's make the most of what we've got,' Gina says. 'Give it the air it deserves. What about the website?'

My mind wanders as Tim explains how the web editor is pushing out clips from the package through social media over the course of the day.

If I'm going to be in the studio tonight, should I go for the red tie or the blue one? And what about an interesting anecdote about Annie? I've not had much to do with any of them in recent years and I struggle to recall anything worthy to recount on air. I might have to focus on how Aunty Cath and Uncle Kit are coping and the support they're getting from the police. That might do it.

'What do you think, Yannick?' Gina asks. Holly and Tim are staring at me.

'Sounds great,' I say, too embarrassed to admit I wasn't listening.

There's a knock on the door and Tim's deputy sticks his head into the office with the flustered look of a news editor on the heels of a breaking story.

'Really sorry to interrupt,' he says, 'but there's been a development. The Press Association is reporting police divers have found a child's shoe in one of the lakes near the school. The police are treating it as a credible lead although they're not confirming it belongs to Annie yet.'

Gina rocks back in her chair and blows out her cheeks. 'Right, well, that changes things,' she says.

Holly looks pained, but I can't see the issue. It's only a shoe. It's not like they've found a body or anything.

'What's the problem?' I ask, irritated.

'If they find Annie's body,' Holly says, 'we obviously can't run your interview as it is. It'll need updating with fresh reaction.'

'Alright, let's not panic yet,' Gina says. 'It's obviously a fluid story. Yannick, get back to Faversham and be ready to get the interview updated with your aunt and uncle if this does develop into something more significant.'

'I thought I was going to be here, in the studio?'

'If they find a body, your interview's going to be out of date,' Tim says. 'Put them on standby and I'll send a dish to the house. Then at least we can take a reaction from them right up to the wire.'

'Tim's right,' Holly adds. 'At least if you're in Faversham it gives us some options. You could always link up with Imogen and the two of you could have a chat about the latest.'

Oh god. Anything but that. The thought of being interviewed by Imogen Moon with her simpering smile and faux concern makes my stomach churn. I'd much rather be in the studio and present a piece in my own right.

'Can't I be in the studio? Think about it. Even if the police did find a body, there's no way they'd confirm an identity by the time we went on air at six.'

Tim, Holly and Gina exchange glances.

'Tim?' Gina says.

'He's got a point,' he says. 'It's unlikely they'd release the identity publicly until they're one hundred per cent certain it's Annie. Or not. And that could take a while.'

'Please,' I beg. 'I can add so much more being here, talking about how the family's coping.'

It's a final throw of the dice. It has to work. I really do not want to be stuck out in Faversham acting as Imogen's sidekick.

Gina tugs at her lower lip as she considers my plea. 'Holly, it's your programme. Your call.'

'I don't know,' Holly says.

'Please, I won't let you down,' I say, clinging to the edge of my seat.

'Fine,' Holly says at last. 'Yannick in the studio with a segment on his relationship with the Warrens, but I need someone in Faversham ready to react to any breaking developments as we go on air.'

Chapter 19

CATHY

'Turn it off,' I grumble.

It's awful watching myself on TV, especially when I'm so ashen-faced and tired. With no make-up, I look pale and ghost-like, my eyes two lifeless beads poked into my skull. And as for the black bags, they're more like sacks. It's like I've been punched repeatedly in the face.

'It's not finished,' Kit says, the TV remote in one hand. He's sitting on the edge of the sofa, glued to the screen, hanging on to every word as a journalist, following on from Yannick's long interview with us, explains in a sombre tone how police divers have recovered a shoe from one of the lakes. The implication hangs suggestively as the presenter, wrapped up in a chunky scarf and thick coat, nods with a concerned knot in her brow.

DS Monkton turned up at the house with it earlier. It was still sodden, a film of condensation forming on the inside of the plastic evidence bag they'd placed it in. He held the bag up by the tips of his fingers so I could see. 'Is it Annie's?'

It certainly looked similar to the shoes Annie wore to school. Black leather. Gold buckle. A row of perforations across a fringed medallion. But that's what most girls' school shoes look like. There isn't much choice.

I shook my head and lowered my gaze.

It's the first lead the police have found, and Monkton's face said it all. He was bitterly disappointed, because if it wasn't Annie's shoe in the lake, it meant they were no closer to finding her.

'Are you sure?' he asked, as if I could have been mistaken about something so important.

'Yes, I'm certain.'

They've clearly not informed the press as they're still reporting it could be vital evidence pointing towards what's happened to Annie. Why haven't the police told them it's not hers? Is it because Monkton doesn't believe me? Or is it because they want the public to think they are making progress, when actually they don't have a clue?

Annie's been missing for more than forty-eight hours now and they've made no progress at all. They've not found anyone who can confirm seeing her after she left school and have no idea where she is or who she's with. I've always been brought up to have utter trust in the competence of the police, but I'm beginning to seriously have my doubts.

Zara, our liaison officer, is sitting on the sofa opposite, watching the TV with one leg crossed over the other.

'Kit, I don't want to see anymore. Please, switch it off,' I say. The long, lonely hours of sitting around the house, waiting for news and imagining the worst, are taking their toll.

All we do is wait and hope, praying for a miracle, trying to push the dark, unwanted thoughts out of our mind. The minutes tick by so slowly, it's painful. But the nights are the worst. Long, dark hours counting down to the morning, every bump and creak the possibility that it's Annie coming home. And of course, it never is.

I wasn't going to watch the interview tonight, but Kit insisted. He said we ought to see how Yannick put together the final edit. What he'd included and what he'd left out. I begged him not to use anything about my father's death and specifically the insinuation that I was somehow an unfit parent. But, just as I expected, my plea fell on deaf ears. I knew Yannick was selfish and self-serving, but this is a new low, even for my nephew. I don't think I'll ever be able to forgive him.

As if it couldn't get any worse, he then popped up in the studio talking about his relationship with me, Kit and Annie, and how worried we all were for her safety.

We?

Yannick hardly knows Annie. He's shown next to no interest in her since she was a baby, and rarely remembers her birthday. When he does, all he ever sends is a cheap card, signed simply "Love Yannick x". He has some gall to claim we're one big family united in concern. He's just using us.

'What did you think?' Kit asks, glancing at Zara.

'It was fine,' she says. That's what people say when they don't want to tell you what they really think, isn't it? She doesn't approve that we did the interview. She thinks it was a mistake, which is funny, because now, so do I.

'People are going to think I'm a bad mother, aren't they?' I say.

Why did Yannick have to bring up my parents? It wasn't my mother's fault that my father's death destroyed her. She did her best, but when he took his own life, shamed and maligned by the hospital and the papers, I think a little bit of her died with him.

'Of course not,' Zara says. 'It's unimaginable how anyone could cope in the circumstances.'

'Why haven't you found her yet?'

It's the same question I keep asking, wondering if she'll give a different reply this time.

'I don't know,' she says, looking away. It's telling that she can't hold my gaze. Is it because she thinks Annie's already dead? She's not said as much, but it's the vibe she's giving off. She's not exactly been falling over herself to reassure us everything's going to be fine, that we'll have Annie back soon. And that can only mean one thing.

Zara uncrosses her legs and leans forwards. 'Cathy, we have every available officer looking for Annie,' she says. 'And there are hundreds of people from the community helping out too.'

'So why has no one found her? You don't think she's still alive, do you?'

'You shouldn't think like that,' she says. 'You need to stay positive.'

I wish she'd just go. We don't need her here, but she seems to think we'd crumble without her constant presence. At least, that's what she wants us to think, although I'm careful about what I say in front of her, wary a misplaced word or the glimmer of a smile is misinterpreted and fed back to Monkton. I'm sure he thinks we have something to do with Annie's disappearance.

There's a knock at the door. Not the urgent, demanding rap of someone here to deliver news, but a soft, almost apologetic knock.

Every muscle in my upper body, from my shoulders to my stomach, tenses. I sit up straight, adrenaline ripping through my veins.

'Who's that now?' Kit growls, putting the TV remote on the coffee table to answer the door.

There's a brief exchange of words, which I strain to hear, followed by the door slamming shut. But the knocking immediately starts up again.

'Go away!' Kit yells, stomping back into the room. 'We have nothing to say.' He throws himself onto the sofa, scowling, his face red.

'Who was it?' I ask.

'More bloody journalists. Why can't they just leave us alone?'

It's obvious why they've come. They've seen our interview with Yannick and now they think we've changed our minds about talking to the press, even though we were promised it would keep them all off our backs. More lies.

Another knock at the door. Louder and more insistent this time. And movement outside the window. Through a crack in the curtains, I see a shadowy face peering in. And then someone banging on the glass makes me jump.

'Mr and Mrs Warren? Five minutes of your time, please?' The words are deadened by the double glazing but still clear enough to hear. Whoever is outside must be shouting.

'This is what I was afraid of,' Zara says.

Bloody know-it-all. I slap my hands over my ears and squeeze my eyes shut. I can't bear this. We're under siege. Our privacy has been stolen. Even in our own home, there's no escape.

When I open my eyes, Zara's standing on the sofa, sealing off the gap in the curtains.

'Can't you make them go away?' I sob, tears of frustration and anger bubbling up uncontrollably.

Kit throws his arms around me and pulls me into a hug. I bury my head in his shoulder, softening into his embrace, letting him envelop me.

'Mr and Mrs Warren, it's the *Mail*.' Someone's actually shouting through the letterbox now. 'We saw your interview and wondered if we can speak to you both? We can offer you a small fee for your time, of course.'

It sounds like he's in the house.

'Let me call someone,' Zara says, 'and see if I can get some uniforms down here to keep them away from the house.'

She ferrets in her handbag and pulls out a mobile phone.

The walls feel as though they're closing in. The house airless. If I stay in the room for a second longer, I'm going to suffocate. I need space. Room to breathe. I push Kit away and run for the stairs.

'Cathy!' he calls after me.

'Leave me alone!'

I dive into Annie's room and shut the door, throwing my weight against it. I slump to the floor in a flood of tears. My shoulders rock and my head falls onto my chest.

I never wanted any of this. I never asked for hordes of journalists to surround the house, leaving me a prisoner in my own home. We're victims in this mess and yet I feel like a worm under the microscope of the nation, public property for people to scrutinise and judge, all because our daughter vanished on her way home from school. It's not fair. Don't they know we're human too? That we have feelings and insecurities? Why can't they go away and leave us in peace? Is it too much to ask?

My head throbs and a stabbing pain from the stress and lack of sleep attacks the back of my eyes. I haul myself to my feet and flop onto Annie's bed. As I bury my face in her pillow and inhale her sweet, stale scent, my heart lurches.

I want her home so badly it hurts like a knife in my chest. She should be here with us, sitting around the TV with our dinner on our laps, laughing at some silly sitcom and making plans for the weekend. All we have left is a gaping black hole in our family.

I never thought it was possible to love anyone as much as I love Annie. It's unconditional and absolute. An iron fist around my heart. Losing her hurts more than I could have ever imagined. My beautiful miracle girl. Without her, life hardly seems worth living.

My fingers wrap around the blister pack of paracetamol in the pocket of my cardigan. I sit up and pop out two pills into my hand.

I hate what we're going through. What they're doing to us. The press. The police. My own nephew. I wish I could make it all go away. To end it here and now.

Maybe I can.

It wouldn't take much, although there's Kit to think about and the fallout for him.

Could I really do it?

I toss the pills in my mouth, shut my eyes and swallow. The blister pack crinkles noisily in my hand.

If I really wanted to end it, I could. And this would all be over, once and for all.

Chapter 20

DELORES

Delores Dean pulls her laptop closer and scrutinises the woman on the screen. Her voice is heavy with sadness, her head hanging in defeat. Her face is pale, her cheeks sucked in with the painful hollowness of an emaciated child. But it's her eyes that draw Delores's interest. Puffy, black bags give the impression they're receding into her skull and even when she glances up at the camera, she hardly blinks. It's hard to watch. A woman in despair. A mother who's lost everything. It's voyeuristic and yet utterly compulsive.

It's an amazing result for the local TV station. The interview everyone else wanted, although Delores wasn't surprised when she discovered the reporter is related to the family. Cathy and Kit Warren's nephew. Annie's cousin. It partly explains why they've refused to speak to anyone else.

Charlie, Delores's ageing ginger tom, jumps up on the table, miaows in her face and rubs his head against her cheek. She's been so preoccupied with analysing the interview, she's completely forgotten to feed him.

She scoops him up, carries him into the kitchen and pours a pile of dried nuggets into his bowl. He purrs contently as he crunches on his dinner, crouched over his bowl with his long, stripy tail extending across the floor. Delores has never had children. She's left it too late now, of course, but her job would have made it almost impossible anyway. She wasn't going to be one of those mothers who never saw their child, relying on the goodwill of friends and family for care while her career took her away for long periods. It wouldn't have been fair. Cats are much easier. Charlie can come and go as he pleases and the woman in the flat upstairs is always happy to keep an eye on him when she has to go away.

With Charlie content, Delores returns to her laptop and rewinds the interview to the beginning, this time advancing the footage forwards a single frame at a time. She's not interested in hearing what Cathy has to say. She's already listened to the interview several times, and apart from the revelation about her father and his untimely death, Cathy's not said much Delores hadn't expected. She's less concerned with *what* Cathy's saying than *how* she's saying it.

She nudges the footage forwards another three frames, and back again, focusing on Cathy's face. The curl of her lip. The shape of her eyes. The rise and fall of her brow.

Most people rate themselves better than average at detecting when someone's lying, maybe looking for a glance to the right or a general shiftiness in the way they speak. But in reality, most people are terrible at determining when someone's not telling the truth. You need to know what you're looking for and to spot almost imperceptible micro-facial signals, or leaks, your body cannot hide.

On the surface of it, there's nothing to suggest Cathy Warren isn't genuine. Her appearance and behaviour are entirely in keeping with a woman who's lost a child. And you can't fake the black bags under her eyes caused by sleepless nights.

But as Delores rocks back and forwards between frames, she sees something maybe nobody else has spotted. Cathy's looking towards the interviewer, her eye line slightly offset, her face a picture of despondency and despair as she pleads for her daughter's safe return. She looks dejected and demoralised. But in the next frame, there's a hint of a smirk. The slight twitch of the cheek muscles. The merest suggestion of a grin.

They call it emotional leakage.

It's hard to spot in real time but easier to identify on film where you can study each individual frame, twenty-four of them in every second, as Delores learned from two criminal psychologists who run a course on the subject at a college in London. It's proved an invaluable lesson in Delores' work as an investigative journalist.

It's clear Cathy's trying to look sad but can't hide her pleasure about something. And in the circumstances, that's odd. Her expression is betraying her. But what exactly is she concealing?

Delores pushes her chair back as Charlie ambles into the room and stops abruptly to wash his back leg. The image on her laptop is frozen on the frame where Cathy appears to be smiling. In isolation, it's totally disconcerting.

Cathy Warren is a little out of Delores' usual sphere of interest. She's more used to investigating the secrets and lies of pop stars and footballers, politicians, businessmen and members of royalty. People who've been corrupted by power, money and influence. She wouldn't normally waste her energy on someone like Cathy Warren, but there's something intriguing about her and the case that's gripping the nation.

Maybe it's the complete lack of progress made by the police. There hasn't been a single sighting of Annie Warren after she left school to walk home alone on the day she disappeared. Nor a shred of physical evidence or a solitary frame of CCTV footage to suggest what might have happened to her. But it's more than that. Delores is fascinated by the woman herself. The depths of her anguish. The coldness of her demeanour. Her reluctance to speak to the press. Most parents in Cathy Warren's position would be falling over themselves to speak to as many journalists as they could, to highlight the appeal for information. But Cathy has remained aloof and detached. Delores wonders why. And like a troublesome mosquito bite, she can't leave it alone.

She snatches up her phone and makes a call.

'Yes?'

'Dave, I'm thinking about doing some digging around on this missing girl story,' Delores says. 'There's something about it that doesn't add up. What do you think?'

'It's a bit left field for you,' he says.

'I've been watching Cathy Warren's interview. I think she's lying about something.'

'What, you don't believe her kid's missing?'

'I don't know. Maybe.'

'That would be some story.' Dave's not easily impressed. Or shocked. After all, he's been running the newsdesk on the country's biggest tabloid for years and has overseen countless stories on scandal and misdemeanour and sat on several dozen more that never made it to print.

'I want to spend a few days in Kent and see what I can turn up,' Delores says.

'What about the Warrens? Think you can get them to talk? We've not had much joy so far.'

'I don't know. I can try.'

'I have something that might help persuade them,' Dave says.

In the shadowy world she resides in, she's not used to the news editors offering their help. More often than not, she's left to her own devices. And as long as she delivers, they tend to leave her alone. They're her stories. Her contacts. Her tip-offs. But she'd be an idiot to turn down assistance if it's being offered. As long as it's not babysitting one of Dave's work experience teenagers. He knows she works alone. And in secret. It's why she's so good. Nobody even knows her real name. Her friends and neighbours all think she works for an online retailer.

'The finer details are still being worked out, but they're talking about putting up a cash reward for information,' Dave says.

'How much?'

'Fifty.'

'Fifty grand?' Delores sucks in air through her teeth. It's a lot of money.

'There's a catch.'

'Isn't there always?'

'It's on the agreement we get full and unfettered access to the family. And I mean twenty-four hour access while Annie's still missing. I was going to send someone down to break the good news, but if you're going, it might as well be you,' Dave says.

'And if they say no?'

'They won't.'

THURSDAY

Chapter 21

CATHY

It takes a moment to remember where I am.

Annie's room.

In her bed.

Did I sleep in here last night? Light spills in through the window, the hint of morning sun falling across my face. And then the memory that she's not here hits me like a thundering avalanche, sending me spiralling back into the depths of despair.

It's hard to believe I've slept at all. Sleep's been elusive ever since Annie vanished, but I must have been shattered. Running on fumes, nervous exhaustion finally catching up with me.

The last thing I recall is crying into Annie's pillow. A flood of tears I thought would never stop. I guess I must have nodded off. Guilt swells deep inside me. I shouldn't be sleeping while my daughter's missing. It's not right. What would people think?

My phone's on the floor. I snatch it up to check the time. It's already gone eight. How the hell have I slept for so long? My mouth's as dry as the Sahara, my teeth coated in a coarse film, and I'm still wearing my jeans and cardigan from last night. I should get up. Take a shower and get changed, but it all seems like such an effort. And what's the point? I have nothing to look forward to but another day of the same. Waiting and hoping, imprisoned in the house, not daring to show our faces outside the door.

Why does everything seem so desperately hopeless?

Eventually, I drag myself out of bed when I hear dishes clattering below. Kit's already up. He's in the kitchen with the radio on and a slice of toast in one hand, studying his phone, which is propped up against the salt cellar.

I shuffle towards the kettle, my feet sweaty in yesterday's socks.

Kit jumps and clicks away from whatever he was reading. More lies and half-truths about us? I guess he's only trying to protect me, but I can't help being suspicious. Is there something else he's hiding? Now I'm being paranoid. What could he possibly have to hide from me?

'I must have dozed off in Annie's room,' I explain, flicking on the kettle. I really need tea.

'I didn't want to wake you. You looked totally out for the count,' Kit says. 'I guess you must have needed the sleep.'

'But you're not supposed to sleep when your child's missing, are you?'

'We all need to sleep.'

I pour hot water over a teabag in a mug and sit at the table opposite Kit. On the radio, a news bulletin is coming to a close and a weather presenter is announcing it's going to be a fine day ahead. If there's anything about Annie, I've thankfully missed it. Kit seems glued to the coverage, but I don't want to hear them talking about my daughter or read any of their lies about us. If there are any developments, the police have promised we'll be the first to know.

Although it's light outside, Kit's left all the curtains and blinds closed with the lights on. I guess it's the only way we can guarantee not being spied on. Is that our life now? Not even afforded the luxury of daylight? How I long for a big house in the country, like we had when I was growing up, surrounded by a deep, dark wood I could escape into and tall fences to keep people from looking in.

The hot tea scalds my lips, but at least it's a distraction from the deeper pain I feel inside.

'Is Zara here yet?' I ask. We might be able to hold the journalists at bay, but there's nothing we can do to avoid contact with our family liaison officer, without eyebrows being raised.

'She should be here any minute.' Kit rolls his eyes. He hates her being in the house with us as much as I do, but we can't protest. She's supposed to be here to help.

'What were you reading?' I ask.

'Nothing,' he says, too quickly.

'Show me.'

'You don't need to know.'

'Obviously I do,' I say with a creep of worry.

'It was just a news report. The tabloids trying to dig up some dirt.'

I bet I can guess. Someone's been raking through the archives and rehashed all my father's old patient case histories, found the old reports about the investigation and subsequent inquiry. So what? At least they will have also found that he was completely exonerated. No case to answer. No evidence of any wrongdoing. His name cleared and his reputation restored, even if he was already dead.

Kit sighs and tosses the crusts of his toast onto his plate. 'You really want to know?'

'No, but I think you ought to tell me anyway.'

He breathes in noisily through his nose. 'Someone's made an allegation,' he says. 'That's all.'

My own breath catches in my throat. 'What kind of allegation?'

'That we were regularly heard shouting and arguing with Annie.' Kit pushes the crust across his plate, clearing a trail through the crumbs.

'What?'

'And that Annie was seen running out of the house in tears a couple of weeks ago.'

I shake my head, casting my mind back. 'That's not true.'

Kit folds his hands on the table and fixes his gaze on my face, almost as if he's waiting for me to remember something I've momentarily forgotten.

'What?' I snap.

'A few weeks ago, you two had an argument. You texted me at work about it, remember?'

I don't recall that.

'Something about Annie wanting her ears pierced because one of her friends had had them done? And you said she left the house upset and I told you to leave it and it would all blow over by the time she was home from school. Remember?'

Oh that. It was a stupid row over breakfast. A tempest in a teacup. I told her she was too young to have her ears pierced, and she flounced off in a huff. By the evening, it had all been forgotten. They were making a big deal about that?

'Let me see,' I say, holding out my hand for his phone.

'It'll only make you angry.'

'Show me.'

Kit reluctantly finds the story and hands over his phone. It's worse than I thought. "Parents abused missing schoolgirl", the headline screams. Under it, a sub-headline makes it sound even more sinister. "Neighbours reveal ten-year-old's catalogue of mistreatment".

'They can't print that,' I gasp.

I scan the story. It's a speculative piece sourced from an anonymous neighbour who says he regularly heard raised voices coming from the house, and on one occasion had seen Annie storm out in tears. But worse is the allegation that he'd noticed bruises on her arm.

Bruises? What the hell?

How can they get away with printing stuff like this? It's outrageous. They can't make up shit like this. Surely there's something we can do to get it taken down? And who is this neighbour anyway? Have they paid him to spout this crap? Or has he done it out of spite?

Of course there have been arguments. Show me a family that doesn't row from time to time. But it doesn't mean anything. We've not been abusing Annie. And she didn't have bruises. That's libel or slander or something.

'Why would they say these things?' My chest tightens in anger.

It's obviously George next door. Who else could it have been? When we refused to talk to the media, they must have gone knocking on the neighbours' doors, trying to rake up some muck.

George has been surly and cantankerous for as long as we've known him. Living alone in the house since his wife died, he seems to have nothing better to do than complain about our bins being left outside his house or the shrubs in the back garden spilling over onto his side. It has to be him.

'It's not worth stressing about,' Kit says. 'Leave it.'

'I'm not standing for this.' I slam my tea on the table and it sloshes out of the mug.

'What are you going to do? Complain to the paper? And what do you think is going to happen then?'

'We can't ignore it or else everyone will assume it's true.' I slap a hand to my forehead, my breath coming in short, ragged gasps. 'And everyone will think we've been mistreating Annie and they'll hate us.'

'If you make a fuss, you'll only end up drawing attention to the story,' Kit says. I can't understand why he's being so reasonable.

'I'm going to deal with this.'

'What do you mean?' His brow furrows. 'Cathy? What are you going to do?'

I'm already heading for the front door, a red-hot spike of anger fuelling me on. I pull on a pair of boots and throw open the front door to the evident surprise of a small cohort of journalists and photographers gathered casually outside. The diehards who won't leave us in peace.

They stare at me open-mouthed like they've seen a ghost, shocked into inaction, until I'm halfway to George's front door.

Suddenly, cameras are clicking and flashing as I hammer loudly with my fist.

'Cathy! What are you doing?' Kit's voice barely registers as journalists swarm around me, sensing something brewing.

Adrenaline races around my veins, and I ball my fists tightly at my side.

'George! Open up!' I yell, banging on the door again. 'I want a word with you.'

Eventually, the door opens a crack and I push it fully open. George stares at me as if I've gone mad.

'What do you want?'

'What the hell do you think you're playing at?' I scream.

He scowls at me, shaking his head. 'I don't know what you're talking about.'

'You know exactly what I'm talking about. Don't treat me like an idiot. It was you, wasn't it, telling the press we've been abusing Annie? Why would you do that?'

His mouth is clamped tightly shut, but the muscle in his jaw is pulsing.

'You're a mean and spiteful old man,' I continue, getting into my stride. 'Well, I hope you're proud of yourself.'

The cameras continue to click and flash all around me. Still George says nothing.

'Keep your nose out of my family's business, understand? I hope they paid you well, you pathetic, interfering excuse of a man.'

He tries to push the door closed, withdrawing into the safety of the house, but at least I've shamed him in front of these journalists. I hope they report every word I've said.

'How dare you speak to me like that,' he hisses, taking refuge behind the closing door.

'You're the one who's been selling lies to the papers.'

'And maybe if you were a better mother, your daughter wouldn't be missing.'

I take an involuntary step backwards. That's unfair. I love my daughter more than anything in this world. I'd never do anything to hurt her.

'I mean, what kind of mother lets their ten-year-old daughter walk to school on their own? You were asking for trouble,' he says, spittle spraying from his mouth.

I can't believe the gall of the man. My head spins with rage. 'To keep them safe from dirty old paedos like you, you mean?'

I shouldn't have said it, but the words leak from my mouth before I stop to think it's not such a good idea in front of a gleeful pack of reporters. But I've not been thinking straight for days.

An arm wraps around my shoulders, gently trying to guide me away.

'Get off me,' I shout, shrugging myself free. I'm not finished with George yet, and from the venomous look in his eye, he has plenty more to say to me too.

'Come on, leave it,' a woman's voice says.

'I'm not done yet.'

'Yes, I think you are.' The arm snakes around my shoulders again, more firmly, pulling me back from George's doorstep.

'No!'

'This isn't going to bring Annie back, is it? Come with me. Let's talk about it.'

George slams the door in my face and when I turn angrily, I'm surprised to come face to face with Pam Buckley.

'Did you hear what he's been saying about me?' I rant. 'He told the papers we've been abusing Annie.'

'Don't worry about it,' she soothes, as I allow her to guide me through the press throng. She uses her free hand to push them out of the way like she's parting the Red Sea. 'This isn't the time or the place to fight your battles. It's only going to make things worse.'

'Where are we going?' She's guiding me away from the creek. Away from my house.

'Back to mine. I think you could do with a break for half an hour, don't you?'

'What about Kit?'

'I'm sure he'll survive on his own for a while. I'll put the kettle on and we can have a proper chat. Anyway, there's something I want to show you.'

Chapter 22

Pam's house is only a short walk away, but the fresh air does wonders to lower my blood pressure. I shouldn't have confronted George in front of everyone, but I'm running on a short fuse. Every tiny thing seems to set me off.

'Did I come across as a lunatic?' I ask with a wince.

'A little,' Pam says, smiling cheerily. 'It's understandable given the circumstances.'

I bury my head in my hands. 'The papers are going to have a field day, aren't they?'

'No point worrying about it. You save your energy for finding Annie.'

Pam lives in a well-maintained red-brick terrace in the heart of the residential estate behind our house. It has white plastic windows and a grey satellite dish over the front door. It's small but clean and tidy, with a neatly clipped lawn at the front and a long, narrow garden with a trampoline and washing line bowing under the weight of drying clothes at the back.

'Come and see,' Pam says, leading me into a dining room where a long table is buried under piles of T-shirts, leaflets and posters, all bearing Annie's happy, smiling face and the words "FIND ANNIE WARREN" printed in bold, capital letters.

'You've done all this?' I ask, amazed. How's she found the time, especially as she's been coordinating the volunteer search effort?

I run my hand over the stack of T-shirts, pricked by guilt. This is what Kit and I should have been doing, not moping around the house fretting, while relying on the generosity of strangers.

'I like to keep busy,' Pam says.

I'm sure she has plenty to keep her busy without adding "Project Find Annie" to her list. Didn't she say she was a single mum?

'I don't know what to say. This is ... humbling.'

'I'm sure you'd have done the same for me.' When she smiles, little creases fold around her eyes.

'Do you ever stop?' I ask.

'Not if it's for a good cause. I can't imagine how I'd cope if it was me.'

'Do you have just the one daughter?' I ask.

'Phillipa, yes. She's seven, nearly eight. I'd have liked more, but, you know... '

My eye catches a collage of photographs in a frame on the wall. Some baby pictures. A few of a toddler with long blonde bunches. Pam, looking younger, slimmer, fresher-faced, appears in some of them, but I can't see any evidence of a man in her life.

'It's just the two of us,' she says, as if reading my mind.

I think she told me Phillipa's father left when he found out she was pregnant. That must have been tough.

'I'm sorry,' I say.

'Don't be. We're happy on our own.'

'And you've not met anyone else?'

'God, no.' She laughs as she ambles into the kitchen and grabs two mugs off the shelf.

'Aren't you lonely?'

'I don't have time to be lonely, not with Phillipa.'

'It must be hard though, bringing up a child on your own.'

'Not really. We rub along pretty well together,' Pam says.

'I'd find it hard. What about Phillipa? Does she ever see her dad?'

Pam laughs again, but it's hollow, bitter and laced with resentment and regret. 'He's not interested,' she says.

'That's so sad.'

'She's best off without him. He's a waste of space. I know what he's like. He'd only end up breaking her heart if I let her see him.'

I don't like to judge, but she's wrong. I don't doubt Pam's doing a great job bringing up her daughter on her own, and I have nothing but admiration for single-parent families, but Phillipa's missing out on so much not knowing her father, or at least having a male figure in the house. You only have to see how many juvenile offenders come from broken homes, and how many of them go on to become serial offenders.

'Are you getting much sleep?' Pam asks, handing me a mug of tea.

I pat my hair down where I feel it sticking up, remembering I'm still in last night's clothes. God knows what she must think of me.

'I slept in Annie's bed last night.'

'You poor love.'

'I haven't managed to get much sleep the last few nights.'

'You need to look after yourself. Are you eating? Are you hungry?' Pam asks. 'I can make you a sandwich.'

'I'm fine,' I say. 'Thank you.'

'I just keep thinking what if it had been my Phillipa. I'd have totally gone to pieces, but you've been so strong,' Pam says.

'Have I?'

'Yes, you've been amazing. I'd have been a blubbering wreck, but you've held it together so well. I saw the interview on TV last night. You were so composed and rational. I really do admire you, Cathy.'

'You do?'

'Of course, but we all need a shoulder to cry on. Even you. I don't know if you have friends or family close by,' Pam says, 'but if you need someone to talk to, I'm here. You know that, right? Pop around any time or give me a call. Or I can come to yours. I know you have Kit, but I don't want you to think you're dealing with this on your own.'

She means it, too. It's coming from a genuine place in her heart. I envy her. A rush of emotion causes a lump to swell in my throat, which I can't seem to swallow. I'd usually turn to my friend Fiona in times of trouble, but I've not spoken to her since I threw her out of the house for trying to take over. I don't need that kind of additional stress in my life right now.

I should get back to Kit. I don't want to cry in front of Pam.

'You're very kind, thank you,' I mumble, glancing at the floor to hide the tears wetting my eyes.

'I mean it. I'm here for you, Cathy.'

'Kit'll be wondering where I am. I'd better get going.'

'So soon? You've not even finished your tea.'

Pam must think I'm so rude, but I can't stay. She's being too kind. Too caring. And I need to hold it together. I put my mug on the side and hurry for the door, pressing my feet into my boots.

'Cathy, you've forgotten something,' she calls out behind me. She rushes into the hall holding up two T-shirts. 'For you and Kit.'

Annie's smiling face on the front of them is a painful reminder of my loss and misery.

'Thank you.' I snatch them from her and run out of the house without a backwards glance, onto the street and, with my head bowed, head for home.

Chapter 23

I can't face running the gauntlet of all those journalists at the front of the house again, so I slip in around the back, grateful Kit's left the back gate unlocked. But as I approach the kitchen door, I can see through the glass that two figures are sitting at the breakfast table. One of them is Kit, but the other is a woman I don't recognise. Curious, I watch them for a moment. She's doing all the talking and Kit looks tense, his shoulders scrunched up to his ears. Another police officer? News about the search?

I tap on the glass and Kit jumps up to unlock the door like he's on a spring.

'Cathy, where the hell have you been?' he asks.

'Who's this?' I size up the woman as she stands and holds out a delicate hand. She's pretty and demure, although not lacking in confidence. She's already made herself quite at home in my kitchen with my husband.

'Delores Dean,' she says, as if she expects me to recognise the name.

I tentatively take her hand, and she shakes it with a firmer grip than I'm expecting. 'Police?'

Her mouth curves into an amused smile, which makes her pretty nose wrinkle. 'No,' she says.

'Delores has been sent by her editor,' Kit tells me.

'A reporter?' The words hiss out of my mouth like hot steam. 'And you let her into the house?' What the hell was he thinking? I've barely been gone an hour.

'I'm sorry. She said she had a significant offer and I thought I ought to hear her out,' he says, hanging his head.

I raise a quizzical eyebrow.

'They want to put up a reward,' he adds.

It takes a moment to process his words. A reward? So she's not here sniffing around for a story? 'Which paper?' I fold my arms across my chest.

'*The Post*,' she says. 'It's all been signed off. We just need your agreement to go ahead.'

My stomach flips and my legs weaken. *The Post*? Is this some kind of joke? It's the biggest and probably the most influential newspaper of them all, but it's also the paper responsible for my father's death. It broke the story about the hospital investigation and even coined the despicable phrase *The Butcher of Brighton*. It's the paper he was reading the day he died. The paper I'm sure sent him over the edge and left him feeling that life was no longer worth living.

'Sit down,' Delores says, as if she's invited me into *her* home and not the other way around. 'Let me explain how it would work.'

Unsteadily, I pull out a chair. Kit grips my hand tightly under the table, his palms hot and sweaty, as Delores folds her hands on top of it and leans towards us like a businesswoman entering a high stakes negotiation.

'It would be a reward of fifty thousand pounds – '

'Fifty thousand?' I gasp. Kit and I had talked about the possibility that one of the news organisations might offer a reward. It's happened in the past in cases like ours, but it was far from a certainty.

Delores smiles with tight lips, her eyes steely. 'But there would be certain conditions attached, which is why I need your consent before we proceed.'

My heart sinks. 'What sort of conditions?'

'Exclusive rights of access.'

I shake my head. She even sounds like she's negotiating in the boardroom now. 'What do you mean?'

'We would require an initial interview with you both, to be run over the course of several days, plus an agreement that you would not speak to any other UK or foreign media,' Delores explains.

My tongue's thick and furry in my mouth and my brain throbs behind my temples. 'An interview?'

'Problem?'

Yes, it would be a problem. It would be a very big fucking problem. How could I live with myself if I agreed to sit down with a reporter from the newspaper that destroyed my life? What would my father say?

I open my mouth to answer, but Kit beats me to it. 'I'm sorry, we can't,' he says. 'It's Cathy's nephew, Yannick. We've promised *him* exclusive rights.'

Delores tilts her head to one side, her chin wrinkling as she presses her lips together. I'm not sure she was expecting us to say no.

'Yes, I saw his interview,' she says. 'And I can understand why you'd choose to talk to him, as he is family, but was there any signed agreement of exclusivity?'

Kit glances at me with panic in his eyes. 'No,' he says, 'but we gave him our word.'

Delores rocks back in her chair. 'In which case, there's nothing legally binding. You can tell him circumstances have changed.'

'I can't do that. He's Cathy's nephew,' Kit complains.

'I'm afraid that's the deal,' Delores says. 'It's non-negotiable. If we put up this reward, we'll want unrestricted access to you both. And, of course, when Annie's found, we'll also need the reunion story exclusively.'

Kit looks frantic. 'What about Yannick?' he repeats, like a stuck record.

'What about him?' I'm not exactly wild about signing our lives away to *The Post* either, but it's a lot of money. A fifty thousand-pound reward could be the key to getting Annie home, the sort of sum that could easily loosen tongues. I don't care about Yannick, any more than he cares about helping us find Annie.

'We made him a promise,' Kit says.

I don't understand where this misplaced loyalty is coming from. All I can imagine is that he thinks he's protecting me by coming up with an excuse why we can't accept *The Post*'s offer.

'Why don't I leave you two to think about it,' Delores says, getting up and pulling on her coat. She slides a business card across the table. 'That's my number. Give me a call when you've come to a decision. But I wouldn't leave it too long. It's a time limited offer. You have until two o'clock tomorrow to make up your minds.'

Chapter 24

DELORES

By a stroke of good fortune, the Airbnb Delores has rented is on the opposite side of the creek with an unobstructed view of the Warrens' house. Unfortunately, she hadn't anticipated there would be a rear access to the house that allowed them to come and go as they pleased, unseen. She'd only discovered that when Cathy returned home while Delores was chatting with Kit in the kitchen. She didn't say where she'd been, which has only deepened Delores' suspicion that Cathy has something to hide.

Delores lets herself into the flat, pulls up a chair in the window and watches the bored pack of reporters and photographers hovering outside the house, like an indolent pride of lions waiting for an unsuspecting gazelle to stray too close.

As she watches, she fishes her phone out of her bag and makes a call to the office.

'What did they say?' Dave, the news editor, asks. The newsroom in the background is humming with activity.

'They're thinking about it. They have reservations about the interview, so I've given them until two tomorrow to give me their answer.'

Dave sighs. She can almost hear him rubbing his big, meaty hand across his stubbly face. 'I hope they don't take that long to decide. We want to splash on it in tomorrow's paper. We don't have time to muck around waiting for the Warrens to decide if they want help finding their daughter or not.'

'I pushed them as far as I could,' Delores says, although she didn't push them at all. She knows if she had put pressure on them, they'd have run a mile. It needed a gentle touch. Not too aggressive. Instead, she'd offered them a ticking clock to focus their minds. 'I'm confident I'll hear from them soon.'

'You'd better.' Dave puffs out a loud mouthful of air. 'How were they?'

'Tired and not exactly pleased to see me,' Delores says, 'until I mentioned the reward.'

'And then?'

'He was worried they'd promised exclusivity to the local TV station, but actually she didn't dismiss it out of hand.' Delores watches a seagull soar on the breeze and glide down to the muddy water on the creek where it lands on the bow of an old sailing barge. 'They know they have no choice.'

It's a lot of money and if they're truly committed to finding Annie and getting her home safely, they'd be insane to turn it down.

Cathy had been everything Delores had expected. Wary. Distrustful. Exhausted. If she is hiding something, she's giving nothing away, playing the grief-stricken parent to perfection. Her face was grey and haggard, her fingernails bitten down to the flesh. And as for the house, the kitchen was a complete state. Dirty cups and plates piled up in the sink. The bins overflowing and stinking. If they're somehow involved in Annie's disappearance, they're playing a cool hand.

It was only a short meeting, but the dynamic between the couple was interesting. Kit's much older than his wife, but Delores isn't sure where the balance of power lies.

At first, she thought it was with Kit, but clearly it's not that simple. Cathy certainly didn't back down when he didn't want to sign the agreement. In fact, she was less resistant to the whole idea than Delores had expected. She knows all about Cathy's father and those supposedly botched operations her paper exposed, which led to his untimely suicide. Is she still bitter about the paper's role in his death? Grieving sons and daughters often have a warped view of reality.

In retrospect, calling him *The Butcher of Brighton* was a bit strong, especially as the investigation had yet to be concluded, but it's water under the bridge. Something that happened more than thirty years ago, long before Delores' time. People have moved on. Times have changed. It's not the same publication it used to be.

And Cathy must know that if they reject the paper's offer, it's going to look bad on them. What parent in their right mind would shun a huge cash reward for information about their missing child? It would certainly raise a few questions. It's probably why she didn't put up much of a fight, despite Kit's reluctance.

'And now you've met them, you still think they know more than they're letting on?' Dave asks.

'They're convincing on the face of it, but there are too many things that still bother me. For a start, how is it possible no one saw Annie Warren once she'd left school? I've taken a quick look around. The school is surrounded by houses. Someone must have seen her.'

'Unless she was picked up by someone she knew and who wouldn't raise suspicion?' Dave suggests.

'But surely *someone* would have noticed?'

'Well, that's the point, isn't it? She was coming out of school with a hundred other kids, all in the same uniform. Loads of people probably saw her, but no one noticed.'

'I suppose. Regardless, I think Cathy Warren *is* hiding something.'

'Like what?'

'That she knows exactly where Annie is. Maybe she even organised her disappearance,' Delores says.

'But why? What's her motive?'

'I've not figured that out yet.'

'Could be they're getting off on the publicity,' Dave says.

Delores scoffs. 'In which case they'd be talking to every journalist with an NUJ card. Cathy hates the press. I think they only did that TV interview because her nephew pressured them into it.'

'What then?'

Delores runs her tongue over her teeth. Every motive she's come up with so far seems so far-fetched. 'They could have trafficked her,' she says. It sounds even more ridiculous when she says it out loud. 'We all know there's an underground market for pretty girls like Annie.'

'Seriously? You think they're the kind of parents capable of selling their own daughter into slavery?'

'Nothing about people surprises me,' Delores says. She's seen too many dark hearts in this job, witnessed the lengths people will go to for money and power, how easy it is for some people to be corrupted and seduced.

'What about Annie? Do you think she's still alive?'

Delores rubs her thumb across her chin. It's something she's thought about. It wouldn't be the first time a parent had killed their own child, accidentally or otherwise, and faked their disappearance to cover their tracks. 'It did occur to me,' she says. 'There was that case in the States, wasn't there, where a mother drove her two kids into a lake and then claimed they'd been abducted?'

'Yes,' Dave says. 'I remember. She did a TV appeal for the safe return of the children.'

'And then a few days later, confessed to their murders. Who knows what was going on inside the Warrens' house. For all we, or the police, know, they could have been abusing Annie for years. What if the abuse went too far and she died, and in their panic they hid her body and made up a story about her going missing?'

Dave whistles through his teeth. 'Now that would be some story, and it ties in with what the neighbour was saying about the mistreatment he witnessed.'

'I'll do some digging, ask around at the school. Talk to her friends. If she was being abused at home, someone must have noticed something. Bruises. Mood changes. That kind of thing.'

'What about your police contacts? Any steer? Are they looking at the Warrens as possible suspects?' Dave asks.

'Everyone's sticking to the script that it's a missing persons inquiry for now and won't speculate on suspects, which makes me think they're also watching the Warrens closely.' Delores stands and rolls her neck. The tide's out and the creek below has been transformed into a river of mud.

'Okay, let's suppose you're right. If Cathy and Kit Warren did kill their daughter, either accidentally or not, what did they do with the body?'

Delores breathes in deeply through her nose, filling her lungs. 'They have a small garden out the back, but to be honest there are loads of places they could have dumped her. They live right on the creek for a start. Plus, there are miles of marshland all around here and several former quarries, now lakes, close to Annie's school.'

'A murderer's paradise.' Dave laughs, but it's not funny. They're talking about a missing little girl. 'Of course, it could be they're telling the truth.'

Of all the possibilities Delores has considered, this seems the most unlikely.

'I need to spend some time getting to know them both. Maybe I can even wring a confession out of them,' she says. It's wishful thinking, but she's done it before. It's a skill, getting people to tell you their darkest secrets.

Just like that woman who killed her husband as his health deteriorated, his future and his humanity robbed by a cruel degenerative disease. She told the police he'd died in his sleep, but eventually admitted to Delores that she'd smothered him with a pillow to put him out of his misery.

'They could have an accomplice,' Dave says.

'True. The flat I'm renting overlooks the house, so I can keep an eye on any comings and goings, although, to be honest, it's under siege at the moment. It's hard to get in or out without being noticed by the press pack.'

The phone beeps in Delores's ear, notifying her of an incoming call. She glances at the screen. It's a mobile number she doesn't recognise.

'Hang on a minute, Dave, I've got another call coming in.'

She puts him on hold.

'Hello?'

'Ms Dean?'

'Speaking.'

'It's Kit Warren. You came to the house earlier,' he says.

Delores catches her breath and holds it. They've reached a decision. 'Have you had a chance to think about the offer?' she asks.

'Yes.'

'And?'

'We'll sign whatever you want if it means going ahead with the reward.'

'That's excellent news,' Delores says, a wide grin spreading across her face. 'You're doing the right thing.'

Chapter 25

YANNICK

I've spent the morning with Harry at one of the lakes where police divers found that kid's shoe, hoping something else will turn up to give us a decent follow up to last night's interview with Aunty Cath and Uncle Kit. But it's been a complete waste of time. Other than grabbing a few shots on a long lens of the frogmen in the water, there's been nothing else newsworthy to report. Maybe I made a bad call and we should have been back in the town digging around.

Harry's packing up his camera kit in the back of his car when my phone rings. It's Tim on the news desk. It's rarely good news when he rings, so I steel myself to answer.

'Tell me we have footage of your beloved Aunt Cathy attacking the next-door neighbour,' he yells into the phone so loudly I have to hold it away from my ear.

I've no idea what he's talking about. 'What?'

'Your Aunt Cathy went full-on berserk with the next-door neighbour this morning after that piece in the paper about Annie being abused by her parents,' he says.

The rising flush of heat causes a rash of sweat to break out across my brow as it dawns on me that I've missed something big.

'I - I - I didn't know,' I stutter. 'Harry and I have been up at the lakes all morning.'

I'd seen the piece in the paper making wild allegations about Cathy and Kit's treatment of Annie, but I'd not taken much notice of it. I thought it was a reporter clutching at straws. The papers have been so desperate after my exclusive, they've been making up all sorts of rubbish.

'You're kidding me. You didn't get the shots? Well, it's all over the BBC and Gina's hopping mad.'

Harry flexes an eyebrow, sensing trouble. I roll my eyes and he grimaces.

'We'll head down there now,' I say.

'What's the point, Yannick? It's over. There's nothing to see now. You were supposed to be all over this story, and you've missed it.'

What am I supposed to do? I can't be in six places at once. If he'd left a camera at the house, we'd have been covered. If it's anyone's fault, it's Tim's.

'You'd better have something decent for tonight,' he continues to rant. 'We're relying on you for a strong follow-up to last night's interview.'

'I'm working on it,' I say, the panic making my heart drum quicker.

'So, what have you got?'

I look at Harry and beyond, through the reeds where the dark silhouettes of several police divers bob up and down in the water. 'I'm with the police dive teams. I was going to build a piece around the shoe they found.'

'Yesterday's news, Yannick. I need something better than that. Get hold of Cathy and Kit and get their take on these abuse allegations,' Tim says. 'At least it will be something nobody else has got. Phone me when it's in the bag. That's tonight's lead, unless there's anything else?'

'No,' I say. How the hell am I going to persuade Cathy to talk on camera again so soon? Maybe I can get Uncle Kit to do something on his own, but I doubt that's going to wash with Gina, especially as it was Aunt Cathy who's been caught having it out with the neighbour. It's the best I'm going to be able to deliver.

'Problems?' Harry asks as I hang up.

'Tim's on the warpath again. But don't worry about it.'

I try Uncle Kit's mobile. It rings and rings for what seems like forever before he finally picks up.

'Yannick,' he hisses, his voice a loud whisper. 'It's not a good time. Can I call you back?'

'I just heard about what happened with the neighbour. Is everything okay?'

'It's fine.'

'And Aunt Cathy? I heard she properly lost it.'

'You know how headstrong she is, and she's been under a lot of stress. I couldn't stop her,' Uncle Kit explains.

I walk in a tight circle, watching my feet kick up the dust. 'The thing is, my news editor's on the warpath because it's all over the BBC and we missed it. Could I pop over and get a quick rebuttal from you of the allegations in the paper this morning?'

Kit groans. 'Not now, Yannick. We've got a lot going on here, you know. I'm sorry, I can't.'

'Uncle Kit, you don't understand. I need this or I'm in big trouble.'

'I'm sorry, Yannick. I've got to go. Later, maybe.'

He hangs up before I can argue any further, and I'm left holding the phone to my ear.

'What did he say?' Harry asks.

I chew the edge of my finger, savouring the pain. 'He won't do it.'

'So, what are you going to do?'

'I don't know,' I snap. 'I'll think of something.'

I twist and turn all the possibilities over in my mind. I desperately need something to keep Tim and Gina off my back, but without an update from either Aunty Cath or

Uncle Kit, I can't think of anything else. I'm screwed if I can't get them to talk to me on camera again.

There's nothing else for it. We're going to have to drive over there and knock on the door. If Uncle Kit won't speak to me on the phone, I'll have to remind him of his familial duties face to face.

Chapter 26

CATHY

I wanted to sit at the kitchen table to put a physical barrier between us and that woman from *The Post*, but she insisted we all sit in the lounge where we'd be more comfortable and could relax.

Relax? Ha!

This is the last thing I want to do, but we couldn't turn down a fifty thousand-pound reward, and no one else is going to put up that kind of money.

Delores Dean, if that's even her real name, seems nice enough on the surface. Amiable and polite, asking how long we've lived in the house and commenting on the original artwork over the fireplace. But I don't trust her with her beautiful hair, enviable figure and expensive dress and boots. She's brought a photographer with her, a balding, pot-bellied man in a leather jacket that wouldn't have looked out of place in the Eighties. He sits quietly with a camera in his lap as Delores takes control.

She crosses her stockinged legs and smiles sweetly as she puts her phone down on the coffee table between us.

'You don't mind if I record the interview, do you?' she asks, pressing a record button without waiting for our agreement.

I hated speaking to Yannick in front of the TV camera and the hot lights, but this is ten times worse. My skin feels like it's crawling with ants and my stomach is tight and bilious. I can just imagine my father looking down on me from above, his face scornful and disapproving. But what choice do I have? This is about finding Annie, not about me holding onto the recriminations of the past.

'Sorry, Daddy,' I mumble under my breath. I lick my dry lips. My mouth's all gummed up and my breathing is fast and shallow.

'Shall we get started then?' Delores says.

There's that sickly sweet, butter-wouldn't-melt smile again, which she thinks puts us at our ease, but which actually has the opposite effect. It makes me think she's here to catch us out. We need to be careful what we say.

She's already made us sign a three-page contract, which I didn't have the heart or the inclination to read. She assured us it was their standard legal document and there was nothing to be worried about. It's not the contract that concerns me.

'Let's start with these allegations made by your neighbour, shall we?' she says.

Straight in with the tough questions, I see. I was right to be worried.

'He says he regularly heard you shouting at Annie and that there were often arguments between you,' Delores says. 'Also, a few days ago, he saw Annie going to school in tears and noticed bruises on her arms.'

I straighten my back, immediately on the defensive. 'All families argue,' I say. 'And there were no bruises. That's not right.'

She shrugs, like it's neither here nor there. 'But not all families scream and shout at each other so loudly they can be heard by the next-door neighbours.'

'He's exaggerating, but I guess some people will say anything to get into the papers.'

Delores smirks, but I don't kid myself I'm winning her around. She's here to trip us up, to make us say something that will make a headline. I'm not an idiot.

'And Annie going to school in tears?'

'She wanted to get her ears pierced. I told her she was too young.'

'I see.' Delores glances at a notebook she has open on her knee. I wish I could read her handwriting and get some forewarning of the questions to come. 'Is that the sort of thing you'd often fight about?'

Kit jumps in before I can answer. 'We didn't fight,' he says, 'but we've always agreed as parents that Annie should have clear boundaries. Like all children, she sometimes likes to push those boundaries and see how far we'll go. Like Cath said, we're no different from any other family.'

Delores steeples her fingers and runs them across her lips. 'Is it possible she's run away? I mean, if she felt you were being too strict – '

'No,' I say firmly. 'She wouldn't do that.'

'Any of her clothes missing?'

'No.'

'What about her favourite toy or cuddly animal? Did she have one?'

'Rocky,' Kit says. 'He's a bear she's had since she was a baby. I can get him, if you'd like?' He jumps up like he's been waiting for an excuse to make himself scarce.

'Yes, please,' Delores says. 'Maybe we could get some pictures of you together on the sofa holding him? It should make a nice image.'

Funny, that's exactly what Yannick and his cameraman wanted. It's like a journalistic cliché.

'Let's say for one moment she has run away. Where might she go, hypothetically speaking?' Delores asks.

'She's not run away.'

'I presume you've checked with all her friends?'

'Of course.'

'What about family? Are there any grandparents she might have been trying to reach?'

She might as well have pulled out a dagger and stabbed me in the stomach. She knows damn well my father's dead and my mother too, overcome by grief at his loss. What a total bitch. I knew I didn't like her. Kit's parents are long gone too. They both died before I met him.

'No,' I say coolly.

'I'm so sorry. What was I thinking? That was insensitive of me.' She feigns a look of mortification. 'Of course, there's a history of suicide in the family, isn't there?'

My hands ball into tight fists, the anger and indignation burning like a furnace in my gut. Forget the reward money. I can't bear this woman in my house, making snide insinuations about my family. I want her out.

But before I can say anything, Kit barges back into the room, his brow furrowed. Agitated.

'I can't find Rocky,' he says. 'He's gone.'

It takes a second to register what he's saying. 'What do you mean, gone?'

'Rocky. Annie's bear. He's not in her room.'

'Are you sure?' He was definitely there the other night. I remember Yannick's cameraman making us pose with him on our laps.

Delores uncrosses her legs and stares at me. 'Could it be that Annie took him with her when she left?' she asks.

'No! We filmed with him. You remember, Kit.'

Kit nods and then shakes his head. 'It's weird, but I've looked everywhere.'

'It doesn't matter,' Delores says. She's plucked a pen from her bag and is scribbling something in the margin of her notebook. I'm sure she thinks we're lying.

'Watch the footage back online. You'll see.' I'm desperate for her to believe us, although now I think about it, I can't remember if Yannick used any shots of Rocky in the piece.

'Of course.' Delores smiles thinly, but it's obvious she's not going to watch the interview back. 'Tell me, what makes you so certain Annie's been abducted?'

'It's the most likely explanation,' I say.

'She could have got lost on her way home.'

'The school's less than a mile away. I don't see how she could have got lost.'

'It just seems a big leap to assume she's been abducted.'

Abducted. There's that word again. Such a brutal, ugly word laden with so much uncertainty and fear. I don't even want to think about it anymore. I don't want to picture someone taking Annie against her will, bundling her into the back of a van or coaxing her into a strange car. But it's what's most likely to have happened.

But who's taken her?

And why? That's the big question I've been avoiding. I don't want to think about why anyone would want to snatch a ten-year-old little girl, nor what she might be going through. The mere thought of it makes me sick to the pit of my stomach.

It's a horrible thing to think, but maybe it's better if she's already dead. Better that than suffering at the hands of a cruel and depraved stranger.

A golf ball-sized lump swells in my throat. Please god, don't let her be dead. But don't let her be suffering either.

'I guess it's a feeling I have,' I croak. 'A mother's intuition.'

'Have you ever raised your hand to Annie?' Delores says, changing her line of questioning quicker than the click of her fingers.

'Are you serious? No!'

'Children can be a handful, can't they? Sometimes we lose our temper and strike out without thinking. It's nothing to be ashamed of.'

'No,' Kit says, his jaw clenching. 'We've never hit Annie. We wouldn't dream of it.'

'Not even a little tap on the backside when she was little?'

'Never,' Kit repeats.

It's something else we've always agreed on. We'd never hit Annie, or any other child for that matter. It's brutal and unnecessary, a surefire way to teach them that violence is the answer when it never is. Plus, Annie has always been so precious to us, I can't ever imagine raising my hand to her. Our miracle baby. Our unexpected gift.

'What are you suggesting?' I ask.

'I'm not suggesting anything,' Delores smiles. 'I'm only asking questions, trying to get a better picture of what home life is like.'

'Our home life was fine,' Kit says, 'until our daughter went missing.'

'The community has been incredibly supportive. There are more than two hundred police officers involved in the search and who knows how many volunteers. How do you feel about so many people giving up so much of their time?'

'We're truly humbled,' Kit says. 'The response of the police, our neighbours and the wider community has been beyond belief, and we'd like to take this opportunity to – '

He doesn't get to finish his sentence, cut off by another question.

'I've seen people wearing "Find Annie" T-shirts and there are posters in almost every window. Is that something you've organised?'

Kit looks at me, and I reluctantly pick up the baton. 'No, that's been done by the residents' association. Pam Buckley, the chair, has been wonderful. She's helped co-ordinate the volunteers and had the T-shirts and posters printed,' I explain, hoping Delores will at least give her a mention. It would be nice if she got some credit.

'Oh, so what have you been doing?'

It's more like an accusation than a question.

What *have* we been doing? The police told us to stay in the house in case Annie returned unexpectedly or tried to call. There's not much we've been able to do other than sit and wait.

'It's been hard to concentrate on doing anything while Annie's missing,' I say, deflecting a bullet. 'We're just trying to stay positive and focused.'

'And how are you coping?'

At last, a sensible question. 'We're surviving. Just,' I say, forcing a smile.

Like any parents, our instinct has been to get out and look for Annie ourselves. But the police instructions were crystal clear. It was important we stayed at the house, even when the walls were closing in around us and the hollow gnaw of helplessness felt like it was slowly killing us both. Minutes and hours drag by, especially at night when neither of us can sleep. And I'm so tired, I can hardly think straight or form a coherent sentence. But we have to keep going, soldier on through, for Annie's sake, while keeping the faith that soon, and against all the odds, she'll be found safe and well and returned home to us.

'Are you sleeping?' Delores asks.

'Not really,' Kit replies. 'Cathy slept in Annie's bed last night. I think it made her feel closer to her, you know?'

What did he have to tell her that for? I wish he'd watch his mouth.

'So, you did sleep?' Delores says, her eyebrow arching. 'I'm surprised you can, with your daughter missing. I'm not sure I'd be able to.' She says it like it's a commendable achievement, but we both know it's a cruel dig.

At least I'm saved from answering by a knock at the door.

'That's probably Zara, our police liaison officer,' Kit says, standing. 'She's helping us through this.'

Delores watches him step out of the room. How much more of this torment do we have to endure? How many more questions?

'Shall we get some pictures when Kit gets back?' Delores asks.

'Sure. Is that everything you need?' I grit my teeth, trying to make it sound as if I'm being co-operative. The last thing I need is for her to paint me as obstructive and difficult.

'For now,' she says.

'When will it be in the paper?' I hear muted voices. Hushed whispers coming from the hall.

'Tomorrow.'

'And is that when you're announcing the reward?'

'Hopefully, it'll be the front-page story.' Delores picks up her phone and switches the recorder off.

The front door slams. Kit scuffs back into the room looking shifty.

'Who was that?'

'Yannick.'

Delores, busy packing up her notebook in her bag, looks up at the mention of my nephew's name. 'What did he want?' she asks, eyes narrowing.

'I don't know. He wanted to come in and talk to us.'

'What did you tell him?'

We're going to have to let him know about the deal we've signed with *The Post* at some point, but now is not the time. He's not going to be happy, but Yannick's tantrums are the least of my worries.

'I told him we were busy and we couldn't talk right now,' Kit says.

'Did you tell him about Delores?' I ask.

'No.'

Delores's smile is less sickly sweet this time. More self-satisfied. Smug. 'Great, shall we get the photos done?'

Chapter 27

YANNICK

All I wanted was to talk, but Kit as good as threw me out on my ear, like I was nothing to him. An annoyance. A pesky fly buzzing around his face. Now what am I going to do? What am I going to say to Tim? I fucked up this morning by not being here and missing Aunty Cath attacking her neighbour. My only chance of redemption is to get her explaining on camera what happened, but how, if they won't even have me in the house?

My heart's galloping like an out-of-control racehorse with a mixture of anger at how Kit talked to me and the fear of having to admit to Tim I've failed.

Something's going on inside the house. I could tell by the way Uncle Kit couldn't look me in the eye. How he couldn't shoo me out of the door quickly enough. They probably had the police in there talking to them. Uncle Kit said to come back later, but that's no good. Time isn't on my side. After the glory of an exclusive the whole country was talking about yesterday, I'm left with crumbs today. I need something to back it up. A strong follow-up. But I've got nothing, and with so many other news organisations digging around, it's only a matter of time before someone dredges up a story that puts my interview in the shade.

'What did he say?' Harry appears at my shoulder with his camera ready as I stand outside the door, fuming. My fist is raised as I seriously contemplate whether to knock again.

'They won't do anything today.'

'Okay, so what's your plan?' Harry knows as well as I do how desperately I need something, and quickly. I chew my bottom lip. I need a new angle. Something no one else is running.

But my thoughts are interrupted by a voice from behind.

'Awww, didn't Aunty Cath want to talk to you today?'

I spin around and recognise a reporter from a rival local news channel. I can't remember his name. Steve? Stefan? Who cares? He must have seen me being thrown out by Uncle Kit, and now he's sneering at me, looking unashamedly triumphant.

'Shame you weren't here for this morning's little performance,' he continues. 'I thought she was going to punch him. Great pictures. I suppose it makes a nice little follow up while there's no news on the little girl.'

'If that's the best you can do, it's probably time to get back to writing up council meetings for the local paper,' I snap back, cross with myself for letting him get under my skin.

The sneering triumphalism drops from the reporter's face. I've hit a nerve, which gives me a small degree of satisfaction. He's just annoyed he doesn't have access to Aunty Cath, although at the moment, neither do I.

'Did you have a camera here?' he asks, exaggerating the rise of his eyebrows. He knows full well we missed it.

'It's not a story,' I shrug. 'And anyway, I have something much bigger.' I tap the side of my nose and wink.

The flicker of concern that crosses his face gives me a zip of pleasure. The problem is, it's not true. I have absolutely nothing up my sleeve.

Harry guides me away. 'Leave it. You don't have time.'

He's right. The clock's ticking. I can't hang around here hoping something will fall into my lap. I need to be proactive and pray for a miracle. It's either that or a tongue-lashing from Tim or Gina. 'Let's get back to the lakes. We'll make something out of the search.'

'Really? There wasn't much going on earlier,' Harry says, frowning.

I turn on him and stare him in the eye. 'Don't argue with me, Harry. Unless you have a better idea?' I know I'm taking it out on him, but there's no one else around to bear the brunt of my stress and frustration.

'Fine, you're the boss,' he says. Thankfully, he's used to reporters having little tantrums. He's developed a thick skin over the years and has learned not to take it personally.

We trudge back to his car, and I climb into the passenger seat with a swelling sense of dread. I'm going to have to phone Tim and break it to him that Aunty Cath won't give me a follow-up interview, and that I don't have anything else.

As the car pulls away, I turn down the radio and make the call with blood throbbing in my ears.

'I'm really sorry, Tim. I tried my best, but they can't do anything today,' I explain, steeling myself for the full blast of his anger.

'What do you mean they won't do it? I don't understand. They spoke to you yesterday. What's changed?'

'I don't know. I can't force them to speak to me. They said they were busy with other things.'

A horrible, gaping silence opens up on the line, as if Tim is trying to process the highly improbable news that I've failed.

'Tim? You still there?'

'Go back and explain we're the local TV news and that they *have* to speak to you. Don't they want to find their daughter?' He sounds genuinely incredulous that they wouldn't be jumping at the chance.

I hate it when he's like this. Totally immovable. Utterly unsympathetic. I'd like to see him do better. It's easy when you're on the other end of a phone, throwing orders around and expecting people to move mountains for you. But this is my career. I can't tell him no. He expects results and if I don't deliver them, I'll be back on that late-night graveyard shift faster than a rogue flash-frame and I can probably kiss goodbye to anymore presenting shifts too. That's how petty and vindictive it can be in news.

'Of course they want their daughter back,' I say. 'We all do. But I can't force them to do the interview.'

'Go back and speak to them again,' he says. He's not heard a word I've said.

I roll my eyes at Harry. Why does it always have to be like this?

'Okay, I'll try,' I lie. I have no intention of returning to the house and facing the humiliation of being told no again, but it's easier than arguing with Tim. I know he won't back down. I'll call Uncle Kit later, see if he's changed his mind, but I doubt it. 'But on the off-chance it doesn't come off, I thought I'd go live from the lakes tonight. I've spoken to a contact in the police who says they're going to be making a major announcement in the next hour or so.'

Of course, it's another lie. I don't even have any contacts in the force, but I need something to get Tim off my back and give me some breathing room.

'What kind of announcement?' There's a catch of excitement in Tim's voice. He's bought the lie, but of course now he wants details. What am I supposed to say?

'A significant one.'

Harry shoots me a sideways look. I shrug.

'Have they found something? A body?'

'Possibly. I'll know later.'

What am I going to do now? I can't magic up a police development out of thin air. But I can't stop myself, now I've started. 'You won't be disappointed,' I continue. 'And as far as I know, nobody else is onto this yet. Can you send the satellite truck? It might be a tight turnaround.'

'Of course, and I'll let Holly know. Great, well done, Yannick.' A smile of satisfaction creeps across my face. Even though it's a complete fabrication, any kind of praise from Tim is a precious commodity.

He hangs up abruptly, and I let out a sigh of relief. At least I've bought myself some time. If I can find something better, Tim might forget all about my half-arsed promise. The problem is, I need something solid and significant, and I don't have a single lead to pursue.

'Is that true?' Harry asks.

'Of course it's not. I had to tell him I had something.'

Harry sucks in air through his teeth as he pulls up at a police cordon near one of the lakes, a few minutes' drive from Annie's school. 'So, you thought you'd lie to him instead?'

'It's fine. We'll go live from here tonight and I'll just have to make sure I've found something half decent to report.'

'Five minutes before we come to you, Yannick,' the director says in my ear.

I give a thumbs up to the camera to show I've heard and understood.

We've found a spot between the trees with a great view across the water to the police activity on the other side of the lake where several emergency vehicles are lined up. All day police divers have been in and out of the water. With the sun setting over the marshes and the reed beds swaying hypnotically in the breeze, it's a great shot. While

I give an update on the latest on the search for Annie, Harry's going to zoom in and focus on the police activity.

I tried to come up with a new, significant angle, but I've got nothing. I called Kit's number a few times, but it kept going to his voicemail and he never returned my calls. I tried to persuade the police to give me an interview with the dive team working at the lake, but that was turned down. And still with no confirmed sightings of Annie, there's next to nothing new to say. I'm going to have to wing it and hope for the best.

I've told Tim the police announcement is still expected but that they've had to delay it for a few hours for operational reasons. He was surprisingly happy with that. My plan now is to reveal live on air that the police are close to a major breakthrough in the case.

It's not true. It's a figment of my desperate imagination, but it's the best I can do. And who's going to remember anyway? There's bound to be some kind of development or new line someone's turned up tomorrow and we'll all move on.

'Coming to you in two minutes,' the director says.

I straighten my tie and pull back my shoulders.

The rush of adrenaline in those few minutes before going live on air is better than any drug. It's a peculiar kind of nervous energy that focuses the mind and makes every nerve in your body tingle with anticipation. That feeling is especially heightened right now, knowing the untruths that are about to trip off my tongue. They're only small lies. Little whitish ones. And for all I know, the police *could* be on the verge of a breakthrough.

'Shit,' Harry hisses. The panic in his voice makes me glance over my shoulder. 'They're packing up.'

'What?'

'The police are leaving.'

A set of powerful spotlights that had been shining on the impromptu camp the dive team had set up, go black and one of the vehicles drives off. One by one, the divers climb into the back of a van. Its headlights come on and the sound of an engine starting up drifts across the lake.

In the studio, Imogen Moon delivers the headlines.

'Coming up in the programme tonight at six...'

Fuck. The beautiful live slot I promised Holly is falling down around us.

'Police on the verge of a major breakthrough in the hunt for missing Annie Warren...' Imogen continues in my ear.

What are we going to do?

We can't stop the police from leaving, but it considerably weakens the suggestion I'm about to make that an imminent police breakthrough is connected to the activity on the lake. If there's no police activity here, it's going to be obvious there is no breakthrough in the case.

'All that and more, including the latest weather forecast, coming up in the next half an hour,' Imogen says, wrapping up the titles.

And then suddenly she's on the story and throwing to me.

'Police divers hunting for missing ten-year-old Annie Warren have spent the day searching the murky waters of a lake near to the little girl's school. A shoe discovered yesterday has been ruled out as belonging to the schoolgirl, but the force has suggested a breakthrough is imminent,' Imogen says. 'We can cross live now to our reporter, Yannick Kellor, who's at a lake in Faversham, where a major announcement is expected within the next few hours. Yannick?'

I gulp noisily, my mouth and throat dry. 'That's right, Imogen.' Behind me, and with appalling timing, I hear the police vehicles driving off.

'As you can see behind me, after two days searching this lake just a few minutes' walk from Annie Warren's school, police divers are tonight pulling out. We were told by police sources that they were on the cusp of making a major announcement this evening, but obviously we're still waiting to hear exactly what they've found, assuming they've found anything at all. Hopes had been raised after the discovery of a child's shoe here, but that has now been discounted from this inquiry.'

I manage to ramble on for another minute and a half without saying anything new. Harry's face remains impassive. He's the only one who knows I've lied live on air, an unforgivable broadcast sin, but I trust him not to say anything.

'And we understand there was a minor scuffle this morning outside the Warrens' house?' Imogen asks.

'That's right. Cathy Warren, Annie's mother, reacting to a story in a national newspaper, we understand, claiming a neighbour witnessed a number of noisy arguments at the house. So far, Mr and Mrs Warren have been unavailable for comment.'

Somehow, I battle my way through the rest of my slot, surviving without any major hiccups. But I know they're going to be furious back at base. It's not the follow-up they were expecting. I've failed to live up to my own hype. With the divers pulling out and no updates from the police, today's been a disaster.

As Harry switches off the top light and I peel off the microphone attached to the inside of my jacket lapel, my heart flutters. It's not the same kind of nerves I get before delivering a live, but a tightening grip of fear.

I'm already in Harry's car, waiting for him to finish packing up, when the inevitable call comes from Gina. I knew she wouldn't be happy.

'You want to explain yourself?' she yells in my ear.

'I'm sorry, Gina, I did my – '

'Not good enough, Yannick. We gave you the opportunity on this story because you promised you had an inside line to the family.'

'I delivered the only interview they've given to the press,' I protest, but predictably it doesn't wash with Gina. She always wants more.

'That was yesterday. You didn't even get the footage of your aunt assaulting her neighbour. Give me one good reason why I shouldn't take you off the story right now.'

'Please,' I beg. 'I know I didn't deliver today, but I can do better. Give me one more chance. I promise I won't let you down again.'

FRIDAY

Chapter 28

DELORES

Delores finds a newsagent in the centre of town with stacks of newspapers lined up on the floor by the magazine stands. The front page that stands out amongst all the others, still giving prominence to the Annie Warren story, is *The Post's*. Her splash.

Missing Annie: £50k reward
"We're prisoners in our own home" - Cathy and Kit Warren Exclusive
By Delores Dean

She buys two copies, tucks them into her bag and heads to the creek. A few news crews are in between breakfast bulletin lives when she arrives at the Warrens' house.

It's been four days now since Annie went missing, but even though the police have admitted they have no leads or significant information about her whereabouts, interest hasn't waned.

The mood in the town is sombre. It's the same with the press. The chances of Annie being found alive are now looking increasingly slim. The police won't say it publicly, but it's obvious they're now looking for a body. In fact, the only people still clinging onto the belief Annie is alive are her parents.

A photographer jumps out of nowhere and tries to snap Delores' picture as she approaches the Warrens' house. She raises a hand to hide her face. The last thing she needs is her image plastered all over the papers.

She bangs on the door. Kit opens it a fraction, peering out suspiciously.

'Delores,' he says. 'We weren't expecting you.'

She shoves a copy of the paper at him. 'I thought you'd like to see the story.'

Kit snatches the newspaper and lets her in. He's not dressed yet, still in his pyjamas and a dressing gown, his dark stubble halfway to becoming a beard. They stand in the hallway while he flicks through the first five pages, which are devoted to the Warrens' interview and peppered with photographs of the couple around the house, plus a selection of pictures of Annie they'd handed over.

Cathy appears from the kitchen. She's not dressed either, the rings around her eyes even darker than before, the sockets sunken and hollow.

'What are you doing here?'

Cathy's hostility is palpable, and she hasn't even read the interview yet. She isn't going to like it much, but Delores isn't here to pull any punches. Her job's to uncover the truth. And sell newspapers.

'I brought a copy of the paper. Has there been any news overnight?' Delores asks.

Kit holds up the front page. Cathy's lips silently form the words as she reads.

'Prisoners in our own home?' Cathy says, frowning.

'You said the police have instructed you not to leave the house.'

'We're not prisoners.'

Delores shrugs. 'Is the kettle on? I could murder a coffee.'

Cathy's face is a picture. Did she really think Delores was going to leave them alone after one brief interview? They should have read the terms of the contract closer. It's all set out in black and white. They've agreed in writing to full and unfettered access for the duration of the search for Annie, and up until both parties agree to end the arrangement.

'I have a few more questions when you're ready,' Delores says. 'We're keen to keep the story in the spotlight to raise awareness. I thought today we could talk about Annie as a baby.'

'Is this really necessary?' Cathy wraps her dressing gown tightly around her body.

'Absolutely. You do want to find Annie, don't you?'

An hour later, the three of them sit at the kitchen table. Delores, on her fourth coffee of the day, is beginning to feel human again. Cathy and Kit are both dressed, and some police liaison woman has turned up, but thankfully is keeping out of the way in the lounge. Delores places her phone in the middle of the table and doesn't even bother to ask the Warrens' permission to record the conversation this time.

'Tell me how you met,' she asks. She doesn't really care. It's an icebreaker to get them talking, although their age gap is curious. He must be at least ten years older than her, if not more. What did she see in him? Delores knows Cathy's father died when she was young. Does she have daddy issues?

'It's a funny story, actually,' Kit says. 'I only popped out to buy a sandwich, but ended up witnessing a marriage and finding a wife.' He smiles thinly. It's obviously an anecdote he's told a thousand times.

Delores plays along, cocking her head and encouraging him to tell her more. He tells her they were chosen randomly off the street by a young couple getting married in the register office in Canterbury, and that afterwards, when they went for a drink together, they hit it off and just seemed to have so much in common.

Delores wonders how much a couple so far apart in age could really have in common, but doesn't say anything. It's a fun story and could make an interesting sidebar at some point. People love quirky stuff like that, especially if there's romance involved. Mills and Boon is still going strong for a reason.

'How old were you when you met?' Delores asks.

'Twenty-seven. Kit was a bit older,' Cathy says.

'Not quite old enough to be her father, but not far off,' Kit laughs, before catching himself and letting his humour evaporate.

'How much older?'

'Fifteen years. He was forty-two when we met.'

So Delores wasn't far wrong. 'Were you single?' she asks Kit. Always a chance that Kit, in a stale marriage, had his head turned by a younger, prettier woman.

'Separated,' he says.

'And are there children from your previous marriage?'

'A boy and a girl, but I'd rather you kept them out of it, if that's okay?'

'Any particular reason?' What does he have to hide?

'This has nothing to do with them. It wouldn't feel right, including them without their permission. And I don't think their mother would be too happy either.'

'How did they take it when you remarried, especially to a much younger woman?'

'Honestly, I don't see how this is relevant.' Kit shuffles uncomfortably in his seat.

She's touched a nerve. It's worth exploring further. Were his kids jealous of a new baby on the scene? Or was it the ex-wife who took exception to Kit starting a new family with a younger wife? She makes a mental note to do some digging into the former Mrs Warren.

'When did you get married?' Delores asks.

'In 2008, after Kit's divorce was finalised,' Cathy says. She's cradling a cold mug of tea and can hardly bring herself to look Delores in the eye. She doesn't want to do this interview, but she signed the contract. She should have known what she was agreeing to.

'But Annie wasn't born until 2012. Is that right?'

'She was our little miracle,' Kit says.

'You'd been trying to start a family for a while then?'

'We agreed we'd let nature take its course and see what happened.' The hint of a smile creeps across Kit's face.

A happy accident then. Fair enough. It doesn't mean they loved Annie any less.

Delores looks to Cathy for confirmation of what Kit's saying, but her face is blank. Unreadable. She's staring into her mug, lost in her thoughts.

'Cathy?'

'What?' She looks up, startled.

'How did you feel when you found out you were pregnant with Annie?' Delores asks.

'Yeah, it was amazing,' she says. 'I'd always wanted to be a mum but didn't think I'd be able to fall pregnant again.'

Kit's phone rings. He checks the screen and dumps the call, turning the phone face down on the table.

'Again?' Delores says.

'What?'

'You said you started to think you'd never be able to fall pregnant *again*. Was Annie not your first pregnancy?'

Kit's phone rings for a second time. He apologises and switches it to silent.

'It doesn't matter,' Cathy says, shaking her head.

'Had you been pregnant before, Cathy?' Delores presses. The fact Cathy doesn't want to talk about it suggests there's a story behind it.

'That's none of your business,' she snaps.

Delores's mind spins with the possibilities. A stillbirth? A child taken into care? A miscarriage?

She pauses for a beat, framing the words carefully in her mind. She needs Cathy to open up and tell her everything. The paper's putting up enough money. She softens her tone and leans forwards. 'It might help build some empathy for what you're going through if you could talk about it,' she suggests gently.

'I don't want to.'

'But it – '

'I said no.'

Okay, no point pushing it at this stage if Cathy's made up her mind. It's something Delores can come back to later, and in the meantime, it's something else to dig into.

'Any complications with the pregnancy or the birth?' she asks.

Cathy shakes her head. 'None.'

'How would you describe your feelings when Annie was born?'

Cathy thinks about the question for a second or two. 'I guess I was numb,' she says. 'In shock. It was a quick labour. It all happened so fast.'

'I meant, you must have been over the moon after trying for so long?'

'Oh, yes,' Cathy agrees.

'I never thought I'd be a father again,' Kit adds, his cheeriness in stark contrast to the mood his wife seems to be in. 'Not at my age, anyway. I thought that ship had passed. But Annie was perfect. She came out kicking and screaming like she was ready to take on the world and we instantly fell in love with her, didn't we, Cath? Do you have children, Delores?'

'Me? God, no.'

'Why not?'

Delores stiffens and pulls herself up straight. 'We're not here to talk about me,' she says, lips so tight her jaw aches. 'I want to hear your story.'

She's always hated talking about herself, which is probably why she became a journalist, so she doesn't have to. She's never liked being the centre of attention.

'There must be a reason,' Kit presses.

'My job takes me away too much. It wouldn't be fair. Now, tell me more about Annie as a baby.'

Kit shrugs. 'She was an angel,' he says. 'A very contented baby. She was sleeping through at four months and never gave us any real trouble. It's a shame we couldn't have had more.'

'Couldn't?'

'I'd have happily had at least two more, but it wasn't to be, sadly.'

Cathy's still staring into her mug.

'What about you, Cathy?'

'Maybe. I don't know. We had Annie and that was a miracle enough.'

'Right,' Delores says, watching her closely, at the way her hands are gripping her mug so tightly it looks as though she's trying to crush it. At the way she's pulled her chin back so close to her chest, as if she's trying to withdraw into herself. And the way she's rounding her shoulders and still can't or won't look Delores in the eye.

She's definitely hiding something. Maybe she'll return to it later or try to catch Cathy on her own, when Kit's not around.

'You run a charity, I understand, Kit?' Delores asks, changing tack back onto safer ground.

Cathy scrapes her chair back, gets up and shuffles across the kitchen to the kettle. If she is responsible for Annie's disappearance, she's putting on a good act. The lank, unwashed hair. The bags under her eyes. The air of misery that hangs over her like a bad smell. And yet, it still doesn't add up. Cathy is playing a game, but Delores isn't sure what, if any part, Kit has been assigned. Is it possible Cathy is behind Annie's disappearance, but he doesn't know? She needs to keep probing, asking questions, in the hope one of them will slip up. But so far, their answers have been textbook.

'We provide services for refugees and asylum seekers.' Kit's voice is almost drowned out by the rush of water from the tap as Cathy fills the kettle.

'That must be very rewarding?'

'It is.'

'Shit!' Cathy slams her mug on the worktop.

'Cathy? What's wrong?' Kit jumps up as Cathy suddenly bursts into tears. They've sprung from nowhere. It's quite the display. 'We've run out of fucking teabags,' she cries.

Kit rushes to his wife's side, gently takes her by the shoulders and turns her around, pulling her into a hug. 'It's okay,' he soothes. 'It's okay.'

Delores watches silently. She's used to people bursting into tears on her. It's all part of the job. Usually she can tell if it's genuine emotion, but with Cathy she's not sure. The way she's sobbing her heart out certainly looks real.

'I'm sorry,' Kit says over his shoulder, still holding his wife. 'It's been a trying few days. Cathy's exhausted. She's finding this whole thing very difficult.'

Delores suspects most people in her shoes would squirm with embarrassment to be witness to such an emotional, tender scene between husband and wife, but actually this could form the opening of the colour piece she has in mind.

With the house still in darkness, the curtains drawn to keep out prying eyes, Cathy Warren flicks on the kettle to make a cup of tea. It should be the most ordinary thing in the world, something that happens in houses every day up and down the country. But this is no ordinary house. And no ordinary woman. Cathy's daughter, Annie, has been missing for four days and as Cathy drops a teabag into a mug, she begins to sob, her hot tears flowing freely with fear, sadness and loss.

'I can't even go out to the shops without being mobbed,' Cathy sobs. 'You're right. We're prisoners here. And all I want is for Annie to come home and all of this to be over.'

'I know,' Delores says, glancing at her phone. It's still recording every word. Every sound. A perfect audio record of this moment in history. She reaches across the table and switches it off. 'It's going to be okay, Cathy. You're going to get through this.'

Cathy sobs louder, sinking her head into Kit's shoulder.

'I could always nip out to the shops for you, if you'd like?' It's a small gesture, but an opportunity to win Cathy around.

Cathy sniffs. 'Don't be silly. You don't have to do that.'

'I don't mind, honestly.' Delores gets up and hooks her bag over her shoulder. 'I'll only be five minutes. I'll pick up some more teabags and maybe a couple of pints of milk. Do you need anything else?'

Cathy shakes her head.

'Thank you. That's very kind,' Kit says.

'It's no problem. We'll pick up again when I get back.' Delores heads out of the kitchen, her boots click-clacking across the stripped wooden floorboards. She's not going to get anything meaningful out of Cathy while she's so upset, so it's probably for the best that she gives them a short break to compose themselves.

She yanks open the front door and yelps in alarm as she comes face to face with a man on the doorstep. He has his fist raised as if she's caught him about to knock. He looks familiar, but she can't immediately place him.

'Who are you?' he demands, looking her up and down.

He's smartly dressed in a suit and tie, his hair styled in a fashionable cut, and possibly dyed where it's greying at the temples. Delores takes an instant dislike to him.

'You're Yannick Kellor,' she says, remembering his face from the TV interview she's watched over and over on her laptop.

'That's right.' He tries to push past her, to get inside, but she holds out her arm to stop him.

'Where do you think you're going?'

'I'm Cathy and Kit's nephew. I need to see them,' he says. 'It's urgent.'

'I'm afraid I can't allow that.'

'What the hell are you talking about? Get out of my way.'

'They've signed an exclusivity deal with us. They won't be talking to anyone else, I'm afraid, and especially not you.' The anger on Yannick's face brings a tingle of pleasure to the tips of Delores' fingers.

'Aunty Cath? Uncle Kit? Are you there?' he shouts.

'It's not a good time, Yannick. Please don't make a scene. Your aunt is upset enough as it is.'

He stares at Delores with loathing, his eyes burning with fury. 'You can't stop me speaking to my own family,' he hisses.

'I can if you're a journalist.'

'Get out of my way!'

He rushes at her, trying to force his way in, but she's ready for him and pushes him back into the street.

'We had a deal, Uncle Kit,' Yannick shouts into the house, backing away from Delores, defeated. 'You can't treat me like this.'

'I think you'd better leave,' Delores says, catching her breath and flicking a stray strand of hair out of her eyes. 'And don't come back.'

She slams the door in his face and drops the latch.

The police liaison woman is standing in the doorway to the lounge, watching.

'What's going on?' she asks, brow knitted in concern.

'An unwelcome visitor,' Delores says. 'No one important. He's gone now.'

As the police officer shrugs and disappears back into the room, Delores slumps with her back against the door.

'Sorry, Cathy, you're going to have to wait for those teabags,' she says, striding back into the kitchen. 'I can't get out of the house at the moment. Too many bloody journalists. Let's crack on with the interview, shall we?'

Chapter 29

YANNICK

The door slams in my face for the second day in a row, but this time I have a far bigger problem on my hands than the sheer humiliation of being turned away without even being able to speak to my aunt and uncle. I've been shafted by my own family, and all hopes I had that this story could be the making of me and my career are hanging by a thin, spindly thread.

The phone call from Tim first thing this morning wasn't the best way to start the day. I was deep in a dreamless sleep when he rang. I answered groggily, rubbing my eyes, and he started ranting at me without drawing breath about how I'd let the entire newsroom down.

I had no idea what he was talking about until he texted me a link to the story in that morning's *Post*. They were offering a fifty thousand-pound reward for information about Annie. But that wasn't the problem. It was the accompanying story. An exclusive interview with my aunt and uncle, revealing, among other things, how they felt they'd become prisoners in their own home since Annie's disappearance.

My jaw virtually hit the floor as I read on, Tim still shouting and raving in my ear. I couldn't believe they'd sold me out and hadn't even told me what they were planning. They must have been offered a big pile of cash. There's no other explanation.

I hurled my phone across the room and screamed with fury. How could they treat me like this? Did I really mean so little to them? I jumped straight in the car and headed for Faversham to have it out with them, but a journalist from *The Post* was already in the house and although I tried to battle my way inside, she point-blank refused to let me in. At least there were no other journalists around to witness my humiliation this time, most of them preoccupied by the arrival of a convoy of police cars that turned out to be nothing of importance.

There's clearly no point hanging around. Whatever deal they've signed, I'm not going to be able to speak to either Aunty Cath or Uncle Kit while that woman's in the house. I've tried calling Kit repeatedly, but he's still not answering. This is a complete and utter disaster. Not what I'd planned at all. Of course I'm worried about Annie, but this was supposed to be my big opportunity and now it's been stolen from me.

I need to get back on the front foot.

I need a story that's going to be so explosive no one's going to care about what *The Post* publishes about Aunty Cath and Uncle Kit. But short of finding Annie and returning her home safely, I'm not sure what I can do.

There must be something.

Anything.

Come on, Yannick. Think.

And then it comes to me in a flash of inspiration, and I chuckle to myself. It's so obvious now, I don't understand why I didn't think of it before. It's been staring me in the face this whole time.

It's certainly explosive and if I play this right, those job offers should finally start rolling in.

Harry sets up his camera on a tripod while I sort out my microphone, coiling the wire up under my shirt and clipping it to my lapel. When I explained to Tim, Holly and Gina on a conference call earlier what I'd found out about the investigation, it was enough to convince them to give me the top slot in the programme, with the warning it was my last chance to prove myself. As if I needed reminding.

'This had better be good, Yannick,' Tim said. 'We're going out on a limb keeping you on this story, so you'd better not let us down.'

'You won't regret it,' I said. 'This is dynamite. I promise.'

I'd already given him an outline of what I was going to say, but I'd kept back some of the more contentious details of how I was going to present the story. The newsroom can be a bit nervy sometimes when it comes to grey areas of the law, but I'm confident in what I'm doing. This is going to put a whole new spin on the story and send every other journalist in the area into a blind panic that they've missed something huge.

'Make sure you keep the top light off until we're ready to go on air,' I tell Harry.

'Are you sure? The gallery's not going to like it.'

'Yes, I'm sure. Stop questioning me,' I snap. 'Just do what I ask without arguing for once, would you?'

I'm painfully aware that if this live goes wrong, it's all over. I can kiss goodbye to a job on national TV. In fact, I'll be lucky if anyone ever lets me in front of a camera again.

I don't want the lights on until the last possible moment because I don't want anyone to know we're here, especially any other journalists. They've all been a bit jumpy since I pulled that interview with Cathy and Kit out of the bag, and they've been keeping a wary eye on what I'm up to. The satellite truck parked a short distance down the street is a bit of a giveaway, but there's not much I can do about that.

I brush a few spots of dust off the shoulders of my jacket, straighten my tie, use the camera on my phone to check there's nothing stuck in my teeth and run a hand through my hair.

This is it. Make or break time.

'Coming to you in five, Yannick,' the director says in my ear. 'You have three minutes all up, linking into various soundbites. Then we'll come back to Immy who'll throw you another question.'

I hold my thumb up to the camera. I'm buzzing. This is going to be so good. Tim, Gina and Holly are going to love it. I can't wait for their phone call when we come off air.

And then suddenly the title music is playing, soft and tinny through my earpiece.

'Good evening. Tonight at six, a prime suspect identified in the hunt for missing schoolgirl Annie Warren. A news exclusive.'

My hearts thumps so loudly, I fear it'll be picked up by the microphone.

I breathe in through my nose and let it out slowly through my mouth. I wet my lips and swallow a build-up of saliva in my mouth. God, I love this feeling. The excitement. The trepidation. The anticipation.

Imogen wraps up the titles, pauses for a beat and I imagine her looking up from her scripts, her face stony serious as she prepares to launch into the opening link.

'Yannick, standby, coming to you in twenty seconds,' the director tells me. 'Harry? We can't see Yannick. Can you get a light on him?' There's an urgency, verging on panic, in her voice.

Harry's poised, his finger on the top light of his camera. I nod and he flicks it on, almost blinding me but more importantly, partially revealing the scrubby house behind me.

'Good evening,' Imogen says, 'and we start tonight with another exclusive report on the search for missing ten-year-old Annie Warren. Annie was last seen leaving school in Faversham four days ago. More than two hundred police officers and an army of volunteers from the community have been searching for the schoolgirl, so far without success. There have been no sightings and police have yet to name any individuals of interest publicly. But tonight, we can reveal police have identified a prime suspect, a local man they believe could be involved in Annie's kidnap. Let's cross live now to our reporter Yannick Kellor, who has details of this major development tonight.'

'And cue Yannick,' the director says.

I nod into the camera solemnly, trying to convey the gravity of the information I have to impart to our viewers. 'Yes, as you say, Imogen, a major breaking development here tonight after police swooped on the house behind me late this afternoon. I can reveal that officers have interviewed a fifty-two-year-old former soldier under caution on suspicion of the kidnap of missing Annie Warren.' I pause for dramatic effect.

I don't know for a fact he's a former soldier, but who's going to correct me? And honestly, it's the smallest of the untruths I've just told. I know I'm taking a massive gamble. As far as I'm aware, the police haven't raided the house yet, but it's only a matter of time, especially after I've outlined all the evidence. I don't see it as a lie, more that I'm jumping the gun a little. Helping the police by moving things along. I needed to do something. I couldn't just sit back and hand over my story to that silly woman from *The Post*.

'My cameraman Harry Collier and I spoke to the man earlier this week as part of our own investigation into what has happened to Annie,' I continue. 'Although we spoke only briefly, what was striking was his claim that he was unaware that Annie Warren was missing, despite the huge amount of publicity the case has generated. The question tonight is, was he telling the truth? Does he know more than he's letting on? And is this the man responsible for Annie Warren's disappearance?'

'On pictures,' the director says in my ear as she rolls the footage of Blair Black peering out of his front door that Harry shot a few days ago.

When I watched it back with Harry, it was far better than I imagined. Harry had done a great job. Blair Black looked every bit like a predatory paedophile with his long grey hair and scraggy beard that hasn't seen scissors or a razor in years.

Holly, the programme producer, had wanted his face pixelated so he couldn't be identified, but I hadn't bothered. What was the point? He's hardly going to sue us, is he?

There are raised voices of panic in the gallery, as if there's some sort of disagreement going on. I guess Holly's just noticed.

'And back on you, Yannick.'

'I also showed him a picture of Annie and asked if he'd seen her in recent days,' I continue. 'Again, he denied recognising her. I asked him if he had anything to say to Annie's distraught parents. I think you'll agree, his answer was rather curious.'

'Cue soundbite,' the director says as I pretend to look down at an imaginary monitor.

I hear my own voice in my ear. 'Do you have a message for Annie's family?'

'Not really. I'm sorry, I have to go,' Black replies.

'And back with you, Yannick,' the director says.

'Well, we can reveal tonight that man,' I glance down at my notes, 'is Blair Black, a man with a string of convictions for sexual offences against young girls.'

It's not something I've managed to confirm with the police but it's what all the neighbours are saying, and there's rarely smoke without fire.

'Yannick, what the hell are you playing at?' Holly screams in my ear. Why does she always want to play it so safe? Is it any wonder I didn't tell her my plan to identify him? 'You can't broadcast this. It's libellous. What are you thinking?' She sounds frantic now. 'Cut him off. Come back to Imogen in the studio and apologise. Say we're having technical difficulties.'

What? She's cutting me off? Seriously?

I plough on in case the director's slow to react.

'And something else strange we noticed about the house is that all the curtains are kept closed during the day,' I say. 'This is what Black had to say when I asked him about it.'

I look down at my imaginary monitor again. Harry peers up from his camera.

'They're off us,' he says. 'They've cut back to the studio.'

'Cowards!' I hiss. 'They've got no balls.'

Harry shrugs. 'I didn't realise Black has been questioned by the police,' he says, knocking a pair of headphones off his ears.

'Strictly speaking, he hasn't been yet, but it's only a matter of time with his history.'

'Are you out of your mind? Tell me you didn't just make that up?'

I shrug apologetically. What's the big deal? My hand was forced. I was on a last warning from the newsdesk. And it's not lying, exactly. It's just rearranging the timeline of the truth.

My phone, still on silent, vibrates in my jacket. It'll be Gina or Tim on the warpath. I'll deal with them later, when they've calmed down and I can make them see sense. The fact is, we've broken another major exclusive. It's not just me everyone's going to be talking about. The whole station's going to be bathed in glory.

'I wouldn't like to be in your shoes,' Harry says, lifting his camera off the tripod.

'Don't worry about it. Are you back up here tomorrow?'

'I think so. I'm on the weekend roster. I'm due to start at ten.'

He's about to head off when a car travelling far too fast, its engine revving loudly, screams towards us.

It pulls up in a squeal of tyres half on the pavement, half on the road, directly outside Blair Black's house. Harry and I watch in horror as four fearsome-looking men in hoodies and dark clothing pile out of the vehicle. They rush towards the building. Over the low brick wall. Up the overgrown path. One of them is carrying a baseball bat. Another has what looks like a hammer.

I step back into the shadows, transfixed but confused.

The first guy to reach the house bangs on the door.

'Black, you nonce, get out here!' he yells. 'We know you're in there.'

The man with the hammer takes a swing at a window. The glass shatters. Shards fly everywhere.

The door opens an inch and a splinter of light spills out onto the long grass. My breath catches in my throat. My lungs tighten as Blair Black appears, terror and confusion written all over his face.

Two of the men grab him by the collar and drag him outside. He stumbles, screaming at them to stop, and falls as he tries to resist.

Now he's on his back, being hauled out onto the street, but it happens so quickly I can hardly take it all in.

The other two men disappear inside the house. Lights come on behind the frayed, tatty curtains and they shout for Annie.

They think she's in there.

They think Blair Black *has* abducted her.

Maybe he has, but this isn't what I planned. I expected the police, not a gang of hammer-wielding thugs.

Blair's trying to curl up into a ball as the men punch and kick, their fists and boots striking his body and his head with sickening dull thuds.

He moans in pain, pleading for them to stop. We should step in. Try to stop them. But I'm frozen to the spot. Terrified. Helpless.

What have I done?

What *have* I done?

And then it's over, as quickly as it all began.

Blair's not moving.

His body's gone limp. His head turned to one side. His eyes rolled up into his skull.

A grotesque sickness blooms in my stomach. My legs turn to water.

The men who were beating him take a step back, not sure if he's faking it.

They look at each other, scared, as the other two men emerge from the house.

'She's not in there,' one of them shouts.

'Let's get out of here,' yells another.

And they pile back into the car, revving the engine, tearing away into the night in a cloud of sooty diesel smoke.

SATURDAY

Chapter 30

CATHY

Pam said I could pop around at any time, so here I am early on a Saturday morning knocking at her door, desperate for a friendly face, now that Fiona and I are no longer speaking. Someone non-judgemental I can talk to.

I had to get out of the house, or I thought I might go insane. We've been cooped up inside for days, but rarely left on our own. If it's not Zara, our police family liaison, loitering around like a bad smell, it's Yannick, constantly pestering us for interviews. And now Delores Dean, that awful, simpering woman from *The Post*. She's hardly been out of our sight since we agreed to talk to her, asking all sorts of difficult questions. About me and Kit. Annie's conception. My pregnancy. The birth. What Annie was like as a baby. If we have any problems with her.

It's been like someone's holding a drill to my temple and slowly boring a hole into my skull. Several times, I've almost told her to leave, especially when she started prying into my previous pregnancy, which I accidentally let slip. I don't want it splashed all over the papers that I had an abortion when I was nineteen, thank you very much. But we're stuck with her. We signed the contract. We agreed to give her full and open access to our lives. What else could we do? We need that fifty thousand-pound reward if we're ever going to see Annie again.

The stress is getting to both Kit and me. Neither of us is sleeping well. We're bickering more than we've ever done. Arguing over the silliest things. Kit wants the TV left on all day with the rolling news. I want it switched off. He's on his phone constantly, which drives me crazy, while he accuses me of not caring enough about keeping track of developments. But I don't care what the media is saying. I only care about getting Annie home. And then last night it all came to a head and Kit stormed out, saying he needed some space to think. I didn't try to stop him.

I don't know what time he came home. I went to bed and must have fallen asleep before he returned, but he was back when I woke this morning, early. I'm not sure I slept much, but when I did wake, I made the mistake of looking at my phone.

Kit's right, I try to avoid the news through the day. It's too much, always hearing about the search for Annie, seeing her face in that photograph we gave out. But I like to check what's happened first thing, to see what they're saying about us, about Annie. I shouldn't do it. Most of it is lies and half-truths because they have nothing else to report. But this morning, I was shocked to read a man had died on the estate behind the house, not much more than a stone's throw from here.

We'd heard the sirens and all the commotion out the back during the evening but hadn't paid too much attention. Sirens and emergency vehicles have become a common sight and sound around here since Annie vanished.

They said it was a vigilante attack, someone who'd been identified as a suspect on the local news. Four unidentified men had rolled up at the house, dragged him into the street, and beaten him to death.

I sat up in bed with a bilious nausea settling in my stomach. A man was dead because Annie was missing. I clamped a hand over my mouth to stifle my sobs and let my tears flow. I had to get out of the house while Kit was still asleep. I didn't mean to come to Pam's, but my feet found their way here, so I guess subconsciously it had always been my intention.

She's lovely. So caring. Friendly. And best of all, she doesn't constantly bombard me with questions or tell me what I should be doing, like Fiona.

Burrowing my hands in my pockets as I wait for Pam to answer the door, I keep my head bowed, trying to look inconspicuous. Everyone around here knows who I am now. A celebrity of sorts, but for all the wrong reasons. Mothers give me sympathetic smiles. Kids point. And the men can't look me in the eye. It's hard to keep your business to yourself in a town like this where everyone knows their neighbours.

A postman saunters past and tosses a cheery 'good morning' my way.

I smile and nod.

Pam throws open the door and her face lights up. I'm glad she's dressed and I haven't dragged her out of bed.

'Cathy, how lovely to see you,' she says. And then her expression clouds. 'Is everything alright?'

'Not really,' I say. 'I'm sorry it's early. Can I come in? I didn't have anywhere else to go.'

I've realised how few friends I have to turn to in a crisis. There's Fiona, of course, but she's been avoiding me since I accused her of interfering and threw her out of the house. And besides, it's easier to talk to a stranger and Pam seems to take me as I come.

'Of course.' She grabs my arm and guides me inside. The smell of toast fills the house.

'I was just getting Phillipa ready for gym club. Tea?'

'Lovely, thanks.'

I follow her into the kitchen, past the lounge where a television set is blasting out cartoons.

'I'm not holding you up, am I?'

It's only been five days, but I've already fallen out of my usual routine in the mornings, making sure Annie is up and dressed, fed breakfast, teeth cleaned and ready for school. Even on the weekends, it's tennis club and shopping. I've been so caught up in my own drama, I've forgotten life goes on for other people.

'No, no,' Pam assures me. She checks her watch. 'We don't need to leave for another quarter of an hour.'

'I'm sorry to turn up without warning, but I needed to get out of the house. It feels like the walls are closing in.'

'You poor love. Any news?'

'Not yet.' I bite my lip and scratch at a loose tag of skin around my thumbnail. 'Did you hear about the guy who died on the estate last night?'

'I did,' Pam says, pouring boiling water from the kettle into two mugs. 'Shocking.'

'Did you know him?' I ask.

'Not really. He kept himself to himself. I heard the police made some arrests overnight. A father and son and a couple of their mates. I know feelings are running high, but I don't like people taking matters into their own hands. Okay, Blair was a bit of an oddball, but you can't judge people by how they look.'

'Was he - ?' I ask, not able to say the words out loud. It feels wrong speaking ill of the dead.

'A sex offender?'

'I heard about Yannick's report last night. The papers are full of it. He said he had convictions for offences against young girls. Is it true?'

'No,' Pam says. 'As far as I'm aware, he's not one of those on the list.'

'So he was innocent?' A lump forms in my throat.

'He's lived here for years. Never been any trouble. He looked a bit strange, and the house was a dump, but he was harmless.'

I take a deep breath and let it out slowly, staring out of the window into Pam's back garden and the trees in the distance swaying in the breeze. The idea of anyone dying so brutally is utterly abhorrent, but at least I had the solace that he wasn't an innocent man. That he was a deviant predator who took advantage of young girls. But it's not true. He was innocent and killed because of Annie. The weight of responsibility bears down heavily on my shoulders.

'It's all my fault,' I whisper.

'Don't say that. The only people to blame are those idiots who thought they could take matters into their own hands instead of leaving it to the police.'

'But he'd still be alive if Annie hadn't disappeared,' I say.

'That's crazy talk. You can't help Annie going missing.'

'Maybe I should never have let her walk to school on her own,' I say. 'Am I a bad parent?'

'Oh, Cathy, don't beat yourself up. Of course you're not a bad parent.'

'It's what some of the papers are saying.' I've tried to avoid the worst of the mudslinging, but it's hard. I've read some horrible things about me being an unfit mother, and it hurts. I mean, it *really* hurts.

'You know better than to believe anything in the papers.'

'Did he have any family?' I ask.

'Blair? I don't know. I think he might have a grown-up daughter, but she doesn't live in the area.'

'It's such a waste of a life. It's not fair.'

Maybe Pam's right. I shouldn't beat myself up. I can't be totally responsible for Blair Black's death. If anyone's to blame, it's Yannick. Why did he make all those claims about him being investigated by the police if it wasn't true?

The tea Pam's made for me is hot and sweet. I wrinkle my nose as I sip it from a chipped mug. I don't usually take sugar, but it seems rude to ask her to make me another.

'Listen, while you're here, I thought I should mention I was thinking about organising a vigil for Annie. You know, getting everyone together one evening with some candles and maybe get the vicar to say a few words and offer some prayers for her safe return. I thought it would be nice for people to show their support. What do you think?'

I shrug. What am I supposed to say? It won't bring Annie back, but if that's what she wants to do, who am I to stop her? 'Sure, if you like,' I say. 'If that's what people want.'

'It's not about them. It's about you,' Pam says. 'People want to show they care.'

'But they've already done that. So many people have given up their time to look for Annie.'

'And they'd do it again in a heartbeat,' Pam says. She pokes her head around the kitchen door and hollers to her daughter. 'Phillipa, turn the TV off now and go and clean your teeth. We need to leave in a minute.'

'I'm in the way,' I say, suddenly feeling as though I've outstayed my welcome.

'Don't be silly. You're not at all.' She takes my empty mug and loads it into the dishwasher with a stack of dirty breakfast dishes.

It's incredible how many people's lives have been affected by Annie's disappearance. There's all the police for a start, and hundreds from the community who've turned out to search for her. Pam, who clearly has her hands full looking after her own daughter, but has organised the volunteer searches, the posters and the T-shirts. And now Blair Black. Murdered on his doorstep. Every one of those lives touched by Annie.

'Pam, there's something I should tell you,' I say. 'I've done something really stupid.'

The words tumble out of my mouth before I can stop them. A little dribble of truth I've been holding inside leaking out.

Pam closes the dishwasher door and frowns. 'What kind of stupid thing?'

'I wish I could tell you.'

'It can't be that bad, surely?'

'You'd be surprised.' The confession is on the tip of my tongue, willing to be spoken.

'Well, you know what they say. A problem shared is a problem halved.' She laughs, but there's nothing funny about this.

'I know but – '

'I'm ready.' Phillipa comes bounding down the stairs and into the kitchen, flashing a gappy smile at her mother.

'Did you do your teeth?'

'Yes.'

'Right, get your shoes on. Sorry, Cathy. We need to get going. What was that you were saying?'

I shake my head. 'It's nothing,' I say. 'Nothing at all.'

Chapter 31

YANNICK

It must be bad. Gina's called me into the studio for a crisis meeting this morning and she never works at the weekend. She didn't have to tell me why. She's obviously angry about last night's live, but it wasn't my fault some boneheads took it all out of proportion and went on a vigilante crusade against Blair Black. I was just doing my job. Reporting the facts, even if they were slightly skewed. I can't be held responsible for other people's behaviour.

She makes me sweat outside her office for more than twenty minutes before inviting me in. She pushes open the door, her face hard like granite, and doesn't even wish me a good morning.

'Come in,' she says with the kind of formality I haven't encountered since she interviewed me for a job more than seven years ago.

I haul myself wearily out of my seat and straighten my tie. I thought it was important to make an effort to look professional this morning, even though I didn't get much sleep. I was too wired. Haunted by the sight of Blair Black lying on the pavement, curled up in a ball as those men attacked him. His eyes rolling back in his head, his skin turning grey. Every time I closed my eyes, I heard the sickening hollow thud of boots and fists pounding his helpless body echoing through my head. I keep telling myself there was nothing I could do, but the fact is I didn't try. I let a man die in front of me and I did nothing to stop it.

Of course, I was brave after they'd scarpered, pumping his chest until the paramedics arrived. Whispering in his ear that everything was going to be alright, if only he could hold on. The ambulance crew said there was nothing more I could have done and that he was likely suffering from a pre-existing heart condition. I don't know whether that's true. It's probably what they're trained to say when someone's done their best and it's still not enough.

Over and over, I've told myself I wasn't to blame. It's what Harry tried to tell me as he guided me away from the ambulance while the paramedics got on with their work. But there's this niggle in my head that keeps tap-tapping away. If I hadn't identified Blair, showed where he lived, broadcast my suspicions about him, he'd most likely still be alive. I've tried telling myself he had it coming. That it was justice. I mean, he was a paedophile with convictions for assaulting little girls, right? But another niggle reminds me I was acting on rumour and hearsay and that I never did manage to get those insinuations stood up by the police.

I trudge into Gina's office with my head bowed. No point walking in like a cocky young upstart. She needs to see as well as hear that I'm sorry.

'Sit down.' She points to a chair that's been positioned directly in front of her desk.

She's not alone. There's another woman behind the desk, sitting with a clipboard and a grave expression on her face. I recognise her. She's from HR. This doesn't look good. Am I looking at more than a slap on the wrist and a furious dressing down?

Gina opens a folder and flicks the end of a pen.

The silence stretches out achingly between us. Outside, the dull hum of traffic buzzes through the window, almost drowned out by the throb of blood through my veins and the beat of my racing heart. Why's my mouth so dry? My tongue feels like it's gummed up to my teeth. I wish the floor beneath my chair would open up and swallow me.

I clear my throat and adjust my jacket. My shirt is already damp with perspiration and the collar is cutting into my neck. Damn, it's hot in here.

'What the hell were you thinking?' Gina's raised voice makes me sit up straight. 'Did you completely take leave of your senses?'

I swallow hard, my head swimming. I need to stay calm and professional. If I can explain the pressure I was under, maybe she'll understand why I did it.

'I'm sorry, Gina,' I say, 'but the thing is – '

'Not only did you name a suspect when Holly expressly told you not to, you blatantly disregarded her instructions to obscure his face in the picture.'

'There was no reason not to identify him,' I say. 'He hadn't been charged with anything.'

'He'd not been charged because he wasn't even a suspect,' Gina screams, slamming her pen on the desk so hard it makes both me and the HR woman jump. 'You fabricated a story, and that's unforgivable. And now a man is dead.'

'But – '

'A man is dead, Yannick. Can you not see how serious this is? I've already had the chief constable on the phone bending my ear, demanding to know how this could have happened. Any trust we had with the police is gone, and it's going to take a lot of work to rebuild those bridges. So let me ask you again, what the hell were you thinking?'

I hang my head. I have no defence other than my ambition to prove myself ran away with me. I didn't stop to think what I was doing. All I cared about was delivering a jaw-dropping scoop. But I have to try. My job's on the line.

'All the neighbours were pointing the finger at him,' I say, my voice wavering. 'And I was frustrated the police weren't getting anywhere in finding Annie, and they hadn't even considered Blair Black as a suspect. They'd not even interviewed him. It's been five days now and my cousin's still not been found. I was desperate.'

'I'm sorry, Yannick, I'm really struggling to get my head around this.' Gina squeezes her eyes shut and shakes her head. 'In all my years in journalism, I've never come across anything like it.'

'I made a mistake,' I mumble. 'But it's been such a hard few days for me. You don't understand the strain I've been under. My cousin's missing and you, Tim and Holly were heaping so much pressure on me. I gave you an exclusive with my Aunty Cath and Uncle Kit, which all the other broadcasters took clips from, by the way, but it wasn't enough. You wanted more. You were never satisfied. What was I supposed to do?'

Gina throws her pen down and crosses her arms. 'I see. So, what you're saying is that this is all my fault?'

'I didn't say that.'

'You're supposed to be a journalist. You're supposed to expose the truth, not fabricate fake news.'

'I just wanted you to be proud of me. It's all I ever wanted.'

'You're not a child,' she snaps.

'I mean it. You know how much I admire you. I just want to prove myself to you,' I explain.

'Don't give me that. All you've ever been interested in is getting yourself on screen.'

'That's not fair.'

'It is, and if you think this is the way to get into my good books, you're delusional,' she says.

'Please, Gina, give me another chance. I won't let you down again.'

Her eyes open wide. 'Another chance? Are you serious, Yannick? A man is dead.'

'I know that. I was there.'

'A man is dead,' she repeats, drawing each word out slowly and clearly. 'The community was already a tinderbox and because of you and your stupidity, vigilantes hunted down that poor man, dragged him out of his home, and murdered him on the street. How can I give you another chance?'

'So what then? You're taking me off the story?'

I'm clutching at straws. Of course I'm off the story. She's got to be seen to punish me. I fully expect she'll bust me back down to production duties. They won't risk giving me any presenting shifts for a while, at least not until the dust has settled. That would be punishment enough. But the presence of the woman from HR is a concern. Surely, they're not thinking of going any further than that? It was an innocent mistake. There was nothing malicious about it.

Gina stares into my eyes, a vein on her forehead throbbing. 'Yes, you're off the story.' She sounds incredulous. 'And I'm suspending you pending a full disciplinary hearing. You've left me no choice.'

Her words hit me like a punch to the gut, catapulting me backwards, spinning, falling out of control. She can't be serious. Suspension?

'W - what?' I stammer. 'You can't suspend me. Please, I'm begging you.'

'Go home, Yannick. You'll be notified of my decision in writing.'

I jump out of my chair, frantic. 'I'll make an apology on air. I'll do whatever it takes. Whatever you want me to do, but please don't suspend me.'

'And keep away from Faversham. I don't want to see you anywhere near there.'

This can't be happening. I knew it was bad when I was called in on my day off, but I never expected this. It's so ... unfair.

'Go home,' Gina repeats. 'And pack up your belongings on the way out. The way things are looking right now, you won't be coming back.'

Chapter 32

YANNICK

As I pull away from the studios, wheels spinning, there's only one thought on my mind. How can I prove to Gina she was wrong to suspend me?

It's not fair that I'm carrying the can for Blair Black's murder. It had nothing to do with me. It was that bunch of Neanderthals who thought it was a good idea to attack him. And I haven't forgiven Aunty Cath and Uncle Kit, either. If they hadn't shut me out and signed that deal with *The Post*, I wouldn't be in this mess in the first place.

Mind you, I bet the station's ratings are through the roof. All the papers are talking about me again, even if it is for the wrong reasons. I was the only reporter to secure an interview with Annie's parents, and now this. The station's currency has never been so high. And yet Gina's threatening to sack me after everything I've done for them.

I slam my hand on the horn as the car in front stalls at the lights.

'Come on, out of the fucking way,' I scream, pulling out around the vehicle, my rear end fishtailing as I speed away. Some people can be utter idiots on the road.

I grip the steering wheel tightly, watching my speed race up, the engine over-revving. Eighty. Ninety miles per hour up the motorway. Hedges and fields flash past in a blur. The speed feels good. A way of channelling my anger. Getting the frustration out of my system.

I just need a plan. Something to restore my journalistic capital and make them forget the Blair Black episode ever happened.

Come on, Yannick, you've got this.

I peer into the rear-view mirror. There's an annoying spot that's erupted on my chin, but it's nothing a dusting of powder can't sort out. My hair's looking good and my skin looks fresh, even if there are bags under my eyes from a lack of sleep last night.

Gina warned me to stay away from Faversham, but she's as good as told me they're going to fire me, so I'm going anyway to put things right and show her she was wrong about me. After all, I have nothing to lose.

What I need is some new evidence, something that proves indisputably that Annie was abducted. A new angle on the story that's going to get Gina begging to take me back.

A plan slowly forms in my mind as I drive, causing my stomach to effervesce with excitement.

It's actually a really simple idea, and although there are a few minor complications that stand in my way, it's nothing insurmountable. This could work.

I pull off the motorway and into the outskirts of the town, struck by the visible police presence still on show, with officers stopping random cars and talking to their occupants, presumably about Annie. Fortunately, I get waved through and make it into the town centre unimpeded. I make a brief stop to pick up a couple of essentials I'll need later and then drive to the school.

It's time to put everything into action and get my old job back.

A few hours later, I make my way back towards the creek, driving slowly and carefully, making sure I don't draw any unwanted attention to myself. I need to find whoever's been dispatched to replace me on the story.

I spot our satellite truck setting up for a lunchtime live close to Aunty Cath and Uncle Kit's house. The surprised look on the truck operator's face when he sees me confirms that the news has travelled quickly.

'I thought you were suspended?' he says, eyebrows raised.

I shrug. 'It's a misunderstanding. Who've they sent today?'

'Molly.' He nods towards the pub on the waterfront.

Molly Beckett's not long been with us. She joined the station last summer from another region when her husband was relocated for his job. She's super keen, always going over and above what's expected of her to impress Tim, Holly and Gina.

I saunter over casually to where she's sitting on a low wall scribbling on a notepad.

'I won't interrupt,' I say, stepping into her eyeline. 'I just wanted to say hello.' I wave in front of her face.

'Oh god, Yannick. Hi. What are you doing here?' she says, startled.

'Moral support for my Aunt Cathy and Uncle Kit.' I hook a thumb over my shoulder towards the house.

'Right. Great,' she says, far too enthusiastically. She's all smiles, teeth and bright red lipstick. Too eager by half, if you ask me, always covering the weekend shifts no one else wants, never saying no to anyone.

'Just thought I'd pop around and see what you had lined up for lunch.'

'Oh, right, yeah. Well, really just a quick update on the search,' she says.

'Has there been a development, then?' She's been parachuted in at the last minute and doesn't have a clue what's going on.

'Not as such. I've got an updated soundbite from the police, but that's it so far. Nothing much is happening at the moment. The police seem to be struggling for any leads.' She laughs nervously. 'And of course I'll have to mention the latest on Blair Black's death. They're still questioning those four men.'

She glances away, embarrassed to have brought it up. At least she's not mentioned my suspension, although I assume she knows.

'Isn't it weird how a little girl can just vanish into thin air? I know Cathy and Kit are beside themselves with worry,' I say.

She puts on a sad, sympathetic face, but it's fake. She doesn't care any more than the other journalists sent here to cover the story. 'It must be so hard for them. How are they?'

The truth is, I've no idea. I've not spoken to Aunt Cathy in days and Uncle Kit still isn't answering my calls. 'Yeah, you know,' I say, 'not great.'

'It was a great interview you did with them.' Molly flutters her thick black lashes. If she's trying to flirt with me, she's barking up the wrong tree.

'Thanks.'

'And how are you coping?' She touches my forearm tenderly.

'You know, you have to keep going, don't you?'

'Well, listen, it's nice to see you, Yannick, but I'd better get back to my script. We're on air in twenty minutes.' She holds up her notebook. I notice lots of crossings out and reworkings.

'Absolutely. Sorry, didn't mean to disturb you. Good luck,' I say, turning towards the satellite truck.

I count out three paces, then stop and turn back. 'Actually, Molly, now you're on the story, would it help if I gave you a bit of a background briefing? Obviously, I know the story inside out.'

'Oh my god, would you? That would be amazing.'

'Of course.' I glance at my watch. 'Why don't I take you for lunch after you come off air and I'll bring you up to speed with everything I know.'

'That would be awesome,' she says. 'Thank you. Thank you so much.'

'No worries. It would be my absolute pleasure.'

Chapter 33

CATHY

The town is quiet and the few people who are out walking dogs or heading for work ignore me as I stalk the streets with nowhere to go. I'm not ready to return home to face Kit or run the gauntlet of a dozen news-hungry reporters. So I wander aimlessly, letting my feet guide me, relishing the freedom after being stuck in the house going crazy.

In many respects, time has moved so slowly while we've waited for news from the police, and yet everything has happened so quickly since we reported Annie missing, and we've been caught up in a maelstrom ever since. First it was the police, and then the press. Even the response of the community, who've taken the cause to their hearts, has been overwhelming. On almost every lamppost there are posters with Annie's smiling face beaming back at me. And in the windows of houses and in the back of cars, reminding me she's gone, as if I needed reminding.

And, in the midst of all this madness, a man is now dead.

An innocent man, caught up in something he had no control over.

It was never supposed to be like this.

People are getting hurt and that's something I never intended. The possibility never even occurred to me. This has to end. Enough is enough. I couldn't stand for anyone else to get hurt. I should never have been talked into it, but that's always been my problem. I'm too weak-willed. Too easily persuaded.

And before I know what I'm doing, I'm at Jake's house, sneaking around the back with a furtive glance over my shoulder. Jake, our plumber, our Mr Fix-It. The man I trust implicitly, and who's always been there for me in my hour of need.

We became close when he was replacing the old pipework not long after Fiona and I opened the coffee shop. It was a messy job that couldn't be done during normal trading hours, and so he'd agreed to work in the evenings. Fiona's daughter was still young, so I offered to stay late with Jake and lock up each evening when he'd finished.

That's when I got to know him properly, when I discovered we shared the same sense of humour and, randomly, that we both despised baked beans, kisses on the end of text messages and squirrels (like rats but with bushy tails). When he kissed me, I should have stopped him. He was married too. But I was flattered and caught up in the moment. It was exciting and dangerous. I couldn't help myself, even though I knew it was wrong.

I hammer on the back door with my fist. If I'd known I was going to be coming, I'd have thought to pick up the key he'd left with me and Kit so we could let ourselves in whenever we needed, although it was only really supposed to be in case of an emergency. That's what we all agreed.

When Jake doesn't immediately answer, I knock again, louder.

Eventually, he appears through the glass, pulling on a T-shirt over his toned body. He peels the door open warily, squinting, his hair all mussed up.

'What's the panic?' he says, yawning.

I push my way inside, shaking. Tears are building behind my eyes, even though I don't want to cry.

'They killed a man,' I sob, 'just because they thought he had something to do with Annie going missing.'

Jake sucks his bottom lip under his front teeth and scratches the back of his head.

'I can't do it anymore, Jake. I miss her so much. I need to see her.'

'But we agreed – '

'I need to see her,' I repeat. 'I hate this. I hate everything about it. I've made such a big mistake.'

'Don't get upset,' he says. 'Everything's going to be fine, just like we planned.'

He moves towards me, as if he's going to wrap me up in those big, strong arms, but I take a step back, out of his reach. 'Don't.'

'I hate seeing you upset.'

'I'm fine.' I wipe my face with my cuff. 'Is she awake?'

'I haven't seen her this morning. I've only just got up. I was out half the night being given the runaround on an emergency call that came to nothing. You want to see her?'

It's been a long five days. Of course I want to see her. I want that more than anything else in the world. I promised Kit I wouldn't. We agreed it was too risky, that anyone could see us and alert the police. But that was before a man died. And anyway, this is all Kit's fault. He's the reason we had to do this.

'Come on, follow me.' Jake leads me through the house and up the stairs to a gloomy landing. He hooks open the loft hatch with a long pole and drops a ladder to the ground.

'Annie,' he calls in a half-whisper, 'your mum's here to see you. Are you awake?'

It was Jake's idea to hide her in the loft. I couldn't go up there myself, not with my fear of heights, but he showed me some pictures on his phone. It isn't like our attic, dusty, dark and full of all the stuff we should have thrown out but hung onto because of some misplaced sentimentality. He'd insulated it, laid a chipboard floor over the rafters, and installed lights on the roof beams. It was perfectly warm and cosy, but most importantly, there were no windows. We couldn't risk Annie being spotted from the street, and up here in the attic, she's well concealed even if the police were to pay an unexpected visit or carry out a cursory search.

The ladder creaks under Jake's weight and my stomach flutters. Even watching someone else going up a ladder makes me feel funny.

I've spent a lot of time imagining what it would be like to finally be reunited with my daughter, sweeping her up in my arms, both of us crying tears of happiness. Cameras clicking. TV news crews filming. Neither of us wanting to let each other go. But I didn't imagine it would be like this, creeping around in secret, sneaking into Jake's loft while nobody's looking. This wasn't the plan at all. But screw the plan. Things have changed.

'Annie, darling?' I call up from the landing.

I thought she'd come running when she heard my voice.

It must be the drugs. We've had to keep her sedated to help her cope with being shut away for long hours, even though I hated the idea of medicating her.

Jake's been giving her pills from an old packet of sea sickness tablets we bought in the Greek islands on a holiday a few years ago. Kit, Annie and I had all taken them before a sightseeing boat trip, but they'd left our brains thick and foggy and for the next twenty-four hours we'd been unable to keep our eyes open. God knows what was in them, but they've done the trick and kept Annie subdued when she might have panicked and given the game away.

'Annie,' Jake says. 'Are you awake?'

He reaches for a switch and a light comes on, spilling out of the loft and onto the landing where I'm standing, waiting patiently.

Kit's going to be furious with me, but this is the right thing to do.

It's time to bring it to an end.

It was madness to think we could get away with it, but if it means finally being able to bring Annie home and stop anyone else from getting hurt, I'm ready to face the consequences. I only went along with it because I couldn't see any other way. Kit was desperate. He said he didn't know what else to do, and I had to save our family. I couldn't bear for Annie to grow up with her father behind bars.

'There's something I need to tell you,' he'd said, when he sat me down at the kitchen table one night after we'd eaten and Annie was in bed.

It was the look in his eye, the heaviness of his shoulders and the way his jaw was working like it always did when he was anxious about something that made my heart sink.

'Are you leaving me?'

'What? No! Of course not. Why would you say that?'

'Because you're worrying me. What is it?'

He took my hand and looked at me like a little boy lost. 'I've done something stupid,' he said. 'Something unforgivable. I'm really sorry.'

I thought he was going to confess to an affair and my mind whirled with so many questions. How long had it been going on? Who was it with? Did he love her? Was it just sex? I snatched my hand back.

My brain raced, thinking of all the times he'd worked late or was unexpectedly called away on business. And he had been evasive of late. Avoiding my touch. Coming to bed late. Absent even when we were in the same room.

I'd put it down to stress. But had there been something else I'd been blind to?

'Just tell me,' I said softly, waiting for the blow that would destroy my life.

'I'm in trouble at work.'

'Trouble? What kind of trouble?' I sat up straight, shocked.

It wasn't what I thought he was going to say at all, and it sent my head spinning in a completely different direction. What kind of trouble could he possibly have landed himself in? He was the charity's chief executive, for pity's sake. It must be a legal issue. Or maybe one of the refugees they were supposed to be helping had been injured. Or worse.

He took a deep breath, his gaze falling to his hands where he was furiously picking at his nails. I watched the rise and fall of his Adam's apple.

'I've been taking money from the charity.' Like a pin puncturing a balloon, all the air seemed to escape from his body, and he folded into himself.

'What?'

'I stole from the charity,' he said.

'I - I don't understand,' I stammered, trying to make sense of his words. Kit wasn't a thief. Why was he saying these things? To test me? To see how I would react?

'I'm sorry. I know you must be disappointed in me.'

Disappointed? Try shocked. Appalled. Angry. I still couldn't get my head around what he was saying. 'How much? Why?' I gasped, a nugget of nausea cramping in the pit of my stomach.

'I could lose everything,' he said, his eyes rimmed red.

'How much?' I repeated.

'Forty thousand pounds,' he croaked, as if the words were burrs stuck in his throat.

'Forty thousand?' I rocked back in my seat as if I'd been physically punched, my head spiralling with the enormity of it all.

He nodded solemnly, wringing his hands until his knuckles were white.

'But why? We don't need the money like that.'

It didn't make any sense. If he'd stolen all this money, where was it? I certainly hadn't seen any evidence of it.

'I don't know,' he said. 'I can't explain it.'

'Why don't you try?' I snapped. He wasn't getting off the hook that easily. 'You don't just steal forty thousand pounds without good reason.'

'I can't.'

'So where is it, all this money?'

'I didn't take it all at once,' he said, as if that was some kind of excuse. 'It happened over months. Years. It started when I took a tenner from one of the donation boxes left in my office, when I couldn't get to the cashpoint. I always intended to pay it back, but nobody noticed it was missing and... '

'And you thought you'd help yourself to more?' I couldn't believe what I was hearing. It wasn't that it was just so brazen, it was that he could even contemplate doing something so wrong. I certainly never had my husband pegged as a petty thief, although forty thousand pounds isn't so petty. It must have been going on for a long time.

'Trust me, you can't think any less of me than I think of myself right now,' he said, his chin falling onto his chest, 'but every time I wasn't caught, it justified in my head that what I was doing wasn't really that bad.'

'You stole from your own charity,' I hissed.

'I know!'

'Are the police involved?'

Kit shook his head. 'Not yet.'

'What's that supposed to mean?' He was still talking in riddles.

'It means the trustee who found out what I've been doing hasn't reported it yet.'

I shook my head and narrowed my eyes. 'Why not?'

'He took pity on me, I guess. We've always got on. We work well together, and he knows this could cost me my job. So he's given me an ultimatum. I have four weeks to find the money and repay it, otherwise he says he has no choice but to call in the police.'

'And you'll be dismissed?'

'Obviously,' Kit said.

'Do you trust him?'

'Yes,' Kit nodded. 'He's a good guy.'

'How did he find out?' There was still so much of Kit's story that I couldn't grasp.

He shrugged. 'He said he'd suspected for a while that money was going missing from the tins because the donations seemed to be unexpectedly drying up, and as they were being stored in my office, he guessed it was me.'

'So he doesn't know for sure?' I said, clutching at straws.

'I confessed everything,' Kit said.

'But he can't have any idea how much you've actually taken.'

'No, but we agreed on a figure of forty thousand, which is probably a little on the high side, but it's the price I have to pay not to go to prison.'

Prison? A hard lump balled in my throat.

I couldn't let that happen. I couldn't let him abandon me and Annie. And, of course, it would be all over the news when it came out in court.

The shame of it. They'd have a field day when they found out the chief executive of a national charity was siphoning off cash intended to help refugees and asylum seekers fleeing from the war-torn corners of the world.

But worse was the thought of Annie being without her father.

No matter how stupid, selfish and dishonest Kit had been, I didn't want Annie growing up without her dad around. I knew from my own experience how difficult that would be for her.

I didn't know how to cope without my father in my life. I became withdrawn, sullen and uncommunicative. I lost interest in school, had a few run-ins with the police myself, and eventually dropped out of college with few qualifications.

I didn't want that for Annie.

I would not let it happen. She deserved so much more.

And so I had to find a way to keep our family together.

'How are you going to find the money to pay them back?' I asked, exasperated.

Kit looked up at me but said nothing.

'There's a small amount in our savings account, I suppose,' I said, 'but that was going to be Annie's university fund. What about selling the car? Although that won't go anywhere near covering it. The only other alternative is to extend the mortgage.'

Kit sighed. 'We can't take out any more on the house. We've already increased it once to fund the coffee shop.'

'There must be something else,' I said, trying desperately to think of something. 'We could sell up and move somewhere smaller?'

'No, that wouldn't be fair to you or Annie,' he said. 'But you're right, there is something else, although I don't think you're going to like it much.'

At that point, I was so desperate I'd have agreed to anything. An image flashed across my mind of taking Annie to visit Kit in prison, watching him emerge from behind heavy metal doors looking haggard and grey. Annie stiff with fear. Me trying to be stoic and brave.

I shuddered.

That's when he suggested we could fake Annie's abduction.

'One of the papers is bound to put up a reward,' he said, like he'd thought it all through. 'Remember Madeleine McCann? And those girls in Soham? All we need to do is keep our heads down for a few days. Then, when the reward is offered, we'll arrange for Annie to be found and claim the money. Simple. No one needs to get hurt and the charity gets its money back in full.'

'Are you serious?' I gasped.

'Absolutely. It's a win-win situation. We get the money, and the papers are bound to sell more because of the publicity. It's the perfect solution.'

What he was proposing was preposterous.

Or was it?

The alternative seemed so much worse. Kit arrested, inevitably charged with theft, and most likely convicted. Annie left without a father during the most important years of her young life and our names and faces plastered across the papers.

I didn't like Kit's plan, but time wasn't on our side and we had no other way of raising that kind of money quickly. And as he said, no one would get hurt, as long as we stuck to the plan rigidly. I certainly didn't care about duping the papers after what they did to my father.

'We'd have to find somewhere to hide her for a few days,' Kit said. 'Somewhere safe where she wouldn't be found until we were ready.'

We needed more than that if we were going to make this work. 'We can't do it on our own. We need someone to help us,' I said, my mind working furiously through the permutations. 'Someone who could look after her and then claim to have found her for the reward. Someone we can trust.'

'What about Fiona?'

'No, not Fiona.' I didn't want her to have any part of this madness and besides, I had a much better idea. 'Jake.'

'Jake Maginnis? The plumber guy?' Kit frowned.

'Trust me, we can rely on him.'

'Are you sure?'

'One hundred per cent.'

'Because he's got the hots for you, hasn't he? I knew it.' It was hardly the time for Kit to get all judgmental.

'Don't be so childish,' I snapped back.

Jake climbs into the loft, his movements quickening, a tension in his muscles.

'Annie?' he calls again, louder.

I don't like the tone of his voice. The question mark hanging over my daughter's name. Something's wrong.

His head reappears, peering through the hatch at me. 'She's gone,' he says. 'Her bed's empty and her sleeping bag has gone.'

'What? Then where the hell is she?' I gasp, my heart rattling with panic.

Jake stares at me, bewildered. 'I don't know,' he gasps. 'She should be here.'

Chapter 34

YANNICK

Molly's lunchtime live is predictably dull. She has nothing new to say and even had to check her notes when she appeared to forget Annie's name. It was a poor performance.

'You were great,' I say, as we enter the pub.

The bar is busy with locals, reporters and photographers. It's become an impromptu headquarters for many of the journalists working on the story because of its proximity to Cathy and Kit's house.

'Really? Thank you,' she says, putting her hands together like she's praying.

I observed her performance from a distance while I kept one eye on the bulletin on my phone. 'You did a really good job. Now what do you fancy to eat? My treat.'

She chooses a prawn salad and I leave her at the table while I order at the bar.

I carry our drinks back and watch carefully as she sips her Coke, leaving a smudge of bright red lipstick on the edge of her glass.

'I heard you had a roasting from Gina,' Molly says, tilting her head to one side like she cares.

'It's a misunderstanding, that's all.'

'What are you going to do?'

I shrug. 'Admit that I made a mistake,' I lie, 'and prove to her the newsroom needs me.'

'That's the spirit.' Molly shoots me a professional broadcast smile, one that doesn't connect with her eyes. 'You must be worried about your cousin. What do you think's happened to her?'

'It's obvious, isn't it? Someone must have taken her,' I sigh. I rotate my glass slowly around on top of the sticky table. 'There are some sick people out there. I only hope and pray she's safe and that by some miracle, we'll get her home in one piece soon.'

'That poor little girl. She must be so scared,' Molly says.

'Yes, it's horrible, but we're trying to stay positive until we know for sure what's happened.'

'I can't imagine what you all must be going through.'

'Thank you. We're just grateful as a family we have each other,' I say.

'Have you always been close?' Molly asks.

'I didn't know my father, and my mother died when I was eighteen,' I tell her. There's no point hiding the truth. 'Cathy and Kit took me in for a while, just until I was able to get back on my feet and make a life for myself.'

Molly's eyes open wide, her glass frozen halfway to her mouth. 'Oh my god, I'm so sorry. I didn't realise.'

'It's fine. They picked up Mum's cancer late and by then there was nothing they could do. Cathy and Kit became my surrogate parents, so I've always thought of Annie as my little sister.'

'I had no idea.'

I can see in her eyes that Molly's buying this crap hook, line and sinker. I don't have anything against Annie, but we're not close. We never have been. She's just a kid. And as for Aunty Cath, she's never forgiven me for becoming a journalist. I wonder if that's why she's punishing me now by cutting me out of the loop and talking to that tabloid reporter?

A young guy with what's left of his receding hair tied back in a lank ponytail arrives with our food. Molly immediately tucks into her salad, but I don't have much of an appetite and push my burger around my plate, munching on a couple of chips instead.

'I knew there'd be a lot of media interest when Annie vanished,' I explain, 'so I've kind of offered my services as their media adviser. It's the least I could do.'

We talk for another twenty minutes about how Aunty Cath and Uncle Kit are coping, the routes Annie could have taken home, and my theories about how she was most likely snatched from the street by someone in a car or a van.

'Anyway, I hope that's all useful background for you now it looks like you're taking on the story,' I say, gritting my teeth.

'It's incredibly helpful and so generous of you,' Molly says, finishing the last of her salad and pushing her plate away.

'It's my pleasure. But I'd better let you get on. I'm sure you have plenty to do.'

She rolls her eyes. 'Holly's already been on the phone. She wants another live into the programme this evening and a package about your aunt's abortion.'

'Abortion?'

'Oh, didn't you know? It's all over the papers about how she lost one child when she was only nineteen and now she's lost another.'

'Right,' I say. 'Of course. That.'

'Oh my god, you did know, didn't you?'

'Yeah, of course I did,' I say, shrugging it off, but she's right. I had no idea Aunty Cath had had an abortion. Another family secret she's kept from me. Did Mum know, I wonder? And who was the father? I guess this was in her wild child phase Mum said she went through after my grandfather's death. I should have spotted the coverage this morning, but I overslept and only had the chance to run a cursory eye over the headlines. How stupid to have missed it. It's a great new angle. If only Aunty Cath had confided in me. That should have been my exclusive.

'I hope I didn't speak out of turn,' Molly says.

'Don't be silly. Anyway, good luck with tonight's show. If you need anything more from me, I'm around in Faversham for the rest of the afternoon, so just call me.'

It's important she knows I'm here and available. In the meantime, I need to put the rest of my plan into operation.

I amble back to my car, drive to Annie's school, park on the road a short distance away and wait anxiously for the end of the school day.

Time creeps along painfully slowly.

I try listening to the radio, but it's an irritating distraction. I just want to get on, but there's nothing I can do until classes end and the children are dismissed. I flick the radio off and go through my plan one last time, making sure I've not overlooked any important details. I have to get this right. There'll be no second chances this time around.

Finally, as it approaches three o'clock, parents with pushchairs and toddlers in tow begin heading towards the school playground for pickup.

I jump out of the car, grab my camera from the boot, and hurry to the school gates, where I loiter, trying not to look suspicious.

A bell sounds somewhere inside the school and finally pupils begin to spill out of the building, running out in small groups to greet their parents. It's frustrating that most of them, the younger ones mainly, have an adult here to meet them.

It's only as the noisy throng of parents and their offspring starts to disperse that the older children appear, strolling casually out of their classrooms, dragging bags and scuffing their shoes. These are the ones I've been waiting for. The kids who no longer need their parents to drop them off and pick them up, even after Annie's disappearance. These are the kids who must have known her.

I set my sights on a group of girls completely blinkered to everything going on around them as they laugh and gossip, heads down, shoulders bumping.

'Hey,' I say to catch their attention as they thread their way through the gates and off the school premises. 'Do any of you girls know Annie Warren?'

They've obviously been told not to engage with strangers and hurry away from me, arm in arm, giggling.

The same thing happens with two boys, one tall and one short, who follow them out. They shake their heads, staring at me mistrustfully.

Several more students ignore me or run off terrified.

This isn't going well, and I'm beginning to attract concerned stares from some of the parents, but my persistence finally pays off when I approach a girl with bushy black hair who emerges from the school alone. Unlike all the boys, who have holes in their trousers, grass stains on their knees and ties hanging askew, she's immaculately dressed, like she's just turned up for school instead of leaving for the day. She's wearing scholarly glasses perched on the end of a pert, freckled nose and floats with the elegance and poise of a ballerina.

'Hello,' I say with a friendly smile.

'Oh, hi.' She smiles back, confidently looking me in the eye.

'I'm hoping you can help me.'

She stops and looks up patiently, waiting for me to explain myself. She has a bag over her shoulder and a coat folded neatly over her arm, like she's out for a day's shopping with friends. Eleven going on twenty-one.

'I'm trying to find someone who knows Annie Warren, the girl who went missing,' I say.

'Oh yes, I know Annie. She's in my class,' she says. She looks pleased to be able to help.

'Really? That's wonderful. I work on the TV news.' I hold up my camera to show her. I don't want to scare her off by thinking I'm some kind of weirdo. 'We're all trying to work out what happened to Annie so we can find her.'

The girl shakes her head. 'I know, it's terribly sad,' she says, with precocious maturity.

She might be mature for her years, but she's also incredibly naive. Haven't her parents warned her about the dangers of talking to strangers, especially after Annie vanished? Still, it works in my favour, so I'm not complaining.

'Did you see her leaving school on the day she went missing?' I ask.

She nods. 'Oh, yes. We walked out of class together, but we go home different ways, so I didn't see what happened to her. I'm sorry.'

Bingo.

'No, that's fine,' I say. 'How would you like to be on TV?'

'Ummm, I'm not sure.' She looks around as if she's seeking someone to tell her it's okay.

'It might help us find your friend. You do want Annie to be found, don't you?'

'Yes, of course,' she says.

With the interview wrapped up and the girl safely on her way home, I have two phone calls to make. The first is to the police. I call the emergency number and get straight through to a call handler.

'I have some information about the missing girl, Annie Warren,' I say. 'I've found a vehicle. I think it might have been used in her abduction.'

She might be used to dealing with high-pressure emergencies and all kinds of crank calls, but I catch the slightly shocked hesitation in her voice.

'You've found a vehicle you think was involved in an abduction?' she repeats back to me. Why do they always do that?

'That's right. It's a white van parked on the outskirts of Faversham.'

'And what makes you think it was involved in the Annie Warren case?'

'I'm a journalist,' I tell her. 'I've been interviewing people about what they remember of the day Annie went missing. One of the people I've spoken to is a girl from Annie's school. One of her friends. She told me she saw a white van driving past the school several times on Monday afternoon. She even remembers part of the registration plate.'

At least she did after I'd suggested it to her. People's memories can be exceptionally malleable, especially if they're young. After half an hour, the girl I'd met earlier was utterly convinced she'd seen a white van driving suspiciously up and down past the school on the day Annie disappeared.

'And when was this?' the operator asks.

'I spoke to the girl earlier today, but I didn't think anything of it until I stumbled across a van that matched the description,' I say. 'I'm sure it's nothing, but I thought I'd better call in it.'

'You did the right thing. What's the location of the vehicle?'

I give her the address of a pub out on the marshes, hoping the van hasn't been moved. After taking my name and contact details, she promises she'll pass on the information to the relevant team and thanks me again.

Of course she'll pass on the information. The police are desperate for a breakthrough, and I can almost guarantee they'll be swarming all over it within the hour.

Things are slowly dropping into place. Now it's time to see how Molly is faring.

I know she's suffering as soon as she answers her phone. I can hear it in the strain of her voice.

'Just checking everything's going okay,' I say. 'Anything I can help with?'

'Not really,' she groans. 'But I'm not feeling so great. I think it might be those prawns I ate at lunch.'

'Oh, really?' I say, feigning concern.

'I've got really bad stomach cramps,' she says. 'I'm just hoping I can get through the live tonight and get home in one piece.'

'You poor thing. Where are you?'

'Still down by the creek.'

'I'll be right there,' I say. 'I'll come and give you a hand.'

I hang up before she can protest. She has no idea I slipped a laxative into her drink over lunch in the pub and there's little chance she'll be able to report live tonight.

Everything is going to plan beautifully.

Molly's pacing up and down outside Cathy and Kit's house, with cameraman Harry looking on concerned. She's clutching her stomach and doesn't look at all well.

'You look awful,' I say, placing a comforting hand on her back as she doubles over in pain. 'Are you sure you're going to be okay for the live tonight?'

'Not really,' she gasps. And then she's off, sprinting towards the pub. As she runs inside, I struggle to conceal my amused grin. I shouldn't laugh. It's not funny, but this is *my* story. *I* should be covering it.

'I'm not sure she's going to be up to this,' Harry says, zipping up his puffer jacket.

'She's not looking too bright, is she? The poor thing.'

Harry shoots me a sideways glance. He has suspicion written all over his face, but so what? He can't prove anything.

Ten minutes later, just as I'm seriously contemplating following Molly into the pub to check on her, she reappears. She doesn't look any better, and the grimace on her face tells me she's still suffering.

'What are you going to do?' I ask. 'You can't do a live like this.'

Her bright red lipstick is smudged, and her hair is coming loose where she's pinned it on top of her head.

'I don't have much choice,' she says. 'I'm the only reporter on duty today.'

'That's a shame.' I chew my lip in mock contemplation. 'Unless...'

'What?'

'No, it's silly. Gina would never agree to it.'

'You could do the live!' Molly says, finally catching my drift.

'I'd love to, Molly. Really I would, but I'm supposed to be suspended.'

'Yannick, please, you have to help me out here.'

'I don't know.' I run a hand through my hair, doing my best impression of looking conflicted. 'I'd better not.'

'I can't do it like this,' she moans.

'I suppose it makes sense, but – '

'Let me call Gina and see what she says,' Molly insists, pulling her phone out of her pocket, and before I can utter another word, she's making the call with her back to me.

It seems to go on forever before she spins around to face me again.

'Yes, he's here right now. Hang on, let me hand you over. You can speak to him yourself,' she says, thrusting her phone at me. 'It's Gina.'

I hold the phone tentatively to my ear.

'Molly says she's ill,' Gina says curtly. 'She doesn't think she can do the live tonight.'

'No, she's not looking too good, I'm afraid.'

Gina takes a deep breath, as if what she's about to say goes against every instinct in her body. 'It leaves us with a major headache for tonight. She was supposed to be putting together a package and linking into it live from location. We don't have anyone else close enough to scramble to take her place.'

She's building up to ask me to do it, but I'll make it easier for her. It's time to play my trump card. 'You've heard about this van the police have found, have you? They think the abductor might have used it. Is that the story Molly was going to package tonight?' I ask innocently.

I let the stunned silence sit awkwardly between us. Of course she hasn't heard. Nobody apart from the police has heard.

'Where?' she snaps.

'Hollowshore. Out on the marshes. In a pub car park. One of my contacts tipped me off. If you hurry, you could reposition the sat truck and take a live from the location,' I say. 'I don't think anyone else knows about it yet,' I add for good measure.

She swears under her breath. 'Are you sure?'

'One hundred per cent. I know I let you down before, Gina, but I promise I have this on very good authority.'

In the background, a dog barks. She must be at home.

It took me ages to find a suitable vehicle, one of a certain age and in the sort of condition that would appear credible. It was streaked with rust around its door seals and front bonnet, and empty coffee cups, cans of soft drink and newspapers were piled up in a mess on the dashboard. Its seats were all ripped and spewing out lumps of foam, it had a soft front tyre and the bodywork was splattered in mud.

It was the sort of vehicle you could imagine being used in a child abduction. It was almost too perfect.

I can see now I went too far when I named Blair Black as a police suspect. On an estate like that, it was asking for trouble, although I could never have predicted what would happen next. But this is different. It's a van. I'm not pointing the finger at anyone, unless you count the owner, but I'm not naming them, and I really need my job back.

First, I dashed around to each wheel, letting out the air. I couldn't risk the owner returning and moving it before I'd had the chance to alert the police, so as a backup I grabbed a bottle of mineral water from my car and flipped open the fuel cap. Frustratingly, it was one of those lockable caps, but I tried it anyway and to my surprise it twisted open in my hand.

The mix of diesel and water should have wrecked the engine and prevented the owner from driving it away, even if they managed to pump up the tyres. At least that's what I found out with a quick search on the internet.

Finally, I needed to convince the police this was the van used by Annie's abductor. It's a good job I kept hold of Annie's favourite teddy bear, Rocky. It was in the boot of my car, wrapped in an old towel and tucked into the spare wheel under the felt liner. Aunt Cathy and Uncle Kit were so caught up in the filming, they didn't even notice me smuggle him out of her room under my jacket and slip him into my bag while Harry was fitting them with microphones. I knew it would come in useful at some point. Of course, there's a chance it's contaminated with my DNA, but I've been careful and it's easily explained. I'm Annie's cousin and I've been to the house a few times. It would make sense that there could be cross-contamination.

I dropped the bear into the undergrowth behind the van with his ear poking out of the thicket, sufficiently hidden so no one would find him by chance, but not too well secreted that the police wouldn't discover him when they searched the area.

'Look, is there any chance you can do the live for us, Yannick?' Gina finally asks.

'I thought I was suspended?'

'Do you want to do it or not?' she snaps.

'Of course,' I say, lowering the phone and holding it to my chest. 'Harry, get packed up. We're moving.'

Chapter 35

CATHY

The sound of sirens cuts through the air, filling my head and sending my pulse galloping. They're close. Coming this way. No, not onto the estate. Beyond it. Out towards the marshes.

Annie?

I glance at Jake, my mouth open.

'Do you think - ?'

'I don't know,' he says.

We've spent the day searching everywhere for her. We've turned the house upside down, hoping she'd simply got bored in the loft and let herself down to find something to do.

We looked around the garden. In the bushes. And in the shed.

And then around the estate.

Everywhere and anywhere we could think she might have gone. But there was no sign of her. She'd vanished.

'What are we going to do?' I whimper as I sink to my haunches with my head in my hands back at Jake's house.

For the last few days I've been acting a part, trying to put myself into the shoes of a mother whose child has gone missing, imagining the distress and agony of not knowing.

Now I don't have to act anymore. The distress is real and a million times worse than I could ever have conceived. I know now that there's nothing more devastating, more gut-wrenching than losing your child and not knowing what's happened to them. Worrying she's hurt or in danger. Afraid and alone.

Upset.

Confused.

Dead?

I had no idea of the utter helplessness, like a gnawing hole at the core of my being. Anxiety twists my gut, the pain and desperation like a thousand daggers in my side. I'm in a living nightmare. A purgatory I wouldn't wish on any parent.

She could be anywhere and if she's still sedated, she's at the mercy of everything and everyone.

'When did you last see her?' I gasped when we found the loft was empty. I grabbed Jake's arms, digging in my nails, imploring him to remember something, anything, that would help us find her.

'I don't know.' He clutched a handful of his own hair as if he was trying to wrench it out of his skull. 'Around six last night, I think. I collected the dirty dishes from her room.'

'Six? Oh my god, Jake. That's hours ago. How was she?'

'Fine. Quiet. No different than normal.' His face was contorted in agony.

He meant she was drugged and sleepy, but neither of us wanted to acknowledge it.

'Why did you leave her in the house alone?' I hammered my fists into his chest in anger and frustration.

'I'm sorry, Cath, I had a call-out. I thought she'd be okay. They said it was an emergency.'

'And did you check on her when you got back?'

He lowered his gaze. 'No,' he said quietly. 'It was late. I thought she'd be asleep. I'm so, so sorry.'

I don't know what more we can do. It's been almost a full day since anyone last saw Annie and we've searched every nook and cranny.

'We have to call the police,' I weep, finally admitting we have no other choice. I don't care about the consequences. All I care about is finding Annie.

'No, Cathy. You can't.' Jake's face lights up in alarm. 'What would you tell them?'

'The truth. It's time they knew what we've done.'

We've made a terrible, stupid, unforgivable mistake. It seemed so simple when Kit suggested faking our own daughter's disappearance to dig him out of a hole of his own making, and I'd glibly gone along with it. Why? What was I thinking? How could this possibly have worked out for the best?

We took our own child away from her family home. Drugged her. Imprisoned her. And all for what? To keep this family in one piece? What a joke. This family was destroyed the moment Kit let temptation rule his head and he took money that didn't belong to him.

I should have called the police myself as soon as he told me. Who knows, maybe he wouldn't even have faced a custodial sentence. No one was hurt. He might have got away with community service or a fine. Now we're both facing prison. And Jake too. But none of that matters one jot while Annie is missing. We have to find her, because if anything bad has happened to her, I'll never be able to live with myself.

'We can't,' Jake pleads, clutching my forearms as he kneels in front of me. 'We're all accessories to kidnap, faked or not. I'll lose my business. My reputation. Everything.'

'I don't give a flying fuck about your reputation, Jake,' I hiss, snatching my arms out of his grasp.

'They'll take Annie away from you.'

'No,' I gasp. 'They can't. She's my daughter.'

'They will if they think you're an unfit mother,' Jake says with an intensity in his eyes that makes me shudder.

Oh god, he's right. Even if we do find her, they'll take her from me. They're bound to. They never take the parents' side. I might never see her again.

I mean, what kind of mother am I, anyway? And how could I ever have thought this was a good idea? I'm no better than a pimp, prostituting my own daughter out. Using her for my own ends.

I thought I was a good mother. A caring mother. The sort of parent who would go to the ends of the earth for her child. But it turns out I'm no better than my own mother.

'Come on. Let's keep looking,' Jake says, pulling me to my feet. 'I'm sure she'll turn up. We could try down by the boat sheds at Oare.'

I shake my head. 'We have to tell Kit,' I say. 'He has a right to know what's happened.'

I'm surprised I haven't heard from Kit all day. Hasn't he been worried about me? Did he not wonder where I've been? I guess he's still angry with me after we argued last night, and figured we could both do with some time apart.

I don't blame him. It wasn't so much an argument as a full-on stand-up blazing row where we stood nose to nose screaming at each other. I had a major wobble after that man was murdered on the estate and told Kit I wanted to end this crazy charade, to call the police and confess everything. To get our lives back to normal.

But he wouldn't hear of it. He told me I was insane. That we were nearly home and dry and to keep my nerve.

'Keep my nerve? A man's died,' I yelled in his face.

'I'm not going to prison,' he screamed back.

'And he'd still be alive if Annie wasn't missing.'

'We're not to blame. He died because some thugs were looking for an excuse to get into a fight. That's not our fault,' he said. 'But if you call the police now, it's over for both of us. We'll both go to jail. And your friend, Jake. Is that what you really want?'

And then he'd stormed out of the house.

That was almost twenty-four hours ago and the last time I'd seen or spoken to him. But no matter how angry I am with him for getting me into this appalling mess, he still deserves to know that Annie has gone.

'You want me to come with you?' Jake asks.

'It's better if I do it alone.' I wipe my eyes dry and moisten my lips. I'd love to have some moral support when I tell Kit I've made up my mind about confessing to the police and won't be talked out of it. But Jake isn't the person I should have with me.

'I don't mind,' he says.

'No, I have to do this on my own. You keep looking for Annie.'

Chapter 36

I slip in through the back garden, avoiding the journalists at the front of the house. The TV's on in the lounge showing the evening news, but I don't pay it any attention. I only have one thing on my mind, and that's speaking to Kit.

He's perched on the sofa, with our police family liaison officer, Zara, sitting opposite, straight-backed and attentive.

'Cathy! Where have you been?' Kit jumps up and mutes the volume on the TV.

'I needed some space. I had to get out of the house for a bit.'

'Is everything okay?' He narrows his eyes at me. 'Cathy?'

I want to blurt everything out to him and collapse on the sofa in a heap of self-pitying tears, but I can't. Not with Zara here. I have to hold it together for a little bit longer.

'Can I talk to you for a minute, in private?'

'Sure,' Kit says.

He apologises to Zara as he leaves the room and follows me upstairs into the bathroom. I lock the door and turn on the taps in the bath, like I've seen in the movies. I don't know whether it works, but I can't risk Zara overhearing what I'm about to tell my husband.

'What are you doing?' Kit asks, bemused.

There's no easy way to tell him. No way to soften the blow. 'Sit down,' I say.

But he remains standing, staring at me like I've grown two heads. 'Cathy? What's going on?'

I sit on the toilet seat and cross my legs, heart thumping, my mind in a spin. I don't know what to think or feel anymore. I'm numb and emotionally bruised and battered.

'It's Annie,' I say, fixing my gaze on a stain on the bathmat. A grubby spot that's persistently remained despite my efforts to clean it off.

'What about her?'

I bite the inside of my cheek and draw in a deep breath. 'I'm sorry, Kit, Annie's gone.' My words trigger a flood of tears and heaving, gasping sobs that rise from my chest and through my shoulders.

'What?'

'I went to see her. After that man died. I went to Jake's,' I wail, no longer caring whether or not Zara hears.

'You did what?' Kit snaps. 'Why? I thought we both agreed it was too risky.' His jaw tightens and his eyes grow dark with anger.

'I couldn't bear it anymore. I had to see her. I had to hold her,' I explain, but he doesn't understand. He just stands there, glowering at me, shaking his head.

'You could have ruined everything!'

'Really? And how much worse could it get? Didn't you hear me? Annie has gone!'

'She can't have,' he says.

'She's gone,' I repeat, throwing up my arms. 'She's vanished.'

'She's probably just hiding. Did you check Jake's house?'

'Of course we checked. We've looked everywhere.'

'Well, she can't have gone far. I thought Jake was supposed to be looking after her. You said we could trust him,' Kit says.

I knew he'd try to blame this on Jake. He's never really liked him.

'He hasn't seen her for almost twenty-four hours.' I take another breath to compose myself and run my sleeve across my cheek, drying my tears. 'We have to come clean, Kit. It's gone too far. We need to tell the police what we've done.'

'Are you insane?' he yells. 'We can't call the police. They'd arrest us on the spot.'

'I don't care! I just want Annie back.'

'No.' He shakes his head furiously.

'We could go downstairs right now and explain everything to Zara. She'd understand. She'd know what to do and she can get the searches reinstated.'

'And we'd lose Annie forever. You do realise that, don't you, Cathy? They'll take her away from us. They'll put her in care, and we'll never be allowed to see her again.'

'We have to do something,' I wail. 'She could be in danger.'

A light tapping on the bathroom door causes us both to freeze, staring wide-eyed at each other in horror.

'Everything alright in there?' Zara's voice through the door is flat.

Has she overheard us arguing? How much did she hear? Oh god, this isn't how I planned it.

'We're fine,' I say, my voice cracking with the effort of trying to sound normal.

'It's just that I thought I heard shouting. Can you open the door?'

I sniff and run my fingers through my hair, trying to put some volume back into it. To look vaguely human again and not like a madwoman who's in the middle of a shouting match with her husband.

Kit unlocks the door and I force a smile as he peels it open.

'Everything's fine,' he tells her. 'We're just a bit stressed with everything. It's been five days now and still nothing. I mean, what exactly have your lot been doing? There have been no confirmed sightings. No leads. No nothing,' he shouts, venting his anger on the poor woman.

It's not her fault the police have been next to useless. Until last night, we had Annie safely hidden, although I'm surprised there have been no recent sightings of her if she's managed to escape from Jake's house.

'I appreciate it's frustrating, but we're doing everything we can,' Zara says in a soothing tone. 'You just have to trust us to do our jobs.' I guess she's used to parents like us taking it out on her. All part of the job. 'Someone taking a bath?' she asks, nodding at the gushing taps that have steamed up the room and fogged the mirror over the basin.

'No, that was me,' I say, lunging for the taps and turning them off.

The silence hisses in my ears.

It's the perfect time to speak up. To make my confession and tell her the awful thing we've done. I should be pleading for her forgiveness and begging her to find my daughter. Instead, I'm paralysed with indecision. The moment I say something, it's all over. There's no taking it back, and they'll probably take Annie away from us.

But I can't leave it another night, not knowing where she is.

'Okay, well, I was just going to say that unless you need me for anything else this evening, I'll be getting off,' Zara says.

I realise now she's already pulled on her coat and has her bag over her shoulder.

'Right, see you tomorrow.' Kit ushers her out of the room and down the stairs with almost indecent haste.

Did he sense I was going to say something?

The front door opens and bangs shut. It's too late now. Zara's gone. We're alone again, but I can't face Kit. I don't want to see him or talk to him. My head's all over the place. I just need to think.

I trudge into our bedroom and slump on the bed shaking, my head in my hands. What the hell am I going to do? I never thought I'd have to choose between my husband and my daughter. All I ever wanted was to keep our family together. It's not too much to ask, is it? A normal life. A quiet life. Annie safe and tucked up in her own bed. No journalists banging on the door. No fear of the police turning up and leading us away in handcuffs.

I don't deserve this. Surely Kit can see that saving his daughter's life is more important than saving his own skin? Or maybe he can't. Is the thought of going to prison really so terrifying he'd rather sacrifice Annie's life? That would be such a cowardly way to think, and I know my husband better than that.

Or do I?

I never thought he was capable of theft either, but that's what's landed us here in the first place.

How do I even begin to choose? Annie's not a baby anymore. She's independent, fiery and single-minded, but still so young and vulnerable. Kit, on the other hand, is old enough to look after himself.

He made the decision to steal from the charity and thought he could get away with it. Annie and I are innocent victims. Collateral damage. And now he's asking me to stand by him again and put him above my own daughter's safety and welfare.

How can I?

She's only a child. Alone in the world. She needs me, like every child needs their mother. Like I needed my mother when she wasn't there for me after Daddy died.

I should never have gone along with Kit's plan. If I'd had the balls to stand up to him in the first place, Annie and I would still be together. Even if Kit had been sent to prison, we'd have got through it. It would have been tough on all of us, but better than this. Anything is better than this.

It's not too late to do the right thing. They must have to give me credit if I tell them the truth, even at this late stage. I can't find Annie on my own. I need the help of the police and the full weight of their authority and manpower, even if it means arrest and the probable sacrifice of my freedom.

My phone's already in my trembling hand. I unlock it with my thumb. This is the right thing to do. There is no other choice. Annie's life outweighs everything else, including my own.

My fingers hover over the keypad. Three numbers and I'd be through, talking to someone. Telling them the truth. Getting help to find Annie.

But now, below, there's another voice.

At first, it sounds like Zara. Has she forgotten something?

No, not her. Another woman.

Delores?

I strain to make out what's being said, but I can't hear the words.

I lower the phone and let it drop onto the duvet.

And then Kit is shouting up the stairs.

'Cathy!' he calls. 'You'd better get down here. Now.'

Chapter 37

DELORES

Delores has no idea how he's done it, but Yannick has stolen a march on everyone again.

There he is reporting live into the early evening news as the police swarm around a white van they say they suspect has been involved in Annie's abduction. In the background, men in white forensics suits pore over the vehicle.

He's obviously been tipped off by someone. Maybe by a contact in the police, but she can't rule out it came from the Warrens themselves, although that would clearly be a breach of the contract they signed. She's annoyed but all is not lost because what the public wants next, besides news that Annie's been found, is Cathy and Kit's reaction as this development appears to finally confirm their worst fears, that Annie was snatched off the street as she walked home from school.

Delores throws on her coat, grabs her bag and jogs across the narrow swing bridge over the creek and slows down as she reaches the Warrens' house. Kit is in the doorway, slipping back inside, with that police liaison woman marching off towards the pub car park. Delores is glad to see her go. She finds her presence suffocating.

'Kit!' Delores calls out. 'Wait!'

He lets her in and swiftly closes the door behind her. He looks even more weary than before, his cheeks hollowed and his eyes dull. The stress is really getting to him.

'Did you hear about the van they've found?' Delores asks.

'They told us something about a vehicle,' he says. 'Up at Hollowshore, right?'

'They think it might be the van the abductor used to snatch Annie. Is Cathy around? I was hoping to get a reaction from you both.'

Kit lets out a tired sigh and rolls his eyes, but at least he's given up protesting whenever she asks for a quote. 'Yeah, she's upstairs.' He leans over the banister and shouts. 'Cathy! You'd better get down here. Now.'

There's something about his tone that's unsettling. Until now, Cathy and Kit have seemed like a tight couple. United. In harmony. But she senses there's a tension between them this evening. Have they been fighting? It's something to watch and explore. It could be an interesting new line to the story if Annie isn't found soon. The couple whose marriage is unravelling under the pressure of losing a daughter.

Cathy emerges, looking pale and fraught. The lack of sleep is hitting her hard. Her eyes are bloodshot and her complexion ashen.

The three of them sit in the lounge in the same places they took when Delores conducted her first interview. Cathy and Kit next to each other on the big sofa. Delores on the smaller sofa with the low coffee table between them.

'It seems like this might be a significant development,' Delores says, placing her phone on the table and switching on the voice recorder, 'especially as they've also found Annie's toy bear.' She watches them both carefully, gauging their reactions. She still has a nagging feeling they're hiding something.

Cathy jolts like she's been stung. 'Rocky?'

'I know this must be hard for you both, but it seems to confirm your worst suspicions. What are your immediate thoughts?'

Delores leans forwards, her eyes darting from Cathy's face to Kit's and back again, hunting for the little cues and leaks that will tell her what's really going on inside their heads. If they're lying, or fabricating any of this, Delores is going to find out. Her reputation depends on it.

Cathy wraps her arms around her body and starts to gently rock, staring into the space above Delores' head, like she's zoned out, lost in her own world. This isn't the same Cathy as before. She's different. More tightly wound up, like she's standing on the precipice of a cliff, deciding whether to jump.

Something's happened. But what? Maybe it's the discovery of this van and the final dawning realisation that Annie has more than likely been abducted. Delores continues to observe her closely.

Kit pinches his nose. 'It's obviously shocking,' he says. 'I don't know what else to say. I'm sorry. We just want Annie back home.'

His eyes redden with tears. He's clearly fighting his emotions. It's the first time Delores has seen this side of him. Previously, he's been the calm, measured one who's kept it all together. It makes her wonder if they know more than they're letting on. Have the police found something else they've not revealed publicly yet?

'It's okay,' Delores says. 'Take your time. What have the police told you?'

Kit shrugs. 'Not much. They said they were looking at a van up at Hollowshore but they weren't sure if it had anything to do with Annie's disappearance.'

'Your nephew seems pretty certain.'

Cathy's head jerks towards Delores. 'Yannick? What's he said?'

'He was the first to break the news about the van,' Delores says. 'He obviously has good contacts.'

'Hmmmm,' Cathy mumbles, but she's gone again, staring into space, looking like she's about to burst into tears.

'Maybe you have a message for whoever's taken Annie?' Delores asks.

'Um, right, yeah.' Kit blinks several times as he runs a hand over his face. 'I'd just say please don't hurt her. She's only a little girl, you know? Our little girl. She's probably confused and upset. Please, just get in touch with the police and let them know she's safe. And it's not too late to do the right thing.'

'What about you, Cathy?' Delores asks. 'Do you have anything you'd like to say?'

She shrugs like a petulant child. 'I don't know,' she murmurs.

'You've said all along that you suspected Annie had been abducted. What made you so sure?' Delores asks.

Cathy meets Delores' eye and fixes her with a long, hard stare. Her tongue is working inside her mouth, but she keeps her lips firmly closed, almost pouting. She's afraid of blurting out what's really on her mind. Holding back. But why?

'Cathy? Don't you have *anything* to say?' Delores presses.

Cathy shakes her head. 'Kit said it all.'

'But you must be terrified? Aren't you worried someone is holding Annie against her will?'

'I'm sure the police will find her,' she says, turning her head pointedly to look at Kit.

There's definitely something going on between the two of them. And Cathy is almost certainly holding something back.

'And a message to her abductors?' Delores asks.

'I just want her home with us, okay? Wherever she is, whatever has happened to her, she should be here, with us.'

'And if Annie could hear you, what would you say to her?'

'I would say I'm sorry. I'm sorry, baby girl. Please come home.' She wipes away a tear that rolls down her cheek.

'Will that do?' Kit says. 'I think we could both use some time to process the news now. Alone.' He stands, looming over Delores. 'Please, we'd like you to leave.'

Delores could remind them of the terms of the contract they signed, that they've effectively waived their right to any privacy, but what's the point? It's not going to get her anywhere and she still needs them onside.

She picks up her phone and pretends to switch off the recording app. 'Yes, that's great, thank you. I'll leave you in peace.' She grabs her bag and starts coughing. 'I'm sorry,' she says, eyes watering. 'Something's stuck in my throat. Could I have a glass of water, please, Kit?'

Kit's hands flex into tight fists and unfurl again. 'Of course.'

He marches off in the direction of the kitchen, and as soon as he's out of the room, Delores turns to Cathy. 'Is everything okay?' she asks. 'Is there anything you want to tell me?'

'Like what?' Cathy plays all innocent, but there's a flicker in her eye that suggests Delores is onto something.

'I don't know. I had the impression while Kit was in the room, there was something you wanted to say.'

'No.'

'Are you sure?'

'Of course.'

'Because believe it or not, you *can* trust me. I know you probably don't think so, but it's true. If you need help, if there's anything you want to get off your chest, I'm here for you,' Delores says.

Cathy picks nervously at her fingers.

'Cathy?' Delores prompts.

A cupboard door opens and closes in the kitchen. The rush of water from a tap. There isn't much time. Kit's on his way back.

Cathy's head bobs up and there's a sudden determination in her eye. 'Yes,' she says. 'Actually, there is something I wanted to say.'

Kit's heavy footsteps thud through the house.

'Go on,' Delores urges.

'It's about Annie.'

'Yes?'

She opens her mouth, but clamps it tightly closed again as Kit stomps back into the room with a glass of water in one hand.

'What were you two talking about?' he asks, eyeing Cathy suspiciously.

'Nothing,' Delores says. 'I was just getting ready to leave.'

She drinks the water slowly, with one eye fixed on Cathy. But she's looking away again, focusing on the corner of the room. On nothing much at all.

She was on the verge of telling Delores something. Something significant. But what? That they know exactly where to find Annie? That Kit has something to do with her disappearance?

Whatever it is, Delores is determined she's going to find out.

'Thank you for the water,' she says, standing. 'I'll be in touch soon.'

Chapter 38

CATHY

I sit frozen on the sofa as Kit shows Delores to the door. I should have said something. She gave me the perfect opportunity, but I couldn't do it. I don't know why. Maybe because she's a journalist. All that nonsense about being able to trust her? Yeah, right.

She knows something's wrong though. The way she looked at me when she managed to get me on my own, pretending she was on my side. Does she suspect we were involved in Annie's disappearance? And how long before she prints something? I can't afford for those sorts of allegations to appear in the papers before I've had the chance to come clean to the police.

Kit storms back into the room, his face thunderous. He stands with his hands on his hips, staring at me murderously.

'What did you say to her?' he growls.

'What?'

'Don't play dumb with me, Cathy. You said something, didn't you? You told her about Annie.'

'Of course I didn't.' I squirm in my seat. I didn't, but I came very close. The weight of guilt has been pressing so heavily on my shoulders, the urge to tell someone, anyone, what we've done is overwhelming.

'Don't lie to me,' he screams, making me jump. 'I heard you whispering. What did you say? Tell me!'

He rushes towards me, grabs my arms and shakes my body like I'm a rag doll.

'I didn't say anything. I promise.'

'Liar!'

I've never seen Kit like this before. He's a man possessed, driven by anger and desperation. It's certainly the first time he's ever laid a finger on me. I jerk out of his grasp and push him away.

'Don't touch me!' I scream.

He stumbles back, clutching his face. 'I'm sorry,' he mumbles, 'I didn't mean... I was...'

'There's no point arguing. We should be putting our energy into finding Annie. She's out there somewhere, all alone. Don't you understand? She could be in danger,' I say, rising from the sofa.

'You're being melodramatic,' he says. 'She can't have gone far. She'll turn up. She's probably on her way back to Jake's house right now.'

Why's he being so blasé? He was more upset than this when we lost her in Bluewater when she was four, a Saturday afternoon shopping trip turning to panic when she wandered off and disappeared into the crowds.

Kit was frantic, running up and down the mall screaming her name. Eventually, we found her in a toy shop with a sales assistant trying to establish her name and where her parents might be. The sense of relief and joy was like every birthday and Christmas rolled into one. Kit vowed never to let her out of his sight again.

'What's with you, Kit?' I ask, trying to read his strained expression. 'Don't you care about your own daughter?'

'Of course I care, but panicking won't help. We need to work out what's happened before we do something stupid like calling the police,' he says.

'Jake and I have been looking all afternoon.' Why isn't he grasping the seriousness of the situation? Our daughter's safety has to be the priority over everything else. Why can't he see that?

'Maybe you were looking in the wrong places.'

I shake my head. 'We've looked everywhere.'

'Have you tried her friends?'

I scowl at him. Now he's being ridiculous. If Annie had turned up at any of her friends' houses, their parents would have been on the phone to the police in seconds. 'I'm worried she might be hurt.'

'I think we need to calm down a bit, don't you?'

'Don't patronise me, Kit.'

'Tell me where you looked.'

'Around the estate. Up by the school. Everywhere,' I say. But every second we spend talking about it, is another second Annie's out there in danger.

'Did you check the new housing estate by the lakes?' Kit asks.

'Yes. And no one's seen her.' This is pointless. We should be asking the police to help, not trying to second guess where she might have gone.

'She can't have vanished into thin air. She has to be somewhere. Are you sure you checked Jake's house properly? You know what she's like. She's probably hiding in a cupboard somewhere, thinking it's all one big joke.' The way he laughs makes every nerve ending in my body prickle with irritation.

This isn't a game. This is our daughter's life. Why isn't he taking it more seriously?

'Please,' I beg. 'Let me call the police. She's not safe. I can feel it in my gut.'

'No! How many times? We can't. Not now. We've gone too far. They'll crucify us. And can you imagine what the press will say?'

Really? He's worried about his reputation? He should have thought about that before he slipped his hand in the till.

I scream in frustration and stamp a foot on the floor. 'Kit! We have to do something!'

'Fine, if you can't find her, I'll go out and look.'

At least that's something, but I don't see how Kit's going to have anymore luck than Jake and I had earlier. We need help and extra resources.

'I'll come with you,' I offer. I can't stay in the house pacing up and down with worry while Annie's out there somewhere.

'No, it's better if you stay here, in case she finds her way home.'

I open my mouth to protest, but he has a point. If Annie is trying to get home, someone needs to be here. We can't abandon the house, even though I know staying here is going to drive me insane.

'Fine, but you call me the moment there's any news,' I say, following him into the hall.

He shrugs on his big coat and sits on the stairs to pull on his walking boots. 'Yes, yes, I'll let you know as soon as there's anything to report,' he says.

'You will find her, won't you?'

'Of course I will.' He smiles, then stands and kisses me on the forehead. 'Stop worrying. Everything is going to be fine. We just need to hold our nerve for a few more days and this will all be over. We'll get Jake to claim the reward for finding Annie and I can pay the money back to the charity and before you know it, everything will be back to how it was before. Trust me.'

I want to trust him. There's nothing I want more in the whole world than to have our family back together and for life to return to some semblance of normality. No more journalists outside the house. No more Zara. No more posters of Annie on lampposts. No more pretending. No more guilt. And no one else getting hurt.

And yet, why do I have this feeling it's not going to be that easy?

The security light over the back garden blazes on as Kit lets himself out and I watch his lumbering frame head towards the back gate, his long shadow stretching out along the path.

And then he's gone, the light goes off and I'm left alone in the house. Totally, utterly alone. A hollowness balls in my stomach as I stand in the cold kitchen, my arms folded over my chest, my mind still in turmoil. I'm in agony, and yet I'm totally helpless to do anything about it. All I can hope for is that Kit has better luck than Jake and me in locating Annie.

I need to find something to take my mind off my worries, so I head back into the lounge and flick on the TV. I don't want to watch the news. Anything but that. Just something for a bit of company and some background noise to take away the creaking emptiness of the house.

My head spirals through all the events of the last few days, playing them over and over. Kit said the plan was foolproof. Annie was supposed to be safe. Nothing could go wrong. Except it has, in spectacular fashion.

If she's let herself out of Jake's house, confused and disorientated, anything could have happened. A listless and dazed child would be such an easy target.

Oh god, please don't let anything bad have happened to her. I bury my head in my hands, letting my hot tears drip through my fingers. How I wish I could turn back the clock and change my mind. If I could have my time again, I'd tell Kit he was being an idiot and talk him into facing up to the consequences of his actions. Not going along with a harebrained scheme that would wreck our family.

A noise at the window sounds like someone throwing gravel at the glass, and then I hear a hissing burst of rain splattering the road outside. I peer through a crack in the curtains. It's a sudden, viciously heavy downpour. And somewhere out there is my precious little girl.

What if she's caught in it, frozen, wet and shivering? I can't bear it. I can't sit here doing nothing in front of the TV while Annie is lost. I don't care what Kit wants. Or that we could both end up behind bars. Annie has to come first.

My only decision now is whether to call the emergency number again and confess to a stranger, or to call Zara.

I have her number on my phone. She made us both put it into our contacts lists for emergencies. The consequences will be the same whoever I call, but it'll be easier speaking to our liaison officer. She'll guide us through it. Make it less painful for us.

My hand trembles as I dial, but I'm doing the right thing. Kit's going to be furious, but he'll come round in time. When he's given it some thought, he'll understand I was only doing what was best for Annie.

The call connects and starts ringing.

This is it. I'm scared, but relieved.

It takes Zara an age to answer. What is she doing? I thought she'd have her phone within reach at all times, but I suppose she has a life outside work too.

Eventually, the ringing stops. There's a click. And Zara's voice is in my ear.

It's functional and to the point.

'Leave a message. I'll call you back.'

What do I do? I swallow the anxiety that's bloomed in my throat. I can't back out now.

'Zara, it's Cathy Warren,' I say. 'Can you call me? It's urgent. There's something I need to tell you.'

I hold the phone to my ear for a moment, listening to the blood flooding through my veins. Should I tell her why? Will she phone back any quicker if I say Kit and I faked Annie's abduction?

But before I can reach a decision, I hear footsteps in the house.

I spin around with the phone still clamped to my ear and catch the flicker of a shadow behind me.

And then I feel a searing, sharp pain at the back of my head and hear the hollow thud of my skull rattling inside my brain.

Darkness envelopes me.

My legs give way.

And I collapse to the floor.

SUNDAY

Chapter 39

I'm on my side, my arm numb and my shoulders burning. I can't move my hands, which are twisted painfully behind my back, and a jagged spear of pain shoots behind my eyes, like my head's being crushed in a vice. Nausea swells in my stomach and my hips ache uncomfortably.

What the hell happened?

I peel open my eyes and try to lift my throbbing head. The unfamiliar room is unlit and there's a strong smell of damp, mould and dust.

Where am I?

Worse than the smell, there's something filling my mouth. A wad of material thick with the cloying taste of old sweat and diesel that's bound around the back of my head, straining against my cheeks and forcing my face into a rictus grin. The hot, moist air from my lungs whistles through the gag as my breath quickens. My panic rising.

I can't breathe.

I need to spit it out.

It's clogging my mouth.

My throat.

I work my jaw and tongue in tandem, pushing and pulling simultaneously until the damp, coarse material slips over my chin and is finally out.

I gasp for air, pushing my head back, the relief like a surging flood through my contorted body.

Slowly, my heart rate comes back under control, my breathing steadies to a rhythmic rasp and my eyes adjust to the gloom. I'm lying on a cushioned wooden bench in a small, square room with dark wood panelling and cupboards on every wall. It looks like the cabin of an old boat.

But that doesn't make sense. Why would I be on a boat?

There's no swell. The room's not pitching or rolling. There's no gentle lapping of waves or creaking of wood. Only the pulsing thump in my head like the world's worst hangover, so I don't think it's afloat.

There's another bench opposite covered in a pile of old blankets and above it a brass porthole, spotted green and tarnished with age. But I can't see anything through it, not even the sky. Only what looks like a sheet of canvas flapping in the wind.

I attempt to sit up by swinging my legs onto the floor, but my ankles, like my wrists bound behind my back, are tied together tightly. I'm trussed up like a turkey, unable to move or do anything. I fight against my bonds, desperate to get free, but the more I struggle, the tighter they become until they cut into my skin and I'm a bath of sweat. It drips off my forehead and runs down my cleavage, soaking my top.

Who's done this to me?

And why?

I have to get out of here. Wherever here is.

But how? I can't move.

I could probably roll over, but I'd only end up on the floor and then I'd be worse off than I am now. At least the bench is cushioned.

'Help!' I cry, but my voice is weak and croaky, my mouth and throat dry. 'Someone, please help me!'

I stop struggling to listen. To hear if anyone has answered. But the only sound is the flapping of the tarpaulin over the porthole.

For all I know, I'm in the middle of nowhere with no one around for miles.

Suddenly, it seems hopeless.

Whoever's left me here doesn't want me to be found.

I don't understand any of this. It's like I've woken up in the middle of a nightmare, my worst claustrophobic fears realised.

I don't know what to do.

'Oh god, please, somebody help me!' I sob. I don't know whether the tears that flow are from frustration, fear or desperation. But they won't stop and quickly they consume me.

Come on, Cathy. Pull yourself together.

I clench my jaw closed and focus on taking long, slow breaths in. Centring myself. Forcing the tears to stop. Crying won't do me any good. I need to think. If I can't fight my way free, I have to use my brain.

The last thing I remember is being in the house on the phone to Zara. Leaving a message. Begging her to call back. My mind made up that I would confess what we'd done and tell her Annie was missing for real.

Oh god, Annie!

How can I help her if I can't even help myself?

I've no idea how long ago that was. An hour? Six? It can't be any longer than that, surely?

I heard footsteps in the house. Someone creeping up behind me. Hitting me on the back of the head. Blacking out. Have I been unconscious all this time?

Everything's so fuzzy, like I'm floating on the edge of reality, or in one of those dreams where you have a false awakening and find you're actually in another dream.

I stare across the room at the dirty bundle of blankets opposite, my vision swimming in and out of focus.

Funny, I imagined for a second the blankets were moving, like a seething pot of snakes. But that's impossible. I must be seeing things. That bang on the back of my head's probably given me concussion.

I blink several times as I lift my head off the bench and tilt it upright for a better view.

No, they're definitely moving. I saw them!

My vision fades from colour to a monochrome silver and darkness clouds in from the edges.

Once again, the blankets quiver and stir. More noticeably this time.

It's not in my head. It's real.

Oh my god, there's something under there.

'Hello?' I whisper loudly. 'Is there someone there?'

As the blankets rise and swell again, I hear a groan. A small, pale arm appears and flops out, and a hand drops onto the floor.

I gasp, catching my breath. There *is* someone else.

A head of hair pokes out, and my heart almost explodes out of my chest. I coil back into the depths of the bench until I realise it's only a child.

A young girl.

No, surely not. It can't be. A thrill of excitement rockets through my veins.

'Annie?' I croak. 'Is that you?'

Another sleepy groan. Her head lifts and twists, and Annie's face appears, her eyes closed in peaceful sleep. My heart could burst with happiness. She's alive! If only I could pull her into my arms, I'd wrap her up in the tightest hug and shower her beautiful head with kisses.

'Annie, darling, it's Mummy,' I soothe. 'Are you awake?'

Her tongue darts out of her mouth and moistens her lips. Her hair is damp and plastered to her forehead.

'Annie,' I say, louder. 'Wake up, sweetheart.'

One sleepy eye cracks open, followed by the other. She stares blankly in my direction, looking beyond me, not seeing me.

'It's Mummy,' I repeat, smiling.

Her eyes narrow and sharpen as she focuses on my face. And then her lips turn up into the most beautiful grin I have ever seen. It's magical.

'Mum,' she mumbles, the word slurring drunkenly from her mouth.

'Where have you been?' I ask. 'I looked you for in Jake's house, but you'd gone.'

Her smile fades as her eyes flutter closed again.

'Annie, darling, wake up. I need your help. I can't move my arms or legs.'

As far as I can see, Annie's not tied up, but she's clearly still sedated. I need her to wake up, to set me free, so we can both get out of here.

I don't know how long we have. Whoever brought us here could be back at any moment. We don't have a second to lose if we're going to escape.

And what about Kit? He must be worried out of his mind. I promised I'd stay at the house. I can only hope he's come to his senses and called the police. With any luck, they should be looking for us both by now.

Annie mutters something incomprehensible and rolls over, turning her back to me, burying herself under the thick blankets again.

'Don't sleep,' I call out, my voice echoing around the tiny room. 'Wake up, Annie!'

I try to sit up again, wincing in pain. With a renewed determination, I finally manage to roll my legs off the bench and onto the floor. My arms twist painfully behind my back, wrenching my shoulders. And as my head comes up, the blood rushes to my feet.

For a second, my head spins and I think I'm going to faint, the spiked spur of pain at the base of my neck returning with a vengeance.

I scream in frustration and sit, gasping. I can see now my ankles have been secured with a thin blue rope, and I'm not wearing any shoes, but that's the least of my worries. I have only one thing on my mind, and that's getting me and Annie out of here.

'Please wake up,' I hiss.

But Annie doesn't stir. If someone's given her one of those sea sickness pills recently, she could be out for hours. But time is a luxury we don't have and unless I can get Annie to unpick the bonds around my wrists, we're not going anywhere. My voice alone won't rouse her. If only I could make it across the cabin to shake her.

I square my knees so they're in line with my hips and swing my body forwards, hoping the momentum will help me stand. My backside lifts off the bench briefly, but almost instantly I lose balance and fall back down. With my hands tied so tightly behind my back, this is going to take more effort than I imagined.

I rock back and try again, gritting my teeth against the pain, throwing myself forwards and bending at the hips, trying to shift my centre of gravity over my knees and propelling my weight up and off the bench.

I reach a tipping point where I'm on the balls of my feet and catch myself before I fall back down at the exact moment a thud against the hull reverberates around the boat. It's hard to pinpoint exactly where it came from. Above? Below? From the side?

It's followed by a softer sound.

What is that? Feet on the deck above?

The blood thrums through my veins as I freeze, paralysed with fear.

The thud of footsteps draws closer. Someone's coming.

Metal rattles against wood and then there's a scraping sound I can't place. I turn my head to watch as a hatch opens in the roof above a short flight of wooden steps and a pair of boots appears, followed by a figure who scoots effortlessly into the cabin.

It's Kit. Thank god.

'Help me. I'm down here. Someone's tied me up,' I wheeze.

'Shut up.'

The sharpness of his tone shocks me into silence. He moves deftly towards me, but not to untie the ropes. He shoves me back down onto the bench with his fingers reaching for my throat.

No, not my throat. For the diesel and sweat-soaked gag I spat out and which is now coiled around my neck.

He's trying to put it back in my mouth.

'No,' I yell, twisting my head and clamping my mouth firmly shut.

'Stop wriggling,' he mumbles.

Panic scrambles my mind. Why's he not helping me? Unless...

Oh no. Not Kit. Not my husband.

'Stop yelling,' he says, fury blazing in his eyes. He gives up trying to put the gag back in my mouth and raises a hand as if he's going to slap me.

I squeeze my eyes shut and tense my body, waiting for the red-hot sting on my face.

He's never hit me before. He's not a violent man. But then, I never thought he was a thief either. How can you share a life with someone and not truly know them? This isn't the man I fell in love with. This is a monster.

I tremble, my body losing control of itself. Fear runs cold through my core, confusion twisting my mind.

Kit must have returned to the house while I was on the phone to Zara and attacked me, tied me up and abandoned me here on this boat. There's no other explanation. But why? Did he hear me making the call?

I crack open my eyes. Kit's stepped away, his hands by his sides. I snort heavily through my nose as I watch him pace up and down, his brow furrowed.

'I told you not to call the police,' he growls, grinding the ball of his hand against his forehead like he's trying to massage away an incessant pain.

'I didn't,' I protest.

'Don't lie to me! I heard you. You were leaving a message for Zara and you were going to tell her everything.'

'I was worried about Annie,' I sob. 'I just wanted her home and safe.'

'She *was* safe, but now you've ruined everything.'

'I don't understand,' I say. How could she be safe? 'Oh god, it was you. You took her from Jake's house, didn't you?'

'What was I supposed to do? We only had to wait a few more days and we could have brought her home,' he says, his incessant pacing making the boat rock gently. 'But no, you couldn't wait, could you? A few more days, that's all!'

And it all slowly makes sense. 'You took her because you were scared I was going to call the police,' I say.

'What else could I do? You weren't following the plan we'd agreed. You'd lost your nerve. I had to do something, or we were screwed. So, yes, I brought Annie here where no one, including you, would find her. I had to keep her safe for a few more days, that's all.'

I shake my head, trying to understand the madness in my husband's mind, but it's like my brain's been wrapped in barbed wire, rattling around inside my skull.

'You hid our daughter as insurance in case I blew the whistle?' I say.

He shrugs. 'If they couldn't find her at Jake's, I figured they'd think you were suffering from stress. Or delusional. I panicked, okay? I didn't know what to do.'

This is a whole other level of desperation.

'How? When?'

'The night we argued. I called Jake out on an emergency.'

The wild goose chase Jake told me about. It had been Kit all along.

'How did you get her out of the house without being seen?'

Kit shuffles his feet and looks away from me. 'I hid her in a wheelie bin and pushed her out to my car.'

'You put our daughter in a bin? What the hell's wrong with you?'

'She was fine.'

A dull throbbing behind my eyes is a reminder of how I ended up here in this stinking boat with my arms and legs bound so tightly I can hardly feel my fingers and toes anymore.

'You hit me,' I say, fixing him with a hard stare, my anger simmering.

'You left me no choice. You brought this on yourself!' He's shouting again. 'I didn't *want* to hurt you.'

'But you did.'

He stares at me for a second and then his shoulders relax and his chin drops. 'I'm sorry, okay? I wasn't thinking straight.'

'Untie me,' I say gently. 'Let me go. You know this isn't right.' I force a smile, but he shakes his head.

'No,' he says firmly. 'I can't.'

'Please, Kit.'

'I said no, alright?' he snaps.

'Alright, fine.' I don't want to push it and get him angry again. I'll just keep him talking and hopefully I can make him come to his senses. 'Where are we?'

He glances around the dingy cabin. 'An old yacht in Iron Wharf,' he says.

'The boatyard?'

'The owner's supposed to be refurbishing it, but he's out of the country most of the year.'

'So what's the plan?' I ask, working hard to keep my tone even. I don't want to upset him again, at least until he frees me. 'Zara's going to wonder what's going on when she finds out I've disappeared too.'

'I'll tell her you're not feeling well and that you're in bed,' he says. 'At least until I can work out what to do.'

'Untie me, Kit. Please. We can work this out together.'

'I can't, Cathy. I don't trust you anymore. You're unpredictable. I don't know what you're going to do next.'

'Come on, Kit. Let me go.' The forced smile is making my jaw ache, but he has to believe I'm being genuine.

'I can't.'

For pity's sake. This is a waste of time. 'Untie me, now!' I scream, yanking at the ropes around my wrists and ankles, thrashing to get free. 'Kit, just let me go!'

I can't stand the thought that he might leave me here like this, unable to move.

'If I do that, you'll go straight to the police, won't you?' he says. 'And who's to say you won't point the finger at me? Tell them it was all my idea and try to blame everything on me?'

'I panicked, okay? That's all. I can see I was wrong now, but a man died because some thugs thought he'd taken Annie. But we can work this out. It's not too late.'

My mind's buzzing with a sudden clarity as I grasp at anything to make him change his mind.

'I can't trust you,' he repeats.

'We'll say Jake found Annie here on the boat when he was doing some work around the yard,' I say, a plan forming in my mind. Yes, this could work, if he takes the bait. 'Then he'll be able to claim the reward for us and in a few days, everything will be sorted. We'll have Annie home and you'll have your money. We can go back to being a normal family.'

'It's not that simple,' Kit says.

'Of course it is.'

'I really wish it was, Cathy.'

'Kit, please. Don't be like this. You're not thinking straight.'

'I tried my best to make this work,' he says, 'but – '

The shrill warble of his phone cuts him off mid-sentence and he turns his back to me to take the call. What the hell could be more important than this?

He listens for a moment with his hand on his forehead and starts pacing again.

'I know, I know,' he says, 'but listen to me, we have a serious problem and I don't know what to do. I really need your help. You need to get over here urgently.'

Chapter 40

The phone call is short and one-sided. Am I the "serious problem"?

'Who was that?' I ask.

Jake is the only other person who knows the truth about what happened to Annie. But he's my friend, and he and Kit hardly know each other. In fact, Kit doesn't even like Jake. Kit couldn't have been talking to him. So who? Nothing makes any sense.

'Shut up,' Kit snaps.

'I'm your wife, for god's sake. Doesn't that count for anything? Untie me and we can work this out together.'

He moves closer, every muscle in his face taut. He's a seething tangle of doubt and uncertainty. If only I can talk some sense into him. Walk him down from the cliff edge.

'Kit – '

He shushes me quiet, putting a finger to my lips, and for a second I think he's going to kiss my forehead. But instead, he snatches the gag around my throat and pulls it back over my mouth.

And then he's pushing my head down and tightening the material so I can't spit it out this time. I try begging him to stop, but all that comes out of my mouth is a muffled howl of despair.

'Don't go anywhere. I'll be back shortly,' he says, before lumbering off.

As if I *could* leave.

He climbs up the steps and through the hatch, shutting it behind him, despite my desperate, muted wailing.

His footsteps thud across the deck above and there's dull clanging against the hull, which I guess is the sound of him climbing down a ladder.

And then I'm left in silence.

Annie didn't even stir at the sound of Kit's voice. I listen for the sound of her breathing. Slow and shallow. Barely a whisper. What have we done to my poor little girl? Is it possible to overdose on sickness pills? I have no idea. None of us thought to check. How could we have been so callous?

Nothing good was ever going to come of this stupid plan of Kit's. Why did I ever agree to be part of it? There was too much that could have gone wrong and we were totally naive to think we could walk away with a reward without anyone getting suspicious. It's as clear to me now as a spring morning, so why couldn't I see it before?

Maybe if I'd kept my nerve, everything would have worked out. If Yannick hadn't pointed the finger at that poor man, Blair Black. If those thugs hadn't dragged him out of his house and beaten him to death. If I'd not argued with Kit. If I'd not threatened to call the police.

So many ifs.

So many could-have-beens.

But here we are, and I have no idea how this now ends.

I collapse on the bench and screw my eyes shut, exhausted and strung out and with the darkness closing in on my consciousness again.

Suddenly, I'm coming back round with a cold sweat of fear that the boat's been launched and we've been abandoned in the middle of the ocean, pitched and tossed on the waves, as part of Kit's grand plan to make me and Annie disappear for good.

But no, the boat's not moving. It's me. Someone is gently shaking me awake.

My eyes spring open in panic. I'm choking. My lungs struggling to draw breath. Bursting. My throat constricted. It's the gag in my mouth. I can't breathe. I'm going to die.

Fuck.

'Mummy, Mummy, wake up. I'm thirsty.'

I blink, trying to focus, trying to remember where I am and what's going on. My shoulders are in agony, my legs strung together, pressing my kneecaps painfully against one another.

Annie?

She's standing over me, frowning, her eyes glazed and dull. With one hand on my shoulder, she's rocking me gently back and forth. She looks like a zombie, half-dead, her limbs heavy.

My heart wants to tear itself out of my chest. It's thudding so hard. I yank my wrists to free my hands, but the rope stings where it's cut the skin and I yowl in pain.

I try begging Annie to remove it, to let the air back in my lungs, but I can't form the words with the wad of material in my mouth and all that comes out is a muffled sound of frustration.

'I can't hear what you're saying,' Annie says.

I roll my eyes frantically down towards my mouth, until eventually she understands and peels the roll of material down my chin, scraping my sore skin, chaffed and red raw where I've been dribbling.

'There you go,' she says, dead-eyed.

'Thank you, darling,' I say. 'I couldn't breathe.'

But she's so out of it, she doesn't seem to care. 'I'm thirsty. My mouth is really dry.'

She looks awful. Her hair is all tangled and her skin pale. Her eyes are puffy and barely open. I need to get her off this boat.

'I know,' I say. 'I'm thirsty too. Have a look around and see if Daddy's left any water.' I try to keep the panic out of my voice. I don't want to frighten her. She's been through so much already these last few days.

She wanders aimlessly around the cabin with her hands hanging limply by her sides, poking her nose into the tiny galley area and under a table near the hatch.

'I can't find any,' she moans.

'Try all the cupboards.'

She throws open one or two and takes a cursory look inside, but the whole place looks like it's been stripped bare and only the basic shell left.

Annie starts to cry.

'Hey, sweetheart, don't get upset. We'll find some water, don't worry. Help me get free and I'll have a look for you.'

She wipes her tears and hobbles back towards me. With another huge effort, I sit up, turn my back to her and raise my hands as far as they'll go.

'Can you untie them?' I ask hopefully.

She kneels on the bench. Her cold fingers brush my wrists. She tugs and pulls, but the knots don't loosen.

'I can't do it!' she says sulkily, after a few minutes. 'They're too tight.'

'Okay, don't worry. Maybe have a look in some of the other cupboards and drawers. See if there's a knife or some scissors.'

It's a vain hope. I can't imagine Kit would have left a knife lying around, but we won't know until she's looked.

Annie pads across the cabin in a daze. I guide her to each cupboard. Each drawer. Each little cubbyhole I can see from where I'm sitting, but she draws a blank. There's not so much as a screwdriver. Seriously? There has to be something or we're never getting out of here.

'There's nothing here,' she says in despair, slamming a drawer shut. 'I want to go home. I don't like it here.'

'I know. Me neither, but it's going to be okay. Daddy will be back soon.'

I say it to reassure her, but I'm not convinced Kit's reappearance is going to help either of us.

'Listen to me,' I say as she throws herself on the floor with her back against one of the empty cupboards. 'I want you to see if you can get out and find someone to help us. Can you do that?'

'How?'

'There's a hatch at the top of the steps. See if you can open it.'

I hate having to ask her to do this, but there's no other way. Any hope we have of escaping is entirely on Annie's shoulders now. But even if she can open the hatch, and by some miracle Kit hasn't locked us in, she'll have to crawl across the deck and climb down a ladder.

I'd never allow her anywhere near a ladder at home, but these are desperate times and Kit could be back at any moment.

And then she'll need to find someone to ask for help. At least her face has been plastered over every newspaper in the country and every lamppost in the town for the last few days. Someone's bound to recognise her and raise the alarm.

Annie pulls herself to her feet like a huffy adolescent. It's a little glimpse into her teenage future. But if that's the worst we have to deal with, I'll be grateful. I can only pray that what we've put her through doesn't leave deep scars. Will she grow up to hate me when she realises what we've done? Will she ever be able to forgive me?

I'd be naive to think life's going to go back to normal after this is all over. The hell we've put Annie through is going to be with her for the rest of her life. And it's all my fault. Maybe with a lot of support and counselling we can get her through it. That is, if we ever get out of here alive.

Annie clambers up the steps and reaches up for the hatch with both hands. When it doesn't move, she tries shoving it open with her shoulder. But it doesn't budge. It must be locked from the outside.

So that's it then. We're stuck here, entirely at Kit's mercy.

'I can't do it,' Annie wails in frustration.

'Leave it. Come and sit with me.'

I want to throw my arms around her and tell her everything is going to be alright, but I can't do that either.

Instead, she comes and sits next to me on the bench and rests her head on my shoulder, nuzzling into my neck.

'I'm sorry, Mum.'

'There's nothing to be sorry for. You tried your best.' A lump swells in my throat.

If we ever get out of this, I'm going to make it up to her. She can have as much ice cream as she can eat. And we'll go on a shopping spree in Canterbury. I'll make sure she's totally spoiled. Maybe we'll even fit in a visit to the animal rescue centre to look for a puppy. She's been nagging us for months about getting a dog.

'Why did Daddy tie up your arms and put that thing in your mouth?' she asks, as if she's only just noticed. Hopefully, it's a sign the drugs are wearing off.

'I don't know, sweetheart. I think he's playing a game, that's all.'

'It's not a very nice game.'

'No, it isn't.'

I try to take her mind off the awfulness of our predicament by reciting pop songs we used to sing along to in the car.

She giggles as I deliberately mess up the lyrics to her favourite Taylor Swift song and when she tries to correct me, I remain adamant Taylor was singing about Starbucks lovers rather than her long list of ex-lovers, which only makes her laugh more.

I've missed Annie's laughter so much. If only I could bottle it up and keep it.

'When are we going home?' she asks, as we finally fall into silence, Annie still nuzzled into my neck.

'Soon, baby girl. Soon.'

We stay snuggled up together for a while, cosy in each other's warmth, even though all my joints and muscles are screaming in agony, until there's another thud against the hull outside and footsteps on the deck.

Annie sits up, stiffening.

The hatch rattles open and sunlight, defused green from a canvas awning above, spills into the cabin.

Kit clumps down the steps and I'm about to yell at him to let us go, when I notice he's not alone.

There's someone descending the steps behind him. Someone in a suit and tie and polished shoes. His clothes look totally out of place on the filthy abandoned yacht.

'What are you doing here?' I gasp as his face comes into view.

'Hello, Aunty Cath,' Yannick says with a sickly grin.

Chapter 41

I shake my head in disbelief. 'What did you bring him for?' I glance at my husband, who's standing with his brow creased.

'What were you thinking, Uncle Kit?' Yannick asks, coming closer and staring at me like I'm an exhibit at the zoo, his hands casually shoved in his pockets.

'I told you, she didn't give me any choice.'

'I know, but we're not barbarians. You didn't have to tie her up. Let her loose,' Yannick says.

'Fine.' Kit roughly turns me around and unpicks the bonds around my wrists.

I rub the feeling back into my skin and flex my shoulders as he coils the rope in a loop and stuffs it in his pocket. Then he works on freeing my ankles.

I should be grateful, but I'm not. I'm seething. It's all I can do to stop myself launching at Kit with my fists flying. But what good's that going to do? Instead, I grab Annie and wrap my arms around her, savouring the feel of her slight body against mine. The smell of her hair. The warmth of her. And I squeeze hard, like I'm never going to let her go.

With my head resting on the top of her head, I scowl at Yannick. 'Do you want to tell me what the hell's going on?' I scream.

He ignores me. 'What are you going to do now?'

Kit shrugs. 'I was hoping you'd have some ideas.'

Yannick tuts. 'Hey, Annie. You look tired.'

She turns her head away from him, like she's embarrassed. I'm not surprised. Yannick's never had much to do with his cousin.

'Hey, poppet,' Kit says, crouching to Annie's level. 'How are you feeling now?'

It gives me a frisson of satisfaction that she recoils from him, burying her face into my shoulder, hugging me tighter.

'Will somebody please tell me what the fuck is going on?' I say, before I can catch myself.

Annie's eyes widen with shock.

Oh well, I'm sure she's heard worse at school and frankly, it's not the time to be watching my mouth. I want answers. And I want them now.

'Shall I tell her, or do you want to?' Yannick says to Kit with a smirk.

'Yannick knows everything,' Kit says.

'You told him? You idiot. He's a journalist, in case you hadn't noticed.'

'I mean, he's known from the beginning.'

Yannick makes a stage cough, covering his mouth with the side of his fist. 'A bit more credit, please, Uncle Kit. It was all *my* idea.'

Kit shoots him a censorious look.

'Keep talking,' I say, fixing my husband with my sternest stare.

'I confided in Yannick about the charity and the money that had gone missing,' he says.

'That you stole,' I correct him. It's news to me they've even kept in touch. I haven't heard from Yannick in months, and even then it was only a belated birthday card.

Kit stares at the floor, drawing circles in the dust with his toe. He doesn't even have the balls to look me in the eye. 'I was desperate, and I thought he might have an idea how I could handle things,' he says. 'He suggested we could fabricate the story that Annie had gone missing.'

'Why didn't you tell me it was his idea?' I say.

'I thought you'd be angry.'

'Of course I'd have been angry. You know what he's like. He could have sold us out at any minute. And that's why I wouldn't have agreed to it.'

'I had his word,' Kit says. 'He agreed he'd keep my secret if we gave him an exclusive interview.'

I might have known. Yannick has never done anything for anybody unless it feathered his own bed.

'To further your own career, in other words,' I say. Yannick's standing with his arms crossed, watching me with a sneer painted across his smug face. 'That's pretty low, even by your standards.'

He puts a hand to his heart and feigns a wounded look. 'Don't say that, Aunty Cath. I was doing you both a favour. And besides, it's a win-win. You get the reward money and I finally get the credit I deserve. And who knows, a cosy show of my own on the network? At the very least, a reporting gig on the national news.'

'So what now? You've kept us both imprisoned here. What next? Are you going to let us go?'

Yannick sucks on his bottom lip. 'You're right. This is a bit of a pickle, isn't it?' He paces the length of the cabin, inspecting the woodwork like he's looking around with a view to buying the boat. 'The problem is, if we let you go, how can we trust you not to go running off to the police?'

'I guess you can't, but I *am* family. Families are supposed to trust each other, aren't they?' It's the only thing I can think to say. Not that Yannick has ever been remotely interested in the sanctity of family, although it's hardly a surprise. Our family fell apart after my father's death. And then, of course, he lost his mother, Monica, my sister, to cancer when he was still young.

'Hmmmm.' He runs his forefinger over his top lip in thought. 'The thing is, I still need my happily-ever-after story. You've kind of screwed that up for me, Aunty Cath.'

'What are you talking about?'

'I need Annie to be found safe and well and reunited with her family. It's what everyone's hoping to see. I was supposed to get the exclusive interview with the three of you together again.'

'You can still have it,' I gasp. 'Nothing's changed. We can say we had an anonymous tip that Annie was being held here on this boat.'

Yannick shakes his head. 'Kit heard you on the phone to the police,' he says.

'I didn't tell them anything. I swear to you.'

He grimaces. 'I wish I could believe you, Aunty Cath. I really do.' He breathes in through his nose, holds it for a second and lets it out slowly. 'You know, none of us would be here right now if only you'd stuck to your end of the deal.'

'What deal?' I ask, confused.

'The deal I agreed with Uncle Kit for exclusivity. Why did you have to sell out to that stupid tabloid reporter and cut me out?'

'Delores? We had no choice,' I say. 'We had to speak to her, or they wouldn't have put up the reward.'

'No, you didn't.' Yannick rolls his eyes. 'You still don't get it, do you? This was never about the money.'

'Yannick, don't,' Kit growls.

'What? Don't you think she deserves the truth?' There's a wicked glint in Yannick's eyes.

'What's going on?' I stare at Kit, trying to read him, trying to work out what he's hiding from me. Is this just

Yannick mischief making or is there something else going on here they're keeping from me?

'I'm warning you.' Kit clenches his fists and turns on Yannick, his eyes narrowing.

'What truth?' I press, confused.

'Shall I tell her?' Yannick smirks again. 'Don't you think she has a right to know after everything you've put her through?'

Kit throws himself across the cabin at Yannick with such sheer force that I let out a small yelp of alarm. His hands wrap around Yannick's throat, his face flushing with anger. Annie screams and buries her head into me as the two men tumble onto the dusty floor.

It's the most unlikely fight I've ever seen. I don't think either of them has ever been in a scrap in their lives, but they're both going for it like they want to kill each other, arms and fists flying, Kit now sitting astride Yannick's chest.

With a snarl of anger, Kit punches Yannick in the side of the head with a sickening whack.

I glance at the open hatch and clutch Annie's hand. This could be our opportunity to escape.

'Come on,' I whisper in her ear, standing awkwardly, my aching muscles protesting. We might not get another chance.

As my husband and nephew continue to grapple on the floor, I guide Annie up the steps, urging her to hurry. The boat trembles as Yannick throws Kit off and he lands heavily on the floor.

I follow Annie out onto the upper deck to find the boat is tented under green canvas, protecting it from the elements and prying eyes. It flaps and flutters noisily with every puff of wind, while dangerous tendrils of dirty rope criss-cross the deck.

With one final look back, I haul myself out of the cabin and into a sunken cockpit dominated by a huge metallic helm wheel. Peering over the side, I see the boat is propped up on metal supports. It's at least the height of two double-decker buses to the scrubby earth below us. It's the first sense I've had of how high up we are. The ground looks a dizzying distance below. My balance falters as my stomach shrinks up into my body.

Oh god.

The only safe way down is by an aluminium ladder that's been strapped to the side of the hull. An old, rickety, unstable ladder.

I think I'm going to be sick. It's the only way to safety, but I'm not sure I can do it. It's such a long way down. What if I fell?

I can't think like that. I have to put my own fears aside for my daughter.

My whole body is slick with a nervous sweat as I take Annie by the shoulders and kneel at her level to look directly into her eyes. What I'm about to say is asking so much of her, but I'm desperate.

'Listen, sweetheart,' I say. 'We need to climb down that ladder, okay? I want you to go first. I know it looks like a long way down, but if you hold on tight and don't look down, you'll be fine.'

I have no idea how *she* is with heights, whether she's inherited my fears, but from the way she's gone quiet and is tugging at her bottom lip, it's obvious she's terrified. But she doesn't complain. She looks down at her feet and nods. Such a brave little girl.

Below deck, there's a loud crash and Kit howls in pain.

'Go down backwards,' I instruct Annie as I guide her under a wire guardrail, gripping her wrists tightly, trying not to think about my own rising sense of panic at being so close to the edge.

Her feet find the top rung, and she descends slowly. It's such a long way down, it makes my stomach lurch. If she was to slip and fall...

I push the thought from my mind. God knows how Kit got us both up here.

Annie's halfway down, but she's moving so slowly. Her knuckles are white, and her breathing is fast and laboured. I want to urge her to hurry, but I don't want to pressure her into making a mistake. And the ladder looks so flimsy, I can't risk starting my own descent until she's safely down. Apart from anything else, I don't trust myself not to fall.

I glance over my shoulder, back towards the sunken cockpit, half expecting to see Kit or Yannick appear, coming for us. Maybe I should try to lock them in the cabin to buy us some more time?

'Mummy!' Annie screams.

I glance back down the ladder and my heart skips a beat. Her feet have slipped off a rung and she's clinging on by her fingertips, looking up at me with wide, innocent eyes filled with fear.

'It's okay, honey, you're doing really well. Just go slowly.' I clasp a hand to my chest, a cold spear of adrenaline running through my body.

Her feet paddle furiously in the air until she finally finds her footing.

I breathe again. After everything we've put her through, it would be beyond horrific if she fell and injured herself now.

She's nearly at the bottom.

Just a few more rungs.

I stand and flex my shoulders, getting ready to follow her the moment she's safely on the ground.

I can do this.

It's a mantra I repeat over and over in my head, willing my body to overcome the part of my brain that tells me I can't. That I'm going to fall. Plunge to the ground helplessly and die.

I don't know where this fear has come from, but I've had it for as long as I can remember. I'm okay in a plane, or at the top of a tower block, as long as I'm inside or behind glass. But I can't face going anywhere I might actually fall, which is why I've always gone out of my way to avoid heights.

But now I must conquer my fears or stay frozen where I am and deal with Kit and Yannick.

'Mum, I'm down,' Annie shouts up. 'Come on, your turn.'

I don't know if I can.

But I can't stay here.

I peer over the side and down the ladder, my head somersaulting. The ladder really doesn't look that safe. I know it's been tied to the guardrail struts, but what if they snap? What if the ladder slips while I'm halfway down? What if my grip loosens and I can't hold on?

This isn't helping.

If Annie can do it, so can I.

Don't look down and take it slow.

Come on, Cathy. Don't be a baby. You can do this.

I make the mistake of glancing one last time at the cockpit and hatch, and spot Kit emerging from the innards of the boat, his hair dishevelled. He has a red, puffy mark on the side of his face. He snarls at me, a fury behind his eyes. The monster showing his true skin. How could I ever have loved this man? I don't recognise him anymore. And I want to be as far away from him as possible.

I edge towards the ladder, my legs pressed up against the wire guardrail, and I'm hit by a vertigo head-flip.

'Where do you think you're going?' Kit barks at me.

'Stay away from me.' I hold up a hand towards him, urging him to back off. 'I'm warning you.'

I cast a glance backwards. Annie's peering up at me, waving for me to come down.

'Mum, come on, hurry,' she calls.

What a choice. Facing my vertiginous fears or my insane husband.

But before I can decide, Kit lunges at me, grasping for my arms. I scream, feeling my balance teeter.

'Mummy!' Annie wails from below.

Kit has me by the wrists, grasping me tightly. A death grip.

'Let me go!' I yell in his face.

'I can't let you go. You know that,' he says, hauling me away from the edge, towards the cockpit.

I can't pull away from him, because if he lets go, I'll surely tumble backwards over the side. So I do the opposite, hoping to catch him by surprise, and throw myself at him, pushing *him* back.

It works.

He loses his footing and stumbles, dragging me down, and we land in a heap of arms and legs on top of each other.

But if I thought it would give me the advantage, I'm wrong. He howls with rage, throws me off and pulls me up again by the wrists.

'Ow, you're hurting me,' I complain.

The look on his face is one of the most horrifying things I've ever seen, the way his lips are twisted in anger, his eyes wide and black and full of poison. This is the man I supposedly fell in love with all those years ago. Who I used to call my husband. The father of my daughter. But he's unrecognisable to me now.

'You stupid bitch,' he spits in my face. 'Why couldn't you just go along with the plan and keep your dumb mouth shut?'

I'm stunned by the brutality of his language. He's never called me that before. I wouldn't have stood for it, especially not in front of Annie. I hope she's not heard. I'd never want her to think it was acceptable for any man to talk to a woman that way, let alone a husband to his wife.

'Annie! Run!' I shout. 'Go and get help!'

'What are you doing? Annie, darling, stay there!' he calls down to her, his tone softening in an instant, turning on the charm.

'Just go,' I scream.

She hesitates for a second, her face veiled in incomprehension. Kit and I rarely argued in the past, so this must be so hard for her to witness. But she knows what he's done and now she can see what he's really like.

'Mummy?' she calls, as if she's seeking reassurance.

'Annie, you have to run and get help. Please, darling. Go.'

'Annie, sweetie, come back here,' Kit shouts, pulling me out of Annie's view. 'Come up and see Daddy. Mummy's just being silly.'

There's a moment of silence. And then I hear Annie running away, her feet pounding across the hard ground.

'Annie! Get back here now!' The real Kit's back, his charm evaporating.

Good girl. I knew she'd listen to me over him. She can see him for what he really is as clearly as I can. It's his own fault, talking to me like that, like I'm worthless, in front of her.

He roars with anger and frustration, but as he raises a hand to hit me, a noise over his shoulder makes us both turn and look.

Yannick's hauling himself out of the hatch from the cabin and onto the deck. He looks dazed. His lower lip is swelling and a thin trail of blood is running down his chin. One of the arms of his jacket has been partially ripped away from its dust-encrusted body and his tie is twisted and loose. As he straightens up, he brushes a hand through his hair. So typical of Yannick to be thinking about his appearance even now.

'Leave her alone,' he says, his words slurring. I wonder if he's lost a tooth.

'This has got nothing to do with you.' Kit's grip on my wrists loosens a fraction as his attention is distracted.

'It's not going to do either of us any good if you end up killing her.'

Killing me? What the fuck?

'She's my wife. I'll deal with her in my own way,' Kit yells.

'You didn't do a great job dealing with it when she had to keep her mouth shut, though, did you?'

'I never wanted any of this, you know,' Kit says, letting go of one of my wrists to gesticulate at Yannick.

He's shaking with rage. My own legs are wobbling too, but because I'm afraid. Not of falling off the side anymore, but of what Kit is capable of doing.

I wrench my arm out of his grasp and stagger back, snatching the guardrail for balance as I almost topple over, sending my heart rate racing.

'It's too late for regrets. You've made your bed,' Yannick says.

'You forced me into it. What choice did I have?'

'I didn't force you into anything. I made a suggestion and you bit off my hand. You're the only one to blame for this,' Yannick says, moving closer until the two men are squaring up to each other again.

I back away, scurrying along the deck, giving them space.

'You're a tawdry, manipulative wannabe whose life amounts to nothing,' Kit hisses at him. 'And you hate that truth more than anything in this world. You're self-centred, self-obsessed and cruel. You use people, even your own family, and then discard them to get your own way. You're sick.'

'Ha! That's rich,' Yannick says. 'Let me remind you that you're the one who faked his own daughter's disappearance.'

'Because you made me! You trample over people and don't care who gets hurt, as long as Yannick comes out looking good.'

'At least I accept what I am. What about you? We both know what you are, but you can't even admit it to yourself. And you're so worried about anybody finding out, you were even prepared to put your own daughter's life at risk.'

'Shut the fuck up.'

'Shall we tell Aunt Cathy what this has really all been about?'

'Don't you dare,' Kit screams. 'I did what you asked. It's not my fault you screwed it up, you talentless piece of shit.'

Yannick throws his head back and laughs like the devil.

Kit flings himself at him again, his thumbs going for Yannick's eyes. I can hardly bear to watch.

'Stop it!' I yell.

Yannick thrusts out both arms to push Kit away and his hands strike him squarely in the chest. I watch my husband's shocked reaction in slow motion as his eyes open wide and his jaw falls loose. His arms fly up as his body pivots backwards, desperately trying to catch his balance as his legs tangle in the wire guardrail pressed against his calves.

And suddenly he's tumbling over the side.

Falling.
Flailing.
Screaming in terror.
And in a split second, it's all over.

Chapter 42

The silence is broken only by the fluttering green canvas over our heads and the tinkle of mastheads and rigging. I crawl across the deck towards Yannick and we peer over the edge of the hull at where Kit landed with an ominous thud, one leg buckled under his body and his arms outstretched. His head is twisted to one side and his lifeless eyes stare into space as a spreading pool of blood seeps into the earth.

Should I be grateful he's dead? Sad? Angry?

All I feel is shocked and numb. My brain can't process what I've just witnessed.

'You killed him,' I say.

Yannick stands eerily still.

'I didn't mean to,' he mumbles. 'You saw. It was an accident.'

He turns on me suddenly, grabbing my shoulders, his face that of a frightened little boy. I've never seen this vulnerable side of him before.

'Give me your phone,' I say gently, holding out my hand. 'I'll call the police.'

'What?' He jumps back like he's been bitten, his face clouding with alarm.

'I'll tell them it was an accident,' I say.

'No,' he gasps. 'I need to think.'

He slaps a hand to his forehead and turns away, walking to the end of the deck and back.

'Come on, Yannick. Kit's dead. Just give me your phone.'

'I can't trust you. You'll tell them it was all my idea to make Annie vanish and that I murdered Uncle Kit,' he says.

'Of course I won't.'

'You promised you wouldn't call the police, but you did,' he says, regaining his composure, the old Yannick back again. 'That's what got you into this mess in the first place. You were given a plan and you couldn't follow it. I have a better idea.'

'This has gone far enough. No more games. No more lies,' I say, my pulse racing. I don't like that frantic look in his eye.

'Imagine this,' he says, holding up a hand, like he's a film director painting a vision of his next great movie to a young starlet. 'I had a tip-off that you'd faked Annie's disappearance for the reward money and you and Uncle Kit were hiding her on this boat.' He casts a glance at me to make sure I'm listening. 'But when I arrived, I found you'd got cold feet and had threatened to call the police.'

'Right,' I say, frowning, not sure where he's going with this.

'And in his panic, Kit killed you. When I got here, I found him with your body. We fought on the deck as I tried to save Annie, and he fell to his death. What do you think?' He smirks at me.

'You're kidding, right?'

'Absolutely not. The more I think about it, it's perfect. And what a story it's going to make.' He slaps a hand on my arm. 'Even better, I can give a firsthand account of how I rescued Annie from the clutches of her evil parents.'

'You're insane,' I gulp. The ladder down to the ground is a short distance to my left. How quickly can I make it down? My head swims and my stomach sucks in on itself. 'And how are you going to explain that I'm not dead?'

The cold, calculated look he shoots me makes my blood turn to ice. 'I'll make it painless,' he says.

'What?' My breath catches in my throat. He can't be serious.

'It's for the best,' he says, so calm and collected. I've always known Yannick was self-obsessed, narcissistic and had an ego the size of Africa, but I never had him pegged as a psychopath. He's out of his mind. 'You saw how easily Kit fell.'

He moves towards me menacingly. I back away, but there's nowhere to run and I can't fight him. He's taller than me. Stronger than me. I'd likely end up going over the edge of the deck anyway. My only option is to talk him out of this nonsense.

'You're not a killer, Yannick.'

One of his eyebrows shoots up. 'Blair Black died because of me. What's another body?'

'Please, I'm the only family you have. You can't kill me.'
'Why not?'

I've edged as far as I can along the deck and now I'm at the bow with a long, terrifying drop behind and beside me. My whole body is trembling with fear. But I'm not ready to die.

'They'll work out what you've done and you'll go to prison for a long time,' I say.

'But you've left me no choice. You understand, don't you?' He looms in front of me, another monster in my life crawling out from under a rock.

'What about Annie?' I wail. 'She's lost her father. Don't let her lose her mother too.'

'She'll survive,' he says. 'She's only a kid.'

'No... no, wait!' I gasp, my mind racing. I have to think of something. And fast. 'I'll take the blame for Kit's death. I'll say it was *me* who pushed him.'

Yannick stops advancing towards me and cocks his head to one side, his eyes narrowing. My chest is so tight, it's as if I'm drawing in air through a straw.

But I can see he's intrigued. He's like a fish on a hook. He doesn't want to risk a murder charge. Now, if only I can reel him in.

'Go on,' he says.

'If you try to stage my death, there's every chance the police will work out the truth,' I say. My mind is churning like a steam train, working through the logic. 'But what if I tell them I found out that Kit had staged Annie's abduction and discovered them here together on the boat? That's much more plausible. I could tell them we argued and when I threatened to call the police, he turned on me, we fought and he fell.'

Yannick nods sagely. 'Keep going.'

'And then, in a panic, I called you. I mean, who else would I call? You came straight over and found me distraught.'

I hope he doesn't remember Annie witnessed everything and could blow a hole a mile wide in the story.

'Yes, that could work,' he says.

'And you'll still get your story. I won't speak to anyone else. Only you.'

'What about that woman from *The Post*?'

'I'll tell her I've changed my mind. Our deal's off. I'm only talking to you.'

The outline of a smile forms on Yannick's face. He's already planning ahead, thinking about how it's going to look for him.

'Yes, this is perfect. Annie's father dead, exposed as her abductor and a full confession with you is going to be gold dust,' he says.

'You'll be the only one with the full story,' I add, cementing the idea in his head. 'Everyone will be talking about it.'

The outline of his smile has become a full-blown beam. He's grinning from ear to ear, his eyes sparkling with excitement. 'And I bet I can persuade them to give me an hour's national prime-time slot. This is so good, Aunty Cath. So good.'

'Better than murdering me, right?' I ask, just to make sure.

He starts to laugh. But his mirth stops as suddenly as it began as a new thought occurs to him. 'I can trust you, can't I, Aunty Cath?'

'Of course you can, Yannick. And the best part is that most of the story is true. I'll be confessing to killing my husband because he conspired to kidnap our daughter, which is exactly what happened, although I wish I'd never gone along with Kit's stupid plan in the first place.'

'My plan,' Yannick corrects me.

'Whatever. Now, why don't you make that call to the police?'

It's finally time to face the music. What I did was unforgivable. I deserve whatever I have coming. And that starts with a full confession to the police. It's the only way I'm ever going to be able to look myself in the mirror again.

Yannick pulls out his phone from his jacket and stabs at the keypad. 'Police, please,' he says.

I stand by his side, shivering, as he gives the details, explains what's happened and tells them where to find us.

'We'd better get you cleaned up before the police get here,' I say as he hangs up. I wipe the blood from his chin with my thumb. 'We wouldn't want them asking awkward questions about why you're bleeding.'

'Good point.' Yannick slips off his damaged jacket, removes his tie, and dusts off his trousers. There's not much he can do about his swelling lip, but that's his problem. He'll have to come up with his own explanation.

Then we sit in the cockpit by the enormous silver wheel while we wait for the police to arrive. Maybe Annie's already raised the alarm. But wherever she is, hopefully she's finally safe.

'Will you still remember me when you're famous?' I ask.

I never want to see Yannick again after today, but it feels important to keep him talking so he doesn't change his mind about me or remember that Annie is a problematic factor in the story we've agreed to spin.

'You'll be famous too,' he says.

I laugh with him to humour him, even though I feel like crying. I've saved my life by sacrificing my future, but I guess that was written in the stars when I went along with Kit's crazy idea in the first place. I always thought I was a good mother, but how could I have so easily been talked into doing something so criminally stupid? And it doesn't even end here. I'm going to prison for what I've done. There's no doubt about that. For how long, I'm not sure. Long enough that I'll miss the best years of Annie growing up, no doubt. And when I get out? Will she still want anything to do with me? Will they take her into care? God, how I wish I could turn back the clock and make different choices.

Above our heads, the green tarpaulin flaps noisily in the breeze. It won't be long before the police are here and the resulting mayhem begins. But there's a question on my mind that's still bothering me. It was something Yannick said to Kit. I had the distinct impression they were keeping something from me.

'There's one other thing before the police get here,' I say. 'You said earlier this hadn't all been about the money. I don't understand. What did you mean?'

Yannick snickers. 'You still don't know, do you? Everything, all of this, was one big lie,' he says cryptically. 'Kit wasn't caught stealing money from the charity.'

'What are you talking about? Of course he was.'

'No, he made it all up.'

I shake my head. Just as I thought everything was becoming clear, I realise I'm still in the dark. What other secrets was Kit keeping from me?

'Why would he do that?' I gasp.

'You really want to know?'

'Yes. I *have* to know.'

'Fine. Well, like I said, there was no missing money. Kit's been lying to you all this time, in more ways than one.'

Chapter 43

Every word cuts likes a knife, peeling away the layers of lies and secrets until I don't know what to believe anymore. At first, I don't believe any of it, because that would mean I've so badly misjudged my husband - even the word sticks in my throat now - that it's a reflection of my own character.

'It's not true,' I gasp. 'How could you say such a thing?'

It's so appalling, I can't get my head around it. I would have known, surely? A wife would see the signs. Was this why his first marriage had ended so sourly? Had his first wife found out? Kit never talked about why the relationship broke down and I never asked. I was in the first flush of love and couldn't bear to think about him being with anyone else, so it was easier to pretend his first wife didn't exist.

'Don't believe me if you don't want to,' Yannick says. 'I don't care. I'm only telling you because you asked.'

'Why didn't you tell me?' Nausea rolls around my stomach like I've swallowed a gallon of poison. But the only poison is in my head.

He shrugs. 'You know why.'

'Because you were blackmailing him.'

Yannick winces. 'That's a strong word. I promised to protect his secret, that's all.'

'In return for what?' But I suspect I already know. 'Has this just been about furthering your career?'

'You don't know what it's like, Aunty Cath. I'm good at my job. Bloody good, but I just wasn't getting the breaks. I'm fed up reading the news in the regions on the graveyard shift. I needed a story to help me stand out.'

'So you used us?'

'Nobody was meant to get hurt,' he says.

The image of Kit lying broken and twisted in a pool of his own blood on the ground below us flashes through my mind. I squeeze my eyes closed, trying to shut it out, but it's something that's always going to haunt me. There are simply some things you can't unsee.

And then there was Blair Black, unfairly victimised and brutally murdered on his own doorstep when he had nothing to do with Annie's disappearance. And Annie herself. Who knows how damaged she's going to be by all of this.

'Why did you point the finger at that guy on the estate when you knew it had nothing to do with him?'

Yannick sighs. 'I needed an angle. The story was getting away from me and my boss was piling on the pressure. I never thought anyone would do anything about it. It's not my fault.'

'It kind of is, Yannick. It's entirely your fault.'

He shrugs like he doesn't care. 'I'll admit, things haven't exactly gone to plan, but with your interview on camera, it's salvageable.'

Even now, with two dead bodies, he's still thinking about himself. I've never known anyone so cold. His mother would be mortified, I'm sure. Monica never brought him up to be so uncaring. Maybe it was because he never knew his father. Or that his mother died at such a tragically young age. Is that why he's become such a cold-hearted adult, in desperate need of recognition and praise? Did Monica not love him enough? Did she make a mistake bringing him up as a single parent? Or does this go further back to *my* father's death? Maybe it sat heavily with Monica too and somehow that filtered through to Yannick. But I'm no psychologist. I guess I'll never know for sure.

'And the theft from the charity. Whose idea was that?' I ask.

'Uncle Kit needed to persuade you to agree to his plan. It was his idea to tell you he'd been caught with his hand in the jar at work.'

The first sirens sound in the distance. We don't have long. I've already made up my mind to tell the police exactly what happened from the moment Kit first told me he was in trouble and proposed the sham abduction. I'll tell them Yannick was involved from the start and how he was blackmailing Kit, and that I foolishly went along with it all. Let them throw the book at me.

I draw in a deep breath, savouring the salty tang of the marsh air. It's going to be a while until I get to experience it again, so I try to memorise it. I imagine the smells inside a women's prison are quite different.

I don't relish going to jail. I don't even know how I'm going to cope. I've heard all the horror stories, the bullying and the violence. The constant threats and mind-numbing boredom, but I know it's what I have to do to make my peace. To pay my penance. To find forgiveness for what I've done.

I'm under no illusions. People hate women like me. Mothers who abuse their own children. But I didn't abuse Annie. She was always safe and well looked after. I love her more than life itself and would never knowingly harm her, but I doubt other people will see it like that.

The sirens draw closer, filling the silence that's settled between us. The first vehicles arrive, crunching across gravel and skidding to a halt.

Car doors open.

Feet thud across open ground.

Babbling on radios.

Orders being given.

I stand up and turn towards the ladder as I hear someone climbing up. An athletic-looking officer in short sleeves and body armour steps on board with a grunt.

'She did it, officer,' Yannick wails, turning on the emotion like a tap. 'She pushed him! And now he's dead.'

My mouth opens instinctively to deny it. But I clamp it closed again. I'm not saying anything in front of Yannick.

'I came straight over when she called me, but my uncle... ' Yannick's knees buckle as he feigns being overwhelmed with grief. 'Uncle Kit was already dead. There was nothing I could do.'

The officer frowns. 'It's alright, sir. Let's get you off the boat, shall we?'

Behind him, a female officer appears. She's small but tough-looking. She climbs onto the deck and snatches a pair of handcuffs from her belt as she stares at me like I'm a filthy, common criminal. She tells me I'm to be arrested.

'I won't be able to get down the ladder with cuffs on,' I say, my heart pattering fast. With my vertigo, it's going to be a challenge getting down full stop.

The male officer escorts Yannick off the boat first and when he's out of the way, the female officer tells me to follow while she watches from above.

It takes me a full five minutes, tentatively taking one step at a time, even though they've put a harness on me so there's no way I can fall.

When I finally reach the ground, Kit's body has been covered by a sheet, but a snaking trail of his blood is still visible, seeping into the mud.

I blink at the number of police cars and ambulances that have gathered amongst the rows of old tugboats, longboats and yachts in the yard, all awash with pulsing blue lights. The female officer who escorted me off the boat grabs my wrists roughly and pulls them behind my back. My aching shoulders protest but I'm in no position to resist.

'Mrs Warren.' I look up at the sound of a familiar voice. DS Monkton, the detective who's been leading the investigation into Annie's disappearance, is striding towards me, his grey overcoat flapping. 'I'm arresting you on suspicion of the kidnap and false imprisonment of Annie Warren and the murder of Kit Warren. You do not have to say anything, but it may harm your defence if you do not mention, when questioned, something you later rely on in court. Anything you do say may be used in evidence. Do you understand?'

I nod.

He stands with his hands on his hips, looking at me like I'm dirt. I can almost see the headlines now, "Britain's worst mother?"

'Take her away,' he says with contempt.

'Wait,' I say as the female officer shoves me towards a waiting police car. 'Have you found Annie?'

Monkton rubs his nose. 'She's safe,' he says. 'No thanks to you.'

Chapter 44

The side of my head bumps against the cold glass with every jolt in the road, but I don't feel it. I don't feel anything. My body is as numb as my mind while hedges and trees, houses and cars flash past.

A gate slides open, and the patrol car slips inside a compound. I guess we're at the police station. I wouldn't know. This is all alien to me.

The car pulls up. The door is thrown open and I'm told to get out. I keep my head down and my eyes on the ground, watching my shuffling feet as they march me into a windowless building.

I wish they'd given me some shoes.

An older officer behind a tall counter takes my details. My name. My age. My date of birth. Asks me about my health. It's all very official.

Then they put me in a cell which is nothing more than a narrow room with painted walls. A toilet and a basin recessed into the wall. A low, flat bench that doubles up as a bed with a blue plastic mattress. I wince as a heavy metal door slams shut, sealing me inside. How long is it going to take to get used to that sound and the overpowering stench of bleach?

Time ceases to have any meaning as I wait for what happens next. But it's not like I have anywhere to be. It gives me time to think.

I think mostly about Annie, and whether she's being looked after well. At least before I knew she was with Jake. What do they even do with kids when their parents have been arrested and there are no other family members around? I mean, there's Yannick, of course, but there's no way he's going to agree to take her. Or at least, I hope he doesn't. I couldn't stand the thought that she was with him.

I suppose that's what social services' emergency care is for. Not that I have any idea how it works. Do they send the kids off to a foster family? Or is there a big children's home they get swallowed up into, like being sent off to boarding school?

My poor Annie. It's going to be horrible for her. She won't have any idea what's going on and I don't suppose they'll tell her what's happening to me either. She's the innocent victim in all of this, and yet she's being punished for my crimes.

When they send me to prison, what's going to happen then? And afterwards, when I've served my sentence, will she be able to come home with me? Or will they make a court order removing my parental rights? That would be the worst punishment.

When I'm finally marched into an interview room, DS Monkton is waiting for me on the opposite side of a table with a woman I don't know. A more senior officer, he tells me, but whose name I instantly forget. She sits at Monkton's side and lets him do the talking while she watches me, taking notes.

First, they remind me of my rights and that I'm entitled to a lawyer. I don't want or need a lawyer. I've already told the custody sergeant. It's only going to slow things down, and I want this over as quickly as possible. I'll tell them everything they want to know. The worst that could happen is the investigation is strung out. The sooner we get to court the better. I just want to begin my punishment.

'You understand the seriousness of the charges, Mrs Warren?' Monkton asks, leaning across the table. My gaze is drawn to the razor rash around his throat, all those little hair follicles angry and inflamed.

'Yes.'

'Shall we start with what happened to Annie?' he asks. 'You made a 999 call on Monday at seven-o-five pm claiming your daughter, Annie Warren, had gone missing. You subsequently claimed to officers that you thought she'd been abducted. But that was a pack of lies, wasn't it? The truth is, you'd removed your daughter from the house yourself.'

'Yes.'

'Can you speak up for the recording, please?'

I clear my throat and push my hair out of my eyes. 'Yes,' I repeat, louder.

'And for what motive? Money?'

'At first, yes. It was my husband Kit's idea. He told me he'd been caught stealing from the charity where he works and needed to pay the money back or they were going to press charges,' I explain. 'He thought we'd be able to claim any reward for Annie's return the papers put up.'

Monkton's eyebrow arches. 'How was that going to work, exactly?'

'We were going to arrange for Annie to be found by a friend and we'd split the cash.'

'What friend?'

I'd promised myself to tell the truth, but I don't want Jake dragged into this. He only agreed to help because he saw how desperate I was. It wouldn't be fair if he was punished.

'I don't know. We hadn't got that far,' I say.

'And where did you take Annie? To the boatyard?'

'Yes,' I lie. It's another half-truth to protect Jake. 'Kit found the boat a few weeks ago. It's being refurbished, but the owner's abroad.'

'So you admit you and your husband kidnapped your own daughter and falsely imprisoned her?'

'Yes,' I say, hanging my head. 'I'm guilty of everything.'

As unbelievable as it seems now, we actually let Annie walk home from school as normal the day she went missing. She took the exact same route past the church and the factory by the creek as she did every day. But not a single person noticed. Why? Because there was nothing to see. Nothing out of the ordinary. Just a little girl walking home from school.

There was no white van pulling up silently behind her. No men dragging her inside. No screams for help. No struggle. She simply let herself into the house through the back garden. The same as she always did.

When I told her she was going on an adventure to stay with my friend, Jake, she didn't want to go, of course, which is why I had to drug her. It was as I was crumbling one of those old sea sickness tablets into her mashed potato that I had my first pang of doubt. She was only ten. I wasn't even sure if you could overdose on sea sickness medication or whether they would have any lasting effects.

Following the plan we'd agreed, I called Kit at around four thirty. He'd gone to work as usual to avoid raising suspicion and had slipped outside to take my call.

'If you follow the plan, nothing can go wrong. It'll only be for a few days. A week at most and then we can go back to normal,' he promised me.

He never mentioned that we'd need to put on a show for the press until it was too late, and I was left with no choice. We were an upstanding, respectable family, he said. The press would lap it up and be falling over themselves to offer a reward, he assured me.

Annie fell asleep on the sofa watching TV and wouldn't wake up even when I tried to rouse her. I called Jake and told him it was time. He came straight over, backed his van up to the rear gate and together we carried her out of the house.

There were so many flaws in the plan, I was amazed we got away with it. What if someone had remembered Annie walking home? Or seen her slip in through the back gate? What if someone remembered seeing Jake's van parked up at the the back of our house at the exact time Annie was supposed to have gone missing?

But they didn't. I suppose unless you give them a reason, most people don't notice the apparently ordinary things going on around them. We're all so focused on our own lives, our own worries, our own little problems, we're usually not paying attention to most other things happening on the fringes of our orbit.

Kit arrived home a little after five thirty and we set out together on our imaginary hunt for our daughter while Jake settled Annie into her temporary home in his loft.

At seven o'clock, back at the house, I took a moment to imagine what it would be like if Annie really had been abducted. My tears came remarkably easily. Kit handed me my phone and nodded at me to make the call.

The police were at the house within the hour and there was no going back. The first night was the worst. I didn't like that we had to keep her sedated, but I accepted it was a necessary evil. I grew into my role as the grieving mother, almost believing it at times. And actually, it wasn't difficult to appear convincing. I missed Annie so much. The house was desperately empty without her and when my tears came, they were genuine.

'This theft your husband was involved in - how much money had he taken?' Monkton asks.

'He hadn't.' I shake my head. 'It was a lie to pressure me into agreeing to his plan. He told me a trustee was onto him and that unless he paid the money back in full, they'd have to report it. But it wasn't true.'

'And why would he do that?' Monkton frowns. I'm not sure if he believes me, but it's the god's honest truth.

'It wasn't Kit's idea to kidnap Annie. It was my nephew, Yannick Kellor. He's a TV reporter. He was blackmailing my husband.'

Monkton sits back and throws a glance at the female detective whose perfectly shaped eyebrows shoot up. She nods at him to continue.

'Blackmail? That's a serious accusation.'

'Yannick had... some disturbing information.' A sick feeling swells in the pit of my stomach as I think about what Yannick told me. 'He told Kit that unless he went along with the abduction, he'd tell me everything. He was worried if it came out, it would be the end of our marriage, his career and his reputation. There might even be police charges.'

'And what was in it for Mr Kellor?'

I shrug. 'He knew it would be a huge story and I guess he wanted the kudos of reporting on it from the inside. Kit promised him an exclusive interview. Yannick seemed to think that would attract the attention of the network and, I don't know, they'd offer him a job or something.'

'You're telling me Mr Kellor facilitated this whole ruse purely for the sake of his career?'

'It escalated out of hand,' I say. 'No one was supposed to get hurt. Yannick spotted an opportunity and exploited it. That's my nephew for you. Have you spoken to him yet?'

'He says none of this had anything to do with him.'

'You need to speak to him again.'

'What information did your nephew have on your husband that he was using to blackmail him?' Monkton asks.

I chew my lip. I don't want to think about it, and I certainly don't want to repeat it, but I'm going to have to tell them. It's the reason for everything that's happened and why I'm facing a long jail sentence.

'Will I be able to see my daughter?' I ask.

'Not for a while,' Monkton says. 'Tell me what Mr Kellor knew about your husband.'

Monkton listens attentively as I detail what Yannick told me on the boat about the depravity of Kit's crimes.

'And you believe him?'

'I didn't want to. Of course I didn't, but it makes sense now. I guess you'll be checking with the charity? If they don't know anything about a theft, then what Yannick told me must be correct.'

'And how did you feel when your nephew dropped this bombshell?'

I wet my lips and look Monkton straight in the eye. 'It made me feel sick.'

'I see,' he says. 'And your husband's death? Tell me about that.'

'That wasn't me.'

'No?'

'That was Yannick.'

I tell him how I lost my nerve after Blair Black's death and was going to come clean to our liaison officer, Zara, and that Kit had caught me on the phone, attacked me and imprisoned me on the boat with Annie.

'I don't think he ever planned to hurt me, but he panicked. He didn't know what to do, so he called the only person he thought could help,' I say.

'Your nephew, Mr Kellor?'

'When he arrived, Yannick started taunting him. I didn't know about the blackmail at this point, but Yannick was threatening to tell me. That's when they got into a fight, and he pushed Kit off the boat.'

Monkton scratches the back of his neck and stares up at the ceiling. 'That's convenient.'

'Convenient?' It's not convenient in the slightest. Kit is the only other person who can verify he was being blackmailed. Without him, it's my word against Yannick's.

Monkton watches me closely, like he's peering through my skin and into my soul. It makes me shudder. 'Look at it from my perspective. You've just found out your husband isn't the man you thought he was. Maybe you argued. Maybe you didn't mean to kill him, but you pushed him, and he fell to his death.'

I shake my head. 'That's not what happened,' I say. I hold his gaze. It's vital he believes me. I'm not going to carry the can for my husband's death.

'Isn't it? You had the means, the motive and the opportunity, and we have a witness. Your nephew's testified that you killed your husband. And that it wasn't an accident.'

'It wasn't like that. Yannick pushed him.'

'But that doesn't make sense,' Monkton says. 'Why would he want your husband dead?'

'It was an accident, I told you. They were fighting.'

'I want to help you, Cathy, but I can't if you're going to keep lying to me,' Monkton says, leaning across the table and lowering his voice like he's my friend.

But I don't trust him.

'I'm telling you the truth,' I shout. 'I've admitted everything Kit and I did and how we planned Annie's abduction. I'm not proud of it, but I'm ready to accept my punishment. I'll plead guilty to it all. I'll walk you through every minute of it, but I'm not admitting to something I didn't do, and I didn't kill my husband.'

Maybe I should have asked for a lawyer after all.

Chapter 45

YANNICK

Gina is like a child in a chocolate factory when I call to tell her that not only has Annie been found safe and well, but that Cathy has been arrested on suspicion of the kidnapping, and Kit is dead.

'Are you serious?'

'I was there when the police arrested my aunt,' I say. 'They'll be releasing more details shortly, I should think.'

'This is brilliant. Where are you?'

'At home. I've just finished speaking to the police. Do you want me to come in?'

'No, stay there,' Gina says. 'And don't talk to anyone.'

When Annie went missing, it became a huge story, but this development is off the scale. There had been the usual conspiracy theories on crank websites suggesting Cathy and Kit were somehow involved in Annie's disappearance, but I don't think anyone could have predicted this outcome. It's the ending to the story I'd always planned on breaking myself, but technically I'm still suspended, so I don't have much choice than to watch from the sidelines, for the time being at least.

It's frustrating after all the effort I put into creating the story in the first place. It was my idea to fake Annie's abduction and to have her found alive and well several days later, after interest in the case had reached a fever pitch. My magnum opus. My passport to the big time.

But it's okay. No one else has the complete inside track. No one else is going to get the full confession from Cathy or be able to provide the eyewitness testimony I'm planning to give. I could even embellish it a little and reveal how I found my aunt about to take her own life and talked her out of it. I'll be a hero.

After taking a long, hot bath and changing into some clean clothes, I collapse on the sofa and start flicking through the rolling twenty-four news channels to see how it's all unfolding.

The police still haven't released much in the way of detail yet, other than issuing a brief statement confirming Annie has been found alive and well and taken into protective care. There's no word on Aunt Cathy or Uncle Kit, but all the stations are tentatively reporting rumours they were behind the plot to kidnap her, and some are even airing unconfirmed reports that Kit has died.

Some are saying it happened during an altercation when police confronted him, but the press is playing a guessing game, desperately trying to fill an information vacuum when there's no concrete information to go on. Only Cathy and I know what really happened, and all this speculation is only deepening the public's thirst for more. It's playing out perfectly for me. They'll be clamouring to hear the story I have to tell. And as much as I'd like to be in the thick of it, reporting on the latest developments, I can wait. It'll be worth it in the long run.

It's late afternoon and I'm still sprawled out on the sofa, dozing, when there's a knock at the door.

It's probably another courier wanting to leave a parcel for my neighbours. I even throw the door open and reach out my hand to take the package, but instead I find two uniformed police officers on the doorstep. I thought I'd finished with the police after I gave my statement.

'Yes?' I ask, both irritated and intrigued as to why they're here. Do they want me to clarify something I said earlier?

'Mr Yannick Kellor?' the taller of the pair says gruffly. It's apparent from his tone this isn't a social call. 'I'm arresting you on the suspicion of the murder of Kit Warren. You do not have to say anything – '

'Hang on. What?'

'I'm sorry, sir. You need to come with us.'

'I've not done anything.'

That stupid bitch has gone back on her word. She's told them I killed Kit, hasn't she? I knew I shouldn't have trusted her. I should have gone with my original plan and killed her when I had the chance.

'Please, sir, don't make this anymore difficult than it needs to be,' the officer says.

I can't afford to panic. I need to think. There's no evidence against me other than Cathy's word, and no one in their right mind is going to believe a thing she's said after she kidnapped her own daughter. I just need to keep calm and stick to my story.

'Could you turn around and put your hands behind your back?' the officer instructs me as he takes a pair of handcuffs from his belt.

I'm sure I spot a couple of curtains twitching as I'm unceremoniously marched out of the building and into a waiting car.

At least it's only a short journey to the police station and they take me straight into an interview room where they sit me on a hard wooden chair in front of a table.

A few minutes later, a detective, a guy called Monkton, who took my statement earlier, enters the room with a woman. A senior officer with a surly expression.

'What's this about?' I demand as they pull up chairs on the other side of the table.

'We'll come to that, Mr Kellor,' Monkton says, switching on a voice recorder and announcing who's present in the room.

He reminds me I've been arrested and reads me my rights.

'I've already told you everything I know,' I say, folding my arms across my chest. I know it looks defensive, but I'm not happy about being treated like a common criminal.

'New information has come to light about the death of Kit Warren,' he says sternly. 'It's been alleged that *you* killed him.'

I snort a derisive laugh. 'That's nonsense.'

'Is it? Perhaps you can tell me again how you came to be on the boat with your aunt.'

I sigh wearily and recite my story. I need to keep to the facts and not be tempted to embellish.

'Your aunt, Cathy Warren, claims the idea to fabricate the abduction of Annie Warren was yours.'

'That's crazy. Why would I do that? She's trying to save herself.'

'She admits full responsibility for her role in the abduction of her daughter, but says you were blackmailing your uncle, Kit Warren.'

'Blackmail?' I screw up my face, hoping to look suitably horrified.

'You had certain information about your uncle that he didn't want divulged to his wife or the wider public, because he was fearful that information would lead to the end of his marriage, his possible arrest and damage to his reputation,' Monkton says.

So Aunty Cath *has* been singing her little heart out, trying to paint it to look like she's accepting full responsibility for taking part in the kidnap while shifting the blame onto me. Too bad for her that there's not a shred of evidence to back up her claims. It's her word against mine.

'I have absolutely no idea what you're talking about, detective.' I smile innocently.

'When did you first become aware your aunt and uncle were responsible for their daughter's abduction?'

'Like I said before, I had absolutely no idea until Aunty Cath called me earlier today from the boatyard,' I explain. He needs to believe I'm being open and honest with him. 'If I'd had the faintest idea what was going on, I'd have let the police know. Of course I would.'

'Why did you insist your aunt and uncle didn't speak to any other journalists?'

'But they did. They signed a deal with the tabloid paper that put up the reward.'

'Without your approval.'

'Look, this is the biggest story I've ever worked on, right? And I had front row seats because it was my family. But I also had a duty to protect them from the press. I thought I could limit their exposure to the worst of it by having them only speak to me. That way, we could get their message out there about Annie, while keeping them from being hounded.'

'How very noble of you,' Monkton says. 'But the truth is you thought it was an opportunity to make a name for yourself. You exploited your family's suffering for your own benefit.'

'Not true.'

'And worse than that, you strong-armed your uncle into agreeing to kidnap Annie because you calculated a story this big would kick-start your career. How long have you worked in the regions? It must feel a bit beneath you, these days. But you saw this story as a chance to showcase yourself to the national networks, didn't you?'

'Wow,' I say. 'You really do have a fertile imagination, detective.'

Monkton pauses for breath and changes tack.

'Let's go back to the phone call you received from Cathy Warren earlier today. Where were you?'

'In Faversham.'

'Why? You'd been suspended, hadn't you? There was no reason for you to be in the town.'

'I wanted to be there for Aunty Cath and Uncle Kit.'

'How did your aunt sound when she called?'

I blow out the air from my cheeks. 'Upset. She was crying. Almost hysterical, I would say.'

'What did she tell you?'

'That she'd found Annie, but that Uncle Kit was dead and she'd pushed him. To be honest, she wasn't making a great deal of sense.'

'And she asked you for help?'

'Yes, that's right.'

'So you went to the boatyard where she told you they'd been hiding Annie?'

'Yes. I mean, no.' I quickly correct myself. It suddenly feels hot in the room. A sheen of sweat is forming across my forehead, but I don't want to draw attention to it by wiping it away. 'She said she'd discovered Uncle Kit had been hiding Annie on the boat. She didn't know anything about it.'

'And what did you find when you got there?'

I shake my head and force my eyes to water, thinking about a pet dog we'd had to have put to sleep when I was fourteen. 'Uncle Kit was dead,' I gasp. A few tears should do it. I don't want to ham it up and overdo it. 'His body was lying on the ground, and there was blood. Lots of blood. It was horrible.'

'And what did you do? Did you check if he was still alive?'

Did I? No, I stayed with Cathy on the boat. Would that make me sound callous? Uncaring? I mean, I was in shock. I wasn't thinking straight. But hang on, I told Monkton I arrived after Uncle Kit had died, so I would have had to walk straight past his body. That *would* have been callous if I'd not checked.

'I mean, it seemed obvious he was dead,' I mumble, 'but I checked for a pulse and listened to hear if he was breathing.' I lower my head and swallow hard, like I'm struggling with my emotions.

'And then what?'

'I climbed on board the boat and found Aunt Cathy on the deck, crying.'

'What did you do to your lip, by the way?'

My hand flies involuntarily to my mouth. Even though I've cleared up the cut and the blood, my lip has ballooned up. There's no hiding it. Kit caught me square in the jaw with his fist. He even managed to loosen a tooth.

'I hit it on a cupboard.'

'Right,' Monkton says. The intensity of his stares suggests he doesn't believe me, but he can't prove I'm lying. 'And what did your aunt, Cathy, tell you about what had happened?'

'She said she'd followed Uncle Kit to the boatyard that morning and discovered he'd been keeping Annie hidden on board the boat. She said they'd argued, and she'd pushed him. He fell over the side and was killed instantly.'

Monkton pushes his chair away from the table and folds his arms, mimicking my own body language. 'Let me give you another scenario,' he says. 'Your Aunt Cathy was a willing participant with your uncle in the abduction of her daughter, encouraged by you, but when a group of vigilantes killed an innocent man they thought was responsible, she lost her nerve. And when she threatened to confess her part in it, her husband attacked her and imprisoned her on the boat with their daughter. Not sure what to do, Kit called you, the only other person who knew the truth. When you arrived, you and your uncle argued. You threatened to reveal his secrets to Cathy. And in the heat of the moment, you pushed him off the side.'

'No,' I say, shaking my head vigorously. 'Absolutely not. That's not what happened. I mean, I feel sorry for my aunt. She was under enormous strain thinking Annie might be dead and then to find out it was Uncle Kit all along must have been devastating. You can understand why she lashed out, can't you? I don't suppose she meant to kill him, but maybe for her it's better that way.'

'You think your uncle was working alone, that he came up with the plan to abduct his daughter and that your aunt knew nothing about it?'

'That's how I understand it, yes.'

'Why would your uncle do that? What possible motive could he have?'

'I've no idea, detective. Isn't that your job to find out?'

They keep making me go over and over the story, again and again and again. I suppose they're looking for holes and inconsistencies, chinks of light in my narrative. But I stick to the facts and repeat them, careful not to elaborate with unnecessary details.

Eventually, Monkton concedes defeat. There's nothing they can pin on me, even if Cathy is conspiring against me.

'Alright, Mr Kellor. That's all. You're free to leave,' Monkton says.

'That's it? I'm not under arrest anymore?'

'No.'

I scrape my chair back and stand. 'I hope I've been of some help,' I say graciously.

Monkton stares at me with ill-concealed disdain. He doesn't believe me, but I don't care. He can't prove anything.

'And please, my aunt Cathy has been through hell the last week. Go easy on her, okay?'

Chapter 46

CATHY

They've let me languish in this tiny custody cell in the bowels of the station for hours. Why don't they just charge me and get it over with? I've admitted my role in Annie's abduction and told them the truth about everything. Well, nearly everything. Obviously, I've not told them about Jake's role or that he helped to conceal her in his loft, but why drag him into it? He was only trying to help. What's taking so long?

Is it because they're questioning Yannick again? Surely they don't believe his lies? He'll have told them he had nothing to do with Kit's death and I pushed him off the boat. The problem is, it's my word against his and unless Yannick confesses, I'm facing a murder charge on top of kidnapping my own daughter. And if I'm convicted of Kit's murder, I'll be going down for a very long time and I'll probably never be allowed to see Annie again.

When the cell door clangs open and I'm marched back to the interview room, I've lost all track of time. The hours have all rolled into one.

Monkton and the senior female officer are waiting for me, both looking weary.

'Sit down,' Monkton instructs me. He sounds pissed off.

'Did you speak to Yannick again?'

'He maintains he knew nothing about Annie's kidnap until you called him from the boatyard this morning, upset because you'd killed your husband and you didn't know what to do.'

'I didn't call him.'

'He says you did.'

'Well, he would, wouldn't he? It's in his interest to blame it on me.'

'It's your word against his.'

'Can't you look at the DNA or something?' I say, my chest tightening with a growing panic. I can't go down for Kit's murder on top of everything else. It's not fair.

'Obviously, your husband's body is undergoing a full forensic examination, but that's going to take some time. And we already know Yannick came into contact with him when he arrived at the boatyard because he stopped to check if he was still alive. There's bound to be DNA cross contamination.'

'They were fighting,' I say, desperately trying to think of something to expose Yannick's lies. 'Kit punched Yannick in the face. Can't you find skin traces or something from his nails or his knuckles?'

'Like I said, Mrs Warren, we're looking into it. We're also examining Mr Kellor's phone records to see if his movements tally with what he's told us.'

I shake my head. At best, they're going to show Yannick arrived at the boatyard earlier than he's claiming, although if they prove he was already at the yard at the time of Kit's death, that might be enough to call into question his version of events.

I guess it depends on how accurately they can determine the time of Kit's death.

But then it hits me. He's made a mistake. A smile creeps across my face.

'Yannick says I called him after I killed Kit, right? Well, that's impossible. I didn't have my phone. I haven't seen it since I was last at the house, when Kit knocked me unconscious. So how could I have called him?'

Monkton glances at the female officer. She keeps her gaze fixed on me, not giving anything away.

'Mrs Warren, your phone was recovered from the scene,' Monkton says. 'And we've checked. There was a call made on it to your nephew's number at around the time he says you rang him.'

'What? How? That's not possible.' I have a sudden sinking feeling. I'm being fitted up.

If Kit used my phone to call Yannick, it's another nail in my coffin. They'll never believe I'm innocent.

'Shall we go over the sequence of events one more time?' Monkton says. He's not asking. He's telling me.

We run through everything, starting with the argument I had with Kit after Blair Black's death and how I rose early the next morning and visited Pam Buckley where I almost confessed to her.

'What did you do after seeing Miss Buckley?'

I need to be careful. I can't tell them I went to Jake's house. I don't want them to know he had any involvement at all. Of course, there's a danger Annie will say something if they question her, which they will, but he kept her so heavily sedated, hopefully she won't be able to recall exactly where she was being held.

'I spent the day walking around, thinking,' I say. 'I couldn't bear the idea of being in the same house as Kit. You have to understand I didn't know what to do. I didn't want anyone else getting hurt, but I knew that by confessing, we'd be facing police charges and vilified by everyone. But more than that, I just wanted Annie home.'

'So you decided to finally come clean?'

I nod. 'I was going to speak to our liaison officer, Zara. I tried calling her. I left a voicemail. And that's the last thing I remember until I woke up on the boat with Annie.'

'Mr Kellor says you weren't involved in Annie's abduction. He says it was all Kit's idea and you only found out earlier today.'

'Why would I confess to something I haven't done? I told you, Kit and I planned it together to claim the reward to pay back the money I believed he owed the charity. I wasn't aware of Yannick's involvement at that point.' But no matter what I say, I can tell they think I'm lying, even when I'm confessing to a crime.

This is worse than a nightmare.

'If I'm honest, Mrs Warren, I don't think either of you are telling the whole truth.' Monkton arches his eyebrows.

'The truth is simple. I faked my daughter's disappearance with my husband because he told me he'd stolen money from his charity and was under pressure to pay it back. I didn't kill Kit. It was Yannick. They fought on the deck of the boat and Yannick pushed my husband over the edge. You have to believe me. Yannick said he was going to kill me too. The only reason he let me live was because I promised I'd confess to Kit's murder.' The words tumble out of my mouth. If I don't change Monkton's mind quickly, he's going to throw the book at me and charge me with my husband's murder.

'You didn't mention that earlier.' The detective lifts his chin and looks down his nose at me. 'You're claiming now that your nephew threatened you?'

'Yes,' I sigh. To be fair to him, I'm not sure if I was in Monkton's shoes I'd believe it either. 'He'd do anything to save himself. He's always been the same. Yannick doesn't care about anyone other than himself.'

'Again, that's all very interesting, Mrs Warren, but it sounds like desperation. The fact is, you killed your husband because you found out he'd been lying to you. He lied to you when he said he'd stolen from the charity.

And he lied to you about his relationship with Yannick Kellor. You were angry and ashamed, and you deliberately pushed him, intending to do him harm. Isn't that the truth?'

'No! Absolutely not!' I slap my hands on the table in frustration.

'You killed your husband and now you're trying to pin his murder on your own nephew to save yourself.'

'No!'

'And, confronted with the truth, you're making up stories to fit your narrative. The fact is, Yannick Kellor had no reason to kill your husband, did he?'

I bury my head in my hands. This can't be happening.

'Mrs Warren? Your nephew had no reason to kill your husband, did he?'

'Like I said, I don't think he meant to kill him,' I say. 'It was an accident.'

'Oh, it's an accident now, is it?'

The walls of the room feel like they're closing in. My chair plunging into a deep, dark abyss. Warm beads of sweat stipple my forehead. My top lip. My throat is dry. Parched. It's hard to swallow.

There has to be a way to make them believe me.

'I can prove he did it,' I gasp, clutching the edge of the table. 'Give me a chance and I can get him to confess to everything.' An idea forms in my head like rain clouds gathering ahead of a storm. 'He wants to interview me. I said I'd give him an exclusive. Let me do it. Let me talk to him and I'll get him to admit everything.'

'Mrs Warren, you're under arrest for kidnap and murder. I can't let you speak to Mr Kellor.'

'Why not? Don't you want the truth?'

'There are rules. Even if we agreed to it, it would never be admissible in court.'

'You'd rather see an innocent woman convicted than bend your stupid rules to get to the truth? What kind of justice is that?'

Monkton glances at the female officer.

She deliberately closes her notebook and puts the lid back on her pen. 'What did you have in mind?' she asks.

It's the first time she's spoken. I hadn't expected her accent to be so strong. A thick estuary drawl.

'Everything has been about Yannick engineering a story to further his career and he manipulated Kit and me to get what he wanted. It's just been one big opportunity for him. He's an egomaniac. But he's still missing an ending to his story,' I say.

'A confession from you about how and why you faked your own daughter's disappearance, you mean?' the female detective says.

'Exactly. It's what he wants more than anything. Let me do the interview and I'll get him to confess his involvement.' I fix her with a steely look. I have to convince her to give me this shot. It's my only way out of being charged with a murder I didn't commit.

'I couldn't agree to something like that, I'm afraid,' she says.

'Why not? What do you have to lose? You don't have any other evidence. It's my word against his, like you said. Give me the chance and at least you'd know for sure.'

'I sympathise. I really do, but it's above my pay grade, for a start. I don't have the authority to agree to something like that.'

'Then speak to someone who does,' I snap, 'because I didn't kill my husband and I'm not going to jail for a crime I didn't commit.'

The officer taps her pen against her knee as she studies me, deep in thought. 'It's completely against protocol,' she says. 'We'd need to consult with the Crown Prosecution Service before we agreed to anything.'

She's coming around to the idea. I need to push home my advantage.

'He'll bite your hand off if you offer him the interview,' I say.

'And strictly speaking, if we've not charged her, it can't be contempt of court,' Monkton says to the other officer, as if I'm not in the room.

'We'd have to release her, pending further inquiries,' the female officer adds. 'Which opens the risk she might abscond.'

'True, and it could be tricky to justify when she's already confessed to the kidnapping.'

'Unless we put her up in a safe house. She might need it for her own protection anyway. When people find out she was responsible for Annie's abduction, they won't take it too kindly.'

I watch them batting the idea back and forth like I'm watching a game of tennis. They're coming around to the idea, which means they're not completely sold on Yannick's version of events either.

'Look,' I say, 'I don't care what you do. I'll take my punishment and I'll have to live with the hatred, but I'm not going down for Kit's murder. Please, let me do this.'

The female officer nods, and Monkton terminates the interview, switching off the recording.

'I can't promise anything,' the female detective says. 'But let me speak to my governor and see what he says.'

THREE DAYS LATER

Chapter 47

YANNICK

My stomach is fizzing with anticipation. I can't wait to get started and see how Aunty Cath will deal with my questions.

Harry switches on a powerful spotlight and angles it so it doesn't shine directly into her eyes while I go through my notes one last time. The network has agreed to find a prime-time slot to show the interview and they didn't even make much of a fuss about replacing me with a more well-known presenter. I think they liked the idea of me, as Cathy's nephew, there on the scene when she was arrested, leading proceedings. It's going to be one of those moments in history that parents will be telling their children about in years to come, like when Princess Diana was interviewed by Martin Bashir or David Frost grilled Richard Nixon.

'Cathy, could you feed this wire up through the front of your blouse, please?' Harry hands her a lapel mic attached to a radio pack and politely turns his back to her while she pulls it up through her clothing.

When she's done, he clips the microphone to the inside of her jacket so it's virtually invisible to the camera.

She tucks her hair behind her ears, and shifts in her chair, pulling her jacket straight. She's put on make-up. Bright red lipstick and heavily kohled eyes. She looks pretty good. Too good, if she's looking for sympathy. I would have advised less, but I'm not here to offer her media advice anymore.

'Could you tell me what you had for breakfast, for sound?' Harry asks, pulling on a pair of headphones and adjusting his camera levels as she tells him she had cornflakes and a slice of toast with butter.

Harry switches off the overhead lights so Cathy is brightly illuminated against a dark backdrop by the TV spot lamps. I turn on my microphone and count down from ten so Harry can check my levels, and then take my place opposite my aunt.

'Are you ready?' I ask.

She finally looks me in the eye and nods. If she's nervous, she doesn't show it. She looks surprisingly composed, if a little distant.

'Rolling,' Harry says, peering into the viewfinder of his camera.

When I first proposed the idea of Annie being abducted, I couldn't in my wildest dreams have anticipated it would have worked out so well. Fortunately, that unpleasant incident with Blair Black has been conveniently forgotten by the newsroom and my suspension overturned by Gina. Not that I plan to stick around in the regions. I've already been approached by one of the twenty-four hour rolling news channels with a job offer, although I'm not rushing into anything. At least not until this interview airs and my currency is riding high.

Even though she'd made a promise, I was surprised my aunt reached out so soon, especially as she's been in police custody. Frankly, I'm still amazed they agreed to let her do it.

It was the police press office who initiated things, offering the interview to me two days ago. The only stipulation is that the interview can only be broadcast after any legal proceedings have ended. In other words, after a trial convicts Cathy and she's jailed, which is fair enough because they wouldn't want a jury influenced by what they'd seen on TV.

At first, I thought it was a trap, but now I realise it must be part of their plan to get Cathy to incriminate herself. Well, let's see if I can help them put the final pieces of the jigsaw together and get her to confess everything on camera.

She might be my aunt, but the atmosphere is definitely strained between us. She's barely said a word to me since she arrived in the hotel room we've hired. I had to stop myself laughing out loud when I heard she'd been smuggled into the hotel around the back by a police officer to avoid running into any trouble. She arrived in the room with a scarf on her head and wearing a big pair of sunglasses, like a Hollywood celebrity trying to avoid being spotted by the paparazzi.

'Cathy Warren,' I begin, reading from my notes. 'Mother. Wife. Businesswoman. Kidnapper. Murderer. Why did you do it?'

I'd played around with a few ideas for an opening question and thought this nailed it. People didn't want to sit through a half-hour preamble as we skirted around the elephant in the room. They wanted to know how a mother could be so callous that she could manufacture her own daughter's disappearance purely for financial gain, and then murder, in cold blood, the husband she'd planned it with.

It wasn't exactly the story we'd agreed, but if she was stupid enough to confess to kidnapping Annie, when she could have blamed it all on her husband, more fool her. As long as she keeps her mouth shut about my involvement.

'I guess I was desperate,' she says, lowering her head deferentially.

That's good. No point trying to be defiant. The public will hate her even more. She needs to show she's contrite.

'My husband convinced me he'd stolen money from his charity and needed to pay it back to avoid jail. He came up with the plan and I stupidly agreed to it,' she says.

'So why did you kill him?'

It's blunt and to the point, but you can't sugar-coat a question like that.

She lifts her head and juts out her jaw. 'I didn't kill him,' she says. Her eyes narrow and she lets a momentary, accusatory silence hang between us. I hold my breath. Thankfully, it's a pre-recorded interview. If she says anything that incriminates me, I'll edit it out and worry about how to deal with Harry later. 'He fell. It was an accident.'

'The police say you murdered him.'

'They're wrong.'

Now I understand why the police were happy for the interview to go ahead. She's still not confessing to Kit's murder, and they want me to tease out a confession. But I need to be careful. I'll come back to it later. I certainly don't want her pointing the finger at me on camera, so I change tack.

'Many people watching this will want to know how a mother could do what you did to your own child. Annie, your daughter, is only ten years old and yet you held her captive in appalling conditions on a dilapidated yacht in a boatyard not far from your home. What kind of mother does that make you?'

Her eye twitches, and her jaw tightens. Did she really think, with this opportunity, I was going to pull my punches?

'I love my daughter with all my heart, and I'll always regret what I did, but I hope in time Annie can forgive me. I know what I did was wrong, but that's why I'm pleading guilty and will happily accept whatever punishment is handed down by the courts,' Aunty Cath says.

'Have you spoken to Annie since your arrest?'

'No.'

'You've not spoken to her at all?' I raise a quizzical eyebrow. I thought they would have at least let them meet, even if it was supervised.

'She's been taken into emergency care and I've not been allowed to see her.'

'A lot of people say you've given up any right to being a mother. Are they correct?'

'They probably have a fair point, but doesn't everyone deserve a second chance? I just want the opportunity to make it up to Annie and tell her I'm sorry,' Aunty Cath says. She puts a finger to her eye, wiping away a tear.

And so we go on for the next hour, me trying to provoke her into doing or saying something that's going to light up the interview, while my aunt parries away my salvos, trying to rebuild her reputation. We both know it's a lost cause. Most people watching will never forgive her.

I ask again about Uncle Kit's death, certain it's what the police want. But she continues to stick to the line that he fell and refuses to admit she pushed him. And no matter how I go at it, she doesn't give an inch.

Eventually, I run out of questions and different ways of asking her if she's an unfit mother, and with time up, I conclude the interview.

'Great,' Harry says. 'Let's get some reverses in the bag.'

He moves the camera, positioning it alongside Aunt Cathy and pointing the lens at me. Then he gets me to ask some of the questions again, filming as I nod, as if I'm listening carefully to her responses.

'All done,' he says, turning on the overhead spotlights and switching off the TV lights.

'How did I do?' Cathy's shoulders slump as the tension leaks from her body.

'You did great.' I shoot her an encouraging smile, trying to hide how much I'm buzzing. The most eagerly anticipated interview, probably of the last ten years, is in the can and it's going to change my life.

'Are you sure? You didn't exactly go easy on me.'

I shrug. 'I only asked the questions everyone wants answered.'

The shrill ring of Harry's phone cuts through the awkwardness between us. He answers and gives a curt reply to whoever's calling.

'Sorry, Yannick,' he says, clamping his hand over the phone. 'I need to take this. I'll be back in a minute to pack up.'

He steps out of the room and, as the door swings shut, Aunt Cathy and I are alone together for the first time since we were on that yacht in the boatyard. Even the police officer who brought her to the hotel has made herself scarce.

'Look, I'm sorry about the way things worked out,' I say. I'm not a monster. I do feel sorry for her. I'd not planned it this way, and if she hadn't lost her nerve and tried to call the police, we wouldn't be here. Uncle Kit would still be alive, and Aunt Cathy wouldn't be facing a long prison sentence.

'Are you?' she says.

'Of course I am.' I yank off my microphone and switch off the radio pack hitched to the belt of my trousers. I coil the wire around my hand and leave it on the floor by the camera.

'Don't you feel even remotely guilty?' Cathy crosses her legs and hugs her knee.

'For what?'

'This is all your doing. I'm facing years in prison because of you, and I'll probably never see my daughter again.'

'Yeah, I'm sorry, but at least I'm helping get your side of the story told.' She's being a bit ungrateful.

She laughs sarcastically. 'Is that what you call it? I lost everything thirty years ago when my father, your grandfather, died. And now I've lost everything again, because of you. You, Yannick. My own family.'

'That's a bit harsh.' I don't think it's fair to blame me.

'You blackmailed Kit and left him with no choice other than to go along with your stupid plan.'

'Blackmail is such a strong word,' I say.

'You threatened to destroy him if he didn't do what you wanted. What would you call it?'

'I can't help who he was, Aunty Cath, and I'm sorry if it's difficult for you to accept he wasn't the man you married, but that had nothing to do with me.'

'Bullshit.' She spits the word at me like it's poison in her mouth.

'I never encouraged him. He came on to me.' He was my uncle, for fuck's sake. And old enough to be my father. He should have known better.

Cathy wets her lips, uncrosses her legs and refolds them. 'I'm thinking about changing my plea and admitting I killed Kit,' she says.

'Seriously? Good for you.'

She nods and looks down at her hands. She's had her nails painted to match her lipstick. 'So you're off the hook. I'll take the blame for it.'

'They probably would have charged you anyway,' I say.

'One thing that still bothers me, though. I can just about cope with the thought that Kit was secretly gay, but you said he liked... young boys?'

I'm not surprised it's still a struggle for her to come to terms with who Uncle Kit really was. Certainly not the man she thought she had married.

'Tell me that's not true,' she says. 'I don't want to believe we were living a lie for all these years.'

'Don't torture yourself.' It's better she doesn't know the details. She's gone through enough already. Ignorance really is bliss.

'Tell me, Yannick. I have to know the truth.'

I sigh. 'It's something he was obviously trying to keep hidden, maybe even from himself.' I check over my shoulder to make sure Harry's not about to make a reappearance. 'And honestly, I didn't even have any idea Uncle Kit was queer.'

Cathy's lower lip quivers.

'It was only when he contacted me out of the blue a couple of years ago to see if we'd run a story about the charity, and as he was my uncle, I didn't like to turn him down. So we met up in Maidstone one evening after work for a drink, but when I got there, Uncle Kit was already quite drunk. Believe me, I was as shocked as anyone when he tried to kiss me.'

Cathy lowers her head and I can see her jaw working, clenching and releasing over and over. 'Go on,' she whispers.

'Are you sure you want to hear this again?'

'Keep talking.'

Fine. If she wants to keep hearing the secrets Kit was keeping from her all these years, then I guess I owe it to her. Maybe it'll help her come to terms with his death.

'He got the message from me loud and clear, I promise. He was my uncle and I told him he needed to go home and sober up. I didn't hear from him again until I bumped into him just before Christmas last year. He was out on the town with some people from his work and we were having a few Christmas drinks and somehow ended up in the same club,' I explain. 'I'd had a few gins and Kit came on to me again – '

'Spare me the details.' Cathy's gone pale and has started shaking.

'Long story short, and I know this was a mistake, but we ended up spending the night in a cheap hotel. Are you okay, Aunty Cath?'

She nods, but she looks like she's going to be sick.

'I wasn't proud of myself, but it's one of those things, isn't it? And it's not like we were related by blood.'

'He was my husband,' Cathy hisses. 'He was your uncle.'

'Only by marriage. Maybe you should have kept him on a tighter leash.'

For a second, I think she's going to slap me. Her eyes are burning with anger and hatred. 'And then?' she asks.

'A week later, he wanted to meet again. I knew it was wrong and honestly, I wasn't interested, but I knew he needed an outlet. So I agreed to take him to a gay bar, to show him the ropes, as it were.' I laugh at the memory. 'His eyes were out on stalks.'

'And that's where you picked up those... boys?' She can hardly bring herself to say the word.

'It was obvious he was into the younger ones. And the younger looking, the better,' I say.

'And?'

'I suggested we all went back to my flat.' I don't tell her about the drugs. She doesn't need to know her husband was whacked on G, parading around my lounge with his shirt off and his trousers around his ankles, cavorting like he was a podium dancer in a high-end club.

'That's when you filmed them?'

It was supposed to be a bit of fun. A souvenir from a wild evening. It was only later I understood the power of what I'd filmed on my phone.

I nod. 'Yes.'

'You knew it would destroy him if that footage leaked, didn't you? You knew I'd leave him and his reputation would be in tatters,' Cathy says.

'The boys were underage, Aunt Cathy. Nobody would have cared that he was gay, but people wouldn't have forgiven him for that.'

'He wasn't a paedophile.'

I shrug. It doesn't matter what you call it. 'I didn't make Uncle Kit into what he was. I only held open the door.'

'You filmed my husband having underage sex with two boys. That could land you in a lot of trouble.'

'I've deleted the film,' I say.

'But not before you'd threatened Kit with ruin. What did you say to him? That you'd release it online? Send it to the trustees? The papers? Me?' Cathy asks, agitated.

'Does it really matter now?'

'Yes, it does. And the plan for Annie's disappearance? When did that idea spring to mind?'

I sigh. I've been over this with her already, but if she needs to hear it again, then so be it. 'I never meant anyone to get hurt, but I wasn't getting the breaks at work. They weren't even giving me a shot at presenting the main programme, Aunty Cath. Just a few crumbs here and there. You don't know what it was like for me. I'm better than that. I just needed to show them. I thought if I could deliver a major story everyone else was chasing, they'd have to sit up and take note. That's when I thought about Annie and how incredible it would be if she went missing for a few days, only to turn up safe and well a week or so later. I knew there'd be huge media interest.'

'And you threatened to release the footage unless Kit went along with it,' Cathy says. 'Well, I hope you're proud of yourself.'

I shrug. What can I say? I'm not proud of the mess I've caused, but sometimes you have to create your own luck. I'm sorry Aunty Cath is going to carry the can and Uncle Kit is dead, but I'm not responsible. If they'd kept to the plan, everything would have worked out and no one would have been hurt.

'Did he tell you how he was going to persuade me to agree to it?'

'I figured he'd find a way, and a couple of stills from the footage sent to his work email seemed to hurry him along with a plan,' I explain with a grin.

There are tears in Cathy's eyes again. She looks up to the ceiling and as she blinks, a solitary tear rolls down her cheek.

'I only did it for Kit. For our family. I couldn't bear the thought of us being torn apart, of Kit being sent to prison and Annie growing up with the shame of knowing what her father had done. But that was the least of my worries, wasn't it? Look at me now. At least I've held my hands up and I'll pay the price, whatever it is.'

'Keep your nose clean and in twenty years you could be out,' I say. It's not that long.

'Or you could do the decent thing and confess that you killed Kit.'

'Are you insane? I'd lose everything,' I say. 'Anyway, we had a deal, remember?'

'I remember,' she says, her eyes narrowing.

I glance towards the door again. It would be unfortunate if Harry overheard *this* conversation. 'I spared your life, Aunt Cathy,' I say, leaning forwards and speaking in a low whisper.

'That's right. You promised you wouldn't kill me if I told the police I'd murdered Kit. But *you* pushed him.'

'It was an accident, Aunty Cath. You know that as well as I do!'

'You killed him.'

'Yes, but I never meant to do it!'

The sound of the hotel door crashing open startles me into paralysis. Half a dozen or more uniformed police officers pour into the suite, yelling. Screaming at me.

'Get down on the floor! Put your hands behind your head!'

Aunt Cathy gets up out of her chair and backs away, watching me.

'What's going on?' I gasp, unable to comprehend.

'Get down on your stomach!' an officer screams in my ear.

I raise my hands and drop to my knees. He pushes my face down into the thick carpet and kneels on my spine as he pulls my hands behind my back.

'Yannick Kellor, I'm arresting you on suspicion of the murder of Kit Warren and for conspiracy to kidnap Annie Warren.'

I turn my head to see a detective in a cheap grey suit holding up his warrant card.

'You do not have to say anything – '

'I didn't do it,' I yell. 'I didn't do anything.'

In the corner of the room, I catch sight of Aunt Cathy, a sly smile playing across her face as another plain-clothes officer helps to remove her lapel mic.

I swallow a hard lump in my throat as my whole world implodes. I have this plunging, sinking, spiralling out-of-body sensation of everything going catastrophically wrong. All my hopes and dreams being wrenched from my grasp.

How could I have been so stupid?

She set me up. Got me to confess while she was still wearing a live microphone, with the police no doubt recording and monitoring in another room. No wonder they were so keen for the interview to go ahead.

And now they know the truth.

NINE MONTHS LATER

Chapter 48

DELORES

A glum, overweight prison officer studies Delores' driver's licence for a few seconds before comparing the grainy thumbnail image to her face. Someone else goes through her bag and a third officer pats down her arms and legs and peers into her mouth. It all seems a bit much, but it's the price she has to pay to visit Cathy Warren.

She joins a small group of friends and family who are taken into a large, airy room with plastic chairs attached to wooden tables spaced evenly apart. Another female guard gives them each a number and tells them to sit and wait in the corresponding seat. She instructs them sternly not to move from their allocated places, but says they're allowed to hug briefly at the start of the meeting. Otherwise, she says, they're to keep their hands to themselves and not attempt to pass anything to the prisoners.

The clock on the wall hits eleven, signalling the arrival of a stream of tough-looking women who shuffle into the room. Some have braided their hair. Others have lost teeth. Almost all have tattoos and piercings. Cathy is the last to enter, shuffling forwards, unsure of herself in a loose-fitting duck-egg blue T-shirt, unflattering canvas trousers and white trainers. She looks like she doesn't belong here. But she does.

They must know who she is, and Delores imagines the other prisoners have probably given her a hard time.

Inmates who've committed crimes against children make popular targets.

'Hey, Cathy, how are you?' Delores says as Cathy heads towards the table.

Delores stands, but they don't hug.

'Thank you for coming. I wasn't sure you would,' Cathy says, pinching up the slack in the legs of her trousers as she sits.

Delores is on Cathy's approved friends and family list, and they've been speaking by telephone for a few weeks. At first, they chatted about how Cathy was coping with life behind bars and mostly Delores listened as Cathy told her how she was having trouble sleeping, how she couldn't get used to the constant noise or the drug taking or the undercurrent of violence that was ever present.

It took her by surprise when Cathy asked if she would visit. Was she lonely? Did she think Delores was her friend because they'd chatted a few times?

'I want to tell you my side of the story,' Cathy explained when Delores hesitated, trying to think of an excuse why she couldn't make it. 'I want to do an interview with you. I want to tell you everything. Nothing but the truth.'

It was an opportunity that couldn't be missed. The chance of a genuine exclusive.

The only other interview Cathy had given since her arrest was to her nephew Yannick, although it had never been broadcast. The police seized it as evidence and refused to release any of the material.

Delores pulls out her notebook and opens it on her knee, conscious they don't have long. They'll probably have to do the interview over the course of a few visits, but that's okay. They have all the time in the world and Cathy's not talking to anyone else.

'How could a mother kidnap her own child?' Delores asks. 'What was going through your mind?'

Cathy clasps her hands in her lap like an old lady, her shoulders hunched apologetically. 'I was actually trying to protect my family, believe it or not,' she says, after a moment's thought.

'You told the court your husband talked you into it because he was hiding his sexual misdemeanours from you. Did you never suspect he might be gay?'

Cathy lifts her chin and looks Delores in the eye. 'I had absolutely no idea. He kept it very well hidden.'

'And you only found out when your nephew eventually told you?'

'After he pushed Kit to his death, Yannick explained everything. That was when I finally understood our whole marriage had been a sham. I'd been desperately trying to hold our family together and all the time it had been based on a lie. The family I'd worked so hard to protect didn't exist,' she says, with surprising candour.

Yannick's currently serving a ten-year jail sentence of his own for manslaughter after a lengthy trial in which he continued to plead his innocence and blame Kit's death on Cathy.

'What's happened to Annie? Have you had any contact with her?' Delores asks.

Cathy's lip trembles, and a sadness glazes her eyes. 'No,' she mumbles. 'They've not let me see her.'

'Do you know what's happened to her?'

'She's in care, but they're trying to get her adopted. We're working on something, but I can't really talk about it, I'm afraid.'

'We?'

'My legal team.'

Delores glances up from her notes. Cathy had chosen to represent herself in court. She said she had nothing to hide and was willing to admit her full role in Annie's abduction and false imprisonment. So it's a surprise to Delores that she has employed lawyers now.

'You're trying to win back custody?'

'I'd rather you didn't report that,' she says. 'I'll tell you anything else you want to know, but I don't want anything to jeopardise any chance of securing Annie's future.'

Delores hesitates. It's a great new angle on the story. The mother who kidnapped her own daughter launching a legal bid from prison to obtain custody of her child. But she scratches through her notes. Cathy's been through enough already. She won't risk destroying this woman's chance of being reunited with her daughter for the sake of a story that will be old news twenty-four hours later.

'How are they treating you?'

Cathy looks around the room at all the other prisoners preoccupied with children, partners, parents, brothers and sisters. 'It's okay,' she says.

'Are they giving you a hard time?'

She shrugs. Delores notices the blue tinge of a bruise on the inside of her arm. 'I did wrong. I have to accept my punishment.'

'Oh, Cathy, be careful.' Eight years is a long time to survive in prison.

'I'm okay. I'm keeping my head down and who knows, if I can keep clear of trouble, I could be out in four years.'

Four years is still a long time, especially when you have a target on your back.

'Why did you reach out to me?' Delores asks. 'What are you hoping this interview will achieve?'

Cathy cocks her head. 'I'm not looking for sympathy,' she says, frowning. 'And I'm not looking for forgiveness. I know what I did was wrong and I'm paying the price, but I've lived with too many lies for too long. I want people to know the truth. The whole truth.'

'And what is the truth?'

Cathy chews her lip and thinks carefully about her reply. 'My husband lied to me, not only about who he was, but about what he'd done, and I was a fool to fall for it. When he suggested using Annie to dig himself out of a hole, I should have said no, but I was a coward. I think about all the people in my community who gave up their time to look for Annie, all the police time that was wasted when they should have been working on more important matters, all the prayers that were said, the good wishes and flowers that were sent, I'm truly sorry for it all.'

Delores writes down every word diligently. This is good stuff. It gets to the heart of who Cathy really is, what she was thinking back then and what she truly believes now.

'I thought I was doing the right thing,' Cathy continues, 'for my family and my daughter, when actually I was doing the opposite. I hope that one day, when she's old enough to understand, Annie finds it in her heart to forgive me, because she is the one person in all of this who I hurt the most, and somehow, I need to find a way to make it up to her. Maybe in time, she'll find these words and realise I only ever acted out of love.'

FOUR YEARS LATER

Chapter 49

CATHY

The air tastes fresher and the trees look different, heavy now with acid-green leaves. I'd forgotten about the changing of the seasons. It's something you don't notice while you're inside.

'Good luck, Cathy.' The prison officer shakes my hand. She was one of the kind ones. I liked her. She turns and slips back inside, slamming and locking the wooden door inset into the gates behind her.

And suddenly I'm alone. It's an eerie, disconcerting sensation after so long without any privacy.

A gentle breeze brushes my bare legs. How strange to be in a dress again. For the last four years, I've lived in baggy T-shirts, flannel sweaters and comfortable trainers. But the dress is all I have. It's what I was wearing when they brought me here in the back of a prison van. A reminder of my last day of freedom. Of being in court. Of the shock at the length of my sentence.

At least the sleeves come down to my elbows and hide the raw, crinkled skin on my shoulder and upper arm from when they threw a kettle of boiling water and sugar at me in the early days of my incarceration. What's more difficult to conceal is the limp I've been left with after my leg was snapped in two places while they held me down in a cell, and the three-inch scar under my chin where one of the women attacked me with a shank.

Everyone knew who I was, and why I was there. And they all hated me. I suppose I can't really blame them. What sort of mother could do what I did to her own child?

A man jumps off the bonnet of his car and waves at me from the car park. It's Jake. He's smiling, but he looks older. His hair greyer. His face etched with furrows. I know I've aged too, well beyond my years, so I shouldn't judge.

He runs towards me and throws his arms around my thin body, hugging me tightly. But I keep my hands by my sides, clutching the plastic bag that contains my meagre belongings and jewellery. I wasn't sure how I'd feel when I saw him again, but I wasn't expecting to be so numb. Imagine what it would have been like if I'd had to serve my whole eight-year term.

'How are you?' Jake says, gripping my shoulders and looking me up and down. 'It's so good to see you.'

'Is it?' It's been a long time since anyone's said that to me. Is he being polite or does he mean it?

He frowns. 'Of course it is. I've missed you. You didn't answer any of my letters.'

'Can we go now?'

'Sure, but first there's someone who wants to say hello.'

Jake skirts behind me with a grin and throws open the rear door of his car. A thin girl with jet black hair, heavy eye make-up and dark clothes is slumped on the back seat, nodding her head in time to the music pumping through her earphones while she scrolls through her phone.

'Annie? It's your mum,' Jake says, tapping her on the shoulder.

She glances up at me, stony-faced. 'Whatever,' she says.

She's changed so much, no longer a child. The girl on the back seat is a teenager with dyed hair and a sulky pout. Her face is different too. It's thinner, less childlike.

The freckles on her nose have vanished and she's started to develop womanly curves.

'Hello, Annie,' I say, but her attention is already back on her phone. A dagger to my heart more painful than anything the lags did to me inside.

She's not forgiven me. She probably never will. But what did I expect? That she was going to throw her arms around me and tell me she'd missed me? I'd dared to hope during all those lonely nights, but who am I trying to kid? She's not seen me for four years and who knows what kind of poison has been dripped into her mind during that time? It's a miracle I'm even seeing her at all.

When I was arrested and they took her away, I thought that was it. I'd lost her forever. Even when my legal team finally secured custody for Jake, I wasn't sure we'd be reunited. Of course, I'd dreamt about it every night. Imagined what it would be like to be a family again. The harsh reality is difficult to swallow.

I refused to let Jake bring her to visit, even though he begged me to in all his letters. I didn't want Annie seeing me in there, reminding her what I'd done. I wanted her memories to be happy ones, of a time long before we smuggled her out of the house and made her sleep on a camp bed in Jake's loft, heavily sedated on sea sickness tablets.

'Come on, Annie, put your phone down for a second and say hello properly,' Jake says, sounding annoyed. 'You've not seen your mum for four years.'

'Dad, just leave me alone, will you?'

Dad?

It sounds so strange to hear her call him that, but I'm glad they've at least been able to straighten out their relationship and that she's accepted him as her father in such a short time. Maybe she'd always suspected Kit wasn't her real dad.

'It's fine,' I say. 'Let's just go.'

Jake sighs and I climb into the car with my bag of belongings by my feet.

'I didn't think you'd want to go back to Faversham, so I've booked a cottage for a few days while we sort out what happens next,' Jake says.

I'm more grateful than he'll ever know. I can't imagine ever going back to the town and facing all those people. To them, I'm nothing but a liar and a cheat. Or worse than that, a child abuser. And I'm not prepared to run the gauntlet of people heckling or threatening me. I know what people are like, especially when they're looking for a vent for their anger and hatred. It's best I move on.

'That's thoughtful of you,' I say. It's been a long time since anyone's shown me any kindness.

Jake tries to strike up a conversation as we drive, but I'm in no mood to talk. He's acting like the moment they let me walk out, I was free. But I'm never going to be free. I'm always going to be that woman who kidnapped her own daughter.

And so, for the next two hours, we drive in silence until he pulls onto a long dirt track and parks outside a stone cottage surrounded by woodland. It's an idyllic spot where we're unlikely to be disturbed. It's so considerate of him, especially as I'd given zero thought to where I'd go when I was released.

'I picked up some clothes for you,' Jake says, hauling a bag out of the boot. 'I had to guess at your size, so I hope they're okay.'

'Anything's better than this dress.' It's too formal. Too dressy. And it brings back bad memories of being in court with all those disapproving eyes staring at me.

He shows me to a room with a picture window, a fireplace in the corner and a door that doesn't get bolted at night.

I open the bag on the soft double bed and pull out a pair of skinny jeans, a plain top and a cotton sweater. He's gone for sizes slightly too big to be on the safe side, not taking into account the weight I've lost in prison, but it's better than having a bag full of clothes that are too small.

That evening, he orders a takeaway, which we eat at a table he's laid with candles and a bottle of wine. The first sip goes straight to my head.

Annie's still refusing to speak to me, treating me with the kind of teenage indifference I imagine she'd normally reserve for one of her father's girlfriends. She's not remotely interested in talking to me and insists on eating in her room.

Does she really hate me that much?

'Have you thought about your plans going forward?' Jake asks as he tops up my glass.

'A bit,' I say.

'I've been looking at properties in East Sussex,' he says. 'I think I could afford something with three bedrooms and some potential for improvement. What do you think?'

'Sounds like a great idea.'

'It does? I mean, I don't want to pressure you into anything you're not happy with, and obviously I've not spoken to Annie about it yet because it's going to mean she'll have to change schools. And being away from Faversham should mean you're not recognised as easily, but maybe in time you'll feel up to getting a job again,' he continues. He's clearly been giving it a lot of thought.

Oh, god. 'I'm not coming with you, Jake.'

The excitement and anticipation on his face leaches away. I feel bad for bursting his bubble, but it would be worse to string him along.

'But I thought – '

'No, Jake. I can't do it.'

'I can help you get back on your feet and maybe, in time, when you're ready, we can be a proper family.'

The note of desperation in his voice is heartbreaking.

'You're a good man,' I say, reaching for his hand. 'I know you'll do a great job of bringing Annie up, but there's no place for us. I'm sorry.'

When Jake kissed me that night in the café all those years ago, I should have pushed him away. Kit had been working long hours at the charity and invariably came home tired and irritable and didn't want to hear about my day. Jake, on the other hand, made me feel like the most important person in the world. He laughed at my jokes. He cared about my opinion. And he clearly enjoyed my company.

The first time we made love, it was on the kitchen floor. It was hardly the most romantic encounter, but it was exciting. Raw and passionate. And, like a lovesick teenager, I foolishly kept going back for more. Until I fell pregnant with Annie and my world came crashing down.

Kit and I had only casually been trying for a baby, and when I hadn't fallen pregnant, I assumed it was my fault. A legacy of my teenage abortion. He already had two grown-up kids, after all.

What else could I do, other than tell Kit the baby was his? I didn't want to leave him, especially for Jake. Jake was just a bit of fun. A bit of rough on the side and a distraction from the strains my marriage was going through. I knew we'd never work. And besides, we were both married, and I didn't want to be a homewrecker. So I figured it was better Jake and I just stayed good friends. That way, at least, he'd be able to see Annie as she grew up, even if it was only from afar.

I had to tell him I was pregnant, but I made it plainly clear I was going to bring Annie up as Kit's, and to his credit Jake didn't argue. He understood the damage it would otherwise cause, and anyway, he said he wasn't ready to be a father. I think he always regretted that decision, especially as two years later his wife, who'd always been dead set against starting a family, left him for another man and quickly fell pregnant herself.

Of all the terrible things that have happened in the last few years, at least Jake has finally been able to connect with his daughter.

As soon as I heard Annie had been taken into foster care, I made up my mind what to do. It didn't seem right that they were going to place her with strangers when she could be with her natural father, although it was still a long, hard battle to get the courts to agree it was in Annie's best interests.

'You'll take care of her, won't you?' I lower my gaze, the familiar twin feelings of shame and guilt consuming me. I've been a terrible mother. Annie and Jake are both better off without me.

'We can do it together,' he says. 'I know it's going to take time, but please, give it a go. We can be a family. Annie needs you.'

'She's better off without me,' I say, shaking my head. 'All I've done is bring her pain and heartache. You're a great father. I know you'll do the best for her.'

'Cathy, please,' he begs.

'Have you asked Annie what she wants? Is she ready to forgive me?'

'In time, I'm sure she'll – '

'Jake, has she forgiven me for what I did? For using her as a pawn? Pretending she'd been abducted? Drugging her?'

His gaze falls into his empty glass, confirming everything I already guessed. There are some things you can never forgive. A parent's betrayal is one of them.

'You can't just abandon her.'

'I'm not abandoning her. She'll be with you,' I say. 'She's better off without me.' I stand and kiss the top of his head. 'One day, you'll thank me for doing the right thing. I'm going to bed.'

I slip into my room and climb, fully clothed, into the big bed with its soft duvet and squishy pillows. I have no intention of sleeping, even if I could. After four years, this all feels too strange. Too quiet.

Instead, I lie staring at the ceiling, listening to Jake clearing away the plates and switching off the lights.

His bedroom door clicks closed, and the cottage is plunged into silence.

Outside, an owl screeches past the window. Wind rustles through the trees. And wooden beams crack and pop as the house settles down for the night.

It's gone three in the morning before I'm confident Jake and Annie must be sound asleep. I roll my legs out of bed and flick on a side lamp. Jake's bought me a heavy-duty waterproof, which I slip on with a woolly hat and a pair of hiking boots he's left by the door.

Then I'm ready.

Silently, I head down the hall, holding my breath.

The front door creaks on its hinges and I slip outside.

I don't look back as I hobble down the long dirt track back to the main road. I have to keep looking forwards. One foot in front of the other. I'm afraid if I don't, I'll lose my nerve.

Am I doing the right thing? I don't know. Walking away from Annie is the hardest thing I've ever done, but I know she's in safe hands with Jake. He'll be a wonderful father. And who knows, one day, when I've learned to forgive myself, Annie might have learned to forgive me too. For now, she needs the space to grow and heal without me in her life.

Some people will think it's the wrong decision. That I'm taking the coward's way out. But there's nothing cowardly about walking away from your own child when you know in your heart it's the right thing to do. For her sake. For Jake's sake.

Who knows where I'll end up or whether I'll ever be truly free from the hurt and the guilt I inflicted on myself, but I can't go back. That would be the second worst mistake I've ever made.

I have to figure out something new.

A new life.

A new identity.

A better me.

A FREE thriller for you

FREE STORY: The last thing Victor remembers is dancing through the streets of Rome with his new wife, Ruby. But now he's back at the airport, alone, with no idea what he's doing there, nor how to find Ruby.

His Lost Wife is yours for free - just let me know where to send it: bit.ly/hislostwife

Acknowledgements

While The Secrets We Keep is an entirely fictional story, it was inspired by true life events.

The kidnapping of nine-year-old girl in Yorkshire in the UK in 2008 dominated the news headlines for weeks.

The whole country was on tenterhooks hoping for good news after Shannon Matthews vanished on her way home from school.

So when she was found almost a month after disappearing it seemed like a miracle – until it was revealed her parents had been behind the kidnapping.

In the subsequent trial, it was suggested the motive was entirely about greed, with the family planning to claim rewards put up by a national newspaper and others.

If you want to find out more about the case, a quick internet search on Shannon's name will tell you everything you want to know.

The story was so shocking, it was definitely a case of the truth being stranger than fiction.

I wanted to explore how anyone could feel justified in exploiting their own child in this way, while also digging deeper into how the media operates when these big stories develop.

As a former journalist, who worked for fifteen years in regional TV news, I've tried to draw on my experience to give the story a sense of depth and realism, as well as a glimpse into what happens behind the scenes.

None of the characters are based on anyone I know, but like any good writer, I've drawn on behaviours I've observed over the years and dialled them up for dramatic effect.

And that's how the plot for The Secrets We Keep came about with all its twists and turns. I do hope you enjoyed reading it.

As always, I couldn't have done it with the support of my wife, Amanda (fellow psychological thriller author, AJ McDine) who keeps my spirits up when they need lifting and provides expert proofreading skills on my final drafts.

Also to Rebecca, my brilliant editor, who not only ensures my stories are the best they can be, but pushes me constantly to be a better writer. In this manuscript, she's pushed me harder and further than ever, and I hope you agree it shows.

Thanks also to my team of advanced readers who have the privilege of reading my books first in return for their invaluable feedback. There are too many to mention, but you know who you are and I'm forever indebted to you.

Being an independent author, responsible not only for writing the books but doing everything else, from marketing and advertising to sourcing covers and editing, can be a lonely business, but knowing I have such dedicated and supportive readers helps immeasurably.

If you'd like to keep up to date with all my writing news, please consider joining my weekly newsletter. I'll even send you a free e-book! You can find more details at bit.ly/hislostwifeor scan the QR code below.

Or follow me on Facebook - @AuthorAJWills, find me on my website ajwillsauthor.com or join me on Instagram at @ajwills_author.

I look forward to seeing you there.

Adrian

Also by the author

Nothing Left To Lose
A letter arrives in a plain white envelope. Inside is a single sheet of paper with a chilling message. Someone knows the secret Abi, and her husband, Henry, are hiding. And now they want them dead.

His Wife's Sister
Mara was only eleven when she went missing from a tent in her parents' garden nineteen years ago. Now she's been found wandering alone and confused in woodland.

She Knows
After Sky finds a lost diary on the beach, she becomes caught up in something far bigger than she could ever have imagined - and accused of a murder she has no memory of committing...

The Intruder
Jez thought he'd finally found happiness when he met Alice. But when Alice goes missing with her young daughter and the police accuse him of their murders, his life is shattered.

Printed in Great Britain
by Amazon